LOVEDAY

"Then you will marry me?"

She withdrew from him a little. "Matthew, it's not as easy as that, is it? Your father won't allow it."

"I'm twenty-one!"

"But you work with him. You can't go against him."

"If I have to, I will. But I doubt it will come to that. My mother and Sybil will be on my side." There's Mrs Morrow, too. Father seems to hold her in high esteem –" Or did, Matthew remembered, before she introduced Loveday into the household. But he would again, no doubt. Mrs Morrow was an attractive woman, of the kind his father had always found hard to resist. One way or the other, it was impossible to conceive of anything that could mar their happiness, now or later.

"I can't help being afraid," Loveday said.

"Of what?" She could only shake her head, unable to find the right words. Of power, perhaps. Of irresistible forces; of the habit of filial obedience; of a life that was different from anything she had known. "Silly one," Matthew murmured against her hair, holding her close again. "Everything will be wonderful. So long as we love each other, nothing can hurt us."

And when he kissed her like that, it was impossible to think that he might not be right.

**Also by the same author,
and available from Coronet:**

The Ring of Bells
The Song of the Rainbird
Freedom Street

About the author

Barbara Whitnell now lives in Cornwall after
years spent in Africa, the West Indies, Hong
Kong and London. Her novels include *The Ring
of Bells* and, most recently, *Freedom Street*. She
and her husband have four grown-up children
and four grandchildren.

BARBARA WHITNELL
LOVEDAY

CORONET BOOKS
Hodder and Stoughton

British Library C.I.P.

Whitnell, Barbara
  Loveday.
  I. Title
  823.914[F]

  ISBN 0-340-55339-1

Printed and bound in Great Britain for Hodder and Stoughton Paperbacks, a division of Hodder and Stoughton Ltd., Mill Road, Dunton Green, Sevenoaks, Kent TN13 2YA (Editorial Office: 47 Bedford Square, London WC1B 3DP) by Clays Ltd., St Ives plc.

To

Sarah Ann Hutton:

*A very dear daughter-in-law
who is always kind enough
to ask for more*

Book One

❦ 1 ❧

Loveday Pentecost, named for the woman they called the Quaker Saint of Cornwall, was neither a saint nor wished to be one. Not yet, anyway. Perhaps later, when she was quite old – say thirty or thirty-five, when surely she might expect to have drunk life's pleasures to their dregs – but not yet, while she was only seventeen; and certainly not on a day like this when every bird and leaf and flower seemed to sing aloud that spring had come, bringing with it a totally irrational feeling of optimism and excitement.

She could not have told why she felt that 1898 would be any different from 1897. She was contented enough, living with her father high on the Cornish moor – or had been until recently, when suddenly the day-to-day routine of the village school had seemed, just occasionally, dull and restrictive. What did she expect of this year, or this day? She didn't know. It merely seemed a morning when anything might happen. The very air shimmered with promise, and her feet in their buttoned boots appeared to skim over the ground. Her father – thin, and growing thinner – was forced to stop and look at the view from time to time in order to catch his breath, though he kept this primary motive a secret when Loveday challenged him.

"It's a sin and a shame to go so fast, with all that loveliness stretched out before you," he said. "Stop and drink a measure of beauty."

"But Carrivick awaits," Loveday cried dramatically, lifting her arms as if she would fly there. "And oh, I can't wait to see it, Papa, can you?"

9

"It seems," said John Pentecost dryly, "that I am not to be allowed to."

We should have brought the trap after all, he thought. But he had begun the day by feeling strong and confident, certain that the lassitude of recent months had gone, even if only temporarily. With the weather so inviting, he had thought himself more than equal to the three-mile walk to the village of St Ninn. It had always been one of his joys, to stride from the schoolhouse at Fourlanesend where the wind never ceased to blow over the almost treeless moorland and the sea was a distant gleam between folded hills, to the kinder, lusher valley where ferns sprang from rocky walls and primroses starred the banks. Loveday delighted in it, too. He could not remember how many times he had seen his own pleasure reflected in her face.

What will become of her when I am gone? he asked himself, as he had asked so many times. Any answer that might have occurred to him was lost in her cry of delight as they turned out of the lane into a drive where the double gates had long sagged on their hinges.

"Oh, Papa, how lovely it is," she breathed. "Just look at those rhododendrons! Did you ever see such colours?"

Her father stopped and gazed and shook his head, his haggard face transformed at the wonder of it.

"'Not Solomon, in all his glory,'" he whispered. And following this came the line that had tugged at his mind so frequently recently. "'Bliss was it in that dawn to be alive.'"

Loveday hugged his arm.

"I knew it would be wonderful, but couldn't imagine anything like this. It's like an enchanted wood."

The grounds of Carrivick Manor had always held for her the fascination of forbidden territory. The late owner, Sir Thomas Trengrose, had been a recluse who thoroughly disliked his fellow men and had fallen out not only with most people in the village but with his family as well. He was related to the Tallons who owned the clayworks in and around Trelew, but none – so village people reported – ever visited him.

How he would have hated to see this day! It was said in the village that he thought nothing of firing a shotgun at unwanted visitors; now every Tom, Dick and Harry had turned out at the behest of a firm of Truro auctioneers, to view the house and its contents before the next day's sale and to shake their heads over the way the place had gone to rack and ruin. A small group of women had entered the drive behind Loveday and her father, cackling together like a flock of geese. Far in front was a farm cart, two men sitting on the tail of it, their legs dangling, clay pipes sending a wreath of smoke over their heads. Was Sir Thomas spinning in his grave? Loveday wondered.

Others might deplore the way nature had taken over the wooded grounds to the right and left of the drive, but to Loveday there seemed a magnificent profligacy about the untamed rhododendrons that rioted brilliantly down in water-falls of flame and coral and purple amid the tangled under-growth and towering trees. It needed little imagination to see it as the setting for a fairy-tale princess, a Sleeping Beauty who awaited the kiss of a prince. What had made the old man so embittered, Loveday wondered, causing him to live here in solitude with only an old retainer and the ghosts of his ancestors for company? Was it a woman? A lost fortune? Some deep disgrace?

"Probably indigestion," her father suggested prosaically when she asked his opinion.

The house seemed very grand to her when finally it came into view at the end of the winding drive. In bad repair, certainly; gossip had not exaggerated that fact. A few of the long line of upper-storey windows were broken and some of the pillars that rose in pairs from the stone terrace to the first floor were chipped and crumbling. Woodland had encroached on the once well-tended garden and in the paved forecourt where carts and gigs were depositing their owners, a small central fountain, rusted and moss-grown, perched impotently in the middle of a shattered stone basin.

People had come not only from St Ninn which lay no more than half a mile from Carrivick, but also from further afield. John Pentecost had come on purpose to see the books and went at once to make enquiries where they might be found, but Loveday was enticed out of the entrance hall into a room on the right.

She found herself in the dining room, the solid refectory table still in its centre, the massive stone fireplace still holding the ashes of a fire long dead. How the silver must have glittered in the light of it, back in the days when Sir Thomas's more hospitable forebears had entertained the foremost families in the county!

Now the table bore piles of plates and cutlery, neatly tagged with their lot numbers, all ready for the sale. The chairs, damask seats faded, were set in four rows of four, desolate and dispossessed. The curtains had been taken down from the lofty windows, the carpet rolled. The huge clock was silent and dust motes hung in the air, while huge, gilt-framed portraits of long-dead Trengroses stared down at the scene below, stern and impassive.

The air buzzed with village voices.

"Tidden fitty, do ee ask me, turnin' over all Squire's old things," one woman said to another, turning them over just the same. "Some awful old trade, idden un? You'd 'ave to be mazed as a brush to bid more than tuppence."

"Oh, but do ee see the silver, though," said her friend. "I d'dearly love a bit of silver. 'Tis some tarnished, but 'twould come up lovely, do ee give un a bit of a rub."

Loveday wandered away from them, her fertile imagination peopling the room with quite different characters: ladies in silks and satins and laces, and men with powdered wigs and velvet knee-breeches. From their portraits she thought they seemed a self-satisfied lot, those old Trengroses; but they had lived and died here in this house, and no doubt had loved and laughed and cried. What had they been like? She would like so much to know.

She ought to be looking for her father, she reminded herself, forcing herself back to the present. She was anxious to inspect the books, too, on her own account. She went out into the hall again and stood for a moment at the foot of the wide staircase, running her hand over the silken wood of the newel post. How many other hands had done the same? Parents, children – all gone to dust. There was a pleasurable sadness in the thought. For a moment she felt she could almost see those shadowy ghosts.

"Can I help you?" The voice that addressed her was undoubtedly of this world. Loveday turned, startled, to find a young man confronting her. "You seem a little lost," he added, as if in explanation.

He was a stranger to her, of medium height, slim, with a lean, lively face. His fair hair was crisp and slightly curled, his face fresh-complexioned, his eyes somewhere between green and grey. His smile was frankly admiring, and Loveday was annoyed to feel the heat rushing to her face in response to it. She had developed a brisk, no-nonsense response to the sheep's eyes of the local youths, but this young man was something different. He was dressed in the country gentleman's uniform of fawn trousers, leather gaiters and tweed jacket.

"I seem to have lost my father," she said.

The young man laughed.

"Now that's what I call exceedingly careless." There was a note of mock severity in his voice, as if he were chiding a child. "Do you think you may have mislaid him in the drawing room? One can find all sorts of objects down the sides of chairs, I find. D'you know, I discovered a cough lozenge, three hair pins and a tailor's bill, all in the space of one afternoon."

Loveday smiled, but with restraint. He was not so different, after all. The young men of Trelew or St Ninn might speak in broad Cornish dialect; they might have rough and reddened hands and wear heavy boots, but almost all tried to impress her with a show of wit, or what passed for it.

"We came to look at the books," she said, "but I was distracted by the dining room."

"The books?" The young man wrinkled his nose in a manner Loveday had to admit to herself was rather engaging. "They're upstairs in the library – a dull lot, I'm afraid. We don't expect to get much for them."

"We?" She was sufficiently interested in the implication of this word to forget her dignity for the moment. "Are you a member of the family, then?"

"Matthew Tallon, at your service." He bowed, elaborately polite.

"Oh!"

To her intense frustration, Loveday could think of nothing

more to say. It was maddening to be struck dumb at such a moment, and quite against her principles to appear to be so impressed by the Tallon name.

"Are you really interested in the books?" He came a little closer. "There are plenty of other things to see, you know. I could give you a conducted tour."

Loveday moved up one step, as if in retreat.

"I think I should find my father."

"Oh, he'll not come to any harm. Are you from St Austell? I swear you can't be, for I should certainly have noticed you there. It's my guess you live locally. Am I right?"

"No." Loveday felt the colour rising to her cheeks again and could have stamped her foot in annoyance. "I mean no, I don't live in St Austell."

"Then you live close by?"

"No – yes –" Oh, what on earth would he think of her? And what had got into her, to behave in such a foolish, witless way? She, who prided herself on the ability to put any forward young man in his place. "Not in St Ninn, that is. My father is the schoolmaster up at Fourlanesend, between St Ninn and Trelew."

Matthew Tallon pursed up his lips in a soundless whistle.

"Good heavens! I've passed that way – it's the last place God made. You're miles from anywhere, surely. Who on earth considered it a good position for a school?"

Loveday found her voice at last.

"The Education Committee, in their wisdom." Her shyness had dropped away and she looked at him directly, not seeing that he blinked a little at the impact caused by her violet eyes with their fringe of dark lashes. "They are of the opinion that it's convenient for both St Ninn and Trelew, but of course they are wrong. It's quite the reverse, convenient for neither. It's over three miles to each of them, and seems even further in bad weather. The Committee says it's good for healthy children to walk and I suppose they're right in that, but they forget that many of the little ones are no older than four and not all have decent boots to wear." She stopped abruptly and bit her lip. "I'm sorry," she said, becoming shy once more. "It makes me angry. I didn't mean to bore you."

"I assure you, you're not boring me in the slightest. Your

indignation does you credit – but what, in heaven's name, do you find to *do* up there?"

"I teach the little ones."

"For entertainment, I mean. I suppose you have to come to St Ninn for any kind of social life. God knows there's nothing at Trelew, and less than nothing at Fourlanesend."

A queer, inexplicable pride made Loveday deny this hotly.

"Oh, we're far from dull, I assure you."

"No? Tell me what goes on then, up there on the moor."

Desperately Loveday searched her mind and found little to offer. There were musical evenings at Roskelly Farm with her friend, Dolly Crowle – but somehow she doubted that the singing of Moody and Sankey hymns around the piano was quite what Matthew Tallon had in mind. There was haymaking and harvest, and the parties that ensued, with Ned Crowle breathing heavily and gazing at her with lovesick eyes. None of it seemed worth the recounting.

"I read a great deal," she said at last.

Gravely Matthew nodded.

"I see I was mistaken," he said. "Your life is clearly one whirl of gaiety. It is to be hoped you don't over-excite yourself."

Loveday caught his eye, considered looking offended, then exploded with laughter.

"You're right, of course," she said. "I suppose it does seem dull, but my father is the best of company."

"Your mother –?"

"She died when I was four years old."

"I'm sorry."

"I don't honestly remember her, though I half-remember coming to Fourlanesend." She had hated it, and had cried inconsolably, wanting her mother and the little house where they had lived all together in London, and Rosie, the maid of all work, and her friends from next door and kind Mrs Tranter from the corner shop. Poor, poor Papa, she thought now. How awful it must have been for him.

"Where did you come from?"

"From London. Chelsea."

Matthew whistled again.

"From the sublime to the ridiculous."

"Or the ridiculous to the sublime, depending on your point of view. My father was born and brought up in Cornwall and always hankered to come back. And talking of my father – I must go and find him. Good day, Mr Tallon."

"Oh, please wait!" Hastily Matthew followed her up the staircase. "You haven't told me your name."

"I am Loveday Pentecost," she said. "And yes" – she added, a world-weary note in her voice – "I was named after Loveday Hambly, whom my father admires greatly, and no, I am not myself a saint, so please don't ask me. Everyone does."

Slightly below her on the staircase, Matthew Tallon grinned up at her.

"Nothing would induce me to be so unoriginal. Besides, there's a hint of devilment in your eyes that makes the question superfluous."

Not entirely displeased, Loveday tossed her head.

"You are, however, easily induced to be impertinent, Mr Tallon."

"Impertinent?" Matthew's eyes widened innocently. "Why should I be impertinent towards the prettiest girl I've met in months. Won't you at least allow me to escort you to the library?"

Loveday looked upwards, towards the ornately-balustraded landing from which there were two corridors leading to the left and right.

"Well –" She hesitated for a moment, and taking advantage of her indecision, Matthew took command.

"Come," he said masterfully, and led the way upwards, smiling and nodding to a well-dressed couple who were on their way down. Loveday did not fail to notice their covert curiosity and smiled inwardly to think that they would undoubtedly be speculating on her identity. The Tallons, one of the wealthiest families and the largest employers of labour in the neighbourhood, were perennial subjects for gossip.

"You know," Matthew said conversationally, "I'm not at all sure that I can forgive my Great-uncle Thomas for not inviting us here when we were children. This banister is simply crying out to have small boys sliding down it, don't you agree? I've more than half a mind to make up for it by doing so here and now."

"You wouldn't!" Loveday looked at him uncertainly. There was something about him that made her think he was not beyond it. Matthew smiled at her again.

"I tell you what. I will if you will."

"Mr Tallon!" Loveday tossed her head again at such foolishness.

"Oh, well." He shrugged resignedly. "Never mind. I shall have to speak kindly to the next owner and perhaps she'll allow me the chance."

"Who is to be the next owner?"

He stopped in his tracks.

"Do you mean to tell me you haven't heard? Well, perhaps it is early days, even for the jungle drums of St Ninn. It's Sarah Sangster."

He waited expectantly for her reaction and was not disappointed. Loveday stopped too, turning to face him with her mouth open in astonishment.

"*Sarah Sangster? The* Sarah Sangster?"

"None other."

"But what would she want to come here for?"

"She's apparently retired from the stage. She recently married a chap called Robert Morrow who's a friend of my father – they were at school together. He spent much of his childhood in Cornwall, it seems, and has always wanted a house such as Carrivick. He's pretty well-heeled, I understand, with interests in tea estates in India, and shipping, and heaven knows what else."

"*Well!*" Loveday was not often at a loss for words, but could find nothing to say to this astonishing revelation. She, personally, had never seen Sarah Sangster on the stage, but naturally had heard of her. Who in the civilised world had not? Her portrait was reproduced on postcards, her gowns were copied, her coiffure was the subject of comment the length and breadth of the country. It was even said that she was a very special friend of the Prince of Wales. "And – and you, you actually *know* her?" she asked reverently.

"I've met her. She's quite charming, I assure you. Perhaps

you'll see her yourself later on, for she said she would be coming here this morning."

"Do you think she can possibly be happy here, so far from London and all the theatres?" They had resumed their progress towards the library. "I know it's beautiful, but it will seem so quiet –"

"And how will Methodist Cornwall accept such an exotic creature? It can be awfully narrow-minded, you must admit. They tend to look askance at actresses down here. She'll find it quite a contrast to the kind of demi-monde she's accustomed to."

"Exactly," agreed Loveday. She was hazy about what constituted a demi-monde, but felt it sounded a suitable habitat for someone as glamorous as Sarah Sangster.

Matthew came to a halt outside the second door along the eastern corridor.

"This is the library. You'll find all the books in here, such as they are."

Loveday smiled and thanked him, making no comment on his expressed hope that perhaps they might meet again. She felt sure that they would not. The Tallons moved in quite different circles from the Pentecosts and she could envisage no circumstances in which their paths would cross in future. It had, she thought, been a pleasant interlude, no more.

A pity, but there it was. For a brief moment she stood at the door to the library and watched his retreating figure, feeling more than a touch of regret. He was undoubtedly one of the best-looking young men she had ever seen, let alone spoken to; but she remembered the exciting news she had for her father and quickly went in search of him, finding him in the far corner of the room bent over a tea-chest.

"Papa, you'll never guess –"

"Sir Thomas seems to have been inordinately fond of sermons. Strange, that. I wonder what he made of those that dealt with brotherly love?"

"Papa, who do you think is buying the house?"

"Hmm?" Abstracted, a leather-bound volume open in his hand, her father straightened up and looked at her. "I think I've found gold here, though. It's a first edition, unless I'm much mistaken."

"Oh Papa, do listen! Sarah Sangster has bought the house. Isn't it exciting?"

"Sarah Sangster?" She had caught his attention at last. "Well, well! That'll put St Ninn on the map."

"I hear she might be coming to Carrivick this morning. Maybe we'll see her. Oh, I can't wait to tell Dolly! What will she think of us all? Just imagine, we're bound to see her in church and walking about the village!"

"My dear child, she is mortal, you know. It's hardly the second coming."

"But Sarah Sangster, Papa! Dolly has collected all of her postcards. She will be thrilled to pieces."

"It's exciting news, certainly. But can I implore you to turn your attention to the books now? They are being sold by the box. I rather think you may care for that lot by the window, but if not then I shall restrict myself to this one. We can leave our bid with the auctioneer's man."

There was a complete set of Dickens in the box her father indicated, most of which Loveday owned already, but there were others that intrigued her: travellers' tales and poetry, even old and fearsome fairy stories.

"I think I'd like these, if they don't fetch too much," she said.

"No one else has been near them while I've been looking at them. But it's early, yet. People will be coming all day, no doubt."

At this Loveday looked out of the window. Even more vehicles had arrived by this time and friends were greeting each other so that the front courtyard had the aspect of a market-place, but immediately her eyes went to the woman who, at that moment, was being handed down from a brougham. She was slim, modishly dressed in a velvet travelling costume of deepest blue, and though her face was veiled there could be no mistaking her identity.

"Papa, she's here! Come quickly."

John Pentecost put down the book he was holding feeling, suddenly, a strange reluctance to see Sarah Sangster after so long. He remembered her, as if from another life, when he had gone with Ruth, his wife, to see her as Portia; it hurt to think of it, they had been so young and so happy, so madly in love.

Sarah Sangster had been young, too; young and vividly alive, lighting the theatre with her glowing beauty and talent.

"Oh, I wish I looked like that," Ruth had whispered to him behind her programme. "She's so lovely."

"So are you," he had whispered back. "Lovelier," he had added loyally, and to him she was; but there was no doubt that Miss Sangster had been something to see.

And now, nineteen years later, here she was – and Ruth was not. It was still a piercing hurt, even after so long. At the time, he had thought he would never recover. He had crawled away from London like a wounded animal, back to the Cornish countryside that he loved, abandoning a career that had seemed promising.

He had not, on the whole, regretted it. Remaining a country schoolmaster had been a conscious decision, born of his love for Cornwall and his commitment to its children. Only now, his future uncertain and Loveday to be provided for, did he wonder if he had been wise in neglecting to build up just a little more treasure on earth.

At Loveday's urging, he joined her at the window.

"She's like a bird of paradise among crows," he said as he looked below. "What will she do with herself here?"

"She's retired from the stage and has married a wealthy man who has tea estates in India," Loveday informed him, and he looked at her amusedly.

"Who gave you all this information?"

"Mr Matthew Tallon. He showed me the way up here."

"Did he, now?" Her father looked at her quizzically.

"We chanced to exchange a few words. Sarah Sangster is a friend of his family."

"Curiouser and curiouser. The little I know of the Tallon family hardly leads me to think they are patrons of the arts."

"Clay Tallon was at school with Sarah Sangster's husband."

"Ah, all is clear." Almost in spite of himself, John Pentecost's interest was engaged. "I suppose that must be the gentleman in question."

"He looks rather nice, doesn't he? I wonder what it must be like, being the husband of Sarah Sangster?"

"Only he can tell. Now, my dear, I should be glad to start on our homeward way –"

"Oh look, Papa. There is Mr Matthew Tallon greeting her now."

"A fine-looking young man."

"Do you think so?" Loveday, unaware of her father's amused glance, was studiously casual. "He's handsome enough, I suppose, but I thought him a little short, and rather too pleased with himself."

"Young men tend to be. They often grow out of it. Now, perhaps –"

"That's Clay Tallon joining them now, isn't it? I saw him once giving away the prizes at Trelew Feast." With undiminished interest Loveday continued to peer at the group below. This latest arrival was doffing his glossy hat as he approached the others. His thrust-forward head was a little too large for his body, his bouncing gait more energetic than elegant, but even from this distance there was an air of power and consequence about him. "How important he looks," she said.

"Yes, that's Tallon." Her father watched the scene below with interest and mild amusement. What was it that could turn a rather short man with prematurely silver hair into such a commanding figure? Perhaps it was the well-brushed moustache, or merely the services of a good tailor, no expense spared. No, there was more to it than that. Clay Tallon had the kind of assurance that a man was born with.

"An impressive figure, I agree," John Pentecost said musingly. "The very model of a modern, successful captain of industry. They used to call them Adventurers, you know, those first clay barons. I suspect it's not altogether a misnomer in Tallon's case." He smiled, seeing the self-consciously charming tilt of the head, a gloved finger stroking the moustache. "He's enjoying the reflected glory of Sarah Sangster's company, I fancy. Now, may I prise you away from this entertaining little sideshow? Don't forget I have to find the auctioneer's man before we can actually start for home."

He was thankful to accept the offer of a lift on a farm cart before they had gone far. The feeling of well-being, clearly illusory, had left him completely, but he contrived to hide the fact from his daughter.

What was he to do about her? They had friends and acquaintances in plenty, but no kith or kin. His parents had been alive when they had first returned to Cornwall, but both had died some years before. Two brothers had gone to America, and he had seen neither of them for years.

Perhaps Ruth's family –? No! They had never liked him, never thought him good enough for her, always obscurely blamed him for her death, even though she had longed for the child that killed her quite as much as he had done. How had people so mean-spirited produced a shining soul like Ruth? He had never understood it.

He looked at Loveday across the width of the cart as they jolted over the ruts towards Fourlanesend, marvelled again at the purity of her profile, the crisp, dark hair, the curl of the lashes that fringed those startling eyes. God, it was hard to think of leaving her! She had the same kind of gaiety that he had loved in her mother, the same spirit, the same bright intelligence.

But she was so young and vulnerable. Who would she turn to for comfort and counsel when he was gone?

He looked away from her and stared unseeingly at the lane with the fields beyond and the darker patch of green that was Carrivick Woods, and the gently curving hills, and the glimmer of the sea.

"Lord, show me the way," he prayed silently. "Show me Thy purpose." And a great sadness possessed him, for what purpose could there be in leaving a life so sweet?

❧ 2 ❧

Of the four lanes that gave the hamlet its name, one led downwards towards St Ninn, and another up towards Trelew and the clay-mining country. To the left, a twisting track meandered across the moor to link several other small clusters of cottages, while the lane to the right led directly to Roskelly Farm, the home of Loveday's friend, Dolly Crowle.

It was said that a gibbet once stood at the crossroads, and when the wind howled down the chimney on winter nights and rattled the Gothic windows of the schoolhouse, it was only too easy to believe that the souls of the wretches who perished there had come back to haunt them. Even more chilling were the days when mist hung over the moor, giving familiar shapes the illusion of menace. Loveday was always thankful when winter was over for another year and spring brought sun and racing clouds. She loved the moor then, with the gorse and heather in flower, the pale green bracken unfurling tight fingers, and the breathtaking view of the sea, all the way from the Gribbin to Trenarren. The air was clean and sharp and intoxicating, like the wine the vicar brought out on the occasions when the Pentecosts went to dine with him down in St Ninn in the ivy-clad vicarage next to the church.

Walter Crowle, Dolly's father, did not approve of their dining with the vicar. As well as farming Roskelly, he was a pillar of the Primitive Methodist Chapel in Trelew, leader of the choir, keeper of the tuning fork, and occasional preacher.

Loveday always went to the chapel with Dolly when she knew that Mr Crowle would be preaching, even though it meant running the gauntlet of Ned Crowle's yearning looks. She would not have missed one of Walter's sermons for the world, for they were delivered in his own highly individualistic style – with utter earnestness and sincerity, but in the vernacular.

"So Boaz seed Ruth," he proclaimed recently. "And he said, 'Who's liddle maid is this, then? She'm doin' some proper job 'ere, dear of un! I ain't leavin' 'er take no chances along with t'other wimmen. She can go and eat and drink where the young men belong to go.' But then a thought comes to un, and 'e says, 'See 'ere, maid,' 'e says, 'if one o' they varmints lays a finger on ee,' 'e says, 'come and tell I of un.'"

Afterwards she would reproduce it for her father's entertainment; but for all their laughter, and all Mr Crowle's disapproval of their ecumenism, there was genuine liking and respect between the two families, and enjoyment of each other's company. All six of the Crowle children had been through the school, and nine-year-old Georgie was still there, just as stolid and good-natured as the rest of them.

Loveday's feeling of optimism and impending change bore no fruit during the months that followed her visit to Carrivick. In St Ninn it was said that a whole army of workmen was busy on the manor house, but there was no sign of the new occupants. The buzz of conjecture concerning them died down in favour of perennial concerns, such as the St Ninn Feast at the end of May when a fair came to the village, and there were stalls that sold sweetmeats and ribbons and gimcrack china and ornaments. There were races on Farmer Williams's field, and a tug-of-war, and a concert given by the St Austell town band, ending with the bandsmen leading the Flora – the dance that had all the younger inhabitants, and those that felt young despite their age, snaking round the village: up through Fore Street, down around Queen Street, up along Church Cross and back again.

John Pentecost, watching Loveday dancing, and laughing as she danced, found joy in the sight despite his heartache. Old Dr Geach, standing next to him, noted the direction of his eyes and looked at him with compassion.

"She'll be well enough, John," he said softly. "Have you told her?"

"Not yet. Let her enjoy the summer. I can last out this term – perhaps next, for you say yourself no date can be set. I shall know when the time is right."

The doctor nodded in agreement.

"Ay, you'll know."

"There are times when I feel no worse. Times when I have hope –"

He glanced at the doctor, but saw no hope reflected in his old friend's face. There was only sadness. Ruefully, he shrugged.

"Well, I have June-month ahead of me," he said. "I have always thought that if I could choose one month of the year to live, it would be June. And if I could choose one place, it would be high on the Cornish moor."

He loved the moor in all its moods, and always had; but even as he spoke he felt a longing to be down by the sea again, to stand on tall cliffs and look down at waves breaking on granite rocks. They would go at the first opportunity, Loveday and he. There might be no time to lose.

A group of women, mothers of pupils at Fourlanesend school, were standing on the opposite side of the street.

"Master looks wisht," said one of their number.

" 'E never 'ad no colour."

" 'E's gone some thin, too."

"No need to fret. 'E's the wiry sort, is Master."

"Thass true. There was never no meat on un."

So they cheered each other, and turned to the dancing again. It was not possible that anything could be seriously amiss. Master was an institution and life without him quite unimaginable.

Loveday saw her father's tiredness and was worried by it, seeking by every means she could to lighten his burden and encourage him to rest.

"I do wish you would see Dr Geach," she said to him one evening as he read his paper while she was bent over her darning.

"I have, my dear." Her father looked up and smiled at her.

"He happened to drop in only last week when you were at Roskelly."

"What did he say?"

"That old age is catching up with me. He's given me a blood tonic."

"Well, mind you take it, then. And it's nonsense to speak of old age. You're not nearly as old as Mr Crowle – or Dr Geach, come to that. I hope he knows what he's talking about."

"I have every faith in him. By the way, have you thought any more about training college?" Deliberately John Pentecost sought to divert his daughter's attention away from his own frail health. "It's not too late for September, you know. If your intention is to stay in the teaching profession, you should undoubtedly become qualified."

Some of the brightness died from her face and she sighed, laying the darning down in her lap.

"I don't know, Papa. If you think it best for me, then I'll go, of course – if they'll have me!"

"But you are not sure it's what you want to do?"

She bit her lip and shook her head unhappily.

"I don't know," she said again, adding quickly: "Oh, I'm happy teaching the little ones for the moment, don't think I'm not. It's just that I can't imagine doing it for ever. I don't think I have your sort of vocation. Still, I suppose if I *did* go to college, it would broaden my experience, wouldn't it? I mean, experience of life." She cupped her chin in her hand, frowningly pensive. "I should be bound to meet more people. One day, I suppose, I might want to get married – and heaven knows, there's no one here I'd look at twice!"

"The thought had occurred to me."

"Not that I am in any hurry."

"I'm quite glad of that."

"But about college – I just don't know, Papa."

"Then let us leave it." He seized gratefully upon her wish to procrastinate. The last thing he wanted, in his heart of hearts, was to see her go away from Fourlanesend at this moment. "After all, you're not yet eighteen. Twelve more months, and we may see our way more clearly."

Loveday sighed with relief and leaned over to kiss him.

"Thank you for my reprieve," she said. "But reverting to the matter of your health –"

"Pray let us not!"

"But I want to lighten your load. What can I do to help you?"

Her father laughed.

"Now, what can you do? Rid me of Henry Tregilgas, perhaps. No –" Hastily he contradicted himself. "I shouldn't say such a thing. He's difficult, admittedly, but the fault is mine."

"Papa, how can it be?"

"I should have devoted more time to him. Or perhaps I should have beaten him more." He gave a somewhat lugubrious smile, to show that this was a joke. He was a schoolmaster, unusual in his generation, who did not resort often to the cane, holding to the decidedly unfashionable belief that children should be drawn to learning, not driven to it. "It's so difficult to break through that barrier of dumb hostility. Sometimes I feel it would be better to allow him to stay away from school altogether, which is what he wants, but the law is the law, and the whipper-in has been more than usually diligent of late."

"Is there any improvement in his reading?"

Wearily her father shook his head, conscious that only a short time ago he would have regarded the boy as a challenge, not the wearisome burden he now appeared to be. Henry Tregilgas had spent four years in the infants' class with Miss Scobie, Loveday's predecessor, and one in his own class. Still the boy could not read or recognise his letters.

Dismissing him as mentally retarded was clearly inappropriate, even though he gave no sign of interest in learning. For most of the day he slouched in his desk and did nothing, slyly disrupting lessons whenever he saw an opportunity.

Other boys were mischievous. They played tricks on the girls – tied their pigtails or apron strings to the chairs, or let loose a fieldmouse to scare them, and while the headmaster dealt sternly with such transgressions, he regarded them as no more than a part of school life. Truancy was always a problem, too, and the farming year a constant counter-attraction to school. If it were not the seed-planting season,

27

then it was hay-making or potato-lifting. Henry was by no means the only boy whose attendance at school was spasmodic.

But he was different from the others. His line was one of dumb insolence, his crimes more subtle and secretive, his absences unaccounted for by farm work. A girl's elbow would be jogged, spoiling the pristine page of her copybook; but she would never be quite sure who was to blame. A boy would trip and fall on his way back from the Master's desk. Marbles would mysteriously disappear, and fights were fermented. Throughout all the ensuing trouble, Henry would sit, arms folded, dark eyes blazing with derision in his pointed, scornful face. He was, it had to be admitted, a total misfit.

"I have such a sense of failure." There was a hopeless note in the schoolmaster's voice. "It irks me. I'm not used to it, Loveday."

"It's not your fault, Papa." Loveday rushed to give him reassurance, but he shook his head, rejecting it.

"I am conscious that I have failed to ignite any sort of spark in him. He has no interest in anything, no – no *aspirations* of any kind. I'm so afraid he'll end up like his brother."

"I hope not." Loveday retained childhood memories of the unpleasant bully who had mercifully left school just as she moved up from the infants' class. "Henry's not as bad as that."

"What chance has he, Loveday? His home circumstances are such that mind and spirit are ignored – even despised, and however humble the circumstances of the other children, that is something that cannot be said of them. Their parents may be poor and unlettered themselves, but for the most part they want their children to do better. For some reason Henry finds reading more difficult than most, I accept that, but I cannot rid myself of the feeling that the absence of any wish to learn is the main source of his problem."

Loveday frowned and chewed her lip in thought.

"I'm not really sure I agree," she said, after a moment. "There are times when it seems to me that he is desperately unhappy. Suppose he really wants to learn, but finds it so difficult that pride makes him pretend he doesn't care?"

"I suppose it's possible." Her father considered the matter

thoughtfully. "I admit that there is a kind of blockage that seems to affect some children, almost as if what they see before their eyes appears different from what others see. I've heard it called word-blindness. No one understands it, or has a remedy for it. Now I think of it, I read an article on the subject once. It tends to run in families, through the male line." He should have considered it earlier, he told himself guiltily. He *would* have done, not so long ago. If only he were not so tired, so drained at the end of the day. Was now the time to give up? He picked up his paper again, but could make sense of none of it, his thoughts were too intrusive.

His basic tenet, the rock on which he built his school, was the belief that every child was of great worth. The fact that the Tregilgas family was well known in the locality for law-breaking and fecklessness and that no one had a good word for any member of it should not, he felt, be allowed to enter into the matter.

They lived not in a cottage but in a shack in Carrivick Woods made from orange boxes and sheets of corrugated iron. Henry's father had been a drunkard who, by his own negligence, had been killed by a threshing machine one harvest-time. His mother was a strange woman who roamed the lanes picking berries and herbs, for what purpose more conventional folk could only guess at. She wore ragged clothes and a man's hat. Some said she was a witch, of Romany stock; others that she was mad. Everyone knew that she operated an illicit still and had served a term in prison for it, and other darker crimes were attributed to her, in whispers.

Henry's brother Joely, the scourge of the school some years ago, had been in and out of prison too, for poaching or causing an affray or being drunk and disorderly. If a rick were fired or farm implements or building materials mysteriously missing, everyone knew Joely Tregilgas was at the bottom of it somewhere. He was an evil, violent young fellow, people said, with no good in him, and though such a sentiment ran against John Pentecost's normal beliefs, he was inclined to think that where Joely was concerned they probably had the right of it.

"Papa, let me see what I can do with Henry. Truly, I would like to do it."

John Pentecost lowered his paper once more and saw Loveday leaning towards him eagerly, her face alight with enthusiasm. So had Ruth looked when she was determined on any particular course. So had she looked when she had told him of the coming baby that had proved the death of her.

"My dear child, you have enough to do," he said.

This was no more than a statement of fact. While the headmaster took the senior class of eight-year-olds and over, Loveday's class consisted of twenty children, the youngest of whom were barely house-trained and hardly any two at the same stage. While little Annie Mills had to be taught how to hold a slate pencil and care had to be taken to dispatch her at frequent intervals to the line of privies across the yard in the care of an older girl, Percy Winter, at the other end of the class, was embarking on long division. Even an experienced teacher would have had her hands full.

"Oh, I don't think I could manage him in class, but I could give him extra lessons – after school, or at midday."

"*Extra* lessons?" Her father gave an astonished laugh. "I can't imagine him taking kindly to them."

"He might, if my theory is right, and if I took care to make them enjoyable."

"I should be the one –"

"No! You must rest and take your tonic and get well. And I must rack my brains to think of some means to capture Henry's interest and make him *want* to learn."

"You're a good girl, Loveday." Her father cleared his throat, finding a momentary difficulty in speaking. He had moments of weakness like this just recently, he found. "And a good teacher. I don't know that I agree that you have no vocation. Any college would be privileged to have you."

"We'll see. Next year, perhaps. When you are well."

And he smiled and nodded and returned to his paper, though only with a great effort did he force the words to make sense to him.

Next year was light years away.

People said that Sarah Sangster – or Mrs Robert Morrow, to give her her correct title – had looked in the mirror and seen the future. Why else would she give up a successful career to marry a dull, if wealthy, merchant, who chose to bury himself in the depths of the country?

"I give you a year," her friend and fellow actress Lucy Villiers said to her before she left London. "Who will you find who speaks the same language?"

Sarah had smiled. She had tried to explain her longing for peace and security and absence of strain without success, and had not even attempted to describe the emotion brought about by her first sight of Carrivick. Lucy would have dismissed as far too fanciful her feeling of total rightness, the knowledge that at last she had come home.

And that was when the place was a ruin. Now the house was more as she had imagined it, that day when she had come with Robert to see what of the previous owner's belongings they wanted to keep. Not many of them, had been their joint verdict. It was a crime, the way the Trengrose man had let the place fall into such disrepair.

He would not have recognised it now. Carpenters and plasterers and tilers, painters, paper-hangers and gardeners had been at work. The double gates at the end of the drive were replaced by others made of handsome wrought iron, and a veritable stream of consignments from Heals and Harrods and Waring & Gillows had been ferried from the station – bolts of damask and velvet to be made into curtains by local sempstresses, carpets of the very highest quality, pictures from the best galleries in St James's.

By August the house was ready for occupation. Staff was recruited – some from the district, but the butler, cook and housekeeper from London, as well as her own personal maid.

No detail was too small to be of interest to the villagers of St Ninn, and there were those whose thoughts were much the same as those of Lucy Villiers. No one as exotic as Sarah Sangster could live happily in the country: and did they want her, even if she wanted them?

"Actresses idn't what you'd call respectable, say what you will," Mrs Penhaligon remarked to Mrs Beswarick when she chanced to run into her at the post office. Letty Foster, the postmistress, overheard her and, according to Mrs Penhaligon, took the parcel she was posting to her son in Australia with quite unnecessary force.

"Well, speak as you find is my motto," Letty said shortly. "And Mrs Morrow do seem a friendly soul, actress or no. She'm a lovely woman, you ask me."

"No one did ask you, Letty Foster," snapped Mrs Penhaligon. ("That Letty Foster," she said to Mrs Beswarick outside the shop. "Always sticking her nose in. She should tend to her own business.")

The Morrows appeared in church, and details of Mrs Morrow's dress were noted and discussed inside every cottage and on every corner for the following week, and beyond. On the whole, though there were some who thought as Mrs Penhaligon, her appearance and demeanour were approved.

"I'll be some delighted, do I look like that at her age," the women said to each other. The men, for the most part, kept their comments and their lip-smacking for the bar of the Trengrose Arms.

Though, naturally, they expressed themselves in different terms, the reactions of such high society as the district offered were much the same as the villagers of St Ninn. In principle, it was felt, actresses could hardly be looked upon with favour.

"Such a *seedy* profession," Lady Bethune murmured to Sir Jeremy. "One cannot think that she is a lady. However, Mr Morrow is well connected, I understand, despite the fact that he is in trade. I suppose we shall have to entertain them."

Mrs Penberthy, wife of Granville Penberthy of the firm of Penberthy & Trevose, rivals in the clay world to Josiah Tallon & Son, looked at the matter somewhat differently.

"What on earth does one talk about in her company?" she demanded of her daughter Gwendolyn, repeating the question to her friends, all of whom had grown up in the depths of the country and had no interests beyond their own small circle. "I mean, is one expected to know all the plays in which she's taken part? I don't suppose I will have heard of any of them."

In the event, their fears were allayed. Sarah Morrow attended their dinners and dances and At Homes and behaved politely and pleasantly, just like any ordinary gentlewoman. Her clothes were elegant and her figure superb, and her manner, it was generally agreed, could not be faulted. She was high-spirited, but not embarrassingly so.

"I confess," Edwin Tallon, more commonly known as 'Clay' Tallon, said to his wife after his guests had departed following a dinner party given in his old friend's honour, "that I feared before I met her at Carrivick that Robert had been cautious all his life, only to make a late and unwise leap into matrimony. I was wrong. Tonight has only confirmed my opinion that Mrs Morrow is charming."

He was looking with approbation in the mirror over the massive marble fireplace as he spoke, smiling faintly, stroking his silky moustache and holding in his stomach. Not a bad figure of a man, he thought, tilting his big, handsome head sideways a little.

In general, he was pleased with the way the evening had gone. Sarah Morrow had sat on his right hand and had proved an easy and entertaining dinner companion, listening to him with flattering attention and appreciating his small jokes in a way poor Millicent had never been able to do.

He had flirted a little, naturally. What else did one do with an attractive woman? But in addition, he had expanded on the processes necessary for the manufacture of china clay, for she had seemed genuinely interested in the subject.

It was a rare thing, he considered, to find such intelligence in a beautiful woman, and he had brought himself to say as much to her before the end of the evening. The modest way in which she had smiled and lowered her eyes confirmed her worth, to his mind. He was pretty damned sure that she was attracted to him, too. Robert Morrow, the old rascal, had done very well for himself. If only Millicent had that kind of style! As it was, she had been her usual ineffectual self that evening. But that was Millicent for you. He should be used to her by now.

Even so, he was irritated by her looks, as he turned from the mirror with a frown, beetling his rather unruly white eyebrows in her direction. Was it really necessary for her hair to escape from its coils and hang about her face, or for her narrow shoulders to droop so dispiritedly? And wouldn't it be sensible to wear dresses that hid the hollows at the base of her throat?

"My dear, I can't say I care very much for that gown," he said, taking care to soften the words with a smile. "Is it new?"

"Oh Edwin, you know it is." Pale hands fluttered nervously at her throat. "You always say that blue suits me."

"There are blues and blues, are there not?" He smiled again. He had a curling puckish smile – a smile that had once made Millicent want to swoon with delight but which now, distressingly, put her in mind of illustrations she had seen of devils, complete with horns and pitchforks.

"And the cut is, perhaps, not as flattering as it might be," he went on. "Alas, we all have to bear in mind the passage of years. None of us are getting any younger. There, there – pray don't look so distressed. We all make mistakes. I think you may congratulate yourself on the success of the evening."

Millicent, still agitated by his criticism, did not reply.

"However," he said, continuing to stand before the fire with his thumbs tucked into the armholes of his waistcoat, "I should be glad if you would speak to Matthew. He had altogether too much to say tonight, don't you agree? I feel sure Mrs Morrow must have found his conversation extremely tedious. Why, he practically monopolised her when we joined the ladies in the drawing room after dinner."

Her own cause for distress was forgotten in this attack on her son.

"She didn't look as if she found it tedious," she said, a touch of defiance in her voice. "In fact they seemed to me to be getting on very well together. I'm surprised you weren't glad to see it. You're always quick enough to criticise if either of the children appear unsociable."

"My dear Millicent!" There was a touch of superiority in his laugh. "Of course Mrs Morrow gave every appearance of interest when they were together. She is nothing if not well-mannered – but that hardly means she welcomed being monopolised by a mere boy."

"Hardly that. Really, Edwin, I sometimes think that nothing Matthew does pleases you these days."

"Nonsense! He needs a guiding hand sometimes, that's all. I was sorry you didn't contrive that Sybil should speak to Mrs Morrow a little more. The influence of a woman like that would do her the world of good. Sybil, in contrast to Matthew, has far too little to say for herself."

"I'm afraid she takes after me, Edwin."

"Yes, well –" Clay Tallon harrumphed and rocked backwards and forwards a few times, heel and toe. "Something can, perhaps, be done about it before it's too late." He flashed his practised, charming smile in her direction. "I mean no criticism, of course."

Millicent did not believe him, but neither did she protest. She knew she was a disappointment to him, that he would have preferred to be married to someone whose appearance he could be proud of, but there was little she could do about it now. She rose to her feet.

"I shall go up to bed now, Edwin. It has all been rather tiring –"

"Wait, Millicent. There is something I wish to say on the subject of Sybil."

Resignedly, Millicent paused on her way to the door, sighing a little as she turned to face him.

"Can't it wait until tomorrow?" she asked, without hope. "It's very late."

"We have so little time in which to talk in private. Come, sit down again for a moment. Wait – I shall serve myself with another brandy. There," he said, settling himself beside her, glass in hand, smiling. "What could be more cosy? We should do this more often, my dear."

Millicent was not disarmed and the smile she gave him in return was forced. The subject of Sybil was not one which, in her experience, could ever lead to harmony between them.

"I confess Sybil worries me," Edwin said now, furrowing his brow and staring into his drink. "What is to become of the girl? She is twenty-five, but as awkward as any schoolgirl." He shook his head. "I watched her tonight and despaired, I don't mind telling you. She hasn't a word to say for herself."

"She's shy, Edwin. She's not at her best in society."

"I'm well aware of that! I must say, my dear, that I regard it as a mother's duty – but I shall cast no aspersions. No doubt you have done your best. Your limited best," he added.

"Sybil has the kindest of hearts, Edwin. She is a good girl."

"The point is, Millicent, that she is not a girl. She is a young woman who has been of marriageable age for the past seven years without, so far as I am aware, any man showing the least interest in her."

"Oh, you can't say that! There was that young nephew of Lady Bethune —"

"The long-haired poet? He wasn't at all suitable. Anyway, he went back to London and married some girl as Bohemian as himself, by all accounts. No, Millicent, we must look facts squarely in the face. Sybil has lost her chance of making a good match. It's sad but undeniably true. If she is to marry at all, we must cast our net a little wider." He took a sip of his brandy. "It occurred to me that it is all of three years now since Captain Hawke's wife died. He must surely be looking for some comfort —"

"Edwin, how could you!" Outrage made Millicent unusually vehement. "Captain Hawke is old enough to be Sybil's father!"

"The man's in his prime."

"Forty-five, if a day, and most unprepossessing. Besides, he's no gentleman. I cannot think how you can consider him for one moment."

"I seem to remember your family saying the same about me." Clay Tallon's mouth twisted with bitter amusement. "But I hardly think you have anything to complain about. You have a fine home and every comfort. Hawke has a decent little house on the Bodmin Road —"

"And children of almost Sybil's age whom she has never liked. It really is unthinkable, Edwin."

"Beggars can't be choosers. He's let it be known that he has an eye for her."

Quivering with agitation, Millicent Tallon clasped her hands together.

"Oh, please dismiss it from your mind! She could never be happy with him."

"You would deny her a husband and children of her own?"

"Don't be absurd, Edwin." With tremulous dignity, Millicent rose to her feet once more. "I should like nothing better for her, but I cannot believe Captain Hawke is the right man. I beg you not to encourage him. Simply because you find it rather demeaning to have an unmarried daughter about the place is no reason for pushing her into an unsatisfactory alliance. I have no wish to discuss the matter further and shall go to bed now."

"Goodnight, my dear."

Clay Tallon did not pursue the argument, but he smiled a little as he watched his wife's dignified withdrawal. Once a Trengrose, always a Trengrose, he thought. Underneath that timid exterior, she was just the same as the others – her father and grandfather, and mad Uncle Tom at Carrivick. No one was good enough.

But the jibe about having Sybil still hanging about the house was a little below the belt, surely? Nothing could be more unjust. He would have liked nothing better than to have a decorative, spirited girl to show off to his friends – the kind of daughter that other men admired. But Sybil! It was hardly his fault that she had grown into the awkward, gawky creature who never spoke unless spoken to.

He poured himself another brandy. He had made his bed, chosen his path long ago. Marriage to Millicent had brought its rewards, he'd be the first to admit, and it was futile now to think that things might have been different.

But by Jove – to have money *and* Sarah Sangster! He sighed and shook his head. His old friend Morrow certainly had the luck of the devil.

"Don't you think I behaved myself rather well?" Sarah asked Robert as they drove home from Prospect Lodge, the square and solidly prosperous house on the cliff between the little port of Charlestown and the somewhat larger one of Par which Clay Tallon had built some years before when it had been clear that there was a fortune to be made from the earth's bounty.

"Impeccably," he agreed. "How did you get on with Tallon, now that you've had a chance to see more of him?"

She was silent for a moment, considering the question.

"He's an attractive devil," she said at last. "If you like that sort of man."

"What do you mean?"

"I hardly know. Oh, I'm sure he is everything that is good, since he is a friend of yours –"

"*But –?*"

She laughed and shook her head helplessly.

"I don't know, Robert. He's an impressive figure, I grant you that, and chock-full of charm. I could see that Mrs Penberthy, on his other side, was delighted with him – but somehow I felt those twinkling blue eyes could very rapidly turn cold. I felt it was all an act – but perhaps I am wrong. You know him better than I."

"I admired him greatly during our schooldays. He was excellent at all sports – particularly cricket, I remember. One of the school heroes! I longed to be able to swipe a ball as he did. And then, of course, we met during the holidays when I came to stay with my grandparents. Impossible to think it was all so long ago. I thought you were getting along like a house on fire. From my end of the table you looked engrossed in his conversation."

"Oh, he's entertaining enough, I suppose, though most frightfully pleased with himself. *His* struggle, *his* business methods, *his* house, *his* view of the sea – I was invited to admire them all. Even the view seemed to be regarded as some sort of personal achievement, nothing to do with the Almighty at all!"

"He has achieved a lot, though I guess marrying a Trengrose gave him a head start."

"That was the most endearing thing about him, actually, his apparent devotion to the clay industry. I learned quite a bit. I had no idea it was used so extensively in paper manufacture."

"It gives the paper gloss and weight –"

"My dear Robert, pray don't think there is anything you can tell me about it! Talking of marrying a Trengrose, one of his less endearing traits was the way he treated his wife. I thought him too offhand for words. Really, he acts as if she were less than the dust, did you notice?"

"Indeed I did." Robert peered out of the window of the brougham to check on their progress. "I thought of asking him how he contrived to get away with it. I imagine that I would be at the receiving end of a divorce petition were I to try it. Or a black eye, at the very least."

"At the very least," Sarah agreed severely, giving his arm a shake. "But you never would. You really are rather a sweet

38

man, and what I am to do when you go away to foreign parts, I really don't know. Do you really have to go to those horrid estates?"

"Those horrid estates will hardly look after themselves, my darling. And we need them to provide our far-from-horrid income, so we must both grin and bear it. By the way, Tallon assured me that you must regard them as your second family while I'm away and not hesitate to call upon them if you need help of any sort."

"How kind," Sarah said, without enthusiasm.

"What did you think of Mrs Tallon?"

Sarah was silent for a few moments.

"I liked her," she said at last. "I think! The poor soul is so cowed by her lord and master that she can barely string two words together without looking at him for approval – but I was impressed at the way she blossomed when the subject of gardening was introduced, if you'll forgive the pun. There is, perhaps, more to her than meets the eye."

"Her appearance does her no favours."

Sarah twisted her lips cynically.

"Well, you said it yourself. She was a Trengrose. No doubt she had other attractions apart from her looks."

"Such things happen."

"It's a pity the daughter is so like her mother," Sarah said after a moment. "And who could have encouraged her to wear that particular shade of green, I can't imagine! I had little chance to speak to her, but it appeared that you were finding it somewhat heavy-going at dinner."

"You could say so," Robert admitted with a laugh. "I asked her if she enjoyed riding; she said 'Yes'. I then asked if she rode to hounds, and she said 'No'. Conversation languished a little after that, though I promise I did my best. The poor girl is painfully shy, though not without a certain dry humour."

"Perhaps I should take her in hand."

"Perhaps you should. You were dazzling, my love. I can still hardly believe it, when I look across a room and realise that you belong to me –"

"*What?*" Sarah uttered the word in a way that made it sound like a whiplash. She removed the arm that she had put cosily through his and turned an icy glare upon him. "I belong to nobody, Robert. I made that clear, surely, before I agreed to marry you. The fact that we are married, that we are lovers and friends and enjoy each other's company, doesn't mean that you possess me, or that I possess you."

"I'm sorry, I'm sorry!" Half-laughing at her vehemence, Robert took her gently by the shoulders and kissed her cheek. "It was a slip of the tongue. I merely meant that I was proud to have you as my wife. Will that do?"

"Only just." She laughed too, and reaching up, kissed his cheek in her turn. "I'm sorry if I snapped at you. I'm too old and too independent to be a submissive wife – but oh, Robert –" remembering Edwin Tallon's compliment, she giggled like a schoolgirl. "Would it surprise you to know that Mr Tallon is astonished to find me both beautiful and intelligent? Such a combination is something of a rarity, he says."

"And what did you reply to that?"

"I blushed demurely and did my best not to laugh."

"You're a wicked woman. Tallon's not such a bad sort of chap."

"No?" Her voice was amused, unconvinced. "Perhaps not."

"He's much liked by his workforce, I believe. He's known as a bit of a card – a character. Always a cheery word. I suppose one can say he has the common touch. His peers respect him, too. He's the kind of man that has made this country prosperous – adventurous, ambitious, but at the same time hard-working, with a solid foundation of common sense."

"A paragon," murmured Sarah, unconvinced. "It sounds as if you still regard him as a hero."

"Hardly that! I believe there is much to commend him, though. And he has been kind to us, as newcomers. I think we should take him at his face value, don't you? I feel sure that his heart is in the right place."

"That always seems to imply that everything else is in the wrong one."

Sarah's reply was flippant, but she followed it with a sigh. Much as she loved Carrivick, it was impossible not to feel a little ill at ease in this new world. The ways of its inhabitants were not her ways.

"We're home," Robert said, as the brougham passed through the open gates; and at once her brief moment of doubt dissolved and was gone.

Her life had been a long and winding road, with many a diversion along the way; but here, at last, was the haven she had always sought. Here was where she belonged.

❦ 3 ❧

"That boy will learn to read if it's the last thing I do," vowed Loveday through clenched teeth, storming back into the house after one of her extra lessons with Henry.

Dolly Crowle, who had called for tea and had been persuaded by John Pentecost to stay and chat with him in Loveday's absence, gave her friend a sympathetic look.

"I don't know why you bother with him, Loveday, that I don't."

"I don't know, either. The child is a monster. Oh Dolly, how lovely it is to see your smiling face! I'm sorry I wasn't here to greet you. Pray, save my life and pour me some tea."

"No improvement?" Her father lifted his eyebrows in enquiry as he passed her cup, and she took a sip before replying.

"D'you know, I thought there was, at first?" She sighed. "Perhaps I wasn't altogether wrong. I've thought up a game he likes to play, fitting together pictures of objects and their names, and while he's doing that, all is well – but oh, how different when we begin writing! He sits there simply *smouldering* with resentment."

"You ask me, you deserve a medal," Dolly said, and Loveday sighed again.

"No, I don't. It's only sheer pig-headedness that's keeping me going. I simply refuse to be beaten by Henry Tregilgas, and that's the truth of it."

"But not the whole truth, if I'm any judge," her father said.

"Well, perhaps not quite the whole truth." Loveday smiled

at him. "There's something –" She shrugged her shoulders. "I don't know! Something truly brave and admirable about the way he refuses to give up. He gets angry, but somehow I never feel it's directed at me. I can't help feeling sorry for him. I have the feeling that underneath his anger and rudeness, he is utterly miserable. The way he glares at me through that tangle of hair makes me think of a small furry animal, trapped in a snare. There, it only takes one cup of tea to make me think kindly of him again – so perhaps that's your answer, Dolly. I go on battling with Henry because I have an outrageously short memory."

"Perhaps we should ask why he keeps turning up for these extra lessons when he's under no compulsion," John Pentecost said. "Deep inside himself, he must want to learn. Keep up the good work, Loveday."

"I've no doubt I will," she replied, a resigned note in her voice.

The following morning when she sat at the teacher's desk to take her class register, her eye was caught by a large piece of paper which had no place there. It was a picture of a squirrel holding a nut between its paws, drawn in charcoal. She picked it up and studied it with interest, wondering where it had come from and who was the artist. Though it had been drawn on the back of an old handbill, it had been executed with far more attention to detail and considerably more talent than she might have expected from anyone in the school, let alone any child in her class.

"Who put this on my desk?" she asked, looking round the room. "See, children – isn't this a lovely picture? Does anyone know anything about it?"

" 'Twas 'Enry Tregilgas, Miss," a voice at the back informed her. "I seen un come in and leave un down."

And where, she wondered, had Henry acquired it? Later on, at midday, she sought him out in the playground where he stood alone and unbefriended, an expression of bitter scorn on his face as he looked towards a group of boys who were kicking a ball about. She was struck by his thinness, and the boniness of his wrists and ankles as they projected from his ragged clothes. She called his name, and he stared at her almost defensively, half-turning as she approached him as if

43

he feared her and would run away, if he had anywhere to run to.

"Henry, is it true that you put that picture on my desk? That lovely squirrel?"

The dark eyes narrowed in his foxy little face.

"What if I did?"

"Just that I wanted to thank you. I like it very much."

A certain tension seemed to go from him, and an expression that was almost a smile came over his face. He turned his head a little as if to hide his pleasure from her.

" 'Tidn't nawthin'," he said gruffly.

She hadn't considered, somehow, that he could have drawn it himself; not Henry, who could not form his letters or apparently recognise the shape of them. Now, suddenly, she realised the truth.

"Henry, you drew it, didn't you?"

He lifted his head, returning her questioning look with one that was both triumphant and scornful.

"Ar," he said.

Loveday shook her head in amazed disbelief.

"It's good – it's very good indeed."

" 'Tidn't me best. Cain't do me best on an old scrap o' paper like that."

"But why haven't you shown us what you could do before this? Why have you made a secret of it? Neither my father nor I had any idea – and you've been in the school so long! You should have told us, Henry."

He shrugged in reply, as if supremely indifferent to the opinion of others.

"Didn't feel like ut," he said. " 'Tidn't no one's business but mine."

"What do you like to draw most of all?"

He shrugged again.

"Birds and cats and rabbuts an' all that trade." His eyes brightened with a kind of sly eagerness. "Tell ee what, Miss. Give I the paper, an' I'll do ee a kitty."

"Thank you. I should like that very much. When you come for your lesson at four o'clock I shall see what I can find for you."

She smiled at him and began to walk back towards the

school, but a sudden thought struck her and she paused, turning to look at the boy once more. "Henry, can you draw a hedgehog?"

" 'Ess," he replied, drawing out the word in a way that suggested utter scorn for anyone who could not.

"Then may I ask you a favour? Please come and draw one on the board for me now. It's nature study next lesson –"

"Cain't ee do it, then?"

"Not nearly so well as you."

The boy gave her a look in which pleasure, contempt and arrogance were evenly mingled and without a word he made for the school and the infants' room. Loveday watched with admiration and increased astonishment as he performed the task she had given him.

"There," he said when he had finished. " 'Tidn't what I call *good* –"

"Thank you very much, Henry. It's a great deal better than I could do."

"I know ut," he said, with a hard, scornful little laugh.

Loveday studied both the squirrel and the hedgehog once again when he had gone, and shook her head slowly. It defied belief that Henry Tregilgas should possess such a talent, yet should have hidden it for so long.

"It was his secret, but he's made a gift of it to you," her father said, when she told him and showed him the pictures. "It's quite an honour. You've won a small battle, Loveday, and you must build on it. At least he's on your side now."

"You wouldn't have thought it, if you'd seen the way he glared at me!"

Still, she pinned the picture of the squirrel in her room, recognising its importance, hoping that it would encourage her when the strength of her purpose faltered. Knowing Henry, she felt sure it would, sooner or later. He would try the patience of a saint, she thought, and – as she had established long ago – she was no saint, and never would be.

The white square of paper, gleaming in the darkness, was the last thing she saw before she went to sleep that night.

"You'll read, my boy," she warned the absent Henry silently. "You'll read, if I die in the attempt."

* * *

Sarah dreaded Robert's departure for India, but she knew it was inevitable.

"Why not go to London for a while?" he suggested, for he had kept his town house and it waited, shuttered and shrouded in dust sheets, for an occasional visit. She shook her head.

"No, Robert. I want to – to consolidate, as it were. Besides, I want to be here when they start on the building work in the garden. I know exactly where I want the balustrades and the flight of steps, and I'd hate to go away only to find they'd put them in the wrong place. There's plenty to occupy me, but you must allow me to miss you wherever I'm domiciled!"

"I very much hope that you will."

It was proving sweet, this September marriage. For a wealthy man, Robert was remarkably sensitive, Sarah considered. He had paid court to her for years, asking her to marry him on more occasions than she could count. For as many years, she had refused him, knowing herself unable to give up a career which was so rewarding on every level.

She knew what people said – that she feared losing her looks and had finally accepted the comfortable option that Robert Morrow offered her; and, in a way, she supposed there was something in it. She hated the thought of a gradual decline, of a slow diminution of acclaim and applause, of people saying 'Isn't it a pity? I remember her when –' But this was far from the whole story. Gradually she had seen Robert in a new light, and had come to appreciate his gentleness and quiet humour – and yes, his simplicity, for it was the simple things that they most enjoyed: country walks, gardening, reading before a log fire. How astonished and amused Lucy Villiers would be by it all, Sarah thought from time to time. And how little she cared *what* Lucy Villiers thought!

No, she would not go to London, but would stay at home and wait for her husband like a good wife should. And she would occupy her time by taking the governess cart and exploring the neighbourhood, driving down the little lanes that so far they had bypassed, discovering odd byways and hidden hamlets, of which there seemed so many in the least expected corners.

"I will write," she promised Robert. "As you must, too.

And I shall spend the time you are away planning a grand celebration ball for your return, since you tell me that it will be Christmas before I see you again."

She drove with him to the station on an October morning when mist still clung to hedges and spiders' webs were spangled with dew. Russet beech trees met above their heads in the narrow lane which led to the main St Austell road, but by the time she returned the mist had evaporated in warm sunshine and the leaves had turned to gold. A perfect gardening day, she thought with satisfaction, and occupied herself happily until weariness brought her indoors to rest.

It was while she was having tea beside the fire that Matthew Tallon was announced, and she welcomed him wholeheartedly, in spite of her tiredness.

"What a delightful surprise," she said. "Mollie, please bring an extra cup and plate. Come, Matthew, sit down and help me eat some of this sinful chocolate cake that Mrs Lane insists on making for me. Tell me, what brings you to these parts?"

"It was business connected with the property my father still owns in St Ninn. When he sold the Manor to you, he retained the cottages that were part of the Trengrose estate, as you know, and now must repair them – and speaking of repairs, I am astounded by all that you have done here! I barely recognise the place. It's beautiful."

"I'm ashamed that we have entertained so little, but we've been in such turmoil. And now Robert is away for two months at the very least –"

"I hadn't realised he was going so soon. I came with a message from my father asking him to come on a shoot."

"He would have loved it, I'm sure. You must ask him again when he returns. How are your mother and father? And Sybil?"

"Very well, thank you. Well –" He seemed to think better of his words, and hesitated for a moment. "Sybil isn't in the best of form. She's had the dressmaker to call today, to make a bridesmaid's dress for the wedding of her friend, Sophie Nugent, and if there's one thing Sybil hates, it's being fussed about her clothes. If she could wear a riding habit for every social occasion, she might be happy – though on the other hand, I don't suppose she would. She dislikes social occasions on principle!"

"Even weddings?"

Matthew laughed ruefully.

"Especially weddings. All her friends seem to be indulging in them, and she knows full well that everyone looks at her and wonders if she will ever catch herself a husband."

"What an inelegant way of expressing it! Do your parents feel the same way?"

Matthew pulled a face.

"Mm. 'Fraid so. Especially Father. It's really very hard on poor Sybil. He would love her to marry into one of the county families. It would have reinforced his own position, you see – given him something to boast about. And it has to be said, Father loves to have something to boast about! However, you've seen Sybil. She simply isn't the type. He's disappointed in her, and she knows it."

"That's a great pity."

"Yes, it is." Matthew was serious now. "She's shy by nature, as you must have seen, and Father's attitude hardly helps her. He keeps urging her to get out and about – go to house parties and tennis parties and so on, but all she really wants to do is go off by herself in the country, or stay in her room and scribble."

"Scribble?"

Matthew bit his lip.

"I shouldn't have said that. She'd be furious with me if she knew I'd let the cat out of the bag. Father's forbidden it."

Sarah stared at him, open-mouthed.

"Forbidden it? But why, for the love of heaven? It's a harmless enough occupation, surely?"

"He thinks it's bad for her. He's only thinking of her good, he says – if she stays alone in her room she'll only become more shy and reclusive, with no chance at all of meeting people. For 'people' read 'husband'!"

"I see."

"There's another reason, too. He found and read one of her stories about a girl who defied her father and ran away from home, which certainly would explain why he's so against the whole business. He doesn't take kindly to defiance."

"Poor Sybil! But she still goes on?"

"In secret. You won't say anything –?"

"Of course not. As if I would."

Sarah was intrigued, however. She felt this cast a different and interesting light upon Sybil Tallon.

"Does your father have any particular suitor in view?"

"Not that I know of. I rather think he's so desperate to push her off the shelf that almost anyone would do, so long as he isn't criminally insane and can keep her in the style to which she is more or less accustomed. She says she understands now how slaves must feel when they're offered in the market to the highest bidder, and that she feels like the puniest, most useless slave on show. Poor old Sybil! It's a shame, for she's a good sort."

"I think," Sarah said, mildly reproving, "that of all insults, being called a 'good sort' is one of the worst. It has a patronising ring to it. Pray don't tell Sybil that she is a 'good sort'. Tell her that she has fine eyes and a beautiful complexion, both of which are true."

"She'd wonder what had come over me if I did!"

"You should try it, even so. And bring her to see me some time." Smiling, Sarah offered him more cake. "And you? What plans do your parents have for your future?"

For a moment Matthew hesitated.

"None, I hope, if you mean marriage plans. Oh, Father throws out the odd hint from time to time about the desirability of my making a suitable match, but I take no notice." He grinned. "Cap'n Noah tells me I should take my time. 'You'm a long time married, boy,' he says."

"And who might Cap'n Noah be?"

"Noah Pascoe – a man who's forgotten more about the clay business than most people ever knew. A terrifying fellow. Everyone jumps when he says the word."

"Why 'captain'?"

"Every mine has its captain. He's captain of Trelew."

"Like a manager?"

"Well –" Matthew considered the matter. "I suppose so, but it's more than that – much, much more. He wields a great deal of power. He can hire men and lay them off, too. A good captain is worth his weight in gold to an owner."

"And this Cap'n Noah – he is a good captain?"

Matthew gave a short laugh.

"A little grudgingly, I have to admit he's the best. The men hate him, but that's because he acts as a kind of whipping boy. It's Father who lays down the rules, replaces equipment or doesn't replace it, and so on; but good old Clay Tallon's a genial, smiling, remote figure whom everyone likes. Cap'n Noah is the man on the spot."

"And he gets the blame for unpopular measures?"

"Exactly. And rather glories in it, it seems to me. Still, everything I've learned, I've learned from him. He joined as a kettle-boy at the age of twelve and has done just about every job it's possible for a man to do. He took me under his wing when I first left school, and I couldn't have had a better teacher, even if I was scared stiff of him. I've seen grown men turn pale when they realised he's caught them out in some way. No one can hide sloppy work or a job half-done, and woe betide anyone who tries."

Sarah studied him, her head on one side.

"Yet, do you know," she said, "there's something in your voice that tells me you quite like this terrifying gentleman."

"*Like* him?" Matthew gave an astounded laugh as if such a thing was out of the question; then appeared to reconsider the matter. "Well, perhaps," he said. "I respect him, anyway. He's absolutely straight with the men, which is more than can be said for some others."

Others like Clay Tallon? Sarah wondered. She offered more cake.

"And how about you? Do you find the business interesting?"

"Yes, I do. I've learned it from the bottom up, Cap'n Noah saw to that – from digging the levels for the slurry, to pumping it and drying it and eventually shipping it. There's a great deal more to it than you might think – and fascinating new uses for it being discovered all the time. It's the shipping that I'm mostly concerned with now."

"Your father must be quite delighted to have you following in his footsteps," Sarah said, Matthew made no reply apart from a noncommittal smile. She tilted her head, narrowed her eyes and studied him closely. "*Isn't* he delighted?" she asked provocatively.

"Oh yes, I expect so. Yes, of course he is. It's just that – oh, I don't know how to say it without appearing quite monstrously disloyal! You must understand, in many ways I admire my father greatly –" He hesitated, and looked at her shamefacedly.

"*But?*"

"There has to be a 'but' after such a beginning, doesn't there? The truth is that my father can make me angrier than anyone else in the entire world if he puts his mind to it, and I'm afraid I have the same effect on him."

"I'm the soul of discretion, if you want to talk about it."

Matthew hesitated for a moment, tempted by her sympathetic presence, but eventually resisted the impulse to confide. There was, he reminded himself, such a thing as family loyalty – but how ironic that he could talk with such ease to a comparative stranger such as Sarah Morrow when communication with his own father was so difficult.

"I suppose it's a problem that time will eventually cure," he said. "One day he'll realise that I do know something about the business, and that not all my ideas are wild and impractical. At the moment he is convinced I'm still wet behind the ears." He laughed and shrugged his shoulders. "I suppose he could be right."

"Well, perhaps," Sarah said gently.

"Do you know what really bothers me, Mrs Morrow? We are too alike, my father and I. I suspect that's why we have such rows."

"Really? It hadn't occurred to me that you were at all alike – except in some physical details."

"Oh, we are, believe me – in some ways, at least." His wry smile seemed to indicate that he was not entirely delighted by the likeness, if it existed.

"In what way are you alike?" Sarah persisted.

He hesitated for a moment.

"I suppose – I suppose in our desire to be liked and admired. We like to be –" He gestured helplessly with his hands. "Oh,

I don't know exactly how to express it! We like to be in control. Top dog, I suppose."

"It's a very human failing, and common to many of us."

"I suppose so. It falls considerably short of my ideal, however. Such things shouldn't matter."

"Well, at least you have ideals." Somehow Sarah doubted that Clay Tallon knew the meaning of the word.

"I must inherit them from my mother," he said, and she smiled uncertainly, feeling as if he must have read her thoughts. "By the way," he went on, "my mother very much enjoyed meeting you the other evening."

"The pleasure was mutual," Sarah responded. "I hope I get to know her better."

"I hope you do, too. She's so kind and really very wise in her gentle way. You would like her, I'm sure, though she's too shy to make friends easily – really far too unassertive for her own good." He gave a brief laugh. "Except in the matter of Piper's Piece, of course."

"And what, may I ask, is Piper's Piece?"

"It's a piece of land – just a rough field, with a stream running through it. It's the stream that's important. Water, you see, is a very, very necessary element in the production of clay, as Mother well knows, and access to this stream just happens to be essential for the works at Trelew. She inherited Piper's Piece along with other Trengrose land, and though naturally she's happy enough to allow Tallons to make use of the stream, she's always refused to make the field over to Father officially, unlike everything else." Matthew laughed wickedly. "Sybil says it's her insurance policy. If Father gets too out of hand, she can always threaten to sell to a competitor. It's something of a family joke, though I don't think it amuses Father as much as he pretends."

"I think she's very wise. We women need every little bit of power we can get."

"Imagination boggles at the thought of anyone bullying *you*!" Matthew said, laughing. "By the by, my father admires you greatly, and I was severely reprimanded for taking up so much of your time that night you came to dinner. I think he would have preferred to be taking it up himself. I hope I didn't appear too – too forward?"

There was a touch of vulnerability in his smile. He was, Sarah thought, a rather endearing young man, not nearly so sure of himself as he tried to make out.

"I *loved* it," she said roundly, bending forward impulsively to pat his arm. "You entertained me beautifully, and I've laughed to myself several times since, thinking of some of your stories. If that's being forward, then you can be it any time you wish."

He left shortly afterwards, leaving Sarah to ponder on the subject of parents and children. Was it only because she had none herself that she saw so clearly where parents were going wrong? Very likely! Mrs Foster at the post office had acquainted her with an old Cornish saying only the other day. 'Everybody do know what to do with a kicking 'oss, save he that got un,' she had said, and it was perfectly true. Nothing would seem so simple if she herself had the responsibility.

But what would it have been like, having children?

It was a question that, uncharacteristically, she found impossible to dismiss during the course of the evening. Suppose she and Robert had married twenty years ago? She could have had a son very nearly the same age as Matthew! It seemed an astonishing thought – but even more astonishing was the fact that, in spite of all the applause and the adulation that had been heaped upon her, suddenly her childlessness, for the first time, seemed a matter for regret, the cause of a vague and formless depression that descended on her unawares.

By morning, after a good night's sleep, she was able to laugh at her foolishness, for it was not her style to bemoan what might have been, particularly when she was perfectly aware of how much she had to be thankful for. She was more than content with her new life, she told herself firmly – and content, too, with her own company if she could not have Robert's.

This was just as well since she had no further callers that week, though an invitation arrived from Millicent Tallon asking her to a small tea party on the following Wednesday.

"I should have asked you before, had I known your husband was already gone," she wrote. "It was only when Matthew told me that I realised you were on your own. I hope very much that you are able to come."

It would, perhaps, make a diversion, Sarah thought, and it would do her good to make some new acquaintances, as well as furthering her friendship with Millicent Tallon. She wrote a graceful acceptance, and on the appointed day took herself in the trap, choosing to drive to St Austell along the higher road, via Trelew.

What strange country it was, she thought, as the lane wound upwards to where the seamed white pyramids of clay-spoil dominated the village of Trelew, where the whole landscape was scarred by pits. It was from these pits, so she had learned from Mr Tallon, that the slurry – presumably washed down by the stream that ran through Piper's Piece – was piped to the drying sheds, one of which lay a little ahead beside the road. Smoke belched from the chimney of the long, low building, amid countryside so whitened by the clay that it looked as if snow had fallen.

Though at her back the distant sea glinted silver, the village itself was bleak and charmless, the Primitive Methodist Chapel the one building of any size in the line of mean cottages, all overshadowed by the clay heaps. It was a relief to leave it all behind as the road dropped down towards St Austell.

The ladies she had been invited to meet were all in some way connected with the clay industry – or at least, their husbands were. Both Mrs Penberthy and Mrs Trevose were there. She had met Mrs Penberthy once before at the dinner party, and her smiling greeting owed more to politeness than to genuine enthusiasm.

She was also introduced to a Mrs Augusta Nancarrow, whose husband was the owner of a small fleet of ships which carried the precious china clay from the ports of Par and Fowey, Charlestown and Pentewan, to the far corners of the earth.

Driving home after the tea party, Sarah could not avoid the conclusion that it had been a strangely unsatisfactory occasion. Conversation with Millicent Tallon was difficult to sustain once horticultural matters were exhausted. Sweet and gentle she might be, as Matthew had said, but she appeared to have no firmly held opinions of her own, or at least no ability to convey them. Sarah felt sure her husband was entirely to blame for her diffidence. He had entirely destroyed her self-confidence.

And as for Mrs Penberthy and Mrs Trevose – well! Their conversation seemed to be strictly limited to idle and small-minded gossip that became tedious beyond belief!

If it had been theatre gossip you wouldn't have minded it at all, Sarah said to herself severely, and smiled a little as she recognised the truth of this. She and Lucy Villiers could talk for hours about the doings of their fellow actors without being bored for a moment.

The trouble is, Sarah thought, that this gossip isn't *my* gossip. She had, if the truth were known, found great difficulty in hiding her boredom at the endless discussion of what unknown ladies had worn at various functions, whom they danced with, whom their husbands danced with and what comments had been made by the world at large.

Mrs Nancarrow was older than the others, and very earnest. She did not attend frivolous things like dances, it seemed, and looked thoroughly disapproving while all the tittle-tattle was being exchanged; but she was not above a little tittle-tattle of her own, Sarah learned. She was astonished and amused at the feuds that were revealed by the worthy Mrs Nancarrow, who eventually seized the opportunity to speak at great length of the petty jealousies that lay beneath the surface of this committee and that bazaar. Had the ladies of the county ever resorted to pistols at dawn? Sarah had asked humorously; but her only reply was a blank and uncomprehending stare.

Thinking over the matter as she drove homeward, Sarah laughed quietly to herself. It was indeed a different world from the one she had inhabited in her previous life; and perhaps Lucy Villiers was not so far from the mark when she had said that Sarah would find no one to speak her language.

The laugh turned to a sigh.

"Oh, come back soon, Robert," she said aloud. "Please come back soon."

She missed his company and conversation sorely, but she acknowledged to herself that the days passed pleasantly enough. She walked into St Ninn and exchanged small-talk with Letty Foster, the postmistress, and Mrs Chenoweth, who kept the general store. Mr Peake, the vicar, had called with his sister who kept house for him and had been persuaded to stay for tea, and the surrounding countryside was a constant source of interest and pleasure.

On a day that was warm for the time of year even though the sky was cloudy, Sarah took the notion to walk in a direction she had not taken before. There was a gate in the fence that bordered the more formal garden, and this led into Carrivick Woods. Part belonged to Carrivick Manor and was private land, an area of woodland with wide bridle-paths, and here she and Robert had often walked together before his departure, enjoying the cool shade in the height of summer and the changing colours of the leaves as the year moved towards autumn.

The wood continued beyond another gate set in a thick, evergreen hedge, and here it was much thicker and wilder. This, like the cottages in St Ninn, still belonged to the Tallon family, held against the day, presumably, when they might want to extend their clay empire. Until that day it was, to the best of her knowledge, used as common land.

She went through the gate and for a while skirted this further wood until she found a steep and stony path, leading upwards between bushes decked with old man's beard, thick brambles which bore wizened blackberries long past picking, and holly trees where berries gleamed as if to remind her that Christmas was not far distant.

For a moment she stopped to catch her breath, and looking back the way she had come, her gaze sharpened. She had seen birds in plenty and once a rabbit during the course of her walk, but the movement that caught her eye could only be explained by the presence of a human somewhere on the path behind her. She waited a moment, but no one appeared, and curious now to see where this path emerged she continued on her way.

At a bend in the track there was a tree she did not recognise, its leaves spiky and almost oriental in their delicacy. She stopped to examine them more closely, and as she did so heard the unmistakable sound of a boot slipping a little on the shaly path. Once more she looked behind her and once more saw the flash of dun-coloured cloth she had noticed before; but it merged into the undergrowth, as if its owner, seeing her interest, remained motionless, waiting for her to turn and walk on once again.

There was no reason why others should not walk this way. Why was this particular walker so shy? It gave her an eerie feeling, knowing that someone was there, following her, keeping out of sight.

She walked on and round another bend came upon a small clearing. Here she waited, concealed by a thick bush, and only a few moments passed before she heard muted footsteps, as if care was being taken not to dislodge any more stones. Soon she could hear laboured breathing, for the way was steep. Her own heart was beating rapidly, and she expelled her breath with relief when into her limited line of vision came, not the predatory monster she had begun to fear, but a boy.

He passed without seeing her in the small hidden corner where she waited, but when she stepped out on the path, herself the follower now, he whipped round to face her like a cornered fox. He was about ten or eleven years old, she judged, very thin, with ragged clothes and wild, unkempt hair. His shoulders were hunched, his fists clenched.

"Good afternoon," she said politely, but he continued to stare at her, unmoving. What did he fear? There was tension in every line of his body, a defensiveness, as if he saw her as a threat. She made to continue her walk and he pressed back into the bushes, his wide, dark eyes never leaving her.

"Don't look so anxious," she said as she drew level with him. "Tell me, does this path come out on the moor?"

A pointed tongue flicked out, licking his lips.

"Ar," he said after a moment.

Since no further information was forthcoming, she smiled at him and went on her way. If the boy was correct, it was easier for her to go on and walk back to Carrivick via the road than to turn back now and return the way she had come. The question, she thought as she gave a worried look at the sky, was more than academic. She had been preoccupied with other things and had not noticed how threatening the clouds had become – how they had massed and darkened. The wind

57

had got up, and quite large branches were stirring and tossing in the wood behind her.

It was clear that the trees were thinning, growing more stunted. The grass beneath them was different, too – spiky and coarse. She was already hurrying, but increased her pace as she felt a large spot of rain. What a fool she was, she thought; how unwise in the ways of the countryside! She was not dressed for wet weather and had no umbrella with her. She had walked on and on without thought of the elements, and it was clear that she was about to pay for her foolishness.

She held her hat on with one hand, picked up her skirts with the other, and half-ran towards the road she could now see before her – the road which led from Trelew to St Ninn and went past the gate to Carrick Manor. She had not realised that the woodland path would emerge so far along this road. She was not more than a hundred yards or so from the schoolhouse, she saw to her surprise – that incongruous, pompous building with its Gothic gables and long, narrow windows like arrow slits that she and Robert had passed many times on their way to St Austell. That meant that there was almost three miles still to go before she was in the shelter of her own four walls.

There was no doubt that the rain was beginning in earnest now, but as she left the shelter of the stunted trees behind her and came to the open road, she saw to her dismay that there was worse to come. Looking towards St Ninn and beyond it to the distant sea, she could see the rain like a solid black line moving towards her, shrouding the countryside as it came.

For a moment she hesitated, the wind suddenly so strong that she could almost lean against it. Despite her efforts to hold on to her hat, it was whipped from her head and sent bowling across the moor. Then all at once the rain was upon her, slashing and driving with such fury that she could barely see her way.

It was all too clear that she would be soaked through in minutes. Already her hair had come down and was hanging in bedraggled locks around her face. Wildly she looked around for shelter. There was a farm and farm buildings at some distance over to the right, but far nearer was the school and it was towards this that she started to make her way as quickly as she could manage it, the wind buffeting her every inch of the way.

Any hopes of getting there before being drenched to the skin were quickly dashed. Climbing the steep woodland path, she had felt too hot in her corduroy skirt and jacket. Now she was icy cold and soaking wet, and as she ran she found herself gasping aloud with the misery of her condition.

Suppose no one was in the schoolhouse to let her in? The children would certainly have gone home long ago. Did anyone actually live on the premises? She thought so, but could not be certain. Heaven alone knew what the custom was in this part of the country.

A gust of wind caught her as she reached the open gate and seemed to blow her inside it. Only a few yards now – and yes, there *was* a house facing the school across a yard, and even as she hurried towards it she saw someone move towards the window and peer out at the torrential rain. Thank God, thank God!

There was a small porch with a steep pitched roof which afforded partial shelter. The door was of oak with iron studs, and had a bell-pull by its side. Sarah stretched out her hand towards it, but before she could touch it, the door swung open.

Never, she thought with relief, had she seen such a delightful sight as the girl who stood there, or heard more welcome words than her urgent invitation to come inside.

❦ 4 ❧

Once beyond the door, it was like a different world. The house was warm and there was a smell of newly baked bread, logs burning, beeswax and books and lamp oil, combining to create an atmosphere that was both comforting and wel-‘coming, a feeling that was enhanced by the concern of the girl who had opened the door to her.

"I'm afraid I'm dripping on your shiny floor," Sarah said apologetically, mopping her face with her handkerchief.

The girl brushed this aside.

"Never mind the floor. You're soaked through. It's – it's Mrs Morrow, isn't it? I've seen you in the village, but I didn't recognise you at first." Loveday forgot her shyness as she took in the visitor's bedraggled state. "Oh, you poor thing! Come through to the parlour and get warm."

"I must look like a tramp," Sarah said. "The wind took my hat –"

"Did you come on foot?"

"Why I should have chosen today to embark on a country walk, I can't imagine! My dear, I really can't come into your parlour like this. Haven't you a kitchen range where I can steam gently until done?" Sarah looked from Loveday towards the door to the parlour where a man, presumably the schoolmaster, had appeared. She dipped her head towards him smilingly.

"Good afternoon, sir. Contrary to appearances I am not a travelling mendicant, but merely an orphan of the storm –"

The man came towards her with his hand outstretched.

"We're honoured to give you sanctuary," he said. His

smile, Sarah thought, lit his ravaged face in the most extra-ordinary way. He was thin – too thin for health – and looked even thinner because of his height, but still there was something about his eyes which made her feel that he was more alive than many who enjoyed more robust health. "I am John Pentecost, and this is Loveday, my daughter. You, of course, are the incomparable Sarah Sangster – though I am aware I should call you Mrs Morrow now."

"I am delighted to meet you, Mr Pentecost, Miss Pentecost –"

"Loveday, is it possible to find Mrs Morrow something dry to wear?"

An enchanting girl, Sarah thought, as Loveday – rather pink with shyness – took her upstairs to the bare little bed-room with its cheap painted furniture and dimity curtains.

"I hate to put you to so much trouble," Sarah said.

"It's no trouble, Mrs Morrow. Your clothes will dry in no time down on the rack. The only thing is that mine are very plain –"

"With the waist, I dare say, several inches too small! I've been casting envious glances at you as we walked up the stairs. My dear, please don't worry. I shall be happy in any sort of packaging, just so long as I can shed this wet skirt and dry my hair a little."

It was not more than fifteen minutes before Sarah re-appeared, dressed in a black skirt and white shirtwaister, her hair combed back and fastened in a simple style that made her look little older than Loveday herself, John thought.

"And no older than you looked when I saw you as Portia," he said, when she was seated by the fire sipping a steaming cup of tea.

"You saw that? My goodness, that must have been all of twenty years ago."

"Nineteen," John corrected her. "My wife and I were newly married. We were – oh, how can I put it? – *elevated* by your performance! Why is it that one finds total perfection so touching?"

"I don't know, but I feel that kind of emotion when I look down on St Ninn and the hills and the sea from the moorland road. I can't tell you what an honour it is to think that someone, just for a moment, felt the same way about a performance of mine."

"And now you've given it all up?"

"Without any regrets – or very few, I promise you. Life moves on."

"Yes."

The lamps were lit, but John Pentecost's face was in shadow so that it was impossible to see his expression. There was something about his monosyllabic reply, however, that made Sarah look at him curiously.

"May I offer you more tea?" Loveday asked.

Gratefully Sarah accepted.

"I was worried that there would be no one at home," she said as she handed Loveday her cup. "I longed for shelter, but had no idea that I would find myself in the lap of luxury. I've never felt so warm and comfortable and cosseted in my entire life."

John flashed his warm smile at her again.

"Only to someone as wet and cold as you were would a fire in an isolated schoolhouse seem like luxury."

"*And* dry clothes, *and* hot tea, *and* delicious plum cake. Did you make this, Miss Pentecost?"

"I'm afraid not. Mrs Rowse from one of the Roskelly cottages comes in and does most of the cooking."

"Is Maisie back?" John Pentecost asked his daughter. He turned to Sarah. "Maisie Foster is our little maid, and we're rather afraid that she might have suffered the same fate as you. She went to see her mother in St Ninn this afternoon, and could well have been caught on the moor."

"Is she the daughter of Mrs Foster of the post office? She who knows all the gossip?"

"The very same. We are quite exceptionally well-informed in this house!"

"And so am I. Mrs Foster told me that her daughter was very happy in her place – a matter on which I congratulated her, for there can be nothing worse than worrying about a daughter who's left home."

"Let's hope she hadn't started out before the rain began," Loveday said.

"If she did, she probably had the sense to be more suitably

dressed than I was. When I set out I had no thought of coming so far, but the further I went on, the more sensible it seemed to keep going. I'm not so sure now, though. That path through the wood cuts off considerably more of the distance than you might imagine. I was astonished when I saw how far along the road it emerged."

"D'you know, I don't think we've ever walked it all the way to St Ninn, have we, Loveday?" John Pentecost looked questioningly at his daughter. "You see," he added for Sarah's benefit, "it comes out on your land, and Sir Thomas Trengrose would have hung, drawn and quartered any trespasser. The common herd are only allowed to walk this side of the fence – not that many people go there, unless it's to pick blackberries."

"I saw a boy there," Sarah said. "A strange, wild creature. He seemed anxious to keep out of sight and looked terrified when I spoke to him."

"That sounds like young Henry Tregilgas. They live in the wood, he and his family – and a rough lot they are, too. Loveday is doing her best to redeem him."

"How many children do you have here? And tell me, for I have wondered about this, is there a difference between St Ninn children and Trelew children? Trelew is such a bleak and ugly place, and St Ninn so much cosier."

Both John and Loveday laughed.

"We've commented on it many times," John said. "One could never mistake a Trelew child for one from St Ninn. The ones from the clay country are smaller and wirier, less sunny-natured, more suspicious. It would make an interesting study."

"A task for your eventual retirement, perhaps?" Sarah suggested.

"Indeed," John agreed pleasantly.

As the rain continued to beat against the windows, conversation flowed without strain and Sarah marvelled at the ease which she felt in the company of this unusual pair – for John Pentecost *was* unusual, she felt sure, even though her knowledge of the ways of country schoolmasters was nonexistent. If she had given the matter any thought, she would not have expected such an urbane or cultured man.

Perhaps it was the rows of books that made her feel at home – the clear proof that here she was in the society of someone who was interested in something other than parochial affairs and the fleeting social scene. Or perhaps it was the sight of a copy of the London *Times* carelessly folded on a side table, a pair of spectacles resting upon it. She had yet to meet anyone in Cornwall who read anything other than the *Western Morning News* or the *Cornwall Gazette* – excellent publications, both of them, but surely indicative of a more limited outlook than that possessed by the schoolmaster.

John Pentecost, from his bleak moorland eyrie, had kept in touch with the London theatre (the only thing he missed, he told her) and was eager to hear a first-hand account of Beerbohm Tree's new production at the Haymarket, of Ellen Terry's latest triumph and of the new realism introduced by the young man Shaw who was creating such a furore. Such conversation was music to her ears and balm to her soul – her language, as Lucy Villiers would have said, which had been in short supply of late.

It was six o'clock by the time the rain had stopped sufficiently to allow Sarah to think of going home.

"I shall take you in the trap, of course," John Pentecost said, and would entertain no refusal.

He was equally dismissive of Loveday's offer to drive Mrs Morrow to Carrivick, assuring her that he had recovered from the tiredness he had felt earlier; had never, in fact, felt more like an evening drive. Loveday, seeing his expression and realising that he had somehow drawn energy from their unexpected visitor, did not argue with him.

Sarah's clothes were almost dry, but she did not change into them. Instead she accepted the loan of a thick shawl, and it was arranged that John and Loveday should go and take tea at Carrivick the following week when all that she had borrowed would be returned.

"Oh, it *has* been fun," she said to John as they drove down towards St Ninn. "I was a little down, to be honest. I mourn my husband's absence quite dreadfully and was beginning to feel rather like Alexander Selkirk, missing the sweet music of speech and starting at the sound of my own. I swear some kind fate led me to your house today. I shall look forward so much to seeing you both next week."

"Thank you. We shall look forward to it, too."

"Loveday is charming – a delightful girl, and a great credit to you. How did she come by such an unusual name?"

"We called her Loveday, firstly because we wanted a Cornish name; secondly because there was once a wonderful woman called Loveday Hambly whom everyone thought of as a saint. She was a Quaker and was persecuted and imprisoned for her faith, but never wavered, not for one moment. She lived near St Austell, and kept open house for fellow Quakers and travellers, the sick and the needy. She was the soul of hospitality and it seems that everyone loved her. I could wish nothing more for my daughter than that, could I?"

Only that I should be there to see it, he added to himself; only that I should know.

It was some weeks later that Sarah brought herself to ask the question that had bothered her ever since they met.

"How ill are you?" she said.

The tea party at which she had returned the clothes to Loveday had led to other meetings, during which her friendship with the Pentecosts had burgeoned like rain-lilies after a shower.

John Pentecost had become a lifeline. He was a kindred spirit who saw humour in the kind of things that she and Robert found amusing and laughed at together. He appreciated the same books and relished talk of the theatre. It was more a recognition than simply a friendship, she thought; rather as if they had known each other always. As for Loveday, she had grown to have a great affection for her. She was her father's daughter, with the same zest and joy in life, even though John insisted that she was the image of her mother.

There was nothing in the least romantic or sexual about her friendship with John Pentecost, though she rather feared that her staff viewed it with some astonishment and considerable suspicious comment. Perhaps it was unusual for the lady of the manor to be so friendly with the village schoolmaster;

but she was far from the usual kind of lady, and he was certainly not the usual kind of schoolmaster.

Now she stood with him at the top of the small, Italianate flight of steps that she had caused to be built on the lawn at the back of the house, leading from one level to another. They were alone on this occasion, for Loveday had gone to St Austell with Dolly Crowle.

For a few moments he did not answer, but continued to gaze in silence at the vista of woods and rolling hills that lay before them.

"How ill am I?" He repeated her words, following them with a long silence as if he was considering what to say. "Very ill," he said at last, in a voice that wavered a little. He cleared his throat. "Very ill," he said again more firmly.

Sarah turned to face him, reached to touch him, then drew back as if fearful of seeming presumptuous.

"What is it?" Her expression was full of fear. "Oh, my dear man, what is it?"

He hesitated again as if he hated to speak of it.

"A malignant growth," he said. "A tumour."

"Are you in pain?"

"Quite often. Please –" He grasped the hands that fluttered towards him. "Don't be distressed. Somewhat to my surprise, it's not that aspect that worries me most, though I know it will get worse. It's the thought of leaving everything: my work, this place. Loveday."

He turned from her, struggling for calm, finally achieving it as he looked on the green loveliness before him.

"How long?" Sarah asked gently.

He shrugged his shoulders.

"In May, Dr Geach said he doubted if I would see the autumn. Now it's the end of October, and I am still alive, still working."

She pulled him round to face her again, angry now and full of determination.

"What does Dr Geach know? He's an old, country doctor, probably years out of touch. You must see a specialist in London."

"I have seen a specialist. A good one, though in Plymouth,

not London. His diagnosis was much the same. There is nothing to be done. I have to accept it."

"Does Loveday know?"

"She realises that I am ill and nags me to rest and take tonics, but I haven't told her the extent of it. Soon I will have to. Even now I am aware that there are things that are beyond me, and I shall not attempt to work after the end of this term. The Education Committee must be told, and Loveday, too. What will happen about the house – where we will live – I have no idea. Perhaps they will be kind to us and allow us to stay there until – until I don't need the house any more. But then" – he turned to her, his face gaunt with anxiety as well as with illness – "what of Loveday? What's to become of her? This is my abiding grief, that I shan't be here for her just when a young person needs most support."

"You have many friends – many people who love you. I have heard them say so."

"I know, and I'm grateful for it. I don't mean to denigrate them in any way. It's merely that for the most part they have such narrow expectations of life, such limited horizons. Oh, I'm aware that love in a cottage is the equal of love anywhere else! Money is no guarantee of happiness, and I've never taught her that it was. I'm not ambitious for her in a worldly way, but I'm fearful that she will settle for second-best."

"Foolish man!" Sarah smiled at him, though her eyes were bright with tears. "Loveday is not a second-best kind of person. And you are taking no account of me. I shall support her, you can rely upon it."

For a moment he looked at her, his emotion raw and undisguised.

"But why should you?" he asked huskily at last. "You've known us such a short time."

"Come." She took his arm and pulled him gently towards the house. "It's time you came in and sat down. You must be tired, for you're beginning to talk nonsense. Friendship is friendship, no matter how short, and well you know it."

He looked down at her and smiled as he fell into step beside her. He looked carefree, almost boyish, and all at once she could see how handsome he must have been before his illness had taken such a hold of him.

"You mean," he said, "never mind the width, feel the quality?"

"Exactly," she agreed, and was surprised to find that they were laughing together as they went into the house.

"You would never believe," Loveday said, standing on the kitchen table at Roskelly Farm while Dolly pinned up the hem of her new skirt, "how nice and friendly and *ordinary* she is."

"Don't talk rubbish." Dolly's usually cheerful face was serious, but only because the job in hand required her concentration. She took a vicarious and good-natured pride in Loveday's friendship with the actress. "How can she be ordinary? She's Sarah Sangster!"

"Well, perhaps ordinary isn't the word. But she's so easy to talk to that one forgets she's famous. I've never met anyone like her. You'd say exactly the same, I'm sure."

"Opportunity would be a fine thing." There was a humorous reproach in Dolly's voice that Loveday recognised immediately.

"Oh Dolly, I will invite you to meet her, I promise! It's just that I've been going down to Carrivick more times than she's come up to Fourlanesend. We've been going through the books that Mr Morrow had sent from London – boxes and boxes of them! I thought we had plenty, but it's nothing compared to their library."

"Just so long as you don't forget your old friends –"

"As if I *would*!"

"Silly! I know you wouldn't really. I was only teasing."

She was being tactless though, Loveday realised, and said no more on the subject of Mrs Sarah Morrow. It was hard not to do so, for she had become, suddenly and surprisingly, an important part of Loveday's life, something between a friend and fairy-godmother, or perhaps a favourite aunt. The woodland path was in constant use now, for it cut the walk to Carrivick by at least a mile. She had felt guilty at first, leaving her father after school to run down it towards the big house, for it worried her to see that all the medicine he had been taking had apparently done him no good at all; however, he insisted that she should go to help Mrs Morrow arrange

68

the library on the days she was not giving Henry his extra lessons, knowing how much she would enjoy such a task, saying that all he wanted to do was rest and that he could do this as easily on his own as in company. Better, in fact!

Collier, the coachman, brought her back to Fourlanesend in the governess cart after each visit, for Mrs Morrow wouldn't allow her to walk the woodland path in the dark, even though Loveday insisted she would be perfectly safe just so long as she had a lantern to light her way. She would rather brave poachers and hidden tree-roots than the silently resentful Collier, Loveday often thought; but his mistress continued to order the governess cart, or even the brougham on rainy nights.

She was walking down the steep path through the wood one day towards the end of October when she suddenly came upon Mrs Tregilgas in her shapeless rags and wide-brimmed hat, a basket on her arm.

Though she knew Henry's mother by sight, as indeed did everyone in the neighbourhood, she had never spoken to her.

" 'Tis Miss, en it?" the woman said. She was short and fat and quite toothless. Her skin was pallid and dull with ingrained dirt, and her shoulders were hunched around her ears as she grinned up at Loveday, sly and ingratiating.

"Yes." Politely Loveday paused to speak to her. "And you're Mrs Tregilgas."

"Thass right." The woman stretched out her hand and grasped Loveday's arm. "Oh, some 'andsome liddle maid you be – an' a good little soul, too. My 'Enry d'think the world of ee. You bin some kind to un, Miss."

She spoke in a rapid, almost incomprehensible gabble, but once Loveday had taken in her meaning, she opened her eyes wide with astonishment. Henry, apart from his occasional gifts of drawings, had shown no sign of gratitude.

"Oh, it's nothing, really," she stuttered. "I've done very little." Not nearly enough, she was uncomfortably aware, for Henry's reading was still erratic, to say the least.

"You'll make a real scholar out of un," Mrs Tregilgas continued, grinning from ear to ear. There was, Loveday thought, something oily and obsequious about her, something deeply unattractive – a thought that she recognised as ungenerous in view of the praise she had received but could do nothing to dismiss. She looked down at the hand that still held her arm. It was stained and scratched, and the nails were black.

"I don't honestly think so," she said. "Henry still has great difficulty –"

"'E'm comin' on. See what 'e wrote –" To Loveday's relief, the woman let go her arm and delved into the bosom of her dress, pulling out a scrap of paper. Proudly she handed it over, and Loveday looked at it. 'MOTER' it read in ungainly and wavering capitals, with the M upside down and the R facing the wrong way. "It d'say 'Mother'," Mrs Tregilgas said proudly.

"So I see." Loveday smiled as she handed the paper back, but her expression changed to one of concern as Mrs Tregilgas stuffed it back in her bosom, for it was impossible not to notice, as her torn and filthy bodice slipped sideways, that the whole of her right shoulder and the top of her breast were badly bruised. The pale, lard-like flesh flamed purple and yellow and red.

Mrs Tregilgas, seeing the direction of her eyes, covered herself up hastily.

"'Tidn't nawthin'," she said. "I bruise easy."

"Did you fall? It must be painful."

"Ess, ess, that's it. I fell." Hastily Mrs Tregilgas assented to this in a way that somehow seemed unconvincing and sounded alarm bells ringing in Loveday's mind. Joely Tregilgas was out of prison, she had heard, and was said to be a violent man. Was it possible –? No, it couldn't be! Even Joely Tregilgas, whose reputation was one of the worst, would surely not strike his own mother.

"Well, I must be off," she said. "And I expect you're anxious to get home, too."

"We live close by." Mrs Tregilgas nodded her head towards an almost imperceptible path that disappeared into the trees. "'Tidn't much, but 'tis 'ome, like. You'm welcome any time."

"Thank you," Loveday said. "But now, if you'll excuse me –"

"Wait. Don't go yet, my bird." The hand grasped her arm

70

once more and held her close. Loveday had to steel herself not to flinch away for the stench of her unwashed body was unpleasantly pungent. "You'm a pretty liddle maid, for sure. 'Ave ee got a boy to love, then?" Offensively suggestive, the woman peered up at her. Loveday shook her head.

"No. Now I really must –"

"I'll tell the future for ee, my 'andsome. Give I yer 'and."

"You're very kind, but I must go."

" 'Twon't take but a minute." Ignoring Loveday's protestations, she transferred her grip to her hand, holding it palm upwards. "There," she said. "I can see fortune and a long and 'ealthy life, and strong babies, boy and girl."

The singsong voice paused abruptly, as if this last matter had taken her by surprise. She peered closer, her widebrimmed hat obscuring her expression; but when she looked up, Loveday saw that her eyes were clouded with uncertainty.

"Strong babies, boy and girl," she repeated, without expression.

She seemed to be searching Loveday's face, not smiling now, but frowning, wondering, and when she continued it was little more than a gabble as if all she wanted to do was get the job done.

"A handsome man will love you all his life – you'll travel far and never leave the clay – there's clouds around you and sadness and heartache, but sunshine comes after –"

"Thank you." Loveday snatched her hand away, overwhelmed by a sudden panic she couldn't explain. She was conscious of evil and darkness and depravity in a way she had never experienced before. "Goodbye, Mrs Tregilgas. I have to go."

She picked up her skirts and ran down the path, intent only on putting as much distance between her and the woman as possible, but as the path grew steeper and she was forced to slow down and tread more carefully, her thoughts slowed too. She began to feel that she had been foolish. Who was Mrs Tregilgas, after all? Just a poor woman who had known nothing but the most abject poverty; a woman who had never had a chance in life; a woman who, at least, had the grace to be grateful for all the extra effort she was putting into attempt-

71

ing to teach her son. It was nonsensical – even wicked – to be so repelled by her.

As for her fortune-telling, it was a joke, a game, nothing more – all that business about a handsome man, and travelling far but never leaving the clay. What on earth could the woman have meant? And all that about sadness and heartache – well, she was on a safe wicket there, for who managed to get through life without their share?

Any thought of Mrs Tregilgas was finally swept from her mind when she arrived at Carrivick. Jenkins, the parlour-maid, admitted her to the house, giving her the usual supercilious inspection which echoed the opinion of those belowstairs louder than any words. Marnie, Mrs Morrow's personal maid, treated her kindly, but none of the others could understand how their mistress could demean herself by making such a friend of a girl who was, when all was said and done, a nobody. Loveday found her intimidating, but was determined not to show it.

"Is Mrs Morrow in the library?" she asked.

"Not today." Stubbornly the girl refused to smile, but folded her thin lips in a sour line as she took Loveday's coat. "Madam said to show you into her sitting room. She's got another caller."

"Oh?"

With an anxious expression Loveday followed the maid as, nose in air, she led the way to the smaller sitting room at the back of the house which gave on to the sweeping lawn. Who could the unknown caller be? She hoped it wasn't one of the high-and-mighty ladies of the county who would no doubt share the domestic staff's opinion of her and her clothes, but she had no intention of giving the unpleasant Jenkins satisfaction by asking her for information.

As they approached the door, she could hear laughter and a masculine voice and her unease deepened. It didn't sound as if there would be much done in the library this afternoon. Should she offer to go away and come again when Mrs Morrow was free? Her resolve wavered.

"Who is it?" she asked urgently of Jenkins' rigid backview. The girl looked over her shoulder and smiled faintly.

"Mr Matthew Tallon," she said, and looked Loveday up

and down again. "He likely won't stay long, now you've come."

Matthew Tallon!

She wished to see him again, but not like this. Not when she was wearing muddy boots and the skirt that Dolly had run up one Saturday afternoon last winter that she had never considered one of her best efforts, and a blouse that she had worn all day. Oh, why hadn't she changed it? She had thought of doing so, but knowing the books were dusty she had decided against it.

Sometimes, between sleeping and waking, she dreamed of waltzing with a handsome man, round and round, her dress a gown of shimmering satin, embroidered with pearls, and her hair piled high, jewels suspended from her ears. In her dreams, her shadowy partner was often curiously like Matthew Tallon – a matter which made her feel shy at the thought of meeting him once more, as if he could look at her and know her secret thoughts.

Oh, the wretched Jenkins was right! He would likely not stay long. Why would he? She looked a fright and undoubtedly he would think it laughable that she thought herself on such friendly terms with Mrs Morrow. Well, let him, she thought, squaring her shoulders. Let him laugh all he wants. It's nothing to me.

It was, indeed, to renewed laughter that she entered the room. Mrs Morrow was dabbing her eyes delicately with a scrap of lace.

"Pray stop," Loveday heard her say as she went in. "I don't believe a single word of this."

"I swear I'm not codding –" Matthew broke off, a comical look of surprise coming over his face as he caught sight of Loveday and rose to his feet.

"Ah, Loveday, my dear!" Sarah stood up too, and with hands outstretched went to greet her. "I'm awarding us a holiday today. Come and sit by the fire and have some muffins – and come and meet Mr Tallon, whom I have made the excuse for not working. Matthew, this is my good friend Miss Loveday Pentecost."

He looked a little taller than she remembered – and hadn't

73

his face become thinner, or was her memory at fault? But the eyes were the same, and the smile. Could he tell, just by looking, that her heart was thudding at a most ridiculous rate? Where now was the aloof dignity that reduced other young men to jelly?

"We have met," he said, and took the hand she offered. "Here, at Carrivick, at the sale. I'm so glad to see you again, Miss Pentecost. Did you buy the books?"

"Some of them. There was a prodigious number of sermons."

Matthew laughed at that.

"Much good they did Great-uncle Thomas!"

"Tell me, Matthew," Sarah said, when everyone was seated again. "What was the cause of the rift between Sir Thomas and your family? Your mother was a Trengrose, was she not?"

"She was. Her father was Sir Thomas's brother, and neither of them ever forgave her for marrying my father. He was in trade, you see. It was the unforgivable sin. And then –" He broke off. Then there was the suspicion of sharp practice, he was about to say, in the way that old Josiah Tallon, Clay's father, had acquired the workings. He changed his mind, however, at the last minute. There was something about Loveday that made him even more sensitive than usual about the dubious way his family had acquired its wealth.

"Then?" Sarah prompted.

Matthew shrugged.

"I think Sir Thomas was a little mad," he said. "I suppose we should be thankful he left his property within the family and not to his pet cat, like a man on the north coast did recently."

"So, in fact," Sarah said, "Carrivick belonged to your mother, not your father? Everything, I remember, was in his name."

"Well, it would be, wouldn't it?" Matthew smiled tolerantly. "I mean, Mama knows nothing about property or legal matters –"

"She knows enough to keep hold of that field – what was it? Potter's Piece?"

"Piper's Piece. Well, that's a bit different. Mama wouldn't want to be bothered with lawyers and rents, and so on, would she? Women don't."

"Don't they?" Sarah's eyes were bright and challenging, her lips twisted in an odd little smile. "Have you ever asked yourself why this is so, Matthew? Does it occur to you that this could be no more than a myth engendered by men, for the benefit of men?"

Matthew looked a little discomfited at this attack.

"Surely," he said in some bewilderment, "it's not in a woman's nature to deal with business matters?"

"I did so for many years – and I do so still, for all that I am married. My marriage to Robert is a union between two equals."

"I think that's perfectly splendid," Loveday said warmly, clasping her hands together in her eagerness. "All marriages should be so."

Matthew said nothing, but his expression was thoughtful – a fact which Sarah noted with a slight twitching of her lips. It could do the boy nothing but good, she thought, to have this picture of marriage displayed for his consideration. She had a shrewd suspicion it was a very different one from that which he saw at Prospect Lodge every day of the week.

"On a lighter note," Sarah said in quite a different tone, "let us now support my husband in the tea trade – the cup that cheers but does not inebriate! Hurrah for tea."

"And hurrah for muffins!" Clearly Matthew was relieved that she had changed the subject. "May I pass you one, Miss Pentecost? Why not two?"

His eyes were admiring and seemed to pose a quite different question in their depths as he proffered the plate. She found herself shy and confused once more, just as she had been at their last meeting, a circumstance which annoyed her considerably. For some reason it seemed hard to be herself with this young man; and it was no use saying that it didn't matter, that she didn't care what impression she made on him, for suddenly she knew, without any doubt, that it mattered a great deal.

Why couldn't she be natural with him? Surely she wasn't in awe of him, simply because of his name? Yet how else to explain this ridiculous uncertainty? He was only young and was, after all, far from perfect. He still seemed a little too pleased with himself, and a little too confident of his ability to charm – and she wasn't at all sure she cared for those chequered trousers!

No, he wasn't perfect; but he was handsome, she had to admit, with a warm and lively personality that she found attractive. There was humour in his face and in his eyes. It would be fun, she thought wistfully, to spend time in his company; but she knew it would never happen.

Nevertheless, he asked if he could give her a ride home in the dog cart when the time came for them to leave.

"Well –" She hesitated, looking towards Sarah for guidance. Her heart had leapt at the offer and it was deflating to see that almost imperceptibly Sarah frowned and shook her head.

"Collier is waiting to take Loveday home," she said firmly.

"Why not give the old boy a night off?" Matthew smiled at her in a way that few could have resisted. Loveday held her breath, willing her to agree.

"I don't think so, Matthew. Going via Fourlanesend will delay you and make you late for dinner, which will not go down very well at home, will it? I'm sure the offer is much appreciated, however."

Loveday assented, with a touch of regret. It was disappointing to refuse such an invitation, but perhaps it wouldn't have done. She trusted Mrs Morrow to know what was right.

"It would have been my pleasure," Matthew said, accepting his defeat gracefully. But as Sarah turned to pull the bell, signalling Loveday's departure, his eyes met hers. Her mouth went dry and she swallowed painfully, for a long moment unable to look away from him. She saw him catch his lower lip between his teeth, saw the small line that appeared between his thick, fair brows.

"Goodbye, Miss Pentecost," he said, and his voice sounded strange, a little husky. He held out his hand and briefly she took it.

"Goodbye, Mr Tallon."

She was almost sure she sounded calm and was proud of her composure. Beneath it, she had never felt in so great a turmoil.

5

"My dear life, Loveday, you'm some dozy today," Dolly said, exasperated by the lack of response to the burning issue of whether she should choose patterned or plain material for a new Sunday blouse. "Where are your wits to, girl? You'm like Tregony band this morning – three scats behind!"

They had been brought into town by a friend of Dolly's father who lived in Trelew and had dropped them at the top of High Cross Street. Now, stopping short as they walked down the hill towards the shops, Dolly stood and glared accusingly at Loveday who took her friend's arm apologetically.

"I'm sorry, Dolly," she said. "I seem to have a lot on my mind – the school, you know, and Henry, and . . ."

The explanations trailed weakly away as Dolly looked sceptical.

"The school be blowed," she said. "You ask me, you'm in love. Not with Joseph Goldsworthy, surely? I saw him making sheep's eyes at you at Meeting on Sunday."

"Certainly not!" Loveday looked outraged as they resumed their walk. "Joseph Goldsworthy, indeed! As if I'd look at him, with his long nose and his squint."

"Who, then?"

"No one, silly. What was it you were saying about the blouse?"

She was anxious to divert Dolly away from this line of questioning and breathed a sigh of relief when the ploy was successful and once more the merits of polka dots or stripes were the subject under discussion.

Of course she was not in love! How could she be? Admitting that Matthew Tallon was an attractive young man and recognising the fact that she would rather like to see him again was something quite different. Anything more was just the stuff of dreams and fantasy, for nothing could come of it. He was as far above her as the moon and the stars –

"There, you'm doing it again," Dolly said reproachfully. "You ent heard a word."

"Pink," Loveday said hastily. "With a navy pattern. Dots or flowers. That'd look nice with a navy skirt."

"It would, wouldn't it?" Dolly looked pleased at the thought. "You'll help me choose it, won't you, Loveday? Let's meet after you've been to the bookshop and I've been to Auntie Jane's –"

"Eleven o'clock on the market steps?"

They agreed, and parted – Dolly towards South Street to deliver a basket of eggs to her mother's sister, Loveday straight on through Fore Street towards the bookshop and stationers in the Truro Road. She had several commissions from her father as well as a few shillings saved up on her own account.

To be let loose in a bookshop with money to spend was her favourite way of spending a Saturday morning and, perhaps for the first time since the meeting at Carrivick, she momentarily forgot Matthew Tallon. She was almost sure that she would buy the new Joseph Conrad book, but indecision was part of the fun. She was determined to have her moneyworth of browsing before finally handing over her hard-earned cash.

A new book of Yeats's poetry diverted her for a while and in turn led to a collection of Shakespeare's sonnets.

'Love is not love
Which alters when it alteration finds'

she read, opening the book at random – whereupon she closed it quickly and replaced it on the shelf, feeling that Shakespeare must surely be in league with Dolly. Both seemed to have love on the brain.

She would stick with Joseph Conrad, she decided, and reached to take it from the shelf.

"A good choice, if I may say so," said a voice behind her.

She whirled round, not believing the evidence of her ears or her eyes.

"Oh – Mr Tallon!" Was he real, or had she entered some dream world, full of people she had conjured up from her imagination? "I didn't expect –"

"*I* didn't expect, either! I dashed out from my father's office for a new ledger, and here you are. What a lovely surprise."

He was hatless, she saw, and clasping a large black book in his hands.

"Yes." She knew she was smiling. Neither spoke for a moment, but it was as if they had shouted aloud their happiness in this chance meeting as they looked into each other's eyes, too surprised to disguise their delight.

Loveday was the first to look away.

"You've read this, then," she said, indicating the book she had chosen.

"It's a rattling good tale. I think you'll enjoy it."

"He puts things so well, doesn't he?" she said. Surely her voice sounded higher and more breathless than usual? "It's strange, isn't it, when you think that English isn't his first language?"

"My goodness, yes –"

"Papa says much of his charm lies in the fact that his thought has a foreign accent as well as his speech –"

She raised her eyes to his as she spoke and broke off suddenly. He was still looking at her with a kind of joyful wonderment.

"Which – which way are you going?" He sounded hesitant and vulnerable.

"Back towards the church. I'm to meet my friend at eleven on the steps of the market."

"May I walk with you? Please!" he added, as she hesitated.

"But you've come from your office. Aren't you in a hurry?"

"Not now. In any case, I'm going along Fore Street too, in the same direction."

Would Mrs Morrow approve? Probably not, Loveday thought, as she paid for her book and for the others ordered by her father. But Mrs Morrow wasn't there to see, whereas Matthew Tallon was standing beside her, as handsome as ever. It was asking too much of any girl to refuse him.

Afterwards Loveday could remember little of the conversation that passed between them – she only knew that in less time than she could have thought possible they had arrived at the corner opposite the church with the Market House only a few yards away.

"Well –" she said, coming to a halt.

"I wish the street were ten times as long," Matthew said, handing over the books he had been carrying for her. "Oh, Loveday – may I call you Loveday? – I hope I see you again very soon. I shall call on Mrs Morrow often, and hope to find you there."

"We've finished sorting out the library," Loveday said, a little crestfallen. Why hadn't she made the job last longer? "I won't be there so often now."

"Well, by hook or by crook I shall find a way of seeing you again. With your permission, of course."

"How?" she asked.

He shrugged his shoulders.

"I don't know. I'll think of something."

The church clock began striking as he spoke.

"I must go," she said, looking over her shoulder towards the Market House. "My friend will be coming any moment. And you must get back to work. Goodbye, Mr Tallon." She held out her hand.

"Matthew," he corrected her as he took it. "And it's au revoir, not goodbye."

"Au revoir," she repeated, a catch in her voice.

She was glad that Dolly was late – that she hadn't seen them together. The teasing and the questioning would have been endless, and she was in no mood for it.

Was she, then, in love after all? No, no, no, of course not! Why, she didn't know him at all – had no idea what he was really like. She and Dolly had long ago each solemnly written a list headed 'Essential Qualities for the Man I will Love', swearing that appearance was of little importance. Both had put kindness and dependability at the top of the list, with a love of children coming close behind. Did Matthew Tallon love children? Was he dependable? Was he kind? How could she possibly tell?

No, she told herself firmly. Of course she was not in love. She was flattered by his interest, that was all; flattered, and amused. Love really had nothing to do with it.

But oh, he was so handsome, and he had the nicest smile. It was quite impossible not to dream a little.

Buttoning his jacket, John Pentecost emerged from behind the screen in Dr Geach's homely consulting room with its Turkey carpet, red velvet curtains and almost lifesize reproductions of Highland cattle framed in ornate gilt, to find the good doctor, plump hands clasped behind his frock-coated back, staring out at the street beyond the window.

He turned at John's approach, stared at him for a moment, then shook his head slowly.

"I would not have believed it," he said. "I wouldn't have put a penny-piece on it." He went to sit at his desk, motioning his patient to sit down beside it.

"On what, exactly? My continued existence?" John looked at him quizzically.

"No one could precisely forecast that. What astonishes me is that there seems to have been no worsening of your condition since I last saw you. You're not cured, you must understand that. There is no cure – perhaps never will be. It's merely that growth of the tumour seems, by great good fortune, to have been arrested for the time being and we can only thank the Almighty for it with wonder in our hearts. It's known as a remission. I've seen it before, but it's far from common."

Eyes bright, John stared at him.

" 'For this relief, much thanks'," he said softly. "Can you foretell how long it will last?"

The doctor shook his head again.

"No one can tell that. We must simply hope, and you must live from day to day –"

"Making the most of each. That's something I have always tried to do. I'll redouble my efforts."

"You look a better colour."

"I seem to have a little more energy. Who would have

82

thought it? Perhaps I shall live to see another spring, another school year. I'd made up my mind to resign at the end of this week, but shall delay a little."

"So long as you don't overtire yourself."

"I won't." John stood up. "I mustn't take up any more of your valuable time. You've genuinely sick patients out there who need your services, not scrimshankers like me –"

"My dear Pentecost!" Dr Geach got up and walked to the door with the schoolmaster, one arm about his shoulder. "You are to come to me at any time you feel the need – and in any case, I shall want to see you in a month's time. I can't tell you how pleased I am at this development. I've not so many old friends I can lose them with impunity."

A little more time! How he had longed for it, prayed for it – and now, it seemed, it had been granted to him. Even the doctor's reminder that he was not cured, would never be cured, failed to curb his elation.

He could have shouted aloud his joy, and indeed, when he had driven up the hill from St Ninn to his favourite spot where he could look back to where the sea sparkled in the winter sunshine and there was none but sheep and the pony to see him, he yelled exultantly into the wind.

A little more time! But enough, perhaps, to see the direction Loveday's life would take. He asked for no more, and full of gratitude, he uttered a prayer of thankfulness and wept as he did so.

He was glad that Loveday was at Roskelly this Saturday morning, helping Dolly with some dressmaking. It would have been difficult to explain his mood to her. He needed time to compose himself.

He longed to share his joy with someone, however, and when he found Sarah at his door soon after his return home, it seemed like a further answer to prayer, and he told her so as he welcomed her inside.

"I insist that you take a glass of Madeira by way of celebration," he said when he had given her the news, marvelling as he did so at the way her expressive face mirrored her pleasure. "To a little more time," he said, as he raised his glass to her.

"A little more time," she echoed; then set her glass down

with a thump that made the precious liquid rock perilously. "No, a *lot* more time! Why should we be modest in our demands?"

"I mustn't hope for too much."

"Well, you do what you like. For my part, I shall hope and I shall pray – and I have instructed Robert to do likewise. Perhaps it's Robert's supplications that have made all the difference, for he is a very good man," she added earnestly. "You will like him when you meet him."

John smiled, amused by her. There was something about her vivacity that always seemed to give him strength.

"I am sure I will," he said. "It's to be hoped he likes me. But tell me, what brings you to Fourlanesend? If it was a chance visit, it couldn't have been more fortuitously timed."

"I rather think," Sarah said, delving into her reticule and producing a square envelope, "that I come in the guise of Cupid. This is for Loveday – an invitation to a ball to be held in celebration of Matthew Tallon's twenty-first birthday party. I received a similar one myself, and a request that I should bring her with me. She did tell you, I imagine, that she met Matthew at Carrivick a week or two back?"

"Yes, she did."

"They were attracted to each other. One could sense it. I felt ridiculously touched by their confusion – oh pray, don't look so worried! Matthew is a delightful young man and I am very fond of him."

"I'm glad to hear you say so. She's met him at least twice more since then, you know – quite by chance, she would have us believe, and perhaps on her part it was. He appears to have taken to driving from St Austell to St Ninn via Fourlanesend, and I can't imagine the additional miles are entirely due to a desire to admire the scenery."

"She's confided in you?"

"Not in so many words – but how could I fail to notice the effect on her? Loveday has the most expressive eyes in the world!" He gave a laugh that ended in a sigh. "But I can't help worrying, Sarah. We are hardly in their circle. Nothing can come of this, surely – and I don't want Loveday to be hurt."

"Oh, nor do I, nor do I! But if you had seen them, as I

did, you would have felt –" she broke off and shrugged her shoulders, hands held out helplessly " – you would have felt that they must have their chance. He wanted to bring Loveday home that night, but I meanly vetoed the idea – not because I thought he would behave in any way unsuited to a gentleman, but because I knew that he would not expect to be given such licence in his own circle. Oh, John!" It was the first time she had used his Christian name and it gave an added emphasis to her plea. "Please trust me! Let Loveday have the chance to spread her wings. You must give her the freedom to fall in love, even get hurt – and even if nothing develops between her and Matthew, she should be allowed the excitement of dressing up and being admired."

When he did not speak but continued to look pensively into his glass chewing the inside of his lip, she leaned towards him and grasped his arm.

"How do you see her future, John? It was you, if my memory serves me rightly, who were bemoaning narrow visions and limited horizons."

He looked up at that and smiled ruefully.

"You are perfectly right. Fear for her makes me inconsistent. But you talk of 'his circle'! Isn't that the operative expression? Loveday doesn't belong in it, no matter how much you attempt to disguise the fact. How can we be sure that Matthew Tallon doesn't regard her as –" he shrugged, choosing his words. "As nothing more than a subject for experiment? I can think of few things that would rouse me to murder, but I'd swing happily for any man who hurt Loveday."

Sarah shook her head at him, denying the possibility.

"Matthew is a fine young man. It's too soon to talk of love, let alone marriage, but instinct tells me that she would be safe with him. Certainly she would be secure financially."

"I suppose that's a factor I cannot ignore, in the circumstances," John said, rather unwillingly.

"It's not something to be ignored at any time. Believe me, I have grown as fond of Loveday as if she were my own child – the daughter I never had. I want to take her to that ball, John."

"And she, I have no doubt, will want to go, once she

hears of it. Well, I shan't be a spoilsport. She can have my permission to accept the invitation. No doubt it will mean a new dress."

"I shall take care of that – no, no, please don't refuse me! Can you imagine a more exquisite pleasure for me than to choose a gown for a lovely young girl's first ball? Oh, the number of times I have wanted to do it! You simply can't deny me."

John looked at her and shook his head.

"You are quite impossible to resist, aren't you?"

She smiled at him and he marvelled as he had marvelled many times before at the way she was able to cheat the years.

"Would it surprise you," she said, "to learn that you are not the first man to say that? And heaven help me, I hope you are not the last."

"Oh, my dear life," Dolly breathed. "I never did see such stuff. 'Tis so stiff, 'twould stand up on its own – and that blue is your colour, Loveday. Oh, 'tis lovely."

"It is, isn't it? I can't believe it's real, not any of it! Not the dress nor the invitation nor anything. Between you and me, I'm scared to death!"

Scared, but thrilled. The dream was going to come true. Undoubtedly Matthew would ask her to dance, and together they would circle the floor, his hand on her waist, hers lightly touching his shoulder, the other holding the skirt of the most wonderful, magical gown imaginable.

She had been right, all those months ago: that morning at the Carrivick sale *had* been the beginning of something exciting.

She could, for instance, never have believed that she would ever possess a ballgown like this, cut cunningly to make her small waist look even tinier, the low, scooped neckline and flying panels embroidered with pearls and a narrow edging of ruffled tulle. The skirt was caught up in the front to give a glimpse of a ruffled underskirt. Oh, there never was such a dress!

She had hung it on the outside of her wardrobe so that it was the last thing she feasted her eyes on at night, and the first thing that met her gaze in the morning. There were pale-blue watered silk slippers to wear with it, and silk stockings, and gloves of white suede with twenty pearl buttons on each, and a little headdress of blue-and-white feathers. She was to carry a fan of white feathers and – the final touch – Mrs Morrow was lending her a necklet of pearls with matching earrings.

On the afternoon of the ball, it was arranged that Collier (no doubt protesting inwardly every inch of the way) was to collect her and the dress in the brougham and bring her back to Carrivick so that she could have her hair arranged by Mrs Morrow's maid, who would also help her to dress.

" 'Tis like a fairy tale," Dolly said, with such a wistful note in her voice that Loveday turned and hugged her.

"I only wish you were going to be there," she said.

"I'd be scared to death, and that's a fact. Sooner you than me, I can tell you. I'd just like to see you dressed up, that's all."

"So you shall, if you really want to. Mrs Morrow says we can drive to the ball by way of Fourlanesend so that we can stop off and show Papa how I look. It's the long way round, but she says it doesn't matter. Isn't she a darling? Only Mrs Morrow would have thought of it. Why don't you come over and sit with Papa? I know he'd be glad of your company. I've been wanting to ask you, but I was afraid you would think I was showing off. Truly, I don't mean it that way, Dolly."

Dolly laughed, digging her in the ribs with her elbow.

"Don't be proper daft, maid," she said. "I'd be blazing mad if I missed you dressed to death and killed with fashion. I'll wager Ned would like to come, too. Or perhaps he wouldn't. The poor lad is miserable enough because you won't walk out with him without having his nose rubbed in it."

"Dolly, I'm sorry about Ned –"

"Well, so am I, but there 'tez and couldn't be no 'tezzer, as Ma says. I always thought, somehow, you'd look beyond Fourlanesend."

There seemed no reply to this and Loveday didn't attempt to make one. Her dreams had always ranged wide. In imagination she had sailed in Spanish galleons, seen the wonders of the Orient, discovered hitherto undreamed-of continents.

The impending foray into Tallon territory seemed no less adventurous and her heart beat faster at the thought of it. She flung her arms wide and twirled around the room in waltz-time, eyes closed in ecstasy.

"Oh Dolly, how can I wait for Friday?" she asked, her voice vibrant with excitement. "How can I wait?"

Marnie was a calm and kindly woman who had served Sarah for many years and was devoted to her. She was, perhaps, the ideal person to help Loveday dress for this important occasion. Her broad, rather plain face exuded the pleasure she felt at the sight of beauty in others which in itself imparted confidence and serenity.

"There, Miss," she said, when with great care and tenderness she had finished dressing Loveday's hair. "Though I do say it, that looks lovely."

Loveday, turning her head this way and that before the mirror, laughed breathlessly.

"I look so different. Older, don't you think?"

"Much older, Miss." Marnie gave no sign of her inward amusement, though the humour of the situation did not escape her. There were not many women she could think of who would look so pleased by such an assurance. "Sophisticated, I would say."

"Do you think so?" Loveday preened for a moment longer. "I think you've done it beautifully, Marnie. Thank you very much."

She had been allocated a bedroom where a fire burned in a large marble fireplace. There was a chaise longue beside it, and a low table on which had been placed magazines and a tray of tea. Everything, from the display of hot-house flowers on the mantelpiece to the silk hangings on the brass bed and the thick carpet under her feet, spoke of luxury and – Loveday searched for the word and could think of nothing better than the one suggested by Marnie – sophistication. Nothing could have been further removed from her own small, utilitarian bedroom; nothing more calculated to enhance her sense of occasion.

Rather self-consciously she arranged herself on the chaise

longue, a wrapper covering her silk underskirt and new petticoat bodice, with its thin straps threaded with satin ribbon. She had needed new underwear as well as everything else, for she had never possessed any gown so low-cut before.

She had time to kill while Marnie dealt with Sarah and her gown, after which it would be her turn. She had already bathed, using soap the like of which she had never seen or smelled before. From Paris, Marnie said. Could anything be more exciting?

The pale-blue dress was waiting in the wardrobe. Loveday knew it was there. She had put it there herself. She also knew every line and every stitch of it, for had she not looked at it in detail a million times? Still, she was impelled to abandon her studiedly sophisticated pose on the chaise longue to scamper across and look at it once more. The thrill of it never dimmed. It was, without question, the most beautiful dress in the whole world.

Would Matthew like it? Her nervousness, almost banished by Marnie's calming influence, returned. It mattered so much. She was quite sure now that she loved him – that the strange and heady emotion she had experienced at each of their meetings signified more than a passing attraction.

She thought of him constantly, holding conversations with him; imaginary, but so vivid in her mind that imagination blurred into reality. In dreams she walked with him, danced with him; was even held in his arms and felt his kisses. It was impossible for her to believe that their relationship had not progressed in some strange, metaphysical way while they were apart from each other, but tonight it would be put to the test. Tonight they would meet once more, face to face. Would all those dreams become reality?

It seemed a long time until Marnie came. She had turned the pages of the magazines without seeing them and had poured herself some tea, forgetting to drink it before it was cold. She had paced the floor, repolished her nails with the little kid buffer that was on the dressing table, used the water closet at the top of the stairs, with its polished mahogany seat and the picture of Windsor Castle in its porcelain depths. At last Marnie came, and the moment had arrived. She was about to be arrayed for the most exciting night of her entire life.

When, dressed in her finery, she arrived at Fourlanesend, there was quite an audience gathered to see her. Maisie, the little maid, came in to marvel at her magnificence, and Mrs Crowle had accompanied her daughter from Roskelly Farm. It went without saying that Dolly was vociferous in her praise in spite of the nervousness induced by her long-awaited introduction to Mrs Morrow, but John Pentecost was struck dumb by the sight of his daughter and could only reach out tremulous hands towards her as he bent to kiss her cheek, careful not to disarrange any detail of her hair or dress.

"What do you think, Papa? What do you think?" Loveday begged.

He cleared his throat and blinked rapidly.

"I think you are beautiful," he said huskily. "Anyone would think so – but I more than most, perhaps, because I am more than a little prejudiced in your favour."

"As is only right and proper," Loveday retorted pertly, returning his kiss. "But you must admit, Mrs Morrow looks beautiful too."

"Mrs Morrow," John said, smiling towards her, "is, as always, incomparable. She has given us much to be grateful for. I hope you both have a most enjoyable evening."

Sitting in the brougham, drawing ever nearer to Prospect Lodge, Loveday was not at all certain that this feeling of breathless anticipation, this sick feeling at the pit of her stomach, counted as enjoyment. There was undoubtedly a certain amount of dread mixed with the excitement.

"It will be strange," she said to Sarah, "going to a function where I know no one. At least, no one but Matthew."

"Shall I tell you a secret, imparted to me by an ageing actress many years ago?" Sarah asked her. "She told me to pause on the threshold when entering a room full of strangers and to say to myself, 'I am beautiful. I am beloved.' You'd be surprised how effective it is."

"But I'm not *really* –"

"Darling child, you are indeed beautiful tonight, and you are beloved of a man who is himself loved and respected by several generations of children as well as their parents."

"You mean Papa? Does that count?"

"I think so. Besides –" Loveday was conscious of the gleam

of Sarah's smile in the darkness beside her " – there will be others, I feel certain."

She did not mention Matthew, but Loveday was as conscious of him as if she had. Very soon, she would see him. Very soon now.

Prospect Lodge was a plain slab of a house embellished with bay windows and a small, irrelevant turret. Architecturally it had little to recommend it, but was redeemed by its incomparable view over St Austell bay. On this festive night, however, it had been transformed and to Loveday's spellbound eyes seemed to possess all the glamour of a castle in Spain.

It was lit from end to end, with a silk canopy outside the front door and a square of red carpet on the front drive, edged with potted palms. Collier, wrapped up against the weather in his driving seat, was forced to take his turn in the queue of carriages waiting to disgorge their passengers at the door, but at last the nerve-racking time was over and they were able to step out on the red carpet where a liveried servant ushered them towards the house.

Sarah greeted a few people in the huge hall, but Loveday could see no sign of Matthew or of any other familiar face though she was conscious of a few curious glances.

They took off their wraps in a room set aside for the purpose and patted their hair into place. Catching Loveday's eye in the mirror they shared, Sarah smiled at her encouragingly.

" 'Once more into the breach'," she murmured softly, and taking Loveday's arm drew her inexorably towards the moment she had dreamed of.

Matthew was at the door of the drawing room, standing with his mother and father to receive the guests as they arrived. Loveday and Sarah joined the line of people that were waiting; it was Mr Tallon who was holding them up, Loveday perceived. He was bending over the hand of a small, fair woman who had to look up to him. She was doing it very prettily, almost with an air of adoration, while Mrs Tallon drooped beside her looking limp and faded by contrast.

Loveday was surprised at the appearance of Matthew's

mother. She had imagined, somehow, that she would be stylish and self-confident, but instead she saw a woman who, though expensively dressed in pale-green ruched satin, still contrived to look uncomfortable and out of place in this reception line. Her smile was anxious, as if she longed to please but knew herself incapable of it.

She stood on the right of her husband, with Matthew on her further side. Loveday hardly dared look at him, he made her so nervous. He looked more handsome than ever in his cutaway coat and clearly he was enjoying himself as he greeted friends and relatives and accepted their birthday wishes.

However, he seemed to be aware, even as he did so, of his mother's unease. As Loveday watched, the direction of her eyes hidden by the man in front of her who partially shielded her, she saw a glance pass between mother and son. There was little difference in their height, yet somehow Matthew managed to look protective as he smiled at Mrs Tallon and for a moment rested his hand on her shoulder, as if in encouragement. Loveday could not hear the words he spoke to her, but the impression made was one of support given and received, and she was warmed by it, almost as much as if she had been the recipient. He was not only handsome and amusing, but kind as well! Not that she doubted it, of course, but it was reassuring to have it confirmed.

Mrs Morrow was greeting a lady in the line behind her who stood with a girl, dressed in white, of much the same age as Loveday. Introductions were made. The lady, whose eager, darting little eyes appeared to miss nothing, turned out to be none other than Mrs Penberthy. Loveday had heard of the firm of Penberthy & Trevose all her life; meeting Mrs Penberthy made her shy, as if she were being presented to royalty, but she did her best to appear at ease and had every hope that she had succeeded.

Catching the daughter's eye, she was not so sure, for Gwendolyn Penberthy was looking at her with an oddly watchful expression, as if she was perfectly aware that Loveday didn't belong here.

"We haven't met, have we?" Gwendolyn said, as her mother and Mrs Morrow conversed. Her voice sounded shrill and almost accusatory, as if Loveday was guilty of some kind of negligence. "Have you come from somewhere else? Are you staying with Mrs Morrow?"

"Well, yes –"

Only for tonight, Loveday intended to say. It had been arranged that she would stay at Carrivick rather than go back to Fourlanesend, thus allowing Collier a shorter drive home; however, Gwendolyn gave her no time to enlarge on the matter.

"Oh well, that explains it," she said, with a small, down-turned smile. "I know how much Matthew thinks of the great Sarah Sangster. Any guest of hers would naturally be welcome. I wondered how you came to be here, and how it was that I hadn't met you before, but now it's quite clear." She looked Loveday up and down, taking in every detail of her dress and her hair. "I suppose you're from London," she went on. "Don't tell me you're an actress too!"

"No, I –"

"Well, that's a relief! One's more than enough, if you ask me. Are you staying down here long? And have you met Matthew yet?"

Gwendolyn, with her insistent voice and curious, probing eyes, filled Loveday with confusion. Which question was she intended to answer first? It didn't seem to matter, for while she hesitated, Gwendolyn rattled on.

"We've known each other since we were little, Matthew and I. Would you believe," she added in a confidential way, smirking a little, "that we used to play hide-and-seek all over the house?"

"Did you?" What was she meant to think or say? To Loveday it seemed an unremarkable way for two children to enjoy themselves. Gwendolyn shot a sly glance at her mother before bending closer to Loveday and giggling a little.

"Such a pity one can't do it now," she said in a voice heavy with innuendo. "But one learns at one's mother's knee to be just a *leetle* unavailable, *n'est-ce pas*? Such a bore!" She smiled, showing small, even teeth, the tip of her tongue caught between them.

Loveday was saved from making any reply by the move-

93

ment of the line, now very close to the reception committee of Matthew and his parents. The hammering of her heart seemed to fill her body.

She was aware now that Matthew had seen her, even though he was laughingly acknowledging the badinage of a gentleman she did not know but who seemed to know Matthew very well. Everyone seemed to know him very well. Well, of course they would, wouldn't they? It was his twenty-first birthday party, after all. No wonder Gwendolyn had been so anxious to discover what she, an apparent stranger, was doing there. It must, surely, be highly significant that he had desired her presence, amid all his family and friends.

And now it was upon her, and Mrs Morrow – 'the great Sarah Sangster', as Gwendolyn had called her with more than a touch of malice – was introducing her to Mr and Mrs Tallon.

"May I present my little protégée?" she said. "This is Miss Loveday Pentecost."

"Charming, charming." Mr Tallon took her hand, twinkling at her in his gallant way. She could see the admiration in his eyes and thought that, after all, what people said of him was probably true. He was one for the ladies. "So glad you could come, Miss Pentecost. Any friend of Mrs Morrow is indeed welcome at Prospect Lodge."

"Thank you. It was kind of you to ask me."

"So glad –" Mrs Tallon had the air of someone enduring an ordeal with nervousness but great fortitude. She wore a brave but tremulous smile, and blinked rapidly. "A great pleasure, Miss – er –"

"Pentecost, Mother." Matthew took possession of Loveday's hand, and immediately all semblance of composure deserted her. For a moment he smiled at her, saying nothing, her hand still in his. It was the moment she had dreamed of ever since the invitation had arrived, but it was passing, passing, and all she had to show for it was a fluttering heart, a dry mouth, and a head that was filled with whirling thoughts, none of which were worthy of utterance. "You will give me the honour of a dance, won't you?" Matthew asked.

"Yes. Yes, of course," she heard herself say in a strange, stiff-sounding voice.

"Put me down for the seventh. And the last waltz."

Silently, unable to speak, she nodded, and passed on.

"There," Sarah said briskly. "That makes a good start, doesn't it? Two dances booked already. Put them down on your programme before you forget."

Forget? As if she could – but oh, she had forgotten to wish him a happy birthday! How awful! How terrible! What would he think?

"You are beautiful," Sarah whispered meaningfully in her ear. "You are beloved. Courage, darling child."

Loveday gave her a weak smile, but straightened her back and lifted her chin, for the first time taking real stock of her surroundings.

It was all very grand. The room, clearly the drawing room of the Tallons' house, was large and was now given the appearance of being even larger as most of the furniture and the carpets had been removed, leaving an expanse of woodblock floor, dusted with French chalk. Gilt chairs were placed in groups beneath potted palms, and double doors thrown open to give access to an almost equally large dining room.

The vast bay window, hung with figured velvet, provided space for four musicians who even now were tuning their instruments. Several maids were circulating, trays in their hands, offering small glasses of sherry to the ever-increasing number of guests. The noise level was increasing, and suddenly Loveday felt better – less conspicuous, more at ease. It was a feeling that was enhanced by several more requests for dances. Mr Trevose, a dapper, dark-haired little man with a pointed beard, was most insistent that she should grant him the second and though she was aware that he asked merely through politeness – he was, after all, quite old – she felt grateful to him.

Then, suddenly, it was as if both she and Sarah were besieged. Mr Trevose had conducted them to chairs at the far end of the room and stayed to sit beside them and converse about local matters, but he was allowed only a short period to do so in peace. In no time others had joined them, drawn like a magnet, all anxious to pay court to the famous actress who had come to live among them.

Loveday's admiration for Sarah grew by the minute. She seemed so vibrant, so spirited compared to the other women in the room. Loveday could only agree wholeheartedly with Mr Trevose, who spent the entire period of their dance together extolling her virtues; though it was rather noticeable that Mrs Trevose, drawn into the little circle that surrounded Sarah, looked less enchanted. Once Loveday and Mr Trevose returned to the group, she rose to her feet and bore him off to speak to other friends, but their chairs were not empty for long. Sarah was a honeypot to which both men and women gravitated. It became noticeable that where she was, there was laughter and gaiety, and Loveday benefited greatly by being a permanent part of it. Her programme rapidly became full, and she was thankful that Matthew had staked his claim so soon, for she would have been in a pretty pickle if he had not.

From time to time she caught sight of herself in the large mirror above the fireplace as she danced, one gloved hand lightly placed on her partner's shoulder, the other clasped in his, and had to bite her lip to prevent herself smiling too broadly in her delighted disbelief. She looked, she thought, so incredibly *right*, as if she had been familiar with this kind of entertainment all her life. Who among her partners would guess that beneath that groomed and scented and curled exterior lurked little Loveday Pentecost of Fourlanesend? If only Papa could have been there! He would surely be so proud if he could see the way she had overcome her shyness and was holding her own amidst all these grand people.

And really, it wasn't at all difficult to smile and respond to the admiration she could see in her partners' eyes. She found her confidence growing with every moment.

Matthew was dancing, too. She saw him with Gwendolyn Penberthy, listening to her with a slight smile on his face as they circled decorously by. As the couples passed each other, his eyes met Loveday's for a brief moment. She was so thankful that she was dancing, even though she was rather intimidated by her partner, a certain Captain Hawke. He was a small, dark-visaged gentleman with a large curved nose and a large curved chin; rather like Mr Punch, she thought, suppressing a sudden urge to giggle. He was an ex-naval man, he told her; and indeed she was not surprised, since his voice was one more suited to a quarter-deck than a dance floor.

He barked rather than spoke, she decided, and did not hesitate to bark his observations on all manner of things ranging from the music, which he considered too loud, to the behaviour of some of Matthew's young cousins, whom he considered undisciplined. She hoped her delight when the time came for them to part was not too obvious; however, he had served his purpose and she was grateful for that. It would have been utterly shaming if she had been sitting out on one of the little chairs, watching Matthew and his partner pass, doing her best to look unconcerned that no one had asked her to dance.

There were several girls engaged in that dismal activity. Some talked animatedly to each other. Others sat, heads and smiles inclined towards the small orchestra, as if they preferred to listen to the music rather than waste their energies in dancing. Matthew danced with one after the other – but Gwendolyn Penberthy was the only girl she saw him dancing with more than once; and she, as she had told Loveday earlier, was an old friend. Surely it must be significant that he asked her for two dances? And the last one, at that!

He was approaching her at last, and it was exactly like the dream, except that they stumbled over each other's feet to start with; but even that didn't matter, for it made them laugh. It was laughter with a little, tremulous shiver of excitement buried in it; excitement that each could see in the other's eyes.

His words, when he spoke, were mundane enough.

"Are you enjoying yourself?" he asked, when finally they were circling without mishap.

"Oh, yes. Thank you for inviting me. I'm sorry I forgot to say happy birthday."

"You're forgiven. It was yesterday, actually."

"Then mine is exactly one month later."

For some obscure reason this seemed to delight them both, as if it gave them a concrete reason for this strange and wonderful bond that had sprung up between them.

"Is it terribly impertinent to ask how old you will be? After all, the whole world knows *my* age!"

Loveday pretended to consider the matter.

"Yes, I think it is," she said at last. "But I shall tell you anyway. I shall be eighteen."

She looked up at him with a smile which slowly died as she saw the expression in his eyes. He, too, was serious now and she saw that he swallowed with difficulty.

"Loveday," he said; and again, with added urgency, "Loveday, Loveday. We must meet again."

Breathlessly, unable to speak, she nodded.

There was a catch in his voice as he went on.

"I'll think of something. Just so long as I know you want it too."

"Oh, yes. Oh, yes, please." The music was coming to an end. Was ever a dance so short? Abstractedly, they applauded politely and Loveday made as if to return to her place but Matthew drew her to the side of the room.

"We can talk for a moment, until the next dance. Have you met my sister Sybil?"

"No. I heard someone remarking just now that she seemed to be absent."

"No, no – elusive, perhaps, but not absent." He was looking around the room as he spoke. "She hates dances and usually ends up sitting in a corner. There she is! Come on – I'll introduce you."

Loveday, who had no idea that Sybil Tallon's abrupt manner was the result of shyness less well-concealed than her own, felt certain that Matthew's elder sister regarded her with disapproval. She was very like her mother, tall and ungainly, with none of Matthew's good looks and easy manner. No one, Loveday thought, would imagine they were brother and sister.

"Matthew told me about you," Sybil said, unsmiling. "You're a protégée of Mrs Morrow. And a teacher."

"Yes. I'm not qualified, though."

"I've often thought I wouldn't mind it myself."

"Teaching? Sybil!" Matthew's voice was amused. "You know perfectly well Father would never allow it."

Sybil shrugged her shoulders despondently.

"Well, that's the trouble, of course. You know perfectly well what I want to do, but he won't allow that, either. Still, teaching would be the next best thing. Almost anything would be better than spending my life doing all the time-wasting, foolish things that are considered suitable for an ageing spinster."

"Ageing!" Loveday laughed. "That's not true!" But it was, she recognised. It was hard to determine Sybil's age, but she was almost certainly in her mid-twenties – and apparently no husband in sight. "What's the thing you really want to do?" she asked; but Sybil merely shrugged and made no direct answer.

"I tell you, Miss Pentecost," she said, "if I never have to arrange another altar flower, or preside behind another bazaar stall, that will be too soon! I envy you, having something worthwhile to do. Could I get into it, do you think? I get on rather well with children and to my mind it would be far better than waiting for a husband to reach up and pluck me from the shelf."

Matthew looked across at Loveday, eyebrows raised, shrugging his shoulders slightly as if to ask what was to be done with his sister and her crazy ideas, but the matter was not pursued since, rather to Loveday's dismay, they were joined by Captain Hawke.

He bowed stiffly – once in Sybil's direction, once in hers, then once more towards Sybil, nose almost meeting chin in an effusive smile.

"Our dance, I think, Miss Tallon?" he said.

Sybil smiled nervously and a pink stain appeared on her cheekbones. She fumbled with her programme as if suddenly her hands felt too large for her wrists.

"Oh, is it? Yes, I suppose it is."

"Awfully crowded," barked the Captain. "Never mind. Find a space. Can you reverse?"

"Poor Sybil," Loveday murmured as she was borne away.

"Father thinks he might *do*." Matthew's eyes were on the couple, his attention momentarily distracted from Loveday. "But I don't think even Sybil is desperate enough for that."

"I should hope not!"

"It would be wonderful if you two could become friends,"

Matthew said hopefully. "It would make everything so much easier. The three of us could go out together."

Loveday assented politely, but without a great deal of optimism. It seemed unlikely, somehow, that Sybil Tallon would want to pursue the acquaintance.

"Leave it to me," Matthew said. "I'll try to arrange something. Who is taking you in to supper?"

"Someone called Michael Morcom –"

"Oh, good for Michael. He always was a lucky swine. He's my cousin, you know, and thinks himself no end of a fellow. He wants to go into politics, so mind how you speak to him – he may be Prime Minister one of these days. Here he comes now. Damn his eyes, I don't want to leave you, Loveday."

Michael Morcom was a dark haired, smooth young man who had been a constant figure on the dance floor all evening, conspicuous because of his height and his handsome profile. Loveday, however, was supremely unaware of the fact that she had achieved something of a coup in capturing him for the supper-dance. With Matthew's voice still ringing in her ears it was all she could do to concentrate on the dashing Mr Morcom's conversation, particularly as it consisted of asking her whether she knew this member of County society, or that member of the hunt, to which the answer was, inevitably, 'No'. How many ways were there of expressing total ignorance? she wondered desperately.

The buffet laid out in the dining room, with its array of food and floral decorations, quite took Loveday's breath away. Nothing looked familiar. There was chicken mousse in the shape of a swan, salad vegetables cut to resemble flowers, thinly sliced ham rolled into fingers, an unidentifiable, piquant-tasting fish, boned and blended with cream and garnished with prawns, shaped like a giant shell. Loveday regarded it with admiration touched with reverence and was thankful that others had desecrated it before her, for she could never have brought herself to be the first to do so.

"I say," Michael Morcom was helping himself liberally. "A jolly good spread, what? My dear girl, you're not taking enough to keep a bird alive. You're as bad as Poppy Anstruther. Thin as a rail, never eats a thing, but *what* a horsewoman! Have you met her?"

They were back, it seemed, to the question and answer game, but eventually he tired of it, much to Loveday's relief, and turned his attention to the British role in Ireland, about which he held forthright views. This lasted very nicely until Loveday felt able to leave him without offence.

"If you will excuse me," she said, rising at the first hint of a pause in his monologue, "I really must retire to freshen up a little."

Thankfully, she left him, making her way to the upstairs bedroom and facilities which had been put at the disposal of lady guests. The Tallons, also, had a mahogany seat, but a rural scene instead of Windsor Castle, with trees and a reclining shepherdess. Would she ever be able to face the outhouse again? Loveday wondered amusedly. Undoubtedly she was beginning to get ideas above her station.

There was a group of girls in the bedroom. She could hear their voices as she turned the handle, but they all looked towards the door and fell silent as she went in.

Gwendolyn Penberthy was in the centre of the group. Some of the other girls were among those she had been introduced to; others she had only seen from afar. All seemed to be staring at her with varying expressions of distaste.

"Well!" Gwendolyn took a few steps towards her. She looked Loveday up and down, her mouth twisted with amusement. "It's little Cinderella, in person."

"Little impostor, you mean," put in a plump, red-haired girl who had been doing a great deal of sitting out. Loveday had noticed her and had felt her eyes upon her more than once while she had been dancing.

She looked from one to the other of her accusers, her mouth open in astonishment.

"Impostor?" she repeated. "I don't know what you mean."

"Impostor and liar," Gwendolyn said, not smiling now, her face sharp with anger. "Passing yourself off as a friend of Mrs Morrow's from London, when all the time you're a little village girl from Fourlanesend! How long did you think you would get away with it?"

"Mrs Morrow *is* my friend – and I never said anything about London. That was your invention."

"Rubbish!" said Gwendolyn.

"She's probably right," said a new voice coolly.

Everyone turned towards a girl who stood at the mirror a little distance from the group, dabbing at her face with *papier poudré*. Though she had not been introduced to her, Loveday had noticed her on the dance floor and had admired her blonde good looks.

"What do you know about it?" Gwendolyn asked angrily.

Unruffled, the blonde girl smiled at her.

"Well, you do go on rather, Gwennie. You tend not to listen, and then get the wrong end of the stick."

"That's right," Gwendolyn said furiously. "Take the word of a girl of this sort, rather than your own kind, Helen Farrar. It's quite clear what *she* came for."

"And what was that?" Helen sauntered lazily across the room to confront Gwendolyn. "Do tell, Gwennie dear."

"To snare a rich husband, of course!"

Helen laughed at that.

"Unlike you, my dear Gwendolyn. There was no such thought in your head, we all know that."

Uneasily, the other girls laughed and drifted away; only the red-haired girl stood her ground.

"My people are very friendly with the Tallons," she said haughtily. "I don't know how you managed to get yourself invited here, but one thing is sure – you'll never be invited again once they know who you really are. It isn't right, asking someone like you."

"Why not?" Helen demanded, taking the initiative on Loveday's behalf.

"Well –" For a moment the girl looked nonplussed. "Well, she doesn't know how to behave," she said. "A teacher in a Board School, of all things! What if she is a friend of Mrs Morrow's? My mother says no actress can be considered a lady."

"Mrs Morrow *is* a lady," Loveday said, in a voice that trembled. "She's a great lady."

"Take no notice." Helen took Loveday's hand and drew her arm through hers. "She's jealous, that's all." She flicked a contemptuous finger towards the red-headed girl. "Why, poor Beatrice has hardly had a dance all night – and oh, *how* she would love to dance with Michael Morcom, the Magnificent."

"How dare you!"

"My dear Beatrice," Helen went on lightly. "Pray control your fury. A bright red face clashes dreadfully with carroty hair."

The door opened just then and two elderly ladies came in together, effectively putting a stop to any more exchanges. Beatrice swept out with her nose in the air, but Helen stayed where she was and continued to look at Loveday in a friendly way.

"Take no notice," she said again, her voice very soft so that the other occupants of the room could not hear her. "I'll wait for you, if you like, and we can go down together."

"Thank you," Loveday said, attempting to smile. She rinsed her hands and did what she could to subdue the flush on her cheeks. It seemed astonishing to her that her reflection could look so much the same, when suddenly the entire evening had gone so wrong. She felt utterly humiliated. She had lied to no one – in fact she had told several of her partners, in answer to their questions, exactly where she lived and why; indeed, it must have been from one of them that Gwendolyn had, at last, learned of her true circumstances.

But what good did that do? She had been branded a liar and an impostor, accused of masquerading as something she was not – 'one of their own kind', to use Gwendolyn's phrase. That would be sufficient for most people to condemn her without trial. Matthew would certainly hear of it and would surely despise her utterly if he thought she had been untruthful – and how would he know that the accusations were unjust? This was his world, these were his friends.

A thought struck her, so shocking that it was a physical pain. What was it that Gwendolyn had said about being 'just a *leetle* unavailable'? She had learned it, she said, at her mother's knee, along, no doubt, with all the other rules that governed upper-class behaviour. But Loveday had received no such lessons, and had certainly not been unavailable, not even a little bit. 'Yes, please' she had said, when Matthew mentioned seeing her again.

How easy, how cheap he must think her! How could she

ever face him again? How could she ever face any of them? However, she couldn't stay here. Somehow she would have to find the courage to go downstairs. She took a trembling breath, and followed Helen through the door.

The hall was being used as an overflow dining room, with still more gilt chairs and still more potted palms. As the two girls descended the stairs side by side, they saw that couples were lingering over their supper. Matthew stood with a group of young men quite near the foot of the staircase. They were laughing and joking together. Mrs Tallon fluttered through, apparently urging guests to leave the hall and go into the drawing room, but few seemed to take any notice of her. Then, as they neared the bottom, Gwendolyn's voice rang out.

"Oh, *there* you are, Matthew," she said. She came through from the drawing room and took possession of Matthew's arm as he turned towards her. "Don't you know everyone's waiting for you? There's to be a speech, and a toast, and everything." She gave him a playful push, and as he went ahead into the drawing room she lingered a moment, looking around the hall. "Come along, everyone," she said. "You're all wanted inside." Her eyes were bright with malice as they rested on Loveday, who had now reached the bottom of the stairs. "Even you, Miss Pentecost," she said. "You might as well come, now that you're here."

"The proprietorial Miss Penberthy," murmured Helen in Loveday's ear. "Take no notice of her."

"Proprietorial?" There was an ominous ring about the word.

"Well, it's not official yet, but it's generally accepted that she and Matthew will announce their engagement now that he's come of age. They've been friendly from the cradle."

The room seemed to tip and spin, and Loveday put out a hand to steady herself on the newel post.

"I see," she said faintly, wanting to die.

✖ 6 ✖

Had the evening at Prospect Lodge ended on as high a note as it had begun, Sarah's pen, which related each smallest detail of her life in weekly letters to Robert, would undoubtedly have swooped over page after page with exuberant fluency. Instead she sat at her desk, lost in gloomy thought, with barely a sentence written.

What had gone so disastrously wrong? All had seemed to be going as merrily as a marriage bell, with Loveday, delighted with herself and her new dress, clearly enjoying the attentions of her numerous partners.

Sarah sighed, dipped her pen in the silver inkwell, paused, and sighed again.

"I could have sworn," she wrote at last, "that Matthew was enraptured, and Loveday likewise. One had only to see their expressions when they danced together! Call me a romantic fool, but it did my heart good to witness it. Then, between one breath and the next, everything changed!

"Oh Robert, never allow me to wish for lost youth, for those that so wish must surely have forgotten the pain of being young and unhappily in love. All the way home, the poor child maintained the fiction that she had enjoyed the time of her life, for she would have considered it hurtful to me to confess otherwise. I could not find the words to question her directly. Perhaps I should have done – but there seemed such a gallant dignity about her that to pry must surely have been a breach of manners. Yet how I longed to comfort her! For how can I avoid the certain knowledge that I am to blame for her unhappiness?

"True, it was not my hand that wrote the invitation – but I encouraged Matthew to think that should it be written, she would accept it. And it was I who persuaded John Pentecost that nothing but good would ensue from such an acceptance. Oh, how do mothers of daughters contrive to exist, when their every hurt, though at one remove, is felt so keenly? *Mea culpa, mea culpa*, waking and sleeping the words echo through my head."

Her pen was flying now. She sat back and considered what she had written. Was she being over-dramatic? It was not, she thought with wry self-knowledge, outside the realms of possibility; but she was, in truth, heartsick at Loveday's patent unhappiness. If she didn't come to Carrivick within the next few days, Sarah decided, then she herself would go to Fourlanesend. One way or another she would discover what had gone wrong.

"Who, may I ask, was responsible for foisting that rather delightful little impostor upon us the other evening?" Clay Tallon asked at breakfast, several days after the ball.

The family were seated at the heavy oak table; parents at each end, Matthew and Sybil facing each other at the centre. Morning prayers had been said in the hall, attended by the four maids – but not the gardener or the gardener's boy, because they tracked mud into the house, and not the cook, because she was otherwise engaged.

The results of her labours – porridge with thick, Cornish cream; bacon, kidneys, hogs' pudding, mushrooms, eggs and fried tomatoes; muffins, toast, marmalade – had been served, and were being dealt with in varying ways. Clay Tallon took plenty of everything and ate with gusto. Sybil had a surprisingly good appetite and, with the exception of the hogs' pudding which she had always found repellent, did much the same. Millicent Tallon sipped weak tea and nibbled delicately at a piece of dry toast, which was her way. Only Matthew, customarily an excellent trencherman, was displaying an unusual lack of appetite.

He felt the familiar tightening of the scalp, the knot of anger forming in his stomach. His father, he knew, was about to be very offensive concerning Loveday, and he would do so with a twinkle in his eyes and a smile curling his lips. Matthew said nothing, concentrating on minutely dissecting a mushroom. Sybil watched him covertly, concerned about him.

"Impostor?" Millicent looked aghast. "Really, Edwin, I don't know what you're talking about."

"I rather think that Matthew does," Tallon said, cocking an eyebrow at his son. "Hardly the thing, was it, old boy? Inviting a girl of that type behind our backs?"

"Oh, *really!*" Matthew slammed down his knife and fork and glared at his father, unaware both of his mother's alarm and of Sybil's glance that clearly counselled caution. "Miss Pentecost is perfectly respectable, the daughter of a schoolmaster and a good friend of Mrs Morrow."

"I must say, she seemed very –" began Millicent, but her voice trailed away as she caught her husband's eye.

"You must learn discretion, my dear fellow," Tallon said easily, picking up the paper and running his eye down the front page. "She's a pretty enough little chit, I grant you that, but we don't want to encourage her, do we?"

"It so happens," Matthew said tightly, "that I rather do. Want to encourage her, I mean. Not that I have a great deal of hope –"

"That's enough, Matthew." Good humour could be exploited only so far. Now was the turn of the beetled brows and the icy stare.

"Be so kind as to watch your manner when you speak to me. Reaching your majority gives you no right to behave like a hooligan – nor does it give you leave to ask any Tom, Dick or Harry to my house."

"Miss Pentecost," Matthew said, coldly amused, "can hardly be described as a Tom, a Dick, or a Harry. I thought her femininity was adequately demonstrated, didn't you? Anyway, Mama said that Mrs Morrow was welcome to bring her."

Carefully expressionless, the streamers on their caps hanging down their backs like four little monuments to discretion, the two maids circled the table.

"I could see no objection," began Millicent, looking anxiously from her husband to Matthew and back again.

Edwin harrumphed and dabbed his mouth with his napkin, his eyes cold and angry above it.

"I made enquiries," he said. "Cap'n Noah reliably informs me that her father, the schoolmaster, has a lasting and quite disastrous influence on the boys he teaches. There is never a suggestion of forming a union, or unrest concerning wages and the like, without it being fermented by one of Pentecost's ex-pupils. The man's an anarchist!"

Angry and unamused, Matthew nevertheless laughed.

"Really, Father, that's the most ridiculous thing I ever heard."

Clay Tallon's face darkened, but he remembered the maids and restrained himself from any further expressions of his anger, albeit with difficulty.

"We shall talk of this later," he said.

Matthew knew there would be no escape, for it had been arranged that he would drive his father into St Austell that morning.

Later, bowling towards the town, the expected interrogation began.

"Am I to understand," his father asked, "that you have some interest in this Miss Pentecost?"

"My feelings," Matthew said tightly, his knuckles white on the reins, "are not something I wish to discuss."

"Nor do I. If they exist, they're best forgotten."

"I cannot imagine why they are anybody's business but mine."

"May I remind you," his father said through gritted teeth, "that for some years now it has been understood that you and Gwendolyn Penberthy will make a match of it?"

"Understood by whom? By you? By the Penberthys? I swear Gwendolyn has no such thoughts –"

"You're wrong. I had it from her father only yesterday that she is perfectly agreeable for the engagement to be made official."

"Whoa!" Without warning, Matthew reined in the horse and turned to face his father, his expression rigid with anger. "I am *not* agreeable," he said. "Gwendolyn and I were childhood friends, no more, and I will not marry her, no matter

how convenient it would be for you, the business, the Penberthys, or anyone else."

"Then you're a fool. The girl's pretty enough, and apparently well-disposed towards you. What's more, she's an
heiress –"

"And I'm to marry her, for a few holes in the ground –"

"For *eight* holes in the ground – and damned profitable
ones, too. Then there's the Bell Quarry –" Clay Tallon
broke off short, and brushed his moustache with an upward
movement of his hand.

"What about the Bell Quarry?" Matthew was momentarily
diverted from his problems.

Tallon cleared his throat and adjusted his cravat.

"I looked into the matter carefully," he said. "For someone
with money to invest, it seems a good proposition."

Matthew tightened his lips, feeling the irritation that
was becoming customary where his father was concerned.
Three months ago he had pressed for the acquisition of the
china-stone quarry which a smaller owner, over-extended
financially and close to bankruptcy, was anxious to sell. At
that time his father had poured cold water on the idea. China
stone was only used in the production of porcelain, he said.
Paper and textiles were clearly the principal outlets for the
future, and Matthew's recommendation was eccentric in the
extreme, hardly worth considering. Now it appeared that
things had changed. He could have *said*, Matthew thought.
He could have discussed it, instead of going off and talking
it over with others without a word. It was typical of the way
that he never gave any credit to anyone, least of all his son.

"The only problem is one of liquidity," Clay Tallon went
on. "I just don't have the cash available at the moment. I was
proposing to ask Penberthy to come in with me."

"It's a good investment. I said so from the beginning. Why
should he allow personal considerations to affect him?"

Tallon glared at his son under beetled brows.

"Have some sense, Matthew! Penberthy is a proud man, a
difficult man. If you welsh on his daughter, he'll never do
business with me again – and I can't say I shall blame him."

"There never was an understanding –"

"Have you any idea how many tons of clay Penberthy is

worth annually? Forget Bell Quarry for the moment. Wheal Vera alone produces two thousand tons, never mind the rest. For the love of heaven, Matthew, use your head for once and marry the girl!"

"I will not do it!"

"Because of this – this nobody? This Miss Pentecost?"

"No." Uncertainly Matthew looked away. "I don't know. Nothing has been said."

"Then forget it, son." Clay Tallon, sensing vulnerability, abandoned anger as a weapon and turned to cajolery. He laid his hand on Matthew's arm and lowered his voice. "It's easy to be carried away, when you're young. A pretty face, a shapely figure –" He chuckled, man to man. "And the little maid's a beauty, I'll admit that. If I were a few years younger, I swear I'd give you a run for your money. But we've all lusted after totally unsuitable girls at one time or another –" A reminiscent gleam appeared in his eye, and he chuckled again. "I well recall a barmaid at the Ship in Mevagissey when I was no older than you are. My God, I couldn't keep out of the place, or my hands off her. Marriage is different."

"Is it?" Matthew felt light-headed with rage at the insult to Loveday. "I tell you there is nothing – *nothing* – remotely similar about Miss Pentecost and your barmaid! You are saying I should marry for money, as you did? That love is to play no part? Is that it? I am to take you as my example?"

"By God, you could do worse." Clay Tallon was growing angry again. "Love!" He snorted derisively. "Romantic poppycock! Take your Miss Pentecost for a tumble in the hay and get her out of your system, for the love of heaven. You're behaving like a half-baked schoolboy. Marriage is a different kettle of fish altogether.

"As for my affairs, well, I've nothing to be ashamed of. Trelew was nothing until your grandfather and I took it over. We risked our capital –"

And swindled Trengrose, Matthew thought, but didn't say. He had heard it all before – how Josiah Tallon, Edwin's father, had become a manager in the seventies for the Trelew Clay Company in which the Trengrose family had a major holding. How he had lived carefully, salting away a few pounds here and a few pounds there, until when a slump hit the industry in 1876 and smaller owners were going into liquidation right and left, old Josiah had shrewdly bought setts at rock-bottom prices. How he had persuaded the gullible Sir Tristan Trengrose, father of Sir Thomas, that the Trelew setts were worked out and worthless and that the best thing he could do was to cut his losses and sell his shares. How Edwin wooed and won the Trengrose daughter, with her sizeable dowry, which had come in very handy when the Treverbyn China Clay Company had run into difficulties and its two directors fled the country, so that even more clayworks had been acquired. One of the pits, Upalong, had even been already equipped with new and valuable mechanical equipment, which had made it a very shrewd investment indeed.

Oh, yes, his father and his grandfather before him had worked hard, that couldn't be denied, and they had boosted the Tallon fortunes until the house in Watering Hill had been exchanged for the imposing villa on the cliff. He had heard it all before, but there were, undoubtedly, some aspects of the Tallon story that struck a sour note. It was not all, Matthew thought, a matter for pride. And *damned* if he would allow his father to insult Loveday.

"Miss Pentecost is worth ten of Gwennie Penberthy," he said.

"You youngsters are all the same – think you know it all, won't take advice –"

Matthew had heard that before, too. He shook the reins and they continued on their way in a silence resonant with thoughts, both angry and rebellious.

I won't do it, Matthew told himself, mutely vehement, jaw set with determination. I won't, I won't.

His anger momentarily blunted the pain that he had felt since that last dance with Loveday. He had held her as before, and they had moved in time with the music as before, but in no way had it been the same.

"I've waited for this all evening," he had said. And: "I hope I dream of you tonight. I must see you again, Loveday."

"Really?" she had said coolly. And: "How kind of you to say so. Such a pleasant evening! But I hardly think our paths will cross again."

And all the time such coldness, such a remote profile. What

had he said or done to deserve it? Had he talked too much? If so, it was only that she should look at him with those startling eyes. Had he been too flippant? It was only to see her smile.

Oh, let her go, he said to himself time and time again. There were other fish in the sea. Who was she, after all? A girl, no more – a silly, vacillating girl who blew hot and cold. He would soon forget her. Then why the fury, why the anguish, when his father spoke so slightingly of her? Why this dreadful, sick feeling of loss – even of bereavement? The pain, when it flooded back, was all but unbearable.

The afternoons that week were dark and sunless, giving a foretaste of winter and the shorter days that were soon to be upon them.

"Perhaps it would be best if we gave up the lessons after school," Loveday suggested to Henry, at which he gave a short laugh and shrugged his shoulders.

"Dark and light, 'tis all the same to me," he said.

"You mean you want to stay on?"

"Don't see why not."

"Very well," Loveday said. "We'll carry on for the time being, at least."

She felt no enthusiasm for the task. In fact she felt little enthusiasm for anything any more – a phenomenon her father noted and worried about. She had even found excuses for not going to Carrivick this past week, which seemed strange. Ever since that damned dance she's not been herself, John thought; and felt angry with himself for agreeing to it – and even slightly angry with Sarah, though he knew that her intentions had been of the best. He should have followed his instincts, he told himself. Something had told him right from the first that no good would come of it.

It was on a late October afternoon that he walked from the school to the house, leaving Loveday alone with Henry. The wind blew cold across the moor so that he hastened his steps, thinking with pleasure of the tea that awaited him, and the saffron buns that Maisie had brought from her mother's house in St Ninn; and realising with even more pleasure that it was some time since the thought of food had held any appeal for him.

Then he saw the man who leaned over the rough stone wall that separated the school from the lane.

"Goodday, Master," the man said, grinning.

"Good day." John changed direction and walked towards him. "Are you looking for me?"

"Don't ee know me, then? Come on, Master, you know me, right enough –"

Of course he knew him, John realised – though it was hardly surprising that recognition had taken a moment or two, for undoubtedly the man had changed. He looked older, as if the three years he had spent in prison had changed him from boy to man. Prison fare was perhaps not so bad as its reputation, for he had filled out, thickened; coarsened, was perhaps a better word. He had always looked unsavoury, with a bad skin and lank hair, and time had not improved him. His hair had thinned and he had lost a few teeth, while those remaining were blackened. His beard was matted, his faded shirt was torn, and the moleskin waistcoat and kerchief around his neck were equally filthy. The eyes were the same, though: watchful, crafty, gleaming with a kind of jeering insolence.

"Joely Tregilgas! You've been away a long time."

"I come back from Bodmin nigh a month ago."

"Have you found work?"

"Work?" Joely laughed at the notion. "Where should I get work to, Master? The likes of me, we'm forced to live on our wits."

"I heard that Tallons were taking on workers at Wheal Charity."

"Naw, Master, I'll not go clay-work, not for all the tea in China. Work my guts out for less'n two shillun a day? A man'd be mazed."

"Yes, well –" John Pentecost had a degree of sympathy for this point of view. "At least it's honest work, Joely. It might behove you to try it. Did you wish to speak to me for some reason?" It was, after all, not unusual for an old pupil to come back, even one as unsatisfactory as Joely Tregilgas. But if he needed a character, John thought, it would tax a man's ingenuity to compose one.

"I come for our 'Enry." Joely grinned slyly. " 'E's a funny little tacker, our 'Enry. 'E d'think the world of your liddle maid, Master. It's 'Miss says this', and 'Miss says that', and 'I'm a-drawin' this for Miss'. So I gets to thinkin' 'tis time I took a look at Miss. Last time I seen 'er, she was naught but a tacker 'erself.''

"Really?" John spoke coldly, hating the thought of those sly, lascivious eyes on Loveday. He could tell by Joely's amused expression that he was fully aware of his feelings.

"I 'ear tell she'm some 'andsome, Master. Daresay she'm just the kind of maid I dreamed I 'ad me arms around, over Bodmin."

"Now, listen to me –" John, slow to anger, felt it now. Needlessly, of course. He forced it away from him, forced his breath to come more slowly. Of course Loveday attracted attention; she was bound to do so, wherever she went. This wretch was no different from the other men who looked and lusted and were ignored by her. He pulled out his watch. "I expect the lesson will continue for another twenty minutes. It's hardly worth your while waiting."

"I'll wait," Joely said. "I got nawthin' else to do."

"Very well," John said after a moment. He looked thoughtfully at Joely, who had grown from offensive boy to offensive man, and he sighed at this evidence of yet another failure. But I tried, he thought. I did my best. That Tregilgas family . . . one felt, sometimes, they were beyond redemption. What could anyone do?

He retraced his steps to the school, told Henry his brother was waiting and that he should leave at once.

"But we haven't finished," Loveday protested.

"Even so," her father insisted, "Henry should go now."

"Then I shall stay on a little to prepare tomorrow's lesson –"

"No. Come home with me." He waited, aware of her bewilderment, until Henry had gone. "I am sorry to interfere," he said when they were alone. It was something he had always tried to avoid, from the moment that Loveday had become his assistant. "I didn't care for the thought of Joely

114

Tregilgas hanging about outside, or for you being alone here." And seeing that she neither smiled nor looked at him: "Forgive the intervention, Loveday."

"It doesn't matter," she replied, dully indifferent. "We were getting nowhere."

"Come to the house, my darling." His voice was gentle. "You look tired."

"Not so much tired as –" She broke off, biting her lip.

"As what?" He came closer to the desk, took hold of her shoulders and turned her to face him. "As what, Loveday? Can't you talk to me? Can't you tell me what's wrong?"

She lifted her head and he saw that her eyes brimmed with tears.

"Oh, Papa," she whispered. "Oh, Papa. What am I to do?"

And flinging herself upon him, she wept as if her heart would break.

Even the sight of laden clay wagons with the Tallon name emblazoned on the side lumbering down from Carclaze in the direction of the port of Charlestown, powdering the road and the houses that lined it, failed to lift Clay Tallon's spirits or dissipate the anger he felt at his son's pig-headedness. The sound of his wife twittering away to Sybil did nothing to help, either. God knew they spent enough on clothes, and were about to spend more, yet neither of them did him credit, with their droopy, beanpole figures and hangdog expressions. What had he done to deserve such a family? He had always felt a certain pride in Matthew, at least – considered him something of a chip off the old block. He had a way with him, got on well with people.

As a young boy Matthew had looked up to his father. Clay Tallon had enjoyed that. It was highly satisfactory to have a personable son who could speak up for himself and attract attention by his charm and his looks. Things had changed sadly in recent years, however. That old, uncritical attitude had gone. What on earth had happened to change him?

And what on earth was to be done about this Penberthy business? Couldn't Matthew see that marriage to Gwendolyn Penberthy would mean he was set for life? Tallons would be the wealthiest and most powerful company in the west, were he to inherit from both sides. It was the outcome that he, Clay Tallon, had planned ever since Matthew and Gwendolyn had played together as children. He must have been aware of it. His protestations simply didn't ring true.

The girl was, by all accounts, more than willing; she had a trim figure and pleasing features. Her voice was, perhaps, a little shrill, rather like her mother's, but for the love of heaven! A man could put up with that, when there were eight pits to be put in the balance. It made no sense for Matthew to be mooning over some little nobody with no dowry but a pretty face.

He found it impossible to put the matter out of his mind, though there were plenty of other questions to occupy him, not least the matter of Bell Quarry. Matthew had been right in pressing him to buy it, though it went against the grain to admit it and he had no intention of doing so openly. A partnership with Penberthy would have been the ideal solution, both financially and socially, cementing the unwritten alliance; but with Matthew proving so insultingly intransigent, it hardly seemed likely that Penberthy would pursue the matter now, keen though he had once been to do so.

Sitting at his broad desk in the window which overlooked Fore Street, Clay Tallon looked down on the little market town of St Austell, his mind far away from the comings and goings he could see below. The more he thought about that quarry, the more he wanted it – and he wanted it quickly, before Penberthy decided to go it alone. There was just this damned lack of ready capital which was causing a temporary problem.

Perhaps all was not lost. Perhaps Penberthy would ignore the more personal considerations. After all, a good investment was a good investment, no matter whom his daughter married. On the other hand, it was a well-known fact that he was a proud man, quick to take offence . . .

Drumming his fingers on the desk, Clay narrowed his eyes in thought, considering the options that were open to him. He was reluctant to approach the bank just at this moment. He had spent more than he cared to think about on Wheal Charity and the new pumping gear, not to mention repairs on the property he owned in St Ninn. Trelew was in desperate need of a new engine too, now that the pit was so much deeper and wider than a few years ago. *Damn* Matthew and his half-baked, romantic notions!

He forced himself to think of other matters, sending for his chief clerk to make a report on sales figures, casting an approving eye on the accounts which seemed to say that his problems were no more than short-term. His spirits lifted a little, especially when he turned to a report in the latest mining journal concerning the paper industry. The introduction of a pictorial press meant that better quality paper was necessary, made by a new process of coating with, among other things, high-grade china clay. It made cheerful reading. Who could doubt that the industry would go from strength to strength?

He summoned his chief clerk again and together they went through the estimates of expenditure, to see if somewhere, in some way, costs could be cut. They were engaged in this task when a junior announced that Cap'n Noah was in the outer office and had called to pay his respects, if Mr Tallon was at liberty to receive them.

"Tell him to come in." Clay Tallon pushed the papers aside and leaned back in his chair in relief. If there was anyone who could solve this problem, then surely it was Cap'n Noah. "Glad to see you," he said. "I need some help from you."

He dismissed the clerk with a wave of his hand, and Noah Pascoe took the vacated chair, filling it with his solid bulk. He was a tall, broad, craggy man, with a big nose and a face that was as seamed as his own clay tips, but burnt reddish-brown by the wind and the weather. He had a thatch of white hair and pale, knowing eyes, as if he had heard every excuse ever made and saw through all of them.

" 'Ow is it, then?" he asked, employing the universal greeting. There were few who felt sufficiently at ease with Clay Tallon to talk so informally.

"Not good, Cap'n Noah. I'm having trouble raising the wherewithal for Bell Quarry."

"I thought you'd got Penberthy interested?"

"I thought so too, but I'm not hopeful now. I told you about Matthew, didn't I? He's dug his toes in about Miss Penberthy. Says he won't marry her, not at any price. Penberthy's been avoiding me, I swear – and can you wonder at it?"

" 'Twould be a good investment."

"That damn-fool son of mine –"

Cap'n Noah ignored this as an irrelevance.

"So what do us do?" he said.

Clay Tallon smiled. He had other captains, but none like Cap'n Noah. Trust him to go straight to the heart of the matter – to see at once that other steps must be taken to make sure that the Bell Quarry fell into Tallon hands. Others might shrug their shoulders under similar circumstances, accepting defeat. Not Clay Tallon, and not Noah Pascoe. They were, he thought not for the first time, a good team.

"Look," Clay said, half-turning the sheet so that Cap'n Noah could see it. "You know the position more than anyone. If Trelew can hold on a year for the new steam engine –"

Cap'n Noah's expression gave no clue to his thoughts. His face might have been chipped out of granite.

"I know it's inadequate now that the area of the pit is so much greater –" Tallon went on.

" 'Twas inadequate when we bought it second hand from old Roseveare up Stenalees. Now there are fractures in the flywheel."

The captain was thinking aloud, not raising objections. He said nothing that was not known to Tallon, who favoured him with his coaxing, puckish smile.

"You can plate it up, Noah. You and your team can fix anything."

"Maybe. It won't be so efficient. Or safe. If it flies apart –"

Clay Tallon cut him short.

"Not *as* efficient, I agree," he said. "But it will do for a few more months. We can't afford a new one, Noah. You can see that."

"Ah." The captain said nothing for a few moments. He seemed lost in thought, his pale eyes seeing not the office and the desk but the wild, white landscape of Trelew.

Tallon leaned forward a little across the desk.

"Fix it, Noah," he said, not coaxing now but with the air of a man giving an order. "You shall have a new one next year."

The captain looked at him and there was a touch of cynical

amusement in his pale eyes and a caustic twist to his lips.

"Seems like I've heard that before, sir."

"This time I swear!" Clay Tallon was smiling again, and he lifted his hand to shoulder-level, palm outward. "You can do it, Noah."

"Oh, I can fix it," Cap'n Noah agreed. "I can fix anything, like you said. There's a risk, though. That can't be denied."

"We've always taken risks, you and I – and my father before me. Tallons was built on risks, and you know it."

"Hm." Cap'n Noah looked thoughtful. "Maybe Mr Penberthy will change his mind."

"Ha! I doubt that, after the slight he's received from Matthew. What can the boy be thinking of? She's a good-looking girl, Noah, and he doesn't dislike her, after all. Anyone would think I was trying to marry him off to some old crone."

"Well, there 'tis." Cap'n Noah sat in his chair, mighty hands spread one on each knee. "Three things I'd never let another man choose for me. A shotgun, a fishing-rod, and a wife. I daresay young Matthew feels much the same. Marriage is a tricky business at the best of times. My advice is to leave un alone to make his own mistakes."

Keep your advice for the clayworks, Tallon thought; but he smiled his curling smile and said nothing. He needed Cap'n Noah quite as much as Cap'n Noah needed him.

The church clock struck one, taking him by surprise.

"Good heavens, is that the time?" He pulled out his watch to check it. "I had no idea. I promised my wife and daughter I would meet them for luncheon at the White Hart ten minutes ago. You'll excuse me, Cap'n Noah? I know I can rely on you to do what you can with the engine."

He'd do it, right enough, Clay Tallon assured himself as he hurried in the direction of the White Hart, so abstracted that he failed to see the figure of Captain Hawke approaching the inn from the other direction. The two men almost collided at the entrance.

"My dear fellow, forgive me!" Clay smiled charmingly, clapping the other man on the shoulder. "I was lost in thought. Are you coming inside?"

"Propose spot of luncheon. Will you join me, sir?"

"On the contrary. You must join me. I'm meeting my wife and daughter."

"Delighted, delighted. If no objection, of course. Mustn't impose. Not my style!"

"Nothing would please them more."

The fates were, perhaps, on his side at last, Clay Tallon thought. All Sybil needed was a chance to get to know Captain Hawke. He wasn't a bad sort of chap, after all; not a gentleman, by Millicent's standards, but who cared for that? He seemed to have a good income. Odd-looking chap, of course, but women set too much store by looks – and as he had said to Millicent, beggars couldn't be choosers.

For one brief moment, as Millicent and Sybil Tallon saw who was approaching across the dining room, their two strikingly similar faces reflected an equal amount of dismay, but they had collected themselves and expressed nothing but polite welcome as the two men joined them.

"Mrs Tallon, Miss Tallon." Stiffly, grinning his Punch-like grin, Captain Hawke bowed first to one and then to the other. "Invited aboard – hope no objections. Great pleasure for me."

"For us, too. Please sit down, Captain Hawke." Millicent smiled her sweet, uncertain smile at him. "I trust you are well?"

"Never better, never better. And you, ma'am? Good, good! And Miss Sybil?"

There was a distinct softening of his voice as he bent his smile upon Sybil, and the colour surged into her cheeks. Honestly, it was too bad of Father to foist Captain Hawke on her, she thought. She had made it quite clear that she was not, and never could be, interested in the wretched man. She gave a brief and meaningless smile in his direction and thereafter refused to look at him, uncomfortably aware that he was making every effort to catch her eye.

It was she who caught sight of the Penberthys first. There was a small stir by the door, and as she looked across she saw that it was caused by Gwendolyn and her mother effusively greeting friends as they made their way to a table in the corner, closely followed by Mr Penberthy.

The smiles which they were distributing to right and left died as, inevitably, their eyes alighted on the Tallon party in the opposite corner. Clay Tallon rose and bowed towards them, while Millicent fluttered her hand in greeting, but a curt nod was Mr Penberthy's only reply and an even colder toss of the head was Gwendolyn's.

"Really," she was heard to say to her mother, her shrill voice clearly audible in every corner of the dining room. "The White Hart is so dreadfully crowded these days. I don't think I care for it any more."

Heavily, and in silence, Clay Tallon sat down again and resumed his meal. His face was drawn and furrowed with anger and his knife and fork clattered angrily on his plate, as if he wished he were attacking Matthew in place of the lamb chops that had been served to him.

At least the question of a partnership with Penberthy was settled. He knew now where he stood. One way or another, Cap'n Noah would have to get that engine fixed.

"Come for a walk with me, Syb," Matthew begged.

"I was going to bath the dogs –"

"*Please!*"

His voice was low but full of urgency, demanding her attention.

"Oh, very well," she said. "We can take the dogs with us and you can help me bath them afterwards."

It was, she thought, about time he confided in her. She had asked him once or twice what was wrong with him and had had her head bitten off for her pains; but she had forgiven him, partly because he was so clearly troubled, and partly because she always had forgiven him, no matter what.

Out of the gates which stood at the end of the drive to Prospect Lodge they turned left, to walk over the cliffs towards Par. It was a dull, colourless day, but the wind had dropped and the sea was in peaceful mood, with barely a ripple on its surface. Smoke from the steamer out of Par harbour that puffed towards the horizon laden with china clay hung almost stationary in the still air.

"Shouldn't you be at work?" Sybil asked her brother.

"Very probably." He slashed at nettles by the side of the path as he strode along. "I've been checking manifests at

Charlestown. I couldn't face the thought of going back to my office desk."

"What's wrong? Is it the girl?" Matthew said nothing, and Sybil looked at him with exasperation. "For heaven's sake, Matthew, stop mistreating those poor plants and tell me what's troubling you! If you're not going to talk to me, I might as well have stayed at home."

They had come to a stone wall, and a gate, and side by side they leaned upon it. The whole of St Austell bay was spread before them. As if in tune with Matthew's mood, everything was in shades of grey: the sea, the sky; to eastward the land beyond Par towards the Gribbin and Fowey, to westward the bulk of Black Head.

"Do you know Father wants me to marry Gwendolyn?" Matthew asked at last.

"Yes, of course! The whole world knows that. You must have known too."

"I didn't, I swear. Anyway, I'm not going to."

"Good for you. I've never liked her much. Are you in love with that girl – with Loveday Pentecost?"

The silence lengthened between them as Matthew considered his reply. Ultimately, there was only one thing he could say.

"Yes." The word emerged as a short, strangled cry, almost as if he had fought against it. He sighed deeply. "Yes," he said again, but firmly, solemnly. "Father says I am a half-baked romantic schoolboy. He doesn't believe in love."

Sybil sighed too.

"I confess to being a bit cynical about it myself. Girls seem to fall into it so easily. They saddle themselves with a husband and before they can look around they have a houseful of babies and no freedom at all. You don't hear so much about love then!"

Matthew was not, at that moment, interested in women in general; only one woman in particular.

"I suppose people would say that I don't know her – but there's knowing and knowing, Syb. I mean, I don't know what her favourite food is or whether she enjoys Gilbert and Sullivan's operettas, but on another level I feel I've known her for always. Can you understand that?"

"I suppose so." Sybil's voice was slow, almost reluctant. This, she supposed, was what poets wrote about – the strange, bewildering emotion that she had never experienced at first hand and found comfort in mocking. A little to her surprise, she felt no desire to mock Matthew. His pain was too real.

"I take it she doesn't feel the same for you," she said gently.

Matthew beat his fist on the top of the gate.

"She does, she does! I'm sure of it! Each time we've met, it's been the same. We've looked at each other and *known* – yet somehow it all went wrong the night of my party. I couldn't dance with her more than twice, could I? It was my party, after all."

"And you had a duty to your guests. She must have understood that."

"I swear that she did. The first time we danced it was heaven; then the next time, everything was different."

"You weren't the soul of tact, you know, when you introduced her to me. When I said I would like to teach, you implied that somehow it was an unworthy thing to do. Father wouldn't hear of it, you said."

Matthew turned to look at her, appalled.

"Well, he wouldn't, would he? Oh Lord, she couldn't have taken offence at that, could she? Do you think that was it?"

Sybil shook her head.

"Truly, I don't know – but it *was* tactless, Matthew. She seemed very young and rather shy. Perhaps, because I'm thin-skinned myself, I expect others to be the same." She paused, and sighed. "You were right, of course," she said, less censoriously and with considerable gloom. "Father would never allow me to teach anywhere at all, and he would certainly disapprove of your marrying a teacher in a Board School. Why, there was a Treffry and a Tremayne at your ball, no less! We Tallons may have embarked on our climb up the social ladder under dubious circumstances, but we're well on our way now."

"God, she must hate me!" Matthew's voice and expression were tragic.

"On the other hand –" Sybil began before she was distracted

123

momentarily by the two dogs barking somewhere out of sight. Frustrated, Matthew waited while she went to look for them. "Only rabbits," she said as she returned.

"On the other hand what?"

"Well –" Sybil paused, frowning. "I'm not sure of this, mind. It's only a conjecture –"

"For the love of heaven, *what*?"

"I think it's possible that the girls may have picked on her. You know, Gwendolyn and Beatrice and that lot. I rather think I saw her go upstairs after supper – I remember thinking that the bedroom would be a bit crowded because the others had gone up just a little while before. Not much room in front of the mirror, I thought."

Stony-faced, Matthew stared at her.

"What do you mean, picked on her?"

Sybil shrugged.

"You know what little snobs they are! Girls can be terribly unkind if they set out to be –" As she should know, she thought, for she had been the victim more than once. Poor Sybil, twenty-five and not married! In their eyes she was a hopeless failure. "And of course, Gwendolyn might have said something – or someone else might have said something – about an understanding between the two of you –"

Matthew gave a hollow groan and put a hand to his head.

"I can see it all," he said.

"I'm guessing, no more –"

"No, I swear you're right. She heard about this mythical understanding, so thought I was philandering."

"Well," Sybil said briskly, as the two spaniels came lolloping out of the undergrowth towards them, their fur full of burrs. "At least you know what to do about it, then. Come on, if you're going to help me with these animals. You did say you would, you know. They're twice as bad now as they were before."

"*You* said I would. I don't seem to remember agreeing – but I'll make a bargain with you." She was already retracing her steps towards Prospect Lodge and Matthew had to call after her. "I'll help with the dogs if you come with me to Fourlanesend."

"To add respectability?" Sybil smiled a little sourly at this heavy underscoring of her old-maid status.

"To add respectability and weight and gravity and propriety and all the other desirable things that fathers set such great store by."

"I'm not at all sure that *our* father would set great store by such a venture. No, I don't think he would like it at all."

"Then he'll have to lump it," Matthew said inelegantly, feeling more cheerful than he had done for some days.

Loveday, gone to Roskelly for eggs on Saturday afternoon, declined to stay for tea. She had work to prepare, she said.

"Then come over later," Dolly urged her. "Go on, do, Loveday. I've seen nothing of you this week. Mother picked up a *Home Chat* when she went to market, and it's got some handsome fashions. What is it?" she added, as Loveday hesitated. "Aren't you well? I must say you're looking a bit wisht: You haven't been yourself since the Tallon ball. Better fit you stick to St Ninn for your fun, you ask me!"

"I expect you're right," Loveday agreed. "To be honest, I'm not feeling myself, Dolly. I'll have an early night and see you in a day or two."

"There's a blouse and skirt in *Home Chat* would suit you handsome. You buy some stuff next time you're in St Austell and I'll make it for you. You could do with something new to wear. 'Tis wonderful how that old brown dress do go on and on."

Dear Dolly, Loveday thought as she went home with the eggs. No one could call her tactful – but she was a dear, quite without guile, a wonderful friend. Was it just possible that, one day, she might feel differently about Ned? It would be very comfortable to be part of the Crowle family; on the other hand –

She was in sight of the schoolhouse now. There was a strange gig outside; Dr Geach, perhaps? No, of course not! It was far too smart, and anyway, Dr Geach's horse was an elderly grey, not a roan.

It was not Mrs Morrow's either, nor the vicar's. Then who could have come to call? Her heart began to thump heavily. It could be no one exciting, she cautioned herself. It was probably someone from the Education Committee, called on school business.

On a Saturday? She quickened her footsteps, then slowed almost to a halt. Suppose – just suppose – it was Matthew. What should she do, what should she say? She felt in a flutter at the very thought, which was quite ridiculous. Whatever happened, she must behave with dignity. He couldn't surely think that he had only to lift a finger and she would come running – not when he was engaged to another girl?

Of course it wasn't Matthew! She didn't even, she assured herself solemnly, *want* it to be Matthew. Hadn't she decided to forget him, put the whole episode out of her mind? She and Papa between them had agreed that she would definitely go to college in Truro the following year, and would become a qualified teacher. They had stayed up late talking it over. A qualified teacher, Papa had said, can go anywhere – London, Australia, *anywhere*!

"Even America?" Loveday had said, her imagination kindling. She had always wanted to go to America.

"Even America," her father agreed. "After all, you have uncles there."

"We could both go," she said; and he had laughed, and said that somehow he didn't see himself moving away from Cornwall. Loveday couldn't see herself moving, either – at least, not for more than a year or two, just to see a little bit of the world. She had always longed to do that. After all, she thought, Mrs Tregilgas, the old witch, said she would travel far.

And never leave the clay, Loveday reminded herself – whatever that meant.

The front door of the schoolhouse stood open and she went inside. There were voices coming from the parlour on the right-hand side of the hall; her father talking of the stream of emigrants, out-of-work tin miners, leaving for South Africa; a woman's voice replying.

Maisie, the little maid-of-all-work, peeped round the kitchen door at the far end of the hall and cautiously emerged.

"Visitors," she mouthed silently, pointing to the parlour, scampering back into the safety of the kitchen when she heard Mr Pentecost's voice.

"Loveday," he called. "Is that you? Come inside, my dear. Some friends have come to see us."

Three pairs of eyes looked at her as she stood, transfixed, on the threshold, but she was only conscious of one.

"Good afternoon, Miss Pentecost," said Matthew, rising from the chair beside the fire.

"Mr Tallon!" For a moment she could say no more. It was like a dream, seeing him there in the familiar surroundings of the shabby, comfortable parlour – a dream when people behave out of character and nothing is as it should be; and as in a dream, she felt incapable of movement or speech. The thump, thump, thump of her heart was deafening. "And Miss Tallon," she managed to say at last with a nervous smile towards Sybil, remembering her manners. "How – how very nice to see you."

"I hoped you wouldn't mind –" Matthew said hesitantly. Her eyes flew back to him and she recognised, with astonishment, that he was nervous too. His eyes were anxious, his lower lip caught between his teeth. "You don't mind my coming, do you, Miss Pentecost? I persuaded Sybil that you would not."

Loveday could feel the joy. It felt fizzy, like lemonade, and it began somewhere in the pit of her stomach and spread upwards and outwards until it was more like a firework, filling her world with a cascade of shooting stars.

And me in my old brown dress, she thought.

7

"Mr Pentecost is a most remarkable man," Sybil said.

They were in the gig returning to Prospect Lodge and so far she had said very little since leaving Fourlanesend, for the simple reason that Matthew had given her no opportunity. Neither had he recognised, in his own exalted state, that his sister, too, was in the grip of unusual emotion.

"What did you think of her? Isn't she a darling?" They had barely driven away from the schoolhouse before, unable to disguise his elation, he had embarked on the subject of Loveday, his hopes and his intentions. "Father must come round, mustn't he? I mean, how could anyone object to a girl so altogether lovely – ?"

And so on, and so on. Sybil had nodded and murmured agreement and encouragement, her thoughts miles away.

"I've never met a man who *listened* with such concentration," she said when Matthew paused for breath.

"*Father?*" Matthew's expression was comical in its bewilderment.

"No, Mr Pentecost, of course!"

"He seems exceedingly pleasant," Matthew agreed.

He was more than that, Sybil thought. But then she had had more opportunity to talk to him than her brother, for after tea Loveday had yielded to Matthew's expressed interest in seeing the school and the classroom where she spent her days and had taken him off, leaving Sybil and Mr Pentecost together in the parlour. Any thought of offering to accompany them had died still-born, for Mr Pentecost had caught her eye and given a glimmer of a smile, as if they were collaborators.

"I think, perhaps, a few moments alone might give them a chance to sort out their misunderstanding, don't you?" he had said, once Matthew and Loveday had gone, and Sybil had agreed.

"They have a great deal to talk about."

"Miss Tallon, I feel sure I may speak frankly to you."

"Please do, Mr Pentecost," Sybil assented at once, but still he hesitated for a few moments, looking down at his hands that were clasped on his knee. They were thin, blue-veined. Sensitive hands, Sybil decided.

He looked up at her, and she saw that his eyes were grave.

"It is totally against my firmly-held beliefs to interfere in people's lives," he said at last. "But Loveday's happiness is the most important thing in the world to me. I must know what your brother's intentions are towards her. Is there any truth in the fact that his engagement is about to be announced to Miss Penberthy?"

"My father would like it to be true, but the fact is that it is not," Sybil said firmly. "Matthew has told me that he will never marry her."

"But no doubt your father is able to exert considerable pressure."

Sybil laughed shortly at that.

"You don't know Matthew, Mr Pentecost. He can be very determined. And as for his intentions towards your daughter, I know that they are honourable. I have never known him so unhappy as during this past week."

"Then I'll question you no more, but leave the outcome to the two young people themselves, for good or ill." He had smiled, the gravity leaving his face. "Now tell me about yourself, Miss Tallon. How do you pass your time?"

"I – I try to write."

Sybil blushed fiery red, embarrassed and amazed at herself. Afterwards she was at a loss to explain the impulse that had led her to confess such a thing to this virtual stranger. Was it an instinctive recognition of his interest and sympathy? She supposed, on reflection, that this was the only explanation.

At the time she could not believe that she had said such a thing – and to a schoolmaster, too. He would surely be amused at her effrontery.

There was, however, no trace of amusement on his face, but merely a lively interest.

"Really? What sort of thing do you write?"

Sybil swallowed nervously and licked her lips.

"Well – stories, mostly," she said. "Poems, too, sometimes, but I know they're not very good. The stories aren't very good either, of course, but they give me pleasure to write."

"What do you do with them?"

"Do with them?" Sybil looked astonished at the question. "I keep them in my desk drawer."

"And no one sees them but you?"

"Oh no." The colour flooded her face again. "My father is much against it. Anyway, they aren't good enough to show anyone. I can't imagine why I mentioned them."

"They may be better than you think. What makes you want to write?"

Biting her lip, Sybil looked around the room as if seeking an answer.

"I don't know," she said at last. "Yes, I do!" she added, her voice strengthening. "There are things – situations – that seem rounded and whole. It's hard to explain. Plots come into my mind, with a beginning and a resolution, and I seem to see them, complete, hanging above my head in a big, shining bubble . . ." Her voice trailed away. "You must think me mad," she said, with a nervous laugh. "Sometimes I think I must be."

But John Pentecost was looking at her intently, smiling a little, but with pleasure, not amusement.

"I don't think you are mad at all," he said. "I don't think I have ever heard a more valid reason to write. I wish you would show me your stories."

"Oh, I couldn't!" Sybil was covered with confusion once more. "I mean, they are very simple things – women's stories – not the kind of thing you would wish to read. They're not in the least clever. Really, I am so ill-educated, you would surely think them quite dreadful. I never show them to anyone, not even Matthew, and to someone as well-read as you must be, they would seem quite laughable."

"I don't suppose they would for one moment. Why not give me the chance? Perhaps I could help a little. Won't you think about it?"

Sybil's hands were clasping and unclasping in her lap and for a moment she stared down at them, her head bent.

"I don't know," she whispered. "I don't know if I can. I would feel –" 'Naked', she had been about to say, but realised in the nick of time that this was hardly a word that a well-brought-up woman should say to a man. She blushed again at the very thought. "Exposed," she substituted.

"Think about it," John repeated gently. "I do understand how you must feel. Why is your father so much against it?"

"He thinks it a waste of time – that I should be doing something more useful, or sociable. He says that writing gives me nothing but rounded shoulders and inky fingers –"

"I imagine it gives you a great deal more than that."

"Oh, yes." It was amazing, John thought, how her plain face was transformed when she spoke of her secret activity. "It's the only life I have, Mr Pentecost. And probably the only life I will have, for I can't imagine that I shall ever marry – which makes me a total failure. Even if I were a brilliantly successful author" – she looked up with a smile, to show that she was merely joking, that she had no such aspirations – "I should still be a failure in society's eyes, so long as I remain a spinster. To my family and to everyone else I would be poor, plain, embittered Sybil who only fills her time with writing because she can't find a husband. You know that's true, Mr Pentecost."

"Do I?" Quizzically he raised his eyebrows. "Society said, at one time, that the earth was flat. Society does not always have the last word. Perhaps it is not your fate to be married, though I must say that I think you are grossly premature in regarding the matter so pessimistically. But assuming you are right in your supposition, can you not console yourself by the thought that to have no husband at all is preferable to having a bad one? I can think of nothing worse for an independently minded woman than to be subject to a husband she has grown to dislike. Clearly you have a mind of your own. It may be that you have talents not given to others. Marriage and motherhood may be the conventional picture of happiness; but think about freedom, Miss Tallon. It has something to be said for it, don't you agree?" He laughed suddenly. "It occurs to me that for one who dislikes to interfere in the lives of others, I have said a good deal too much."

She was looking at him, tentatively smiling, suddenly hopeful.

"You should smile more often," he said. "No one then would dream of calling you plain."

"Oh!" The compliment threw her into confusion, silencing her for a moment. "You're most kind, Mr Pentecost – most kind."

"Not at all. I am being truthful, and intensely practical. If you are given a talent, then you should use it, and delight in using it. And much as any daughter should respect her parents' wishes, it is my sincere belief that you should fight to the death for your right to do so."

Sybil stared at him, open-mouthed. This was not the pious kind of talk that she would have expected from anyone of his generation, nor even from her own.

"The thing is," she said at last, "I don't know if I have anything worth fighting for. It seems impossible that I should have."

The schoolmaster smiled at her, but there was the firm note of authority in his voice when he replied to her.

"I think you should try," he said.

The barely believable joy remained, but there was constraint, too; a shy silence as Loveday and Matthew crossed to the school, broken only by silly, superficial remarks. Yes, Loveday agreed, the wind was cold up here. No, she couldn't say she looked forward to winter.

And me in my old brown dress and my hair all anyhow, she thought again, and bit her lip and lowered her eyes, pretending to be absorbed in finding her way around the potholes that pockmarked the playground between the house and the school.

She opened the heavy door, and though there was a world

of difference between Matthew's old seat of learning and this school on the moor, still there was a familiar smell about it, as if books and chalk and inky desks gave off their own bouquet.

They walked through the wide porch with pegs on the walls where the children hung their shabby coats, and two long forms on either side underneath the pegs. Beyond was the main classroom.

"And this is where you spend your time?" he asked.

"No, not here. This is the big class. We all have prayers here in the morning, and sing a hymn –"

"Who plays the piano?"

"I do. Not very well, but enough for 'Onward, Christian Soldiers' and 'Fight the Good Fight'."

"How very martial!"

"Oh, I'm quite good at 'All Things Bright and Beautiful', as well. And I'm already practising for Christmas. 'Once in Royal' is quite easy, but 'Oh, Come All Ye Faithful' beats me every time."

"So where do you go after prayers?"

"My class is in here." She crossed the room as she spoke, and opened a door, revealing her domain. There was the desk, just as she had left it, facing the three rows of small desks where the children sat two by two. There were the high windows, the hated, tyrannical round stove that sulked and smoked and roared in turns and had to be constantly tended and placated. On the walls there was the picture of the Queen, the map of the world with vast areas coloured red, and a few arithmetical tables; all exactly the same as ever, yet never to seem quite the same again now that Matthew had stood here beside her.

"I'm glad to have seen it," he said. "I can imagine you, now –" She said nothing, but stood, head bent, tracing the outline of a stain on the lid of her desk where Miss Scobie, years ago, had spilled green ink. It was exciting, the realisation that Matthew thought of her, wanted to picture her.

He covered her hand with his and pulled her round to face him.

"Loveday," he said softly. "What happened? I thought we were friends."

She saw that the hand that held hers trembled a little, and marvelled at it. He had always been so much in command, so sure of himself; but now he was not.

He took her hand and kissed its palm, cupping it, pressing his lips lingeringly on her flesh; and now she trembled too, knowing this was only the beginning.

"Oh, Matthew," she whispered huskily, and could say no more.

Tenderly he pulled her towards him, and she did not resist but lifted her face to receive his kiss, wanting only to feel his lips on hers. His arms closed round her and she heard his indrawn breath as his mouth covered hers.

All the doubts and fears of the previous days fell away as if they had never been. She was conscious of nothing except Matthew, the feel of him, the sharp, clean scent of him, the wanting him. This, only this, was reality.

Now her arms encircled his neck and her lips were as eager as his.

"Oh, my darling, how I love you!" he said at last.

Wonderingly she looked into his face.

"But they told me –"

"I can guess what they told you. If it concerns Gwendolyn, there's no truth in it."

"No? Do you promise?"

"I promise!" He kissed her again, small butterfly kisses on her lips, her cheeks, her hair. "There's no truth in it at all. It was a stupid scheme of my father's, no more. It's you I love and want to marry."

But you can't – how can you? – your father – a Board School teacher – and me in my brown dress –

Her head was like a whirlpool with thoughts and emotions swirling round and round, until they disappeared into the vortex as he took her into his arms and kissed her again.

"I love you," he repeated. And laughed a little, bending to drop a light kiss on the end of her nose. "That's three times I have said it, with no word of response from you. Maidenly modesty is all very well –"

"You know that I love you!"

"I know no such thing." Despite his words, he was confident again now. He smiled at her, his eyes devoured her, lingered on her eyes, her mouth. "There were times this week when I felt quite sure you hated me."

She put her hand against his lips, and he twisted his head to kiss it again.

"Don't talk of this week," she said. "I thought I would die."

"Then you will marry me?"

She withdrew from him a little.

"Matthew, it's not as easy as that, is it? Your father won't allow it."

"I'm twenty-one!"

"But you work with him. You can't go against him."

"If I have to, I will. But I doubt it will come to that. My mother and Sybil will be on my side."

"You don't know that –"

"I know! How could they help loving you? There's Mrs Morrow, too. Father seems to hold her in high esteem –" Or did, Matthew remembered, before she introduced Loveday into the household. But he would again, no doubt. Mrs Morrow was an attractive woman, of the kind his father had always found hard to resist. One way or the other, it was impossible to conceive of anything that could mar their happiness, now or later.

"I can't help being afraid," Loveday said.

"Of what?" She could only shake her head, unable to find the right words. Of power, perhaps. Of irresistible forces; of the habit of filial obedience; of a life that was different from anything she had known. "Silly one," Matthew murmured against her hair, holding her close again. "Everything will be wonderful. So long as we love each other, nothing can hurt us."

And when he kissed her like that, it was impossible to think that he might not be right.

"Yes, yes, of course I liked him," John Pentecost assured his daughter. "I thought the first time I saw him that he was a fine young man, and I found nothing today that made me change my mind. There's an openness about him that some-how inspires trust – and a kind of enjoyment of life that is very appealing. I can quite see the charm that he has for you.

But having said that, my darling, it cannot be denied that you don't know him, neither does he know you."

And whatever difference does that make? he asked himself. Did I know Ruth, when I saw her at the Geographical Society lecture, where I was supposed to be hearing of Baker's expedition to Central Africa but was conscious of nothing except the curve of her cheek beneath that ridiculous hat? And has any woman touched me since, more than superficially?

"Mrs Morrow knows him," Loveday said reasonably.

"Yes, of course she does. And likes him, I know. But Loveday, you are both so young. You must be sure of your own minds."

"We are sure," she said. "But we know it may be difficult to talk Mr Tallon round. Matthew hopes to win his mother's approval first. Oh Papa, be happy for me! I care for nothing, so long as Matthew loves me and you approve."

"How about Miss Tallon?" her father asked. "Does she approve?"

"I suppose she must do, or she wouldn't have come here with him. I have hardly spoken to her, to be honest, and when I did, I thought her – difficult. Did you find her difficult, while we were away?"

"No," John Pentecost said, after a moment's thought. "Not at all. I thought her most interesting."

Matthew saw the ring in a shop in Falmouth where he had gone to meet the agent of a Dutch manufacturer regarding a contract for the supply of china clay. It was a sapphire set with diamonds and seed pearls, and the moment he saw it he knew that whatever its cost he must buy it for Loveday even though their engagement had not been officially announced.

He had been looking for a suitable birthday present, but having seen the ring nothing else could please him. I can call it a birthday present, he thought. And though she won't be able to wear it on the fourth finger of her left hand, still she must have it. It's the loveliest thing I have seen.

"The lady will be pleased with this, sir," the jeweller said, looking at it lovingly before snapping shut the little velvet box that housed it. He winked, leaning confidentially towards

Matthew across the counter. "It belonged to a member of the aristocracy, fallen on hard times."

"Then I hope it's not unlucky!"

"Bless you, no, sir! We make our own luck, I always say. I've no time for superstitious nonsense."

"I'm inclined to agree with you."

"Thank you, sir." Both for the agreement and for the money, he implied, banging the till drawer shut with a flourish. "I hope the lady wears it in health and happiness."

Matthew repeated the wish as he handed his present to Loveday on the evening of her eighteenth birthday. They had been granted a few precious moments to themselves, as John Pentecost was not yet quite ready to be taken down to Carrivick where Sarah had invited them to a birthday dinner and where, with the far-seeing cunning native to lovers, Matthew had contrived to drop Sybil before coming up to Fourlanesend to collect the Pentecosts.

"Oh Matthew, it's beautiful," Loveday gasped, when the full glory of his present was revealed. "It's just – it's just – *beautiful*!"

"Try it on." Matthew took her left hand and slid it on to the fourth finger. "If it's too big I can have it made smaller in St Austell."

"It's not a bit too big. It's just absolutely right – but Matthew, I can't wear it, not until we are engaged. Oh, how can I bear not to?"

"You must keep it secret, just for a little while longer. That's why I've bought you a subsidiary present, so that when people ask you what Matthew has given you for your birthday you can tell them 'Hardy's *Wessex Poems*'."

"Oh, dearest Matthew! You think of everything – and I've *longed* for the poems. I should have been more than happy with them alone, but to have the ring as well . . . words fail me! I know. I'll put it on a chain round my neck, then at least you and I will know that I'm wearing it, even if no one else does."

She rushed away to her bedroom, flushed and excited, coming downstairs just as Matthew and her father emerged from the parlour ready for the short journey to Carrivick, where dinner was to be served at a round table in Sarah's sitting room.

"The dining room is all very well for a banquet," Sarah said. "But for a more intimate meal with friends I find it totally intimidating. Robert and I always dine here when he is home – and I have had wonderful news from him today! He sails from India this very week – in fact he should already have sailed by this time, so will be home by mid-December."

"Then this is a double celebration," John said. "I'm delighted for you." He raised his glass. "To your husband's return."

"No, no – we'll drink to that later. First we must drink to our dear Loveday. Many happy returns of the day, my dear; and may this coming year be the happiest you have yet known."

"Thank you. It will, I'm sure it will," Loveday said, conscious of the ring between her breasts. And no one seeing the look that passed from her to Matthew and back again could doubt that it would.

Sybil felt a pang – not of jealousy, exactly, for she did not grudge Matthew the happiness that shone from him these days, but certainly of longing. How wonderful it would be if one day a man would look at her in that way! But she had only to look at herself in the mirror, to see the heavy features and the mouth that seemed to fall naturally into sulky lines no matter how cheerful she was feeling, to realise the improbability of such a thing.

The pain of this realisation was not quite as great as it had been. After talking to John Pentecost about her writing, she had returned to her desk feeling hopeful and encouraged. She had read through everything she had written; had been elated by some of the material, which seemed better than she remembered, though equally, some had seemed unbelievably poor. One story had seemed particularly promising, she thought, and she had set about reworking it. The result she had handed to Mr Pentecost before dinner. His opinion of it loomed, at that moment, far larger than her non-existent marriage prospects.

It was not, after all, as if she had ever seen a man who appealed to her particularly. Any desire for marriage was linked solely to the status it would impart – and even that was of less importance now. Oh, why couldn't her own father be as kind and as wise as John Pentecost? How different life would be if he would only value what gifts she possessed, instead of constantly disparaging them.

The others were talking of Robert Morrow's return and of the Christmas ball that Sarah was planning. It sounded as if it would be very grand, with a house party from London as well as all the local notables – who would undoubtedly accept any invitation offered, Sybil thought cynically, despite a residue of doubt about Sarah Morrow's status. None of them would pass up the chance of meeting famous names of the theatre, face to face.

Wouldn't it be wonderful, Loveday was thinking, if I could go to the ball as Matthew's fiancée, announced and acknowledged? Was it too much to expect? She knew Sybil was on their side, for she had lent the propriety of her presence several times during the past month. Together the three of them had walked on the moor and in the woods, for the weather had been unseasonably kind; and on another occasion they had driven to Charlestown, the busy little port in St Austell bay built by Charles Rashleigh during the latter part of the last century. They had strolled on the quay and watched the boats, interested spectators of all the activity. Matthew had been in his element here, had taken on a new stature, for this was his world, among the heavy wagons that delivered the clay to the dock, and the boats that transported it to all points of the globe.

Later they had picked their way over the pebbly little beach at the side of the harbour, playing like children at skittering stones across the water, Sybil every bit as high-spirited as they were. She was quite different, Loveday thought, once one got to know her; and not too straight-laced to turn a blind eye when Matthew kissed her behind a rock.

They had gone back to Prospect Lodge to tea on that occasion. The house itself looked far less attractive than it had appeared on the night of the ball when it had been given glamour by the lights and the carriages and the guests arriving. Now she was conscious of its angles and proportions, of the mournful, dead hydrangeas that bordered the drive, of the heaviness and darkness of its furnishings. The one light and hopeful touch had been provided by the table that stood in the window. It was covered by a large, half-worked jigsaw puzzle.

"Father adores them," Matthew explained. "He always has one on the go." He was hanging over it as he spoke, a piece of blue sky in his hand. "There," he said, fitting it neatly into its appointed place.

"Matthew, do leave it," his mother implored. "Don't do any more. You know your father hates anyone else to meddle."

Loveday was intrigued and rather amused. It bore out the general opinion of Clay Tallon: that he was charming and friendly and approachable – a different kind of picture, it had to be admitted, to that painted by his children. Who was right and who was wrong?

The prospect of this social occasion had made her nervous, but the reality was far less frightening than she had imagined, at least at first. Mrs Tallon had a shy manner, but Matthew displayed the same almost protective attitude towards her that Loveday had noticed at his birthday dance, and before long the four of them were chatting without restraint.

"Matthew has told me all about you," she said to Loveday, smiling at her in the nervous, sideways manner that was characteristic of her. "I – I want you to know, my dear, that, that really I – well, I do feel quite – I mean –"

"What Mama means," Matthew said, smiling at his mother affectionately, "is that she is quite delighted that you have agreed to marry me. Isn't that so, Mama?"

"Oh!" Mrs Tallon flushed. "I would not have put it – well, there will be difficulties, nobody can deny –"

"Father, you mean?" Matthew raised his eyebrows quizzically over his teacup.

"He does have other ideas, you know. I cannot possibly encourage you to disregard them. But on the other hand –"

"On the other hand, you are pleased that I shall not be introducing Gwendolyn Penberthy into the household! Admit it, Mama – you were never very keen on her."

"I would never admit to anything so discourteous." But she smiled a secret smile into her cup and Loveday received the distinct impression that Mrs Tallon had little affection for Gwendolyn.

"Naturally," Loveday said, "we hope to gain Mr Tallon's approval."

"Eventually," added Matthew.

"Your father's a strong-willed man," Mrs Tallon said.

"Stubborn," said Matthew.

"Like you," said Sybil. "Well, you'll need to stick to your guns. He'll try to browbeat you, you know."

Were they really speaking of the man who adored jigsaw puzzles? Somehow it didn't add up.

"Sybil," Mrs Tallon protested faintly. "Pray don't speak of your father in that way."

"Well, it's true, Mama."

"A man should be the head of his own family. His children's happiness is his main concern, and his wisdom greater than theirs. It's merely that, in this instance, I feel he has too little regard for Matthew's own feelings."

"So Loveday and I can rely on your support?" Matthew said.

Mrs Tallon wore a hunted expression.

"I – I suppose so, dear," she said. "But you know your father, when he makes up his mind – Oh dear!" She broke off, looking with some dismay towards the window which overlooked the front drive. "Here he comes now. I hardly expected him yet."

The four occupants of the room watched as the gig passed the window, coming to a halt somewhere out of sight. For a moment there was a charged, apprehensive silence, then Matthew turned towards Loveday and smiled at her encouragingly.

"Don't worry," he said. "He doesn't actually eat people."

"He can chew them very thoroughly," Sybil said dryly.

Loveday smiled at her in acknowledgement of the jest, but uneasily. Surely Clay Tallon couldn't be as difficult as they implied?

There was silence again. They were all listening for him, she realised; and when the door opened only Matthew continued to sip his tea nonchalantly.

"Well, dear, this is a surprise!" Mrs Tallon said, as her

husband stood immobile on the threshold, taking in the scene before him. "We have an extra cup – no need to ring – and there's the Battenberg cake you like so much. You remember Miss Pentecost, of course –"

"Of course." Clay Tallon bowed towards Loveday, smiling and urbane, at his most charming. "How do you do, Miss Pentecost? How delightful to welcome you once more."

There, Loveday thought. What can his children be thinking of? He could hardly have been more friendly.

She smiled in return.

"Good afternoon, Mr Tallon."

He radiated power and determination and self-confidence. Such a *polished* man, she thought as she looked at him – not meaning accomplished in this instance, but groomed rather like a valuable horse, dressed in finest cloth with a gold pin glinting in his cravat and a gold watch-chain spanning his stomach. One would have thought, looking at him, that he was the aristocrat who had stooped to marry a lowborn wife. Yet the reverse was true, as everyone was aware.

"Will you stay and take tea, Edwin?" his wife asked as he did not sit down, but prowled around the room, his silver head thrust forward, the curling smile on his lips. He went to the window to survey his puzzle, moved to the fireplace and stood in front of it. And all the time, it seemed to Loveday, there was a strange feeling of suspense, as if his family waited, breath held, to see what he would say or do.

"I think not, my dear," he said pleasantly in response to his wife's question. "Much as I should like to stay and chat to the lovely Miss Pentecost, I have work to do in my study. My, my – I was never so fortunate in my teachers when I was at school! The children at Fourlanesend are indeed much blessed to have someone as pretty as you to instruct them, Miss Pentecost."

"Oh!" Loveday laughed nervously, not knowing how to respond to this. "You're – you're very kind, Mr Tallon."

"And have you some budding genius among your pupils? A young Rembrandt, perhaps? Such a responsibility it must be, Miss Pentecost, to look at your young charges and to know that their future lies in your hands. I feel sure that in years to come our universities will ring with the name of

Miss Loveday Pentecost, without whom great scholars would never have learned their ABC."

"I doubt that," Loveday said. "Great scholars are not numerous at Fourlanesend."

"Really?" His voice expressed polite amazement. "Well, I'm sure you do your best with the material at your disposal."

He bowed and withdrew, and as the door closed behind him Loveday could swear that there was, among his family, a collective sigh of relief.

Somehow, however, it seemed impossible to revert to the easy atmosphere that existed before he came home, and it was not long before Matthew suggested that he should drive Loveday back to Fourlanesend.

"I apologise for my father," he said rather stiffly after they had gone a short distance.

"Why?" She smiled at him. "He seemed very pleasant."

Matthew sighed.

"You were fooled, weren't you? Everyone is always fooled." Loveday looked at him in mild exasperation.

"No, I wasn't," she said, not smiling now. "I know he was patronising me. I'm not entirely stupid. I know precisely what he thinks of Board School teachers, but I could hardly do other than to smile and accept everything at its face value, could I? Oh," she added, her voice a disconsolate wail, "I do so want him to like me! He'll try to change your mind about me."

"Well, he won't succeed. He'll come round."

"I hope so. Matthew, why are you all so frightened of him? I could feel it there, in that room, the moment he came in. Even you –"

Hotly Matthew denied it.

"I'm not frightened. Well –" He laughed briefly. "All right, I admit it. I think it's the very pleasantness you referred to. All that false charm, all the bogus smiles. It fools the world at large, but it doesn't fool us. We know that sooner or later the charm stops and the sarcasm and the rage begin."

She stared at him apprehensively.

"He'll never come round," she said. "He'll never agree to your marrying me."

"We don't need his agreement."

"But we do! It's a family business. You work together."

"Darling, don't worry. Everything will be all right. I'm sure of it!"

Loveday would have given a great deal to be convinced. She had the feeling, however, that even Matthew was not nearly so sure as he would like to make out, and it was unlikely, therefore, that any announcement of their engagement would be made in the near future; but still there was enjoyment to be had in talking of the Christmas ball at Carrivick, for clearly Mrs Morrow was determined to make it the social event of the season. And she, Loveday Pentecost, would be among those present, no matter what Mr Tallon thought of the matter.

And this time, when she and Matthew danced together there would be no shadow of misunderstanding between them.

"Well, Mrs Machiavelli," John Pentecost said to Sarah when after Loveday's birthday dinner the three younger members of the party had gone over to the piano to sort through the sheet music that lay on top. "Are you satisfied with your work?"

"Very." Sarah smiled at him. "If ever two young people were meant for each other –" She looked at him more closely. "You're happy about the match, aren't you?"

"How could I be otherwise? One might say that the day Matthew Tallon came to ask me for my daughter's hand was the happiest of my life, for he loves her and she loves him, there can be no doubt about it." Yet in spite of his words there was a deep sadness in his voice. "One always wants just a little more, Sarah. Six months ago, I would cheerfully have settled for this – yet now I want to know how it works out. I want to see them married, want to see my grandchildren. I'm never satisfied, am I?"

"You could see all of those things; who can tell? I'm so glad you like Matthew."

"There's still his father to contend with. I can't see him giving his blessing to this match."

Sarah twisted her lips and raised her eyebrows in one of

the fleeting, mischievous changes of expression that made her such a delight to watch.

"Don't worry about him," she said.

"You're up to something!"

"I?" She turned towards John with a look of exaggerated innocence, then laughed and shrugged her shoulders. "No, not really. I only wish I could think of something to be up to – something that would make Clay Tallon give his approval. I'm not despairing, though. I feel certain things will somehow resolve themselves. Oh, who said that life in the country was dull?"

"If ever it was," John said, laughing, "then it is far less so, since you came among us."

Just as Sarah intended, the ball at Carrivick was talked of for weeks, for it put all other seasonal festivities in the shade. Small, gold-trimmed Christmas trees with wreaths of holly and ivy decorated the hall and ballroom where a platform had been built to accommodate the six-piece orchestra brought down from London. Extra staff was taken on, for there were fifteen house guests, four of them famous names of the London theatre.

If any lingering doubts remained as to Sarah's acceptability in society, they were swept away entirely, for no one wished to refuse her invitation, thus raising doubts in the minds of others about whether they had been invited at all. In almost every great house in the neighbourhood and far beyond it, dinner parties, or even house parties, were held for those attending, and the guest list sounded like a roll-call of aristocratic families: the Rashleighs, the Treffrys, the St Aubyns, the Tremaynes, the Robartes – all were represented.

And the Pentecosts, Loveday thought with mischievous delight. Whoever would have believed it? She had been co-opted to help write the invitations.

"You'd think she was the daughter of the house," remarked the servants; but with less rancour than before. She was becoming accepted at Carrivick, just as Sarah was becoming accepted in the county. Matters such as this were not quickly resolved in Cornwall.

"Wait till Mr Morrow comes," had been a constant

cry beyond the green baize door during Robert's absence. "He'll not take too kindly to the Pentecosts becoming so familiar."

But now Mr Morrow had come and had apparently been as charmed as his wife, content, it seemed, to spend hours locked in friendly discussion with the schoolmaster.

"There's no accounting," the servants sighed to each other, perplexed but increasingly acquiescent.

"I'm relying on you to speak to your old friend," Sarah told Robert. "Now that you've seen Loveday and Matthew together, you must agree that they are ideally suited. Surely you can make Clay Tallon see reason?"

Robert looked dubious.

"I'm not at all sure that he'll regard it as any business of mine, however favourably I may look upon the young couple."

They were in the bedroom which, with all the preparations for the ball in full swing, was almost the only place where they had any privacy. Robert was already in the wide, canopied bed, enjoying the sight of his wife brushing her hair before the mirror, but at this she swung round to face him.

"You know John Pentecost's position. It's his dearest wish to see Loveday happily settled."

"My love, I know – and I sympathise! Loveday is pure gold, I can see that. I thought, perhaps, that your letters might have exaggerated her charms, but I was wrong. Even so, it's Tallon's business –"

"Business!" Sarah clamped her lips together angrily and returned to brushing her hair with renewed vigour. "That's what it's about, Robert. Just business. Clay Tallon was hoping to make an alliance with Penberthy, who's equally powerful in the china-clay world. Apparently the two men had made a cosy arrangement, whereby Matthew would marry Gwendolyn Penberthy and the two fathers would go into partnership over some wretched quarry. Matthew has made it clear he won't marry the girl, and feelings are hurt. The prospect of going into partnership is apparently disappearing before Tallon's very eyes. It's not Matthew's happiness he's thinking about at all. You will talk to him, won't you?"

Laughing, Robert held out his arms to her.

"When you look at me like that, how can I resist?" he asked. "And now, do you think you could forget the star-crossed lovers for a few moments and concentrate on your poor, old, travel-weary husband?"

"Of course," Sarah said, the anger leaving her face. In the mirror she could see him waiting for her, and was moved by a rush of love and gratitude. Thank heaven, she thought, that he had so little in common with his old friend.

She lay down the silver brush and in a whisper of silk moved across the room towards him.

With deliberate defiance, Sarah had invited both the Tallons and the Pentecosts to the dinner party which was being held at Carrivick prior to the ball.

"Let Clay Tallon see how well accepted the Pentecosts are by ordinary mortals," she said.

When the Tallons were announced, however, she sailed forward to greet them with a slight feeling of trepidation, for she was aware that Clay Tallon's admiration of her had cooled in the light of her championship of Loveday and was well aware that he could, if he chose, make the evening less pleasant than she was determined it would be.

"My dear Mrs Morrow!" The warmth of his greeting took her by surprise. "How delightful you look – and how wonderfully you have decorated the house!"

"Thank you. I'm so pleased that you could all come."

"Morrow, my dear fellow –" Charming as ever, gleaming with health and prosperity, Clay Tallon moved to take his old friend's hand, while Sarah greeted his wife, pleased but astonished that this meeting was going so well.

"Father's up to something," Matthew said quietly to Sarah when the opportunity arose. "He's like a cat who's got at the cream. Is Loveday here?"

"Not yet. Oh yes, she is! Look, she and her father have just come in."

"Mr and Miss Pentecost," announced the liveried servant at the door.

The Tallons had barely moved away from the door themselves and Sarah could not avoid a quick, anxious glance at Clay Tallon. To her total astonishment he was looking towards the Pentecosts, beaming with what she could swear was complete approval.

She moved swiftly to greet the new arrivals, extending both her hands towards Loveday.

"My dear, you look wonderful," she said. Her smile did not change as she looked at John, but her heart gave a small lurch. He did not look wonderful. There was something about him – a greyness – that she had not seen for some time. Oh God, no, she prayed silently. Please, no. "Welcome to you both."

What happens now is in the lap of the gods, she thought, as they advanced further into the room, moving closer to the Tallons. Fervently she hoped that Clay Tallon would remain amenable and on his best behaviour.

As she greeted others, she could see out of the corner of her eye that Matthew had drawn the Pentecosts into his family group, that they all appeared to be talking in a most friendly manner.

"I told you this ball was a good idea," she murmured to Robert as the latest arrivals moved into the room. "But I am surprised, aren't you?"

"Not entirely," Robert said. Sarah looked at him sharply. Clay Tallon wasn't the only one who looked like a cat who had found the cream.

"What do you know that I don't?" she asked.

"Aha!" Robert tapped the side of his nose. "My dear, shouldn't we be circulating?"

"Don't be infuriating, Robert. Tell me what's going on." Relenting, he smiled at her.

"Well, it's only right you should know," he said, "since it's a Christmas present from me to you. I shall expect you to tell me it's just what you have always wanted –"

"*What* is just what I have always wanted?"

"A china-stone quarry. Well, half of one. Well, almost half! You are now in partnership with Clay Tallon."

Her astonished, amused eyes held his.

"So he doesn't need Penberthy?"

"No – nor his daughter. And he doesn't have to skimp on necessary repairs, which was his only alternative."

"He must have been utterly delighted."

"Yes, I think he was, even though I did make conditions."

"Conditions?" Sarah looked at him suspiciously. "Robert, stop being so infuriatingly mysterious. What conditions?"

"He's agreed to withdraw his objection to marriage between Matthew and Loveday."

Sarah suddenly found his image was blurred.

"I have said it before," she said huskily, "and I will say it again. Robert Morrow, you are a very sweet man. I can't think of any present I would rather have."

8

"I think a spring wedding," Sarah Morrow said. "There seems little point in long engagements, don't you agree, Edwin?"

The smile she turned upon Clay Tallon when he called on her to discuss their business partnership was both innocent and engaging, but beneath it was a purpose that was as hard as steel. John Pentecost had said nothing about any deterioration in his condition, and indeed, on the occasions she had seen him after her momentous Christmas ball she had thought that, after all, he looked no worse. Perhaps that grey look had been merely tiredness, or a trick of the light.

Still, it brought home to her the fragility of his health, and reinforced her determination to pin the Tallons down to a definite date for the wedding between Matthew and Loveday.

"I want John to be alive and well and able to enjoy it," she said to Robert in the privacy of her sitting room, when Edwin Tallon had left them. "Clay Tallon is far from enthusiastic about the wedding. He had set his sights on the kind of union that would be advantageous to him, socially as well as financially. I wouldn't put it past him to postpone it indefinitely, given only half a chance."

"And do you really imagine Matthew would stand for that?" Robert looked amused at the idea. "I think both he and Loveday have a few ideas of their own on the subject."

"I'm sure they have – but your dear friend Edwin is a clever devil. I can't quite think what he could do to put a spoke in the works, but I'm not inclined to risk it."

"Dearest." Robert came to sit beside her. He took both her

hands in his and turned her to face him, his expression serious. "Dearest, I know more than anyone how well-intentioned you are, but you really must allow them to work out their own destinies –"

"You're a fine one to talk!" Sarah's eyes flashed indignation. "Who was it made their marriage a condition of buying shares in the quarry?"

"I made Tallon's withdrawal of his objections a condition. The rest I feel we must leave to Matthew and Loveday, no matter how sure we are that we know best."

Sarah, having thought this over for a moment, sighed.

"I suppose you are right," she said. "It's foolish of me to become so involved." She was, however, unable to sustain this uncharacteristically passive acceptance for more than a few seconds. "But Robert," she went on, giving his hands a quick, determined shake, "I've grown so fond of them all! How can I help being involved? If John, heaven forbid, should grow worse again within the next month or two – if he should even die – Loveday would be devastated. It is precisely then that she would need Matthew most, but undoubtedly the marriage would be postponed – can't you see Edwin persuading her of the impropriety of it, no matter how nonsensical that would be? And once postponed, who knows when it would take place?

"Look," she went on, as Robert did not speak. "We must accept the fact that John Pentecost is under sentence of death, perhaps within months. Believe me, I am not interfering frivolously when I say that I want to see Loveday married to Matthew before the worst happens."

"And she truly does not know how seriously ill her father is?"

"He refuses to allow her to be told. She is aware, of course, that he has been suffering from some mysterious malady and I know she was worried about it a little while back; but she is happily certain now that he is on the mend and that by spring he will be better. Apparently Dr Geach has no such conviction."

It was Robert's turn to sigh heavily and shake his head.

"I don't know," he said at last. "Perhaps you are right."

"I'm *sure* I am! It's not as if the two young people are

reluctant, after all. I'm merely looking after Loveday's interests in the way a mother would."

Robert laughed at her.

"I detect an inconsistency, however," he said. "It seems strange that you, who avoided matrimony for so long and are quite the most independent, liberated, self-determined woman I know are yet intent on pushing an eighteen-year-old girl into that very state."

"Pushing?" Sarah, snatching her hands away from him, was outraged. "I would never do that!" She thought over what he had said, however, and laughed a little ruefully. "I suppose it is inconsistent, as you say – but Robert, did you ever see two young people more made for each other? I feel it in my water that it's right for them; besides, has it not occurred to you that I have become a very ardent convert to the concept of marriage?"

Robert laughed softly and took her hands again, leaning forward to kiss her gently on the lips.

"A spring wedding, then," he said.

"Jonquils." Millicent Tallon's face lit up. "Do have jonquils, Loveday. They are quite my favourite flower –"

"But a cloying scent," said Aunt Clara from Tregony. "You'd be better off with Cornish lilies."

"Well, they may cost more, but I always say there's nothing like roses," put in Aunt Jane, who with her portly lawyer husband had driven over from Truro for Sunday luncheon.

Aunt Eveline, come from the far west at great inconvenience for the express purpose of looking over the girl her nephew was going to marry, disagreed.

"For a *spring* wedding she should have *spring* flowers," she said. "And the bridesmaids could carry little posies of primroses. I was at a spring wedding last year where this was done, and I assure you it was sweetly pretty."

"I – I don't think I'm going to have any bridesmaids," Loveday stammered, daunted by this array of Tallons.

"*What?*"

"You can't mean it?"

"But what about Sybil?"

Loveday quailed at the three accusatory faces that were

turned towards her, but her future sister-in-law was less intimidated.

"Sybil," said that lady, "flatly refuses to be a bridesmaid, ever again, under any circumstances whatsoever."

There was silence for a moment in the face of this unequivocal statement.

"Well, dear," Aunt Clara said with heavy tact, "you may be right. It's not always suitable. I'm sure you know best."

"But you're Matthew's sister!" Aunt Eveline had no time for tact. "You *should* be a bridesmaid. Besides, weddings often lead to other weddings, I've noticed it time and time again."

"I agree with Sybil," said Aunt Jane, even less conscious of her niece's finer feelings. "After all, she is past her first youth, and considerably taller than Miss Pentecost."

"Thank you, Aunt Jane." Sybil gave her aunt a bitter smile. "How nice to have your approval of my decision."

Families! thought Loveday, glancing towards the door and longing for Matthew to put in an appearance. Was this the usual way they went on? She had always rather envied those who had them, but realised now, more than ever, that there was much to be said for the untroubled camaraderie that existed between her and her father.

The aunts were undoubtedly a formidable trio who shared Edwin Tallon's forcefulness and assurance – even Aunt Clara who had married a tenant farmer and lived very humbly compared to the others. Her husband, Joseph Yelland, was a quiet, slow-spoken, man who gave the appearance of living in his wife's shadow.

"But I much prefer him to the other uncles," Sybil told Loveday privately before luncheon, when she had accompanied her upstairs to remove her hat and coat on arrival. "I used to like going to stay at Blackberry Farm because he was so kind and always had time for me. Uncle Algernon, on the other hand, scares me stiff!"

"That's Aunt Eveline's husband? I must admit I feel much the same way. He – he doesn't smile very much, does he? When he said, 'So *you* are the young lady I've heard so much about,' I knew quite well he had heard nothing to my credit, he looked so sternly disapproving."

"Uncle Algernon always looks stern. He is a pillar of the local Methodist chapel in Penzance. Father doesn't care for him much." Sybil, who seemed to be in an unusually light-hearted mood and had been trying Loveday's hat on before the mirror, pulled a face at herself. Whether this was a comment on her appearance or on Uncle Algernon, Loveday didn't know.

Neither did she know, in detail, what her father's verdict had been on the latest piece of work that Sybil had submitted to him, though she suspected, from the effect it had had on her, that it had been complimentary. She was not mistaken.

"This version is so much better than the last," John Pentecost had written to Sybil. "I loved your heroine, and Miss Pinkerton is a joy! Very good description p. 3, but perhaps paragraph 2 on the following page just a little wordy? You have a most attractive, readable style of writing . . ." Sybil had only had the time to skim through it, but what she had read had made her happier than anything she had known.

"Poor Loveday!" she went on, taking the hat off and placing it on the bed. "It must be an ordeal for you, meeting the Tallons en masse. We're a dreadful family."

"Oh, I'm sure you're not. What a thing to say! Your mother has always been very kind to me."

Sybil had smiled at that.

"Mama is kind. She is also totally *diminished* by the aunts. You'll see. They all have the Tallon gloss, which neither I nor Mama can claim – that air of somehow being more alive and more important than other people. Father has it, and so has Matthew."

Looking at them around the dining table, Loveday could see exactly what she meant. Though Mr Tallon must be in his fifties and his sisters older, they were all stylishly dressed and all radiated energy and determination. Even the smallest and least important matter seemed to generate argument.

"I *never* serve onion sauce with mutton," Aunt Eveline said. "Caper sauce is the only accompaniment suitable."

"But not everyone likes capers. I mean –" Millicent fluttered her hands helplessly " – I seem to remember your saying they were indigestible, Eveline."

"I have given up both onion and caper sauce." This was

Aunt Clara, just as forceful as her sisters despite her more humble position in society. "The flavour of celery, I find, enhances that of the meat. Allow me to give you my recipe afterwards, Millicent."

"Then," Matthew said, helping himself to the onion sauce, "it would undoubtedly be a waste of time offering this to any of you!"

"*In the absence of anything else* –" said Aunt Clara, in a voice full of deep meaning.

Millicent looked distraught.

"I'm so sorry. I never thought – Matthew, do pass your aunt the onion sauce."

"I was under the impression," said Aunt Jane, "that Edwin didn't care for mutton. He never would eat it when he was young. No, pray don't contradict me, Edwin, I remember it perfectly –"

"You're thinking of Cousin George," said Aunt Eveline. "Surely you remember the time when everyone came to us on New Year's Day and he quite ruined the party –"

"I've never been to your house on New Year's Day in my entire life," averred Aunt Jane. "We always spend New Year at home."

"Oh, you were there on this occasion." Aunt Eveline gave a short laugh. "You fell out with George's wife because she advised you to consult a doctor about Angela's squint."

"Really, Eveline, I can't imagine what you are talking of! Angela never had a squint. Herbert, did you hear what Eveline said? Did you ever hear anything so ridiculous?"

Loveday, catching Matthew's eye across the table, was grateful for his conspiratorial wink. It was less dispiriting to find the aunts funny than to be intimidated by them; nevertheless, she found it an uphill battle to hold her own once the meal was over and the ladies were in the drawing room. Having disposed of the matter of the flowers she would carry, the subject turned to the venue at which the ceremony would take place.

"You will, I suppose," said Aunt Jane, "be married at St John's. The Tallons have a pew there and have always been regular attenders."

"The wedding is to be at St Ninn –"

"*St Ninn!*" For once the three aunts seemed to be in agreement, for all the faces turned to her bore the same look of horrified astonishment.

"But it's such a funny little church –"

"The Tallons have always been Methodists! We've been going to St John's from time immemorial!"

"St Ninn's won't be large enough –"

"Such a long way to drive back here for the reception. I presume the reception will be held here?"

"You presume wrong," Sybil said, answering on Loveday's behalf with clear enjoyment. "There'll be no need to drive back here. The Morrows are giving the reception at Carrivick. Mrs Morrow insists. Loveday is her protégée, you know."

"Well!" the aunts exclaimed almost in unison, pausing only momentarily to draw the deep breath that would allow them to bombard Loveday with questions. Much to her relief, Matthew appeared in the drawing room before she could answer, bearing her off for a walk on the cliff and a turn around Charlestown harbour. Even braving grey skies and cold winds seemed preferable to staying at home to undergo such an inquisition.

The news regarding the reception caused something of a sensation in St Ninn as well as among Matthew's aunts. Master's daughter, not only to marry a Tallon but to be married from Carrivick!

"My dear life!" said Mrs Beswarick when she heard the news. "You could knock me down with a feather. I've known Loveday since she was a little tacker –"

"And a more 'andsome liddle maid never lived," averred Letty Foster. "My Maisie says Master's some pleased."

" 'Tis like Carrivick's come alive again," Mrs Chenoweth said, but Mrs Beswarick wasn't so sure the matter called for rejoicing, and she shook her head gloomily.

"Marry in haste, repent at leisure."

" 'Tidn't all that hasty," Mrs Chenoweth protested. "I heard 'twas to be in spring."

Letty Foster looked over her shoulder as if checking for Boer spies, and finding none leaned towards the other women.

"April." Agog with importance, eyes shining with the drama of it, she mouthed the word silently. "Just after Easter."

"I s'pose your Maisie told you that." Mrs Beswarick's voice verged on the belligerent. "I s'pose Master d'know 'e'm got a spy in the 'ouse? . . . That Letty Foster!" she went on to Mrs Chenoweth as they left the post office. "I don't b'lieve she d'know, no more'n the rest of us. Master don't tell Maisie Foster everything there is to know. Always the same she was, even at school. 'As to be one up."

"Well," said Mrs Chenoweth, "Carrivick won't have seen many brides as pretty as Loveday Pentecost, say what you will."

"Pretty she may be, but she treated Ned Crowle some 'eartless."

"Well, given the choice of Ned Crowle or young Mr Tallon," said Mrs Chenoweth, "which one would you choose, Aggie Beswarick? Tell me that."

It was a question Mrs Beswarick did not attempt to answer, nor did Mrs Chenoweth expect her to for Matthew Tallon must surely rate as the catch of the county. Little Loveday had done very well for herself – and she, for one, didn't grudge her the good fortune.

"You'm leavin', then," Henry said to Loveday.

Christmas had come and gone, and the year was beginning on the long climb uphill towards spring. It seemed to have rained for weeks on end and there was no colour anywhere. The children arrived at school wet and cold and Loveday seemed to spend a great deal of time trying to dry their outer garments – those that were lucky enough to possess any.

Henry invariably arrived at school with a sack over his shoulders, and Loveday felt certain that his anxiety to stay on for his extra lessons was as much a reluctance to leave the warmth of the schoolroom as a desire for learning. He had developed a rasping cough, which worried her, though he assured her that his mother had put a poultice of goose grease on his chest which would have him better in no time. Loveday somehow doubted it, but at least was glad to have an explanation of the strange and repulsive smell that emanated from him in waves.

"I'm not leaving just yet, Henry," she assured him. The boy said no more, but looked away from her, his expression closed and remote, as if she were guilty of desertion. "By the time I go, I feel sure you will be able to read."

He looked at her then, a look of grim amusement on his face. He doesn't believe me, she thought. But he *is* improving, there is no doubt about it.

"Look, let's try these words again." She produced a set of cards that she had made; on each card was printed a word, none of which bore any relation to the others. "Now, what does this card say?"

Henry gave the card a brief, contemptuous glance.

"Cart," he said, with only a momentary hesitation.

"Well done. This one?"

"House."

"This one?"

"Fire."

They progressed through the pile of cards, only the words 'school' and 'shoe' presenting difficulties.

"That's very good, Henry," Loveday said when they had reached the end. "You see, you are improving. Shall we try the reader now?"

Henry shook his head.

" 'Tidn't no good," he said. "There's only the one word on the cards, that's 'ow I can do em."

Loveday stared at him.

"Yes. Yes, of course! Why didn't I think of that?" Henry watched with a baffled expression as she delved into her desk, found cardboard and scissors, and snipped away for a moment or two. Triumphantly she held up a strip of card with a narrow window towards the top of it. "There," she said. "That's a sort of bookmark. Try putting it over the word you are trying to read in the book, so that only one word shows through. Here, let me show you."

Her stomach heaved at the smell of the goose grease as Henry came even closer to the desk, but she managed to quell the nausea. The result of her efforts with the cardboard was hardly miraculous, but undoubtedly Henry derived some benefit from the device.

"I can't imagine why I didn't think of it before," she said to her father afterwards. "It seems so logical. He's getting better and better at recognising single words, so it makes sense to block out everything but the particular word or syllable he's trying to read."

"I wonder what will become of him?" John Pentecost mused. "You have done wonders for him, Loveday. He is so much more co-operative now. He even plays with the other children sometimes. I would feel it a great achievement if he could find a decent job when he comes to leave school, however ill-paid. I hate to think of him ending up like his brother."

"He tells me Joely has gone away – down to Camborne to his auntie to find work, Henry says."

"Work?" her father gave a short laugh. "Joely Tregilgas doesn't know the meaning of the word. I feel sorry for his aunt. Still, I'm glad he's gone. He's a bad influence on Henry and nothing but trouble for the rest of us."

He spoke in an uncharacteristically impatient way and Loveday looked at him with surreptitious attention. He still looked far from well, she thought.

"I hate to leave you, Papa," she said.

She could see the effort it cost him to smile at her gaily in return.

"Nonsense! At last I shall have some peace."

"Papa, don't say such things."

"My dear child –" He caught hold of her hand and pulled her close to him. "You know full well I was joking. Of course I shall miss you. I hate you to go as much as you hate to leave; but equally, I am as happy that you are marrying Matthew. What father could ask for anything more than to see his daughter married to the man she loves, particularly when that young man is as worthy as Matthew Tallon? Believe me, this has given me more pleasure than I can possibly express."

"Oh, I hope Matthew can persuade Mr Tallon that we should live in St Ninn!"

The young couple's place of residence had been a vexed

question, the subject of much discussion. Mr and Mrs Tallon could see no reason why they should not live at Prospect Lodge for the time being. They could, they said, have their own suite. Think of the convenience, they said.

Loveday thought, and shuddered. She always felt strange at Prospect Lodge, never comfortable or at ease. The thought of beginning her married life there filled her with foreboding and she was relieved to find that Matthew was equally determined to be independent of his parents.

They had looked at a house in Charlestown, close to the harbour, and Loveday had been charmed by it even though it was further from her father than she would have liked. Mr Tallon had, however, pronounced it damp – and since it was he who would be buying it on their behalf, the deal fell through.

Now, suddenly, one of the properties in St Ninn already owned by the Tallon family had fallen vacant.

"Father won't approve of our taking it," Matthew said warningly. "He wants me closer to him, under his thumb –"

"St Ninn's not so far away."

"It's convenient to Trelew and Wheal Constance, and the new quarry. I shall try to convince him it will be better all round. But Loveday, the place isn't very big."

"It's quite big enough. And in good repair."

"Indeed it is. It had a new roof only six months ago. You should have heard Father groan at the cost!"

"I've always thought it a pretty house."

In common with most other Cornish towns and villages, though the main street of St Ninn was flat enough, it was almost impossible to leave it in any direction without either ascending or descending a hill. Fore Street was narrow at its western end, but widened as it approached the almshouses and the old coaching inn. It was here that Mrs Chenoweth kept her general shop, and Letty Foster held sway over the post office. Here, too, was Snell's Butchery and Roberts's Bakery, where those that lived close by ran with their meat and potatoes on a Sunday and their pasties during the week, to cook in the baker's oven.

A steep and winding lane led to the church of St Ninn, but a quicker way was by the steps close by the almshouses. Both led to an area known as Church Cross: a square of houses of varying size, unexpectedly elegant. There were two larger houses, sharing one side of the square with the church. One was the vicarage, occupied by Mr Peake and his sister – pink, smiling, grey-haired replicas of each other who seemed perfectly content that marriage had passed them by. Dorothy Peake was quite certain that she could never have found a husband as kind and as generous as her brother Nicholas, while Nicholas often was heard to say, in his humorous way, that Dorothy must surely be the best vicar's wife that never was.

Next to it, almost its twin, was the house occupied by Dr Geach. His dining room served as a waiting room, his parlour as a consulting room. When his wife was alive a screen was drawn around his desk during the evening and all traces of his calling shielded from the couple's off-duty gaze; however, he bothered less now. He had a good fire, and the leather armchair that had stood beside it for the last forty years, and he asked for nothing more. His work had always been important to him. Now it was everything.

Opposite was a row of dwellings, more than cottages, less than houses, with odd, irregular roofs. All were part of the Trengrose estate, but had been retained by Clay Tallon when Carrivick was sold. Two were old; Tudor, the vicar said, and he was probably right. The rest were Georgian, built in a burst of optimism when it appeared that clay would make everyone wealthy.

It was the end one of these that had become vacant following the death of old Mrs Trembath, and Loveday wanted it so much that she hardly dared think of it, for fear of disappointment. She knew that the rooms were small, for she had visited Mrs Trembath several times over the past few years when her health was failing, but they were well proportioned and there was a pretty walled garden. She found herself in abstracted moments scribbling 'Mrs Matthew Tallon, 7 Church Cross, St Ninn, Cornwall', as if she were addressing an envelope to herself.

"Oh Dolly, I do hope Mr Tallon agrees," she said to her friend. "It's such a pretty house – and I wouldn't be too far from Papa."

"Or from me!"

"Well, you won't be at Fourlanesend for ever, if what I hear is true."

Dolly giggled, and blushed. There was a young recruit to the coastguard service whom she had met on a joint chapel outing, who had been haunting the Crowle household recently. He was a little older, a little more serious than other suitors, and though she affected to be indifferent to him, Loveday suspected otherwise and was glad. It was high time that Dolly had a share of the good luck which seemed, recently, to be directed exclusively towards her friend.

There were times when Loveday had to pinch herself to make sure she was awake; times when it seemed impossible to believe all the wonderful things that had happened during the past year. Less than a year, in fact; there was still one month to go before the anniversary of the day on which she and her father had walked down to Carrivick.

She had fittings for the dress which, on this occasion, her father had insisted on buying for her but on which matter she had accepted Sarah's advice. The invitations had been engraved and written and were now ready for the post. Arrangements for the reception at Carrivick had been discussed in detail. A honeymoon in London and Paris was even now being arranged. Flowers had been chosen for her bouquet (jonquils, to please Mrs Tallon, but also roses and Cornish lilies to please everyone else); but in spite of all these things, it was not until she stood with Matthew in the empty rooms of No. 7, Church Cross, that she knew, without doubt, that all would take place as arranged, and that they would be happy ever after.

"We will, you know," said Matthew, holding her close. "I never imagined I could love someone like this. I thought it was make-believe; something that poets wrote about."

"Did you guess, that day on the staircase at Carrivick?"

"I never forgot you, but it was when I saw you again I knew for certain."

"When Mrs Morrow refused to let you take me home!"

"And you were so solemn on the subject of marriage – do you remember? A marriage is between two equals, you said –"

"So it is, so it is!" But she was laughing as she beat her

fists against his shoulders, utterly confident that no matter what problems they faced in the future, none would be insurmountable.

"Well, as head of this household I have a pronouncement to make. Argument is useless. I will be master in my own home. I decree that you will marry me on the fifteenth day of April, 1899 – no ifs or buts – and that we shall live in marital bliss at 7, Church Cross, St Ninn –"

"Oh yes, yes –"

"And that the bliss shall last, so long as we both shall live."

Laughter faded and died. For a long moment they looked into each other's eyes until Loveday, standing on tiptoe, reached up to kiss him.

"Never, never," she said, "could anyone be happier than I am at this moment."

It was only a day later, when she had gone down to the house in Church Cross to take measurements for the curtains that Dolly had enthusiastically volunteered to make for her, that Clay Tallon succeeded in diluting that happiness.

She had just begun her task when she heard a key in the front door and was surprised at his arrival, accompanied by a workman with a bag full of tools.

"Well, well!" He glinted his puckish little smile in her direction. "I didn't expect to find anyone here."

"Matthew gave me the key." Loveday was annoyed to discover that she seemed to find it necessary to explain her presence – almost apologise for it. "I came to measure for curtains."

What was *he* doing here? That was more to the point! Clearly he did not feel the same compulsion to explain and, together with the workman, he went upstairs and out of her view. She could hear their voices and the sound of their footsteps as they moved about the empty house. After a while the workman came downstairs, bade her good afternoon, and left.

It was foolish, feeling so uncomfortable because she knew her future father-in-law was in the house! She would go upstairs, speak to him in a natural way, ask him what jobs remained to be done – but before she could do so, she heard him coming downstairs and went into the hall to meet him.

"Your duties at the school are over for the day, are they?" he asked.

"Oh, more than an hour ago," she replied. He always seemed to have a special note in his voice when he spoke of her work – condescending, slightly amused, as if he thought it beneath contempt. Resolutely she ignored it. "Is something wrong upstairs?" she asked.

"Some skirting boards need replacing," he said. "I thought it best done before you move in. If you move in." He moved away from her as he spoke, into the little parlour at the side of the hall, still apparently engrossed in inspecting the woodwork. Frowning, she followed him.

"If? Surely there's no doubt that we can have the house?"

He turned to face her with a little flourish of his gold-topped cane. He was smiling, but his eyes were watchful, assessing.

"You are quite sure you want to go through with this marriage?" he asked. Astonished, she stared at him.

"Of course I'm sure. And so is Matthew."

"Matthew," he said, "is sometimes less than wise. It's not too late for you to change your mind, you know."

"Why should I change my mind?"

"My dear child –" Deliberately he took out a cigar, cut it and lit it. His actions were unhurried, his faint smile unwavering. "It merely appears to me," he went on when at last his cigar was alight, "as surely it must to any rational being, that if you go through with this you will be making the greatest mistake of your life."

"That's not true!"

"Think about it. What have you in common, you and Matthew? You come from different backgrounds, have different interests. In a year's time you will both be wondering how it all happened. Have you asked yourself, what will you do when Matthew starts regretting his foolish marriage? As he undoubtedly will. How long do you imagine he will be faithful to you? And how will you feel when you discover that he is not?"

Loveday had paled. She was still standing in the doorway, holding on to the jamb as if for support.

"He won't regret it," she whispered.

"No? I wonder!"

"We love each other."

"Love!" He laughed softly. "My dear child, why not admit it? You're wild to go to bed with each other! It amounts to no more than that."

She could feel the colour flood into her cheeks. This was sweet and secret territory he had no right to enter.

"Listen to me. Break off the engagement to my son and I will pay you five hundred pounds. By the look of your father, it won't go amiss. You can buy some expert medical advice for him instead of relying on that old fool, Geach."

Loveday did not move. Oh, clever, clever Clay Tallon, she thought. He had hit on the one thing that could have moved her, but she knew it wasn't lack of funds that was preventing her father from seeking further advice, for she had urged him many times to do so, and as many times he had assured her that he had perfect faith in Dr Geach and in any case was improving steadily. Her impending marriage, he had said, was the best tonic he could have had.

"How dare you, Mr Tallon," she said shakily at last. "You know nothing about love – and you certainly know nothing about my father's love for me. He'd be the first to tell me to have nothing to do with your offer."

She stepped aside and held the door as if inviting him to leave, but for a moment he stood and glared at her without moving.

"You're making a mistake," he said harshly. He lifted his cane and shook it towards her. "Don't come crying to me when you recognise the fact. Clay Tallon's son deserves better than you. He could have married anyone – *anyone* – yet in his youth and ignorance he chooses a nobody! You're both as foolish and pig-headed as each other."

So he'd tried this on Matthew, and failed just as miserably! Loveday lifted her chin and laughed at him. Inwardly she was shaking with anger and distress, but knew she must not allow him to see it.

"Please go away," she said. "And take your bribes and your threats with you. I'm not frightened of you, Mr Tallon."

For a few moments his eyes held hers, but it was he who looked away first. He left without another word. For some time she stood, unable to move, still clinging to the doorknob, shocked by the whole exchange, yet at the same time triumphant. She had said she wasn't frightened of him, and it was true. The realisation was a heady one, even though she now knew, without doubt, that it had done nothing to make Clay Tallon regard her with any more favour. His expression made it clear that the reverse was true.

His enmity was now open and undisguised.

Henry was absent from school from the last week of March. Loveday asked the other children about him, but no one seemed to have any information.

"We ent seen un, Miss," they said.

"I hope he's not ill," Loveday said to her father.

"Most likely he feels like a holiday. This must be the longest period of time he has ever put in an appearance at school. If he's not back by the end of the week, I'll write a report and then it'll be up to the whipper-in. Don't look so worried," John Pentecost added, seeing that she still looked concerned. "I'm more amazed when a Tregilgas comes to school than when he stays away."

"He's had a cough these past weeks."

"It must be wet and cold in Carrivick Woods. Still, they'd no doubt rather be there than in St Austell Union – and spring is coming, after all. Don't worry about him, Loveday. The Tregilgases have survived many a worse winter than this one."

Her father was right, Loveday knew; it was much more believable that Henry was simply playing truant than anything else. On the other hand, he had appeared highly delighted with his improved reading skills. Was it likely that he would choose a time such as this to stay at home if he were in a fit state to come?

The weather turned drier and brighter. The sky was suddenly a clear, pale blue in colour, strangely distant after the lowering clouds of recent weeks, and bare trees were clearly seen to be sprouting buds and lambs' tails. Along the banks there were aconites and even a few early primroses; all evidence that the days were passing and that, before long, April would be upon them.

A thin, bespectacled young woman with red hair and a

strange hat rather like a deerstalker bicycled over to the school from Trelew. She introduced herself as Miss Pinnock, the teacher who would take Loveday's place. She had a twitching nose and a high, nervous laugh.

"She seems amiable enough," John Pentecost said heartily after she had gone. "I'm sure we will rub along very well."

"At least she's qualified," Loveday pointed out.

"Oh, indeed. No more putting up with less than the best."

Loveday wrinkled her nose at him in recognition of the joke. She recognised, too, that his heart had sunk to his boots at the sight of Miss Pinnock and that he was doing his best not to show it. What a pity, she thought, that things were never absolutely, completely perfect, and dropped a kiss on the top of his head as she passed by his chair. It was hard to think that the date for which she longed with such excitement marked the beginning of a very different kind of life for her father. She had no need for him to put into words how he would miss her.

She was glad, really, that she was spared the extra lessons with Henry, for there was much to do. Still, she thought of him from time to time and would have been glad to know that he was well. None of the other children had news of him, which was not as strange as it would have been in the case of any other pupil. The Tregilgas family kept themselves to themselves.

The good weather continued. Who could blame Henry for staying away from school? Spring, Loveday thought as she picked her way down the muddy woodland path towards Carrivick, was a very special time, and evidence of it was all around. There was quite definitely a green shimmer on the branches that were bare only a week before, and the primroses and celandines were clustered thickly beneath the trees.

This time last year she didn't know of Matthew's existence. What of this time next year? She stopped short, suddenly. It had just struck her with all the force of an express train that by this time next year, she might have a child.

It was a terrifying thought, but exciting, too, and it was the excitement that was uppermost. She would, she thought, like lots of babies – a boy first; then, after a suitable interval, a little girl called Sarah, after Mrs Morrow who had been so good to them. They would have to call her Sally, so that there was no confusion. And after that it didn't really matter, so long as they had a house that rang with children's voices and laughter.

She was not fearful or ignorant, like so many girls of her generation; a country upbringing and freedom to read widely had seen to that. Ardent by nature, she longed for the moment when at last she and Matthew were free to love each other as husband and wife. It was hard to imagine how it would be. She supposed it might be a bit embarrassing at first – how *awful* it would be with someone you didn't love! – but with Matthew it would be wonderful, she was sure of that. Matthew's kisses were wonderful enough. She had never imagined that she could ache so with wanting him – Clay Tallon, she had to admit, had been right in some respects, but she had been right, too. Much as she wanted him, there was a great deal more to their love than that. It was hateful, the way he had tried to spoil it.

She continued on her way, realising that she was reaching the place where she had seen Mrs Tregilgas all those weeks ago. Why had she run from her in such a panic? She smiled at her foolish, immature self. The woman had been harmless – rather sweet, really, with her pride in Henry's attainments, and her gratitude to his teacher.

"Come any time," she had said; and suddenly, thinking of Henry's cough, Loveday felt that she had been callous in leaving it to the Attendance Officer to find out the cause of his absence. She could at least venture down the path that Mrs Tregilgas had indicated to see if she could find the cabin in the woods. If it proved difficult, then she would abandon the search – but at least she would have tried.

Even then she almost missed the path, for it was narrow and concealed; but realising she had gone too far she retraced her steps a little, found the narrow track, and followed it easily until it emerged into an open glade. Here she stopped and looked around her. There appeared to be no sign of any kind of dwelling. Perhaps, she thought, it was the kind of temporary shelter that could be taken up and put somewhere else. Perhaps they had gone – moved for the winter into less inhospitable surroundings.

She was about to give up the quest when she saw that the path continued at the far side of the glade. She would go just a little further, she decided, and had hardly taken half a dozen steps when she saw through the almost bare branches the gleam of a tin roof.

She quickened her steps and the full squalor of this woodland dwelling-place was soon revealed to her. It was dilapidated beyond belief. There was one window, stuffed with rags. The roof was scabrous, patched with odd pieces of rusty tin and a few planks, and the whole building seemed to lurch to one side as if it were about to fall down altogether.

Outside there was an odd assortment of objects, none of which seemed to have any practical use. An old chair, sagging on three legs with the horsehair spilling from its guts; buckets, eaten away with rust, a broken dog kennel, casks and kegs smashed beyond repair and a hencoop in the same condition, all in piles or leaning against the walls of the hut. There were rabbitskins pegged out to dry and a tattered blanket hanging on a line strung between two trees.

A curl of smoke rose from the metal chimney and the door was hanging open as if the hinges had rusted. A little tentatively now, Loveday approached.

"Hallo," she called. "Is anyone at home?"

There was no reply; only a robin trilled from a branch that overhung the roof. She took a few steps nearer, and called again:

"Henry, are you there?"

Still there was nothing. Mrs Tregilgas couldn't be far away in view of the smoke, she thought; but the place looked deserted and she was disinclined to venture further. On the other hand, suppose Henry was ill? He might be lying there alone, waiting for his mother to return from one of her mysterious expeditions. Perhaps she ought to look inside.

She approached the door and was almost on the threshold when she knew, instinctively, that she was not alone. Swiftly she turned. No more than ten yards behind her stood a man, mouth agape in a grin above a matted beard, hair straggling to his shoulders. From a strap across one shoulder he carried a bundle of furze he had cut from the moor for kindling; in his hand the hooked pole that was used for such a task.

He looked at her as if he enjoyed seeing the panic that must be showing in her eyes, but he said nothing.

Loveday swallowed nervously.

"I'm looking for Henry," she said. "He – he's been absent from school. Is he well? It's – it's Joely, isn't it?" she added as he did not speak. "I barely recognised you."

"Ess," he said at last, putting down his burden and swaggering slowly towards her. "I'm Joely." He stopped when he was so close that she could almost feel his breath on her cheek and she tried to move away; but the hut was at her back and he put his arm up, holding a branch of the same tree on which the robin perched, to block her only other way of escape.

"Is Henry here?" she asked, making an attempt to ignore his unwelcome nearness.

"Naw." He stank of woodsmoke and tobacco and stale spirits and unwashed body. "Ma and 'Enry's gone. Took it into their 'eads two weeks or more ago to go down Camborne to me auntie's. 'Enry 'ad a cough and Ma worried about the damp."

"Someone said you had gone there."

"I went, but I come back. I'm here now, and all on me own, Miss Loveday Pentecost. No one 'ere but me, Miss Loveday Pentecost."

"Please excuse me." Loveday looked around helplessly as if seeking for a way out. "I really must go now. May I pass?"

"Naw." Still he smiled.

"Please, Joely." She smiled too, and hoped he did not discern the edge of panic in her voice. "I really do have to go."

"Naw." He continued to block her way, solid as a rock.

"Please move. Now. At once." She spoke with all the authority she could muster, but still he did not move.

"Don'ee come all school-ma'amish with me, Loveday," he said. He bent his head towards her, forcing her to strain back against the door. "Give I one liddle kiss, an' I'll let ee go. You'm a lovely liddle maid –"

"No – no!" Loveday twisted her head this way and that to avoid the hateful mouth that was seeking hers. She pushed at him with all her strength, but he was the stronger.

"I d'dearly love a maid with a bit o' fight to un," he said, laughing to himself. He pulled her towards him with a grip like iron, fumbling at her breast. "Come on, my bird, give I a treat. I'll be kind to ee, you see."

"No, no – leave me alone – don't touch me –"

But the more she struggled, the more his determination grew. His smile died as they grappled together and his breathing became hoarse, his eyes fixed as if he were in the grip of some obsession. Her fingernails raked his cheek, and he responded by dealing a stinging slap to her face. Wildly she reached for the furze-cutting tool that leaned against the wall of the hut, but he took it from her as easily as if she had been a child; took it with one hand, and with the other forced her inside the hut.

"Now us'll see oo's master, Miss Loveday Pentecost," he said, pushing her with such strength that she fell to the ground.

He stood over her with his legs astride as she lay on the ground, his hands already fumbling with the buckle of his belt, pushing her with one filthy, booted foot as she attempted to raise herself.

"Now us'll see," he repeated, laughing softly.

The rest was a nightmare, a jumble of hateful images; of his nakedness, of matted black hair and the gross obscenity that jutted from its centre. And the power of his hands that ripped at her clothes, and the stench of him, and the heaviness of his heaving body.

And the pain, the pain, the pain.

🙦 9 🙤

It was the noise that first penetrated Loveday's consciousness; the strange, keening sound that seemed to express a grief that was beyond tears, a despair far beyond the reach of humanity. It took a few moments for her to realise that she was the author of this sound, and that she was quite incapable of stopping it.

She was also chilled to the bone and shivering uncontrollably. Yet though she wanted more than anything else to be away from this place, she did not know how she would ever move. A paralysis seemed to have invaded not only her bones, but her mind as well. The effort needed to rise to her feet and walk away seemed utterly beyond her.

At least she was alone. The monster had taken her and used her. He had satisfied his lust and had gone; but the nightmare was still with her. Shudderingly she lived again the horror of it. She felt the bile rising in her throat and turned her head to vomit helplessly on the earth floor.

She had splashed her sleeve, she noticed dully. But of what consequence were more stains when already she felt filthy and sullied beyond any imagining?

She started suddenly, thinking that Joely had returned; but it was only the wind blowing over one of the pieces of assorted junk outside the hut. It frightened her, though. What was there to prevent his coming back at any time?

Panic gave her the strength to stand up, to set her feet on the path which led back to the main track. The light was fading now, and bushes took on man-like shapes, appearing to her half-crazed eyes to advance and retreat. Sobbing, gasping for breath, she stumbled in rabbit holes and over tree-roots, ignoring the lesser torment of twisted ankles and barked shins. What did such things matter, compared to the greater hurt?

She could not have told why she turned towards Carrivick when she reached the track. It was not a conscious choice, but rather a dogged adherence to her original plan. She had set out with the intention of going to Carrivick and seemingly without thought continued in that direction even now. It was only afterwards that she wondered if she had done so to save her father pain – or was it that she craved, above all things, for a woman's care?

For whatever reason she turned downhill, her panic subsiding a little as she reached the gate that led into the grounds of the mansion. On the far side of it, the side of safety, she paused and for the first time took stock of herself; of her hair that had fallen down about her face, of her skirt that was ripped from waist to hem, of her blouse from which the monster had wrenched the buttons and which he had blackened with his filthy hands. There was little she could do to improve matters.

She had lost track of time, but judged that it must be a little short of six o'clock. At any moment Mrs Morrow would be going upstairs to dress for dinner; perhaps she had already done so. There was a chance, however, that she would still be in her sitting room, and it might be possible to go around the side of the house and attract attention without presenting herself at the front door. If she were to be seen in such a state of dishevelment it would make her the talk of the servants' hall for weeks, Loveday was well aware.

The foolish thing was that she couldn't move. Blind panic had galvanised her into action, but now that surge of energy had deserted her. Her limbs trembled uncontrollably and she clung to the gate for support. She bit her lip to stop the sobs that racked her and forced herself to make one more effort. Safety was very close now.

"There's someone lurking in the shrubbery," Sarah said, standing at her bedroom window. She had gone up to change, but though Marnie had drawn the curtains she had not been able to resist pulling them aside to see the effect of the sunset over the smudgy elms, and the skeins of little birds wheeling in the evening sky.

It was still light enough for her attention to be diverted by the movement in the rhododendron bushes closer to the house and the figure that seemed to be trying to conceal itself.

"Lurking?" Robert came from his dressing room into the bedroom. He was fresh from a bath and clad in a red silk dressing gown. "I expect it's one of the gardeners. Darling, do shut the window, unless you wish my early demise!"

But Sarah was leaning out, peering towards the shrubbery.

"It's not one of the gardeners," she said. "It's a woman. I do believe it's – oh surely, it can't be!"

"There is a *very* chill wind –" Robert began, but stopped and stared in amazement as Sarah turned and ran from the room. "What the – ?"

"Back in a moment," Sarah called from the corridor.

Robert scratched his head and shrugged his shoulders. He went to close the window, peered out into the gathering gloom. There was no one lurking that he could see, and he saw nothing to explain his wife's headlong flight. He laughed to himself. Life with Sarah was one small drama after another – but at least no one could say it was dull.

"My dear child, what on earth has happened? Hush now, don't cry so! Have you had a fall?" Full of solicitude Sarah put her arm around Loveday. "Come, let's get you into the house."

"I – I don't want anyone to see me," Loveday said between sobs. She was shaking again, and could not stop. "I'm filthy, filthy –"

Sarah took in the torn skirt, the open blouse.

"Did a man do this?" Her voice had hardened, her arm tightened about Loveday's shoulders. "Was it a man, Love-day? *Who?*" she added urgently, as Loveday nodded her bowed head.

She could not speak, and seeing this Sarah, making rapid plans, took her to a side door. Still holding her, whispering caution, she led her down a narrow passage and up a flight of stairs, from the head of which it was only a few yards along an empty corridor to the bedroom that Loveday had occupied temporarily on the night of the ball at Prospect Lodge.

She whipped the eiderdown from the bed and wrapped it about Loveday's shoulders, urging her to sit down on the chaise longue while she put a match to the fire that was already laid in the grate.

"You are safe," she said comfortingly, coming back to put her arms around the girl again. "It's over, and nothing can harm you now."

"I'm so dirty," Loveday wept.

"You shall have a bath – a hip-bath in front of this fire. And I shall wash you myself, just as if you were a little girl again. There, don't cry so, dearest. I'm going to leave you now for just a few minutes while I arrange matters, but I shall be back in no time."

It was Marnie who brought in the bath and filled it; dear, discreet Marnie who could be trusted to keep her mouth shut. Loveday barely noticed her. Protesting, she had drunk a glass of brandy and now seemed to float a little in a world that seemed more dream than reality.

One of the stable-boys had been dispatched with a note to Fourlanesend. Loveday had suffered a minor fall, Sarah wrote to John Pentecost. It was absolutely nothing to worry about, but it had shaken her a little and she had been persuaded to spend the night at Carrivick. How wonderful to be young, she wrote, and suffering from such stars in the eyes that the stones beneath the feet are rendered invisible!

The fiction of the fall was repeated for the benefit of the servants.

"She is thoroughly shaken," Sarah told Mrs Lane, venturing through the green baize door and into the kitchen. "If you can produce some soup I will take it up myself."

Warmed, bathed and fed, not only with the soup but with a draught which Sarah had taken from time to time in her previous life when sleep was sometimes elusive, Loveday finally slept.

"Without dreams, I hope," said Sarah to Robert.

"That can't be the end of it, surely! Did she tell you who was responsible?"

"Joely Tregilgas. The jailbird son of that strange woman who roams about the fields. You remember – you commented on her some time ago. He's also the brother of the child that Loveday has been tutoring. They live in the woods."

"The police must be told without delay –"

"No!" Sarah did not raise her voice for they were still at dinner and the servants were coming and going. Even so she was able to convey a degree of determination that made Robert raise his eyebrows in astonishment.

"Why on earth not? God knows it's a crime. The man should be punished."

"I agree. But how often does the man in question get his deserts?" Her voice was bitter. "There was a case in the *Gazette* only a couple of weeks back. A woman, mother of eight, was raped by some ne'er-do-well tinker while she was taking a pasty to her husband out in the fields. The all-male jury agreed with the defence, that she had been a willing party. Can you believe that? Do you imagine they thought the woman insatiable?"

"No one could say that in Loveday's case."

"Couldn't they?" Sarah gave a short laugh. "Your faith in British justice is touching. I am not so sanguine. Talk of something else until we are alone, I beg you.

"Think!" she went on when at last they were left with their coffee in the small sitting room and the servants had withdrawn. "Loveday is to be married in less than three weeks. Imagine, if you will, what any publicity regarding this matter will do to her – and to Matthew! And think what Clay Tallon would make of it! It would be a gift to him."

"But it can't be hushed up. Justice must be done."

"Robert, justice is *seldom* done in these cases! Win or lose, the woman suffers – and you have only to open your eyes and read the papers to know that it is more likely than not that the woman will lose. Until there are women jurors and women judges –"

"We're not dealing in fantasy, Sarah. Here we have a young girl who has been gravely sinned against; that's the reality which we must face. The man must be punished."

"There must be ways of seeing that he is repaid, I agree. But I refuse to go to law about this, or to allow Loveday to."

She leaned forward and grasped his arm with both hands. "Don't you see, Robert, it would ruin her life? Don't you understand that? Oh!" Frustrated in her search for the words that would force him to see her point of view, she jumped to her feet and ranged about the room, unable to sit still. "Don't you understand that if Loveday should report this crime, she will immediately come up against a masculine wall of disbelief? Yes, even in the case of someone like Joely Tregilgas, though if someone's purse was missing he would be immediately suspect. 'She must have asked for it,' people will say. 'Men have needs and urges. A pretty girl, walking through the wood on her own –' Oh, can't you hear them, Robert? The humiliation would be absolute. Even the necessary medical examination takes place in an atmosphere that reeks of disapproval and disgust."

"One would think," Robert said slowly, "that you had personal experience."

For a moment she said nothing, but continued her pacing. Then she came to sit down again.

"Yes," she said, looking at him full in the face. "You could say that, in a manner of speaking. *There!*" She leapt to her feet again, pointing an accusing finger at him. "I saw the look on your face! You are appalled at the thought that *your* woman could have been violated."

"Dearest!" He reached out to pull her down beside him. "Of course I'm appalled."

She shrugged away from him with a short, hard laugh.

"Well, you may breathe again, for it wasn't I who suffered but a close friend, a young girl in the same company. Still, I made my point, didn't I? Even you – a mature, sophisticated, free-thinking man – recoiled from me when you thought I was the victim. No, don't deny it! I saw your face. Oh, I can't blame you, I suppose. It seems a typically masculine response. At least you have the sense to move on from there – to understand that it is possible for the woman to be blameless, but surely you can understand how Clay Tallon would react? How a young man like Matthew Tallon would feel about the rape of his future bride?"

"Won't you tell me what happened?"

She succumbed to his gesture of appeal and went to sit

beside him. For a few moments she said nothing but from her expression he guessed that bitter, hated memories had risen to haunt her.

"It was horrible, Robert," she said at last, her voice no more than a whisper. "Mary O'Mara was young and innocent, knowing nothing of life or men. She'd had a hard, miserable life, brought up by an aunt who treated her like a skivvy, but she had a voice like an angel and when the company went to Birmingham she ran away from home and joined us."

"And you befriended her?"

"Yes, I did. She was sixteen and I no more than twenty or so, but so much older in experience. I think she regarded me as the mother she never had, for all I was so young. And I let her down!"

"How so? I don't believe it."

"I behaved as you are doing now. I insisted she go to the police. It was in respectable Cheltenham, of all places. She was raped by a man – an actor – of forty-two who seriously advanced the defence that she led him on. Oh Robert, if you'd seen Mary, you would know what a ridiculous claim that was! She was the dearest, sweetest little thing, a good Catholic who told her beads and went to Confession."

"What happened to her?"

"You may well ask. Only her extreme youth and innocence persuaded the judge to let her off with a little homily. Otherwise, he said, she would stand accused of bearing false witness. The man was exonerated completely, of course. Mary's wiles were entirely to blame – no matter that she was barely out of the schoolroom and had no precise idea of what constituted the sexual act. The poor child felt utterly used and soiled and degraded – by the questioning she received at the hands of the police as much as anything else, and by the cross-examination when the case came to trial. The local paper reported everything."

"You're not going to tell me she was dismissed?"

"No, no, of course not! Why would she be, when so many people flocked to see the little temptress? We were in the town for the whole of that winter. Even I was conscious of the lubricious curiosity of the audiences coming in waves over the footlights. Can you imagine what it was like for her?

Or how often I wished I'd told her to keep quiet about it and tell no one?"

"You did what you thought was best."

"Yes." Agitatedly Sarah got to her feet again, unable to sit still. "Yes, I did," she repeated. "I kept telling myself that. Until the day I arrived home from town to the digs I shared with her. The house was full of gas and she was dead and cold –" She whirled round and faced him. "I've never got over the grief and the remorse. *I* did that to Mary! I caused her death just as much as the man did – and you want to take the same risk with Loveday? No, I will not allow it."

"But my dear Sarah –" Distractedly Robert ran his hand through his hair. "The matter can hardly be kept secret. Loveday is bound to tell her father, at the very least –"

"No!" Eyes hard and bright, Sarah stared at him. "Tomorrow when she is rested, I will talk to her. I will not have her telling John. It would break his heart! I will not allow her to ruin her life because of this one, tragic circumstance. *I will not allow it, Robert!* Is that clear?"

Robert expelled his breath in a short laugh. Sarah, a forceful personality at any time, looked more formidably determined than even he could have imagined.

"It is possible she may have her own ideas."

Sarah laid a hand on his arm.

"Leave this to me. Promise that you will – I beg you, Robert. Do you swear to say nothing yourself?"

Seeing the resolution that had hardened her face and brought out the lines around the eyes and mouth that were usually disguised by laughter, Robert shrugged his shoulders in defeat.

"I'll say nothing," he agreed. "I would not have done, anyway, for my view is that anything that has to be said must be said by Loveday. But I can see how deeply you feel. Perhaps you are right."

Sarah was untroubled by any doubts.

"There is no 'perhaps' about it," she said firmly.

"And the man?"

"Ah! the man." Sarah looked at her husband. "The man I leave to you. There is no chance whatever of making the punishment fit the crime, which to my mind would be to shoot him like a rabid dog, or castrate him at the very least. However, in the absence of such a solution, just get rid of him, Robert. Get him off that land."

Robert returned her gaze, a gleam of amusement in his eyes.

"My dear Sarah," he said, "Heaven preserve me from falling into your bad graces. You have the look of an avenging angel."

She lifted her chin and her magnificent eyes flashed.

"And rightly so," she said.

"Say nothing."

Sarah's voice was forceful as she confronted Loveday who, pale-faced, propped against pillows, stared at her uncomprehendingly.

She had slept long and dreamlessly, but still felt strangely exhausted. She was more conscious today of her physical pain – of the bruised tenderness of her body where she had been flung to the ground, and the delicate, torn tissue of more intimate parts. She was angrier, too. Surely Joely Tregilgas should be punished for what he had done?

"Say nothing? How can I say nothing?" Her voice sounded weak and fretful.

She had been drinking tea. Now Sarah took the empty cup from her hands and sat down on the bed.

"You can say nothing," she said, "because you have nothing to gain and everything to lose."

Loveday frowned in bewilderment.

"I don't understand," she said.

"Then I will explain."

Clearly and cogently, Sarah laid before her the arguments she had rehearsed with Robert the night before.

"I refuse to allow you to ruin your life because of this one, worthless man," she finished passionately, clasping Loveday's hands. "It was a nightmare, and it is over. Bury it deep. Forget it. Speak of it to Matthew, and it will always be there – maybe out of sight, but just over the horizon, ready to sour everything that's good. And then there's your father. He's far from well, Loveday. Don't give him this added burden of sorrow, just when he is so happy on your behalf."

For a long time Loveday did not speak but lay back against the pillows with her eyes closed, tears forcing themselves under her lids. Tenderly Sarah wiped them away.

"Believe me, darling," she said softly. "In these matters I am wiser than you – and unhappily more experienced."

"I'm not sure that I can keep it to myself. Papa will know there is something."

"I have told him you suffered a fall and are very shaken. The servants think that, too, except for Marnie –"

"And she'll not tell?"

"No, she'll not tell."

"Won't Matthew know?" Her tears, which had stopped flowing, began again. "He will, won't he? Oh, this has ruined everything! I love him so. I wanted him so. And now –"

"Now you must be calm and sensible and very brave. Matthew, I firmly believe, is as innocent and inexperienced as you are yourself and may well not question your physical condition. You must realise that what Joely Tregilgas did to you bears no relationship to the act of love. To speak of it, to let it affect your marriage in any way would be an act of gross cruelty, not only to Matthew but to yourself as well. Believe me," she said urgently once more, tightening her grip on Loveday's hands. "Believe me, I'm right, dearest. You have a wonderful future ahead of you. In a way it would be sheer self-indulgence to speak of what happened yesterday to those that love you."

Wearily Loveday sighed.

"I suppose you're right," she said. And looking at Sarah Morrow, so strong and certain and utterly determined, her doubts weakened. "I'm sure you're right," she amended. "It's just that I don't know if I have the strength."

"You have the strength." It was as if Sarah willed her own determination to pass into the heart and mind of the girl.

For some moments Loveday said nothing, staring unseeingly at a point somewhere beyond the foot of the bed. Then she sighed again.

"It seems so sad," she said bleakly at last; and this time it was Sarah's tears that flowed.

* * *

St Ninn was *en fête* for the wedding between Loveday Pentecost and Matthew Tallon. Even the elements appeared to be rejoicing, for it was a day of bright sunshine and a clear blue sky, with only a light breeze to set the Cornish lilies nodding in the cottage gardens and grass that surrounded the church.

Not only were the schoolchildren enjoying a day's holiday, but the clayworkers as well; and as for the housewives for whom Saturday was normally a busy day with pasties to be made for the menfolk to take to the fields throughout the week – they had postponed their chores for a few hours, for there was not one of them who did not wish to see Master's daughter in her wedding finery.

Carriages had been arriving at the church since eleven – even a wagonette with all the Tregony Tallons.

"You can tell a Tallon a mile away," Mrs Penhaligon remarked, as Aunt Eveline and Aunt Clara met up with Aunt Jane at the lychgate. "They'm all what I call *showy*."

"Where's the bridegroom to?" asked a latecomer.

"Gone inside. Oh, some 'andsome, 'e looked."

" 'Ere comes Clay Tallon. 'E'm still a lovely lookin' man, en un? My Gor, that's never 'is wife, that long streak o' pump water?"

"Millicent Trengrose, as was." Letty Foster again, always ready with the information, and entirely above herself, according to her associates, because her Maisie was actually invited to the wedding – was, indeed, already inside the church complete with a new hat, bought last week in St Austell market. "Ent you never seen un before? 'Twas always said Clay married for money. And there's Miss Sybil Tallon, just as tall as her ma."

Even Letty was unable to put a name to all the guests who were arriving, though there were many who recognised the Treffrys and the Rashleighs. St Ninn had never seen a day like it.

A small cheer went up as Mr and Mrs Robert Morrow arrived in the governess cart, for the brougham was reserved on this great day for the bride and her father. It was warming to the heart, Robert thought, to receive such acknowledgement, but he did not delude himself that he had much to do with it. The cheer was a tribute to Sarah; to her unpretentious, outgoing sociability and lack of condescension – but perhaps, most of all on this day of days, to her splendid appearance. She waved to the crowd like royalty as they marvelled at her heavily embroidered grosgrain dress, dove grey with a spectacular lace jabot, and the tilted hat which bore a pair of bird's wings nestling in a froth of white roses.

"Don't she look a picture?" demanded Letty Foster of no one in particular.

" 'Tis easy when you've money to spend," said Mrs Penhaligon; but her acid comment was lost in the wave of excitement as the Carrivick brougham was seen to be approaching, and the long-drawn-out 'Aahh' of appreciation that arose as Loveday stepped out beside the lychgate.

Afterwards, in the *Gazette*, it was reported that the bride wore a full-trained dress of white peau de soie in the Princess style, with lace fichu and gigot sleeves; that her tulle veil was fastened with orange blossoms and that her bouquet was composed of mixed spring flowers.

Although the finer details might have passed them by, the villagers were unanimous on one point. There never was a lovelier bride.

"Or a liddle maid who do deserve more happiness, dear of her," said Letty Foster fondly. "They'm an 'andsome couple, and no mistake."

"Marriage ent all beer and skittles," Mrs Penhaligon said bitterly. But no one paid any heed to her.

Book Two

Book Two

❧ 10 ❧

Oliver Tallon, shivering a little in his nightshirt, knelt on the window-seat with the soles of his two small feet facing the cavernous room and his nose close to the window-pane where he had pulled the curtain aside so that he could see the night sky and the roaring, white-flecked blackness that was the sea.

He did not care for it at all in this mood.

"Heaven help the sailors on a night like this," Susan had said when she had come to tuck him up, and he couldn't get the words out of his mind. He thought of the clay boats in Charlestown harbour, and that nice Mr Hunkin who had taken him and Sally and Mummy out in his boat at Mevagissey –

Mummy! His eyes widened in horror as the thought struck him. Suppose she was out there! Oh, he knew that she *said* that she and Daddy were going to London in a train, but you never really knew with grown-ups. Suppose they had changed their minds? Suppose they had suddenly taken it into their heads to go to France, or China or somewhere? Or Venice. Mummy had said more than once lately that of all the places in the world, she wanted to go to Venice. One day, she'd said to Daddy; one day we'll go.

Suppose that 'one day' was now?

He looked over his shoulder towards the bed where Sally, his twin sister, slept in unthinking oblivion.

"Sally," he hissed in a penetrating, agonised whisper. And again, more urgently, when he received no response, "*Sally!*"

Her dark head moved a little on the pillow but she slumbered on, and defeated, knowing that she would wake in her own good time and not before, he turned back towards the window, miserably hunching his thin shoulders until they almost reached his ears.

The sound of carriage wheels on the drive, so close that they could be heard above the sound of the sea, distracted his thoughts and quickened his heart. He craned closer to the window and peered outwards and downwards.

Perhaps this was Mummy and Daddy, coming to take them back to St Ninn. Perhaps they'd finished their business more quickly than they'd thought and, knowing how he hated staying at Prospect Lodge, had come hurrying home.

Hearing his grandfather's voice, raised to combat the noise of the wind, shouting instructions at the coachman about the time he would be required the following day, Oliver sagged back on his heels, disappointed, conscious suddenly of the cold.

They weren't going to come. He'd known that all along, really, but he couldn't help hoping. There weren't any trains at this time of night. Mummy had said they would be back in four days, and she always kept her promises. He climbed down from the window-seat with a sigh, and padded back to a bed grown cold in his absence, and huddling under the blankets curled himself into a little ball, while outside the sea continued to roar.

"Georgina says – and I have to say that I agree *completely* – that Art is the sensuous embodiment of absolute truth in philosophy and religion. She cannot approve of the Impressionists, however."

"Poor old Impressionists," Matthew said. Carefully expressionless, he caught Loveday's eye across the expanse of shimmering white damask as he signalled to the waiter to refill the three glasses. Could this really be Sybil speaking? And on the strength of three novels that, entertaining as they were, wouldn't stretch the intellect of the average parlourmaid?

"Why doesn't she approve?" Loveday asked. "I love their use of light and colour."

"They catch only a *fleeting* moment, Georgina says, and

have little knowledge of drawing techniques. She feels they are undisciplined."

"So sensuous whatsisname is acceptable only if disciplined?" Matthew pursued the matter with an earnest air which earned him a frown from Sybil and a surreptitious kick on the ankle from his wife.

"It sounds," Loveday said, smiling with affection at her sister-in-law, "as if you have a very full life in London. Such interesting friends, and so much intellectual stimulation!"

"My dear, I could no more live in Cornwall again than fly to the moon. Georgina says that it's quite astonishing how receptive I am to new ideas, considering the restrictions of my childhood."

"When are we to have the pleasure of meeting Miss Burrell-Hobbs?" Matthew asked. "Though, of course, I dare swear she would find us too provincial for words –"

"No, no, not at all," Sybil hastened to assure him earnestly. "I have told her how liberal you are in your dealings with the work people. She approves thoroughly of your attitude towards unions."

"Well, that's a relief," Matthew murmured dryly.

"And of course," Sybil went on, "I have told her how well-read Loveday is, and how much I owe to dear Mr Pentecost."

Her face softened and she caught her lip between her teeth, the London mask suddenly dropped. Briefly she touched Loveday's arm.

"You must miss him so," she said. "He was the very best of men. Even now I think of things I long to tell him, and reach for my pen before I remember that he has gone."

"I know." Loveday, all tears shed, was able to smile at Sybil consolingly. "There'll never be anyone like him, but at least I comfort myself with the thought that he lived for three years longer than Dr Geach originally predicted. He saw how happy Matthew and I were, and was able to play with his grandchildren."

"And didn't he love it?" Sybil smiled reminiscently. "Now, pray tell me all the news of home. Has Father forgiven my defection?"

Matthew opened his mouth to reply, but Loveday jumped

in quickly, giving him a cautionary look that only a husband would recognise.

"He is not without pride in your achievements," she said. "I caught him reading the little piece about you that appeared in *The West Briton* and he looked highly delighted by it, I thought, though he quickly put the paper down when he saw me. I feel sure he'll come round, Sybil."

"You must become famous," Matthew said. "That'll do the trick. He'll enjoy boasting of your accomplishments to all his cronies."

Sybil looked loftily amused.

"My dear Matthew, fame is ephemeral and ultimately worthless. It's Georgina's belief that to seek it is positively harmful to the creative process. On the other hand," she added more mundanely, "I wouldn't say 'no' to the money it might bring with it."

"Are you short?"

"No, no." Sybil shook her head in emphatic denial. "*Two Hearts in Harmony* paid quite well – really a great improvement on the previous two books – and *The Quiver* has taken several of my short stories in the last few months. As for the novel I am engaged on at the moment –" She paused for a moment, looked confused and gave a nervous laugh.

"I long to read it," Loveday said encouragingly.

"I wonder. It's different from the others. Much more honest and worthwhile, Georgina says, and I feel sure she is right. But I hate to talk of it at this stage – and to discuss money is so sordid. Georgina and I have decided never to do so. We simply contribute what we can afford and manage accordingly."

Matthew had dropped his flippant air and looked at her now with sympathy.

"It's quite indefensible of Father to have discontinued your allowance. I know that it worries Mother dreadfully."

"Then you must tell her that I am well and happy – as, of course, I tell her myself in letters. No doubt she will take your word for it, even if she distrusts mine."

"She misses you, Sybil."

"And I miss her. I shall come home for a visit soon, no matter what Father says, but nothing would make me stay.

Sometimes I think of what my life might have been, and go cold with horror! Life is so exciting in London." She paused and leaned forward confidentially. "Don't say a word at home, but Georgina and I have joined Mrs Pankhurst's WSPU."

"You're a suffragette!"

"Yes. Oh, you should hear her speak, Loveday. It's thrilling!"

"Are you one of the militant ones?"

Sybil laughed, her eyes bright.

"Oh, I've marched and held one half of a banner, but I haven't fallen foul of any policemen yet."

"And you won't, if you have any sense," Matthew said. Sybil pouted at him.

"Trust you to disapprove."

"I'm not at all sure that all this marching and shouting and making a nuisance of yourselves will achieve the desired end, but I don't disapprove of the principle involved, I assure you. I can see no reason whatsoever why women shouldn't have the vote."

"*Well!*" Sybil looked astonished. "I never expected you to be so enlightened. I can see that Loveday has worked some kind of miracle."

"I'm not arguing with that," Matthew said.

"But oh, you can see why I find life so exciting," Sybil went on. "Just imagine if I were married to Captain Hawke! I hear from Mother that he has embarked on a second family, with his poor wife expecting her fourth child – and they not married for more than four years." She shuddered. "I found him totally repellent. How Father could ever have thought I would take him I cannot imagine. He would certainly have been disappointed if he expected *me* to produce a baby a year."

"You realise," said Loveday between mouthfuls of *Filets de Petit Coq de Bruyère à la Financière* which she had chosen from the newspaper-sized menu, not because she had any idea of what it was but because it seemed to be the dish furthest removed from anything she was likely to be served at home, "that your father blames me – and my father of course – for the fact that you turned Captain Hawke down?"

Sybil raised her eyebrows in surprise and bewilderment.

"Why on earth?"

"We are supposed to have influenced you. Poor, darling Papa seems to have been cast in the role of a kind of general purpose *éminence grise*. Any little flurry of discontent among the clay workers – any mention of trades unions, and you can be sure he gets the blame. Likewise with your rebellion and flight from the nest."

Matthew enlarged on the theme.

"Father is of the opinion that the Fourlanesend school was a hotbed of anarchism, with Mr Pentecost wholly responsible for turning out boys unaware of their place in society, lacking respect for their betters, full of dangerously anarchic ideas."

The three of them who had known and loved John Pentecost laughed together.

"What nonsense," Sybil said. "He encouraged my small gift, it's true, and made me believe in myself. It's also true that he suggested to Sarah that she should bring me to London as a kind of companion when she came for the Christmas of 1901 – and *that*, by the way, was something Father heartily approved of. He felt I was bound to find a husband in the biggest city on earth. Staying on, however, was my own idea entirely. I'd made some friends by that time, even if I hadn't found a husband, and sold my first story. A whole new world was beginning to open up. It's been over five years now that I've lived here – yes, *five years*! Isn't it amazing? Time goes so quickly. I simply couldn't face the thought of going back to church bazaars and other people's weddings now.

"Of course," she went on, the animation in her voice becoming even more marked, "meeting Georgina was the most incredible piece of luck. Oh, she's such a fine, fascinating person! You would both love her, I know. Such a pity she has had to go to Bournemouth to nurse her sick mother this week, for I'm so anxious for you to meet her. Especially you, Loveday. Georgina has read everything – just *everything*! You and she would have so much to talk about."

"I shall look forward to it another time," Loveday said politely.

Plates were removed, others brought. The meal proceeded, more wine was poured. The ambience was one of solid comfort, with the cutlery, napery and crystal of the highest quality. The service was impeccable, the other diners clearly prosperous in a quiet, unostentatious way.

"Father recommended this place to us," Matthew said. "At least he knows a good hotel when he sees one. He stays here when he comes up on business."

Sybil looked sceptical.

"I know Father's sort of business," she said. Matthew raised his eyebrows, but did not pursue the matter. "And are you on business?" Sybil asked. "Or is this a holiday?"

"Business."

"A holiday."

Matthew and Loveday answered together, then looked at each other. Only Matthew was aware of the warning light in Loveday's eyes.

"A little of both," he said.

"You haven't said one word about the twins," Sybil went on. "I thought parents were supposed to talk of nothing but their offspring. Are they well? Oh, how I'd love to see them! They must be growing so big."

"Indeed, they are," Loveday agreed, the touch of tension in her expression replaced by maternal pride. "And as artful as several wagonloads of monkeys, I assure you."

"They must be old enough for school."

"Six – seven in November. I teach them myself. There's nowhere to send them but Fourlanesend, and it's a different place these days – a stern and unbending headmaster and that dreadful Miss Pinnock. Besides, I enjoy it."

"You should see our daughter –" Matthew began.

"The apple of his eye!"

"But without the smallest amount of prejudice, Sybil, she is bright as a button and quite the prettiest child you ever saw! Dark curls, Loveday's eyes –"

"And a father she can wrap around her little finger! One flutter of her eyelashes and Matthew is putty in her hands."

"Everyone is putty in her hands, including Father. Can you believe that, Sybil? Can you imagine him being the perfect grandfather, giving her rides on his shoulders and playing Blind Man's Buff?"

"Never!"

"I promise you it's the truth. She's enslaved him."

"And is he the same with Oliver? He must be thrilled to have a grandson."

"Ah!" Matthew took a sip of wine. "Well now – Oliver. He's quite different from Sally. Quiet and timid. A nervous little boy."

"With the sweetest nature," Loveday put in quickly.

"Oh, agreed. One can't help wishing, though, that he would stand up for himself a little more. No one in the world would guess that he and Sally are twins."

"They're not alike?" Sybil asked.

"Not at all. He's dark, like Sally, but quite, quite different in every other way. Different in looks, different in temperament. He's a lot smaller, for one thing –"

"He was smaller at birth, wasn't he?" Sybil looked at Loveday for confirmation, but Loveday's eyes were on Matthew, her mouth pursed a little, her eyes clouded, as if she sensed the bewilderment he felt with regard to Oliver and was hurt by it. "I remember it so well," Sybil went on. "He wasn't expected to live, was he?"

"No." Loveday's brief confirmation was brusque.

"But our Oliver had other ideas." Matthew was smiling now, as if recounting Oliver's determination to live had, after all, given him cause to be proud. "Old Dr Geach and that nurse he had to help him dumped him down at the end of the bed, thinking he was already a goner. They knew by that time that there was another on the way, of course. So typical of Sally! She let Oliver do all the hard work and made sure of a reasonably easy passage for herself."

Matthew's tone was one of amused and affectionate indulgence, and Sybil gave a brief laugh in response to it.

"How different from our family," she said. "You were the golden-haired pet, Matthew, and I the awkward one. Perhaps you two have it the right way round. Good looks are wasted on a man. Better far if Oliver is intelligent and industrious and Sally is the beauty of the family. In any case, it was a miracle that they were both alive and well, and that you came through the ordeal safely, Loveday. I shall never forget my poor brother's worry and anguish until the wonderful news came that you were out of danger. Oh, how happy we were that day!"

Matthew smiled ruefully.

"I vowed that I would never worry about anything trivial again," he said. "I think I aged ten years in those few days."

"Father broke out a bottle of his best claret at dinner. I've never seen him more pleased."

Loveday heard the voices but sat silent, taking no part in the reminiscences. It was an episode in her life she would prefer to forget, and usually succeeded in doing so. The fears and doubts that had plagued her were the stuff of nightmares, as were the voices she had heard outside her bedroom door the day after the twins were born.

"Not married eight months!"

"She's not the first, when all's said and done."

She could hear the penetrating whispers now – could see herself in bed, and the open door giving on to the passage from where the voices came. Who had spoken? The maids, she supposed; or one or other of the women who were caring for her and the babies. Drifting in and out of sleep as she was, she could not tell, but as normality returned she knew there would be speculation and smirking far beyond her own four walls. At least no one suspected that Matthew might not be the father of her twins.

No, no, no! They were clearly premature. Dr Geach had said so, and he had said it with such authority, such conviction, that no one could possibly doubt him. It was totally impossible for her or Matthew or anyone else to pinpoint the moment of their conception.

Sarah was right, and had been right all along. That dreadful violation had had nothing to do with love or procreation and was best forgotten, buried as if it had never happened. For the most part she was able to do so. It was only sometimes that she felt this tremor of doubt and guilt and fear, like a goose walking over her grave, and was conscious of a roaring, gaping pit that lay in wait for her, a pit called 'Retribution'.

She had heard nothing of Joely Tregilgas for years, or of Henry. She only knew that by the time she and Matthew had returned from their honeymoon (and a strange, awkward time that had been! If ever Matthew had needed to exercise love and forbearance, it was then), the hovel in the woods had been razed to the ground – by the Council, people said, who had decreed the dwelling illegal and insanitary, not only a violation of the laws governing common land but clearly a repository for stolen goods. Joely was once more in prison and there was no word of Henry or his mother.

She became aware of Matthew and Sybil looking towards her, laughing at her.

"She's miles away," Sybil said.

"I'm sorry." Smilingly, Loveday apologised for her abstraction. "I'm a little tired."

"It's been a long day," Matthew agreed. There was tenderness in the smile he gave her and warmth in the hand that reached out to clasp hers. All the doubts of the honeymoon had been long resolved.

"Will I see you again before you leave London?" Sybil asked.

"I'm not sure. We'll be in touch with you, I promise."

"Perhaps you would like to meet me to go shopping, Loveday, or to a gallery, while Matthew is busy –?"

"Forgive us, Sybil. Our plans are very vague." Matthew stepped in smoothly, saving Loveday the need to answer. "It has been wonderful to see you."

"I do so wish you could have met Georgina."

"Another time, perhaps."

"You would like her so much."

"I'm quite sure she must be a paragon, if only half of what you say is true!"

Upstairs, with Sybil handed into a cab and safely on her way back to the flat in Bloomsbury which she shared with Miss Burrell-Hobbs, he was less restrained.

"I feel I *have* met the worthy Georgina, don't you?" he asked Loveday. "I'm quite sure she wears greenery-yallery dresses and uncompromising hats –"

"And a very sensible line in footwear!" Laughing, Loveday sat on the bed and removed her own far from sensible, pointed, sparkling slippers. "Still, whatever she's like, she's done wonders with Sybil. You have to admit it, Matthew, she's a different woman. So confident, so sure of herself! And really rather stylish in an arty, rumpled kind of way."

"Can we thank Georgina for that, or is it her little bit of success?"

"Both, perhaps." Loveday's laughter had died. "I hope Sybil wasn't hurt that I didn't leap at the opportunity to meet her again. It may be possible, after all." She sighed heavily, and Matthew at once came to her, putting his arms around her and holding her close.

"Darling, I know how you feel about tomorrow, but you mustn't worry. I keep telling you that I'm happy with my family as it is, and I'm not the least bit anxious for you to try to change things. I'm no Captain Hawke. The pitter-patter of two little pairs of feet are quite enough for me – it's you who are important. Talking to Sybil tonight brought it all back to me. When I thought I might lose you, I nearly went mad –"

"But we always wanted a big family, didn't we?"

"We have one of each! There aren't any more kinds, after all."

Her cheek pressed to his shoulder, Loveday fell silent. It was totally impossible to express how much she longed for another baby – a baby that had no question mark hovering unseen over his cradle. It was not that she did not love Sally and Oliver. She adored them both and had done so from the beginning, for what did question marks matter when two tiny, helpless beings were placed in the crook of each arm, utterly perfect, utterly dependent? No one could help loving Sally. She had smiled her way into their hearts, growing from contented baby to captivating toddler and delightful little girl. And as for Oliver, there was something about his timid vulnerability that she found overwhelmingly appealing – the more so because she was aware of Matthew's unexpressed disappointment.

Boys, in Matthew's book, were expected to be bold, even aggressive. They were supposed to kick balls about, to make too much noise, to fall into puddles and come home covered in mud. He had looked forward to having a son, Loveday knew, so that he could take him fishing and shooting once he was old enough.

Oliver, however, took up so little space that one hardly knew he was there. He seldom dirtied his clothes or made any noise and seemed to have no wish to kick a ball about. As for fishing or shooting, at six he was not old enough for either, but Loveday doubted that he would ever have the temperament for such activities. He was such a sensitive child that he could not bear to crush so much as an ant beneath his foot, and had cried bitterly the first time, at the age of three, he had seen a catch of silvery pilchards threshing and wriggling at the bottom of a boat, still trapped in the net.

Heaven send that tomorrow, at the exclusive, horrendously expensive clinic in Harley Street to which she had been recommended by Dr Geach, she would hear good news. After all, the good doctor would only say that it was unlikely that she would conceive again, not that it was impossible. Medical science had progressed since he had qualified, he was the first to admit. It was possible that a small operation would rectify the damage done by the twins' precipitate arrival. She drew away from Matthew, smiled at him to show that she was in control of herself once more, and rose to prepare herself for bed.

"Will you undo my buttons, darling?"

"Nothing I should like more." He kissed her, once on each shoulder, as he bent to his task.

"You know," she said, "I really ought to go shopping. No one in that dining room was wearing this kind of neckline. Did you notice the girl at the corner table in that glorious yellow dress?"

"I?" Matthew spun her round to face him, a look of exaggerated astonishment on his face. "Can you really imagine that I would notice other women when in the company of the most beautiful, fascinating, adorable –"

"Yes." Loveday was laughing at him. "I can imagine it all too well."

"Well, you are wrong, madam. I recall no girl and no yellow dress."

"And no corner table? Oh, very well!" She reached up and kissed him briefly. "Just take my word for it that it was a lovely gown."

"Then you shall have one just like it."

He would give her anything that was within his power, she knew. Whatever the outcome of tomorrow's consultation, life had been good to her. How many women had found themselves married to selfish tyrants? How many women lived lives of drudgery, subject to every whim of their husbands? She, by contrast, had a husband who loved her as much now as he had done on their wedding day; more, perhaps, if her own feelings were any guide. Certainty and familiarity had only made his touch more exciting.

She kissed him again, but not briefly this time. And as passion flared between them, as clumsiness grew with his desire and he swore frustratedly at the buttons, she took pity on him and helped him with the task, faster and more urgently. Oh, fortunate woman, she thought, when at last their passion was spent and they lay contentedly in each other's arms. Was it wrong to ask more when she had so much?

Perhaps the richness of the food was to blame, or the airlessness of the room; but for whatever reason, it was a long time before sleep came to her, and when it did she was plagued by frightening nightmares. She woke with her heart banging against her ribs, certain that she had cried out; but Matthew slept on, undisturbed. Perhaps she had dreamed that cry of terror.

But of what had she been so afraid? Already the details were fading from her mind and she could remember nothing; only unease remained, only a feeling of dread that she could not dismiss. Was it fear of what she might be told tomorrow? Or was it dread of that pit that always yawned at the edge of her consciousness?

Sunday. Tomorrow Mummy would come back.

Oliver, early awake, sucked his thumb and gazed happily towards the window. He could see blue sky, pale but cloudless, and the sea was no more than a peaceful, shushing, distant presence, speaking of buckets and spades and sand-between-the-toes – quite unlike the monster of the previous night. Susan had promised a walk to Charlestown that afternoon. Then there would be tea and bed, and only one more day to get through – after which he would make Mummy promise never, *never* to go away again.

He would explain to her how much he disliked staying at Prospect Lodge – how he hated the big rooms and the wide, dark corridor which led to the bedrooms. No one ever put the lights on until it had grown so shadowy that it was impossible to see for sure whether or not there was a ghost behind the grandfather clock. Or a lion. And there was a horrid picture on the stairs: two dead pheasants lying on a table beside a basket of vegetables and a brown jug. He always hurried past it with eyes averted, but knowing it was there was bad enough.

The cupboard was another worry. It was built under the eaves in the room he shared with Sally. Funny noises came from inside it from time to time. Susan had said that it was the pipes, and had opened it to show him that there was nothing there but a big square tank, but you could never really be sure that something frightening hadn't slipped in when no one was looking.

Then there was Grandfather. Oliver knew quite well that Sally was his favourite. He played with her and teased her; sat her on his knee and called her his little sweetheart. Oliver didn't mind that at all – in fact he would have been perfectly happy if Grandfather had ignored him altogether, but unfortunately this didn't happen. Grandfather was of the opinion that he needed toughening up.

"The sooner that little Miss Nancy goes off to school, the better," Oliver had heard him say to Grandma. "His mother is ruining him." Oliver had hung his head, his cheeks burning, overcome with misery and shame. Meantime, Grandfather took measures of his own, designed to harden him in body and spirit. He insisted on cold baths (not for Sally, of course), and shot questions at him such as how many apples were left in a box if there were twenty to start with and two boys had six each.

Such mental arithmetic was beyond Oliver anyway, but sheer terror paralysed him to the extent that he never even took in the question properly. Neither could he catch the balls that Grandfather, in playful mood, would suddenly throw in his direction. All in all, he was aware that he was a sad disappointment.

Helping with the jigsaw puzzle, the only activity at which he might have excelled, was barred to him. Grandfather had found him looking at it the other day – only looking, not touching – and had shouted at him, and hadn't listened when he had tried to tell him that he could see where the piece of the soldier's flag went.

"He's rather fussy about his puzzle, dear," Grandma had said apologetically when the storm was over. "It's one of his little ways."

Grandfather, in Oliver's opinion, had altogether too many little ways.

Grandma was different, of course. She was kind and quiet and liked to spend time in her garden. If only, Oliver thought, he could be allowed to stay with her, then things might be all right. He was perfectly happy digging for worms and watching them wriggle about, and he loved planting seeds and patting the earth down to give them a warm, comfortable bed. Grandma had shown him how. But in one sense Grandma was just as bad as Grandfather, for she was always urging him to 'run along and play a nice game'. She tended to ask other children to tea – children who liked rushing about and pushing and shoving – and he was supposed to join in. But not for much longer, for today was Sunday –

Sunday!

Oliver shot up in bed, eyes and mouth wide with panic. He hadn't learned the text! Grandfather had announced it two days ago and said that he would require both children to repeat it at breakfast on Sunday before going to chapel. How could he possibly have forgotten it? How could Sally have forgotten it? No one had said anything more about it and Grandma hadn't mentioned it again, but there was no hope, no hope at all, that Grandfather had been equally forgetful.

Breathing quickly, face set, Oliver climbed from his bed and scampered across the room to the shelves that were filled with a mixture of books, many that had belonged to his father when a child. An old and battered Bible was among them. Seizing it in both hands he ran to the side of Sally's bed and jabbed at the arm that was flung outside the coverings.

"Sally, Sally, wake up. We forgot the text. Wake up."

The startling blue eyes opened at once, clear and alert. There was never any halfway house between sleeping and waking for Sally. She sat up immediately, lip caught between her teeth.

"Oh, my!" she said helplessly.

"Find it, find it." He jabbed the Bible at her again.

"Stop it, Ollie, that hurts."

"Well, find it!"

"I can't remember which one it was."

"Yes, you can. It was the 'Suffer the little children' one. Look, Susan put the ribbon in the place. Read it, Sally. Out *loud!*" he implored as he saw her eyes find the verse, her lips move.

"All right, all right. Just shut up a minute." Impatiently he fidgeted by her side. "Listen, then," she said at last. " 'Suffer the little children to come unto me, and forbid them not; for of such is the kingdom of God. Verily I say unto you, whosoever –' " she stumbled a little on the unfamiliar word, " – 'who-so-ever' " she repeated carefully, " 'shall not –' " again a hesitation while she spelled the word out " ' – receive,' " she said triumphantly at last, " 'the kingdom of God as a little child, he shall not enter therein.' That's it. That's what we've got to learn."

"Say it again, Sally."

She repeated the passage with more fluency this time, and then once more. Then with great solemnity and earnestness they gazed at each other and repeated it, line by line.

The degree of solemnity decreased as their confidence grew. Soon the Bible was on the floor and Sally was bouncing in time to the words.

" '*Suffe*r the *li*ttle *chil*dren to *come un*to *me* –' "

Oliver joined in, flushed and happy now that he had the words by heart. Even the knowledge that they would undoubtedly desert him when faced by Grandfather's terrifying jocularity failed, for the moment, to dampen his spirits and together they bounced joyfully, the bedsprings groaning in protest.

There was a rasping noise and the bed lurched a little. Suddenly they were still, the game forgotten.

"We'll catch it," Oliver whispered, despairingly; but Sally was more sanguine.

"It's a very old bed," she said. "Daddy used to sleep in it.

He told me. I shall tell Grandma that it was all wore out and they'll have to get a new one."

"Well, don't tell Grandfather. We'd better get up. Where's Susan?"

"Everyone's late, 'cos it's Sunday."

"The sun's shining." Oliver had wandered away and was now kneeling on the window-seat. "Susan's taking us to the beach this afternoon. And Mummy and Daddy are coming tomorrow." His world, for the moment, seemed full of the promise of happiness. "Why 'suffer'?" he asked suddenly, turning round and looking at his sister with a frown. "Why did the children have to suffer? What does it mean?"

Sally pulled a face, blowing out her cheeks, lifting her shoulders.

"*I* don't know, *you* don't know, *no*body knows," she sang out, beginning to bounce again.

"Such a racket! What do you think you'm up to, Miss Sally?" It was Susan, bustling in with a flurry of white starched apron. "You'll rouse the whole house. Come now, it's best bib and tucker today."

"Mummy and Daddy are home tomorrow." An excess of high spirits seemed in order, Sally implied.

"Don't I know it!" Susan was picking up and folding and straightening as she spoke. "Tomorrow night we'll all be back in our own beds in St Ninn, and thank heaven for that, I say."

"Don't you like it here either, Susan?" Oliver asked her; but Susan, discreetly, gave nothing away. She folded her lips and took clean clothes from the drawer. "*Don't* you, Susan?" Oliver insisted.

"Be it never so humble, there ent no place like home," Susan said with finality – adding, almost to herself, "and if I don't never see that cook's face again, it'll be too soon for me. Come on, now, Master Oliver –" recollecting herself. "Wash your face and get your clothes on."

"That suit tickles," Oliver said, looking with disfavour at the new sailor suit she had laid out for him.

"You'll look a real gentleman in it, and no mistake. What's a little tickle between friends?"

Reluctantly, Oliver dressed, and despite his earlier feeling of happiness, his spirits drooped. Before the excursion to the beach, there was the morning to get through. Hours and hours of it, beginning with the reciting of the text, continuing with the ordeal of eating breakfast – not in the kitchen with Susan, as on weekdays, but under Grandfather's all-seeing eye – and culminating in the service at St John's Methodist Chapel in St Austell.

Sally recited the text first and managed it perfectly, earning a hug and a kiss from her grandfather; but despite having the opportunity to hear it again, Oliver ground to a halt after 'forbid them not'. Grandfather, he saw, was looking at him with his mouth twisted in the little smile that he had learned to dread. Panic seized him, as it always did when he saw that look of scorn. He could make no sense of the whispered prompt from Sally, could formulate no words. The silence seemed to go on endlessly.

"Never mind, Oliver," Grandma said at last, sounding distressed on his behalf. "You remembered part of it. Really Edwin, I don't think that's at all bad for a little boy of six."

Her husband continued to smile coldly at the boy.

"Your sister managed all of it. Am I to assume she is a better man than you are, Oliver?"

"We can't all be the same," Grandma said. "Sit down, Oliver, and eat your porridge, there's a good boy."

"And we'll try again this evening, before you go to bed."

Grandfather still smiled, but his voice was hard and the scornful look was still there in his eyes. Oliver sat down, but he had no appetite for his porridge, though dutifully he took several spoonsful. This evening would be no better, he knew. Even if he stayed indoors all day, not going to the beach but repeating the text over and over, he would still forget it when he saw Grandfather looking at him like that. The thought of it lay like a cold, heavy, undigested mass in his stomach.

"I think," he said faintly after a few moments, laying down his spoon, "I am going to be sick." And neatly, without fuss, he returned the porridge to the bowl from whence it came.

The day was more like summer than spring, with the sun pouring through the windows and an air of somnolence about the congregation.

Oliver had been right about the suit; it tickled his neck in a nasty, unremitting sort of way that made him wriggle despite his grandmother's restraining hand. And once he had had his fill of staring at the choir, set up on high in the galleried pews above the pulpit, there was little to occupy his mind. Sally, sitting beside him in a feminine, and clearly less irritating, version of his sailor suit kept herself reasonably amused by reading the hymnbook or adding up the hymn numbers on the board; but such diversions were not for him. Even she, however, sighed wearily from time to time and was glad to accept the violet cachous that Grandma kept for such occasions. Oliver couldn't make up his mind whether he liked them or not. They smelled of scent and the inside of Grandma's handbag, and left a funny taste on the tongue, but he accepted them anyway, simply to pass the time.

The voice of the minister, by name Mr Large – which Oliver thought an excellent joke, since it was obviously what he was not, being a thin, desiccated-looking man – seemed to have a dying fall. Could he possibly be coming to the end of his sermon at last? He had a particularly active Adam's apple which had held Oliver's interest far beyond his usual attention span. However, fascination with this peculiarity had died long since. Hope stirred in his breast; and a certain lightening of the atmosphere and a few coughs seemed to indicate that he was not alone in this. But if an early end to the sermon was expected, the congregation was to be disappointed.

"And thirdly, brethren," intoned Mr Large, about to embark on a further instalment of his harangue. He paused for a moment in order, presumably, to draw breath; and in the silence Oliver yawned.

It was not a silent yawn such as many others had indulged in during the course of the sermon, nor the kind of yawn that hid itself behind delicately raised fingers. It was, instead, a full-blooded, open-mouthed, vocally explicit yawn that turned heads and invoked shocked stares or sympathetic grins, according to the nature of the donor.

Clay Tallon might – almost certainly would – have grinned had the malefactor been any other child. He'd been forced to stifle a few yawns himself that morning, and as a reaction to Mr Large's sermon, he had to concede that it was fair comment.

But this was *his* grandson! Trust that niminy-piminy little mollycoddle to let him down in front of half his workforce – not to mention the Penberthys, as well as others among his peers. Yawning was understandable, but he could at least have made some attempt to hide it. Oliver hadn't even got the sense to dissemble.

He leaned forward to glare at Oliver, and glancing fearfully sideways, the boy caught the full force of his grandfather's silent anger. His face flushed scarlet, then turned deathly pale. For a moment he feared that he would be sick again, but his attention was distracted by a nudge from Sally.

"Mr *Large* has a *large* nose," she whispered, to cheer him.

It seemed exquisitely funny. The sickness and the shame were forgotten as he bit his lip to keep from laughing. Sally could always make him laugh. He must remember the joke to tell Mummy, though in his heart he was conscious of a feeling of resignation, for it was almost certain that if there was a joke to be told or news to be imparted, it was Sally who would be doing the telling. Those were the only times that he really became angry with her; angry enough to push and shove and shout – for surely he ought to be allowed to tell his own news? There was that time when Mr Williams's cows broke through the fence into Dr Geach's back garden and from there wandered into the churchyard. He was the one to see them first, but it was Sally who beat him indoors to spread the tidings.

He wasn't, therefore, in the least surprised when, having watched for the station fly the whole of Monday, he somehow managed to miss the actual moment of arrival. Susan had packed the wicker hamper with the clothes and belongings they had brought with them, and the sight of it standing ready for departure in the back hall had filled the day with excitement.

It was the window on the square upstairs landing that gave the best view of the drive, and it was here that the twins had spent all afternoon with their noses pressed against the glass, even though they knew that the train wasn't due until half past three.

"After all, you never know," Sally said. "They might have caught an early one."

To which Oliver could only agree. Mummy, he knew, would be just as anxious to get back to them as they were to see her. Not that he blamed Daddy for taking her away and keeping her in London for four whole days. Business was business, he knew that. Daddy had to work hard to make pennies to buy them things. But he hoped he wouldn't have to stay with Grandfather, ever again. The reciting of the text had gone just as badly as he had expected and he had been sent to bed without any supper – a punishment which had been somewhat nullified by the fact that not only Sally, but Susan and Grandma had smuggled him titbits in bed so that in fact he had eaten rather more than usual. However, it had been a terrifying business all round, with many tears resulting. Guiltily he was aware that he hated his grandfather, and in a mood of rebellious defiance, he left his name off his list of 'God blesses' when he said his prayers.

It was, Oliver felt, just his luck that he had gone to answer the call of nature when the fly turned into the drive.

"Wait for *me*!" he called desperately, fumbling with buttons and braces, hearing Sally's joyous shout as she fled along the landing and down the stairs towards the hall with its red Turkey rugs that skidded on the polished floor if one didn't take care.

But she didn't, of course, and by the time he was in a position to follow her, she was already clasped in Mummy's arms.

It didn't really matter. Daddy was only just behind and took over the hugging of Sally while Mummy opened her arms, allowing him to rush into them.

He felt like crying, he was so happy; but he managed not to because he was a big boy of six, and Daddy wouldn't have liked it. Not that it would have mattered, because he was fairly sure that Mummy was crying a bit herself; but then, she was a girl, and girls were different.

"My dear," Millicent Tallon said, finding herself at last able to greet her son and daughter-in-law. "I hardly need to tell you how welcome you are! You'll want to go upstairs and wash, I've no doubt, then you must take a little refreshment before going home. Tea is quite ready."

She opened her mouth to add something more, thought better of it and caught her lip between her teeth, hands clasping and unclasping indecisively as she watched them. Loveday, Matthew and the two children, apparently determined not to let their parents out of their sight, were moving up the wide staircase together when she finally found the courage to ask:

"Was it a successful trip, dear?"

Loveday, a little behind the others, turned with one hand on the banisters and looked down on her mother-in-law. She, too, tried to speak, but seemed to have difficulty in finding the words. Millicent saw her lips tremble and the glint of tears in her eyes.

"I'm afraid not," she said, as the tears spilled over.

§ 11

"I," Sarah Morrow said dramatically, looking at herself in the full-length pier glass, "am going to seed. I am growing fat and repulsive, and there is not one theatre-goer in London who would recognise me. And shall I tell you something, Marnie?" Smiling, she turned from the mirror, adjusting the cream lace jabot that decorated her blouse. "I simply don't care! Kindly take that green dress I was wearing last night and do with it what you will. The colour should suit you very well."

"Oh, no, madam!" Marnie looked at her reproachfully. "It's almost new. I can ease the seams over the hips, easy as anything."

"They need a great deal more than easing, my dear. I thought I was going to die at Lady Bethune's dinner table! I already had my corsets laced as tight as humanly possible and quite expected acres of billowing flesh to burst into view, thrusting themselves under the fishy eyes of Sir Jeremy."

"I expect he would have enjoyed that, madam." Mistress and maid who had, over the years, shared many ups and downs, laughed together.

"Lady Bethune would have undoubtedly taken a different view. She has never quite been convinced that I am respectable. No, take the green dress, Marnie. We are going up to town very shortly and I shall have more made there. Two inches larger, at the very least."

Sarah shrugged herself into the tailored jacket that Marnie held for her, and reached for her hat which she adjusted with care so that it tipped a little over one eye. For one moment she considered the effect, head on one side; then looked at her maid and winked.

"Perhaps not so repulsive," she said.

"You look lovely, Mrs Morrow, and well you know it." Marnie's voice was tartly amused. "Are you going to see Mrs Tallon while you're in St Ninn? I happened to run into her the other day, and I thought –" She broke off and hesitated for a moment, but continued in reply to Sarah's enquiring expression. "I thought she looked – wisht, as they say down here. Not herself, somehow."

"No." Sarah smoothed on her gloves. "She hasn't been herself for months – not since she and Matthew got back from London in the spring. It was a great blow to her to find that she had no chance whatever of any more children and it seems to have affected her spirits. Before, I suppose, there was always hope."

"Poor dear," Marnie said. "Still, she has the two; boy and girl. Are you taking the trap, madam?"

"No, I'll walk." With one last adjustment of the jacket, Sarah went to the door. "The exercise will do me good," she said over her shoulder.

It was, of course, happiness that was to blame for the excess weight, she thought as she walked briskly towards the village. It was contentment that had put on those extra inches, though she would probably have a hard time convincing Lucy Villiers of that fact when next she saw her, for her old friend still found it astonishing that there was any contentment to be found outside the West End of London. Robert, gone that day to Truro on business, found that happiness had an equally deleterious effect on his avoirdupois.

"I suppose if we tried we could make each other miserable – just for the sake of our figures," he had said on the way home from Lady Bethune's dinner the night before.

"Just so long as we don't grow smug in our contentment," Sarah had replied. "What do a few extra inches matter?"

Loveday, she saw at once, had no such problem. She did, as Marnie had said, look wisht, and had undoubtedly lost weight; however she was delighted to see Sarah and welcomed her warmly.

"I mustn't stay," Sarah said. "I know you are busy with the children in the mornings."

"Oh, not too busy to stop and take a cup of coffee with you. I've set them some work to do. That will occupy them for a while, then they can have a break too. I – I've been wanting to talk to you. There's no one else I can possibly – oh, pray sit down, Sarah, while I settle them."

"May I come and say hallo?"

"Well –" Loveday hesitated. "Just so long as that's *all* you say! You know what you're like. You'll make them laugh, and they'll get so excited that they'll never finish their work."

"I shall be the very model of decorum," Sarah promised.

The children were upstairs in the bedroom that had been made into their schoolroom and were dutifully seated at a table working at an arithmetical exercise when Loveday and Sarah looked round the door. Sally immediately abandoned hers and rushed to fling her arms around the visitor.

"Aunt Sarah, Aunt Sarah –"

Loveday, a resigned expression on her face, raised her eyebrows in Sarah's direction.

"Work!" Sarah said sternly, turning Sally around so that she faced the table again. She gave the small, serge-covered bottom a pat. "Off you go, young lady. I only came to see if you were being good and getting on with your lessons – which I see is exactly what Master Oliver is doing."

Oliver, who had looked up bright-eyed at her entrance, struggled for honesty.

"Not really," he said. "I was, but I'm not now that you've come."

"Then you'd better start again. I want to see how beautifully you can do your sums."

"You may come down for your milk when you have finished the work I've set," Loveday told them – adding firmly: "and when it is done well, if you please. It may take a little thought, but there is no sum there that you can't do if you try."

"Angels!" Sarah said as they went downstairs together, knowing perfectly well that they were not. Loveday's brief laugh was muted, and ended with a sigh.

"There's something I want to show you," she said as they

entered the sitting room where the maid had placed a tray of coffee. "Something that's been worrying me to death. I suppose I should have realised earlier, but I wouldn't allow myself to see it."

"What are you talking about, Loveday?"

"Wait one moment." Loveday left the room, returning only a moment later with two sheets of paper in her hand. "Look," she said, handing Sarah one of them. "This is Oliver's latest attempt at writing."

She went to the window, looking out at the square beyond it as if she couldn't bear to see Sarah's reaction.

"Well, he is only six," Sarah said at last. Loveday turned round, her face pale and set.

"Seven in less than two months. This is Sally's attempt at the same exercise."

Sarah looked at the second paper and laughed.

"Yes, well, we all know that Sally is bright for her age."

"No, not particularly," Loveday said. "Averagely intelligent, I would say – perhaps a little forward with her reading, but no genius, I assure you."

Sarah sank down on the sofa, drawing Loveday down beside her, her expression serious.

"What are you trying to tell me, my dear?"

Loveday took the papers once more, and lip caught between her teeth, studied them again.

"Oliver can hardly write his name," she said in a low voice. "And those of his letters he recognises, he writes upside down or back to front. Look at that R! And when it comes to reading – well, I deluded myself that he was learning because he could rattle off the words in his reader. Then light dawned and I realised the truth. Only last night he read to Matthew – not a word missed, no hesitations. His father was delighted. He didn't know, as I suddenly did, that it was all recited from memory. Sally had read it to him, he had memorised it."

"Children develop at different rates, Loveday. You must know that."

"Of course." Loveday stood up and moved restlessly towards the window again. She turned to face Sarah. "I've made excuses and allowances for him over and over again. I've wanted to deceive myself. But ultimately I have had to admit that I recognise word-blindness when I see it, too. Oliver is word-blind, just as Henry was. Remember Henry?" Her voice rose. "Henry Tregilgas?"

"My dear child!" Appalled, Sarah swallowed and licked her lips. "You mustn't put too much weight upon this. Come, sit down and let me pour you a cup of coffee."

"No, no – forgive me." Abstractedly Loveday poured each of them a cup and sat down once more on the sofa. "Sarah, for weeks – months – I've tried to convince myself that Oliver is just a little slow. But he's *not* slow! He's timid and lacks confidence, it's true, but up here –" with one finger she tapped her head, "up here, in his mind, he's quite Sally's equal. He's a thoughtful boy, anxious to learn. He studies flowers and insects and wants to know about them, and about how things work, and he has the most amazing imagination. Yet he is quite unable to express himself on paper, simply because he can't remember his letters. Exactly the same as Henry."

"But didn't your father say that he had come across such a condition several times?"

"He also said that in his limited experience it tended to run in families." She put her coffee down untasted. "You see what this means, Sarah? Yes, of course you do! It's proof positive – all my questions answered. No doubt now about who fathered my children."

"I – I wouldn't call it positive, exactly."

"Oh, come! The coincidence is too much. I can see a likeness, too, if I look for it. Matthew's mother keeps saying that her grandmother had the same dark, rather bony look to her – but it's a Tregilgas look. Henry had it too. And his expression, sometimes – oh, what on earth am I to do?"

"Do?" Very deliberately Sarah also put her cup down and turned to face Loveday, her face set and serious. "Do? Why, you do nothing, Loveday. What is there to do?"

"Matthew should know!"

"No!" Sarah grasped her shoulders, eyes blazing, mouth rigid with determination. She gave Loveday a shake. "No, Loveday. What purpose could it serve? I said then that you must bury the past, and you did so. It must stay buried. You've managed it all these years."

"But I convinced myself that Matthew was the children's

father! He so easily could have been. Now I know for sure, and it changes everything."

"I can't see why." Sarah spoke softly, but her words were forceful. "Telling Matthew might relieve your conscience but would ruin four people's lives: your own, his, and the children's. He is their father, Loveday, in every way but one. Oh, think what it would do to them! And to him!"

"Do you think I haven't? I seem to think of nothing else."

"Then you must surely have come to only one conclusion."

"I wish I'd been honest from the beginning."

"No!" Sarah's voice left no room for doubts. "It would have spoiled everything. You and Matthew have a good marriage and two lovely children, in spite of Oliver's disability. He loves them both."

"Does he? I see him looking at Oliver sometimes with the strangest expression. Sally, of course, he worships this side of idolatory. He struggles hard not to show his partiality, but he can't hide it, not from me. He dotes on her." Loveday turned her face away from Sarah, but could not hide the tears that forced themselves from beneath her eyelids. "Think of the blood she has, Sarah. Criminal blood. Think of that weird, horrible Mrs Tregilgas; her grandmother!"

"And think of the home she has – the love, the privileged surroundings. Dammit, think of the *food* she has!" Sarah gave Loveday's shoulders a shake to emphasise her words. "Doesn't it occur to you that generations of poor conditions and starvation might have made the Tregilgases what they were?" Sarah put her arms around Loveday and held her. "I knew a duke in London, years ago," she said with apparent inconsequence. "He used to tell the story of how an ancestor in the reign of Charles II contracted a secret marriage with a friend of Nell Gwynne's, a fellow orange-seller. Do you imagine for one moment that there was any record of *her* parents?"

"I can't see –" began Loveday.

"My point is that no one knows about their ancestors. Matthew's grandfather, I gather, was something of a rogue, was he not? His beginnings in the clay industry were questionable, but because he was successful no one paid any heed."

Loveday disengaged herself and wiped her eyes.

"I see your point, Sarah, but I still think you're begging the question. Surely I should be honest?"

"When honesty can only hurt people? Oh, be careful, Loveday, I implore you! I can't bear to think of the damage you could do by just a few, ill-considered words."

The sound of scampering footsteps on the stairs prevented Loveday from replying further. The door opened and Sally burst in upon them, waving her exercise book, Oliver a few paces behind her.

"I checked Oliver's," she said importantly. "And he had three sums wrong, so I helped him with them. You understand now, don't you, Oliver?" Her manner was protective, almost maternal.

"Yes, Sal. Look, Mummy, they're right now."

"So they are. Well done, Oliver. And well done, Sally. Yours are right, too."

"I know."

"Perhaps they were too easy," Sarah said, amused by her air of satisfaction. Sally considered the question seriously.

"I don't think so," she said after due reflection. "I had to think hard."

"Well, such hard work calls for a reward." Sarah delved into her bag and brought forth a small box of peppermint creams. "Fair shares for all, mind, and only when Mummy allows."

"Oh, *thanks*, Aunt Sarah!" Oliver's small, pointed face glowed and his eyes shone. No, Sarah thought as she looked at him. He was by no means dull, though there was a vulnerability in his face that made her fear for him. "They're my favourites. And Dad's too."

"Then you must save some for him."

"You certainly must," Loveday agreed. "Now go into the kitchen and have your milk, children."

There was a small silence when they had gone.

"Loveday, don't spoil what you have," Sarah said quietly. For a moment Loveday did not reply.

"It's like a river, isn't it?" she said at last. "All clear and bright on the surface, but at the bottom, on the bed where no one can see, there's filth and slime and mud."

Sarah gave a brief, mirthless laugh.

"Well, my dear; you possess the only stick that will stir it. I shall never say a word. I couldn't bear to."

Loveday sighed, long and deep.

"I don't suppose I can either," she said.

Old Dr Geach died suddenly just after Christmas. His house-keeper found him in his chair, rug over his knees, hand placed on the page of an open book on a table beside him, as if death had caught him unawares.

"He was just as usual when I left un," Mrs Pollack wept. "He was tired, he said, and felt cold; so I brought un the rug and stoked the fire and told un to be sure to have an early night. Oh, what'll us do now he's gone?"

The whole village mourned the doctor who had cared for them for almost fifty years, but in fact he had already delegated much of his work to young Dr Hargreaves who had come to St Ninn four years previously. The new doctor had married the daughter of a St Austell trader – a prosperous provision merchant – who owned property in St Ninn, including the house where he and his wife lived happily with their two small daughters and a baby son.

"And another on the way," the residents of St Ninn told each other. " 'Er'll never want to move to the doctor's house now."

Indeed, there was no reason why the Hargreaves should move, since their own house was equally central, if not nearly so attractive – at least in Loveday's eyes.

"I have always loved looking out on that house," she said to Matthew. "It has the most satisfactory, satisfying lines of any building I have seen. Pure Georgian, of course."

"With Georgian plumbing, no doubt."

"There's a tap in the kitchen!"

"Such luxury!"

"And Dr Geach told me, only a week before he died, that he was going to get the gas laid on. He said it was cheaper than he thought."

Matthew lowered his newspaper.

"Why do I get the feeling that you're trying to say something?" he asked.

"Oh, Matthew!" Loveday came close to him and took his arm. "You know how badly we need a larger house."

It was something, indeed, that no one could argue with. Not only was the accommodation at 7 Church Cross inadequate for a family with servants, but – in Clay Tallon's opinion, at least – it was less than suitable for someone of Matthew's status.

On several occasions he had brought other houses to his son's notice, substantial villas on the outskirts of St Austell which he considered more in keeping; but always it had been Loveday who fought against moving. Much as she wanted a larger house, she had no wish to be any nearer the senior Tallons. And she loved St Ninn, a preference which Clay Tallon found incomprehensible.

"I see no merit in the place," he often remarked.

"But it's home," Loveday said in explanation. "I know everybody and everybody knows me."

Now Dr Geach's house was on the market and it seemed that it provided the answer to their accommodation problems. It was a substantial, graceful village house; a gentleman's residence of which even Clay Tallon must surely approve.

"It will need a great deal of refurbishment," Matthew said. "Dr Geach let it go to rack and ruin. He only used part of it."

"Those front rooms are beautifully proportioned. They say there are two attics as well as four good bedrooms, plus a little one we could make into a bathroom."

"And do 'they' say how much is being asked?"

"No. But solicitors in St Austell are handling it. Hocken & Thomas, I understand. You could easily find out."

"I could," Matthew agreed, smiling at her, thankful to see the brightness of her eyes and her eager smile. Such good spirits had been in short supply lately, a matter which he attributed to the bad news given her by the London specialist.

This verdict had, in fact, relieved him considerably. Much as he would have liked a larger family, he had no wish to live through another experience like the birth of the twins, during which time he had been forced to face the possibility of Loveday's death – a prospect which had plunged him into unutterable despair. Such an outcome had seemed almost inevitable and the death of at least one of the babies a certainty; yet all had survived against the odds, and his instinct was to ask no more of the fates.

He didn't dare to think of a world without Loveday. From the first he had been enchanted by her looks and her gaiety, and the passing years had only deepened his love. To him she was the focal point of a home that provided warmth and laughter and loving acceptance; everything, in fact, that his own home had lacked. The sight of her gave him as much pleasure now as it had done when they were first married. To watch her from a distance stirred a particular joy in him, she moved with such grace.

She was his conscience, too, as well as his delight. He was aware that, almost imperceptibly, his view of life had changed since his marriage. Among the workpeople, he was known for his sympathetic understanding of their problems, his ability to listen, his determination to see that conditions were improved; and his interest was not confined to the clay industry alone. Only the previous week he had enraged his father over Sunday lunch by venturing to disagree with him over the School Meals Act, whereby the children of the very poor were to be given free school dinners; and as he had told Sybil, he was as ardent as Loveday in his support for women's suffrage.

He was aware that his father failed to appreciate his wife, but even he barely guessed at the antipathy he still felt.

"She's addled his brains," Clay Tallon grumbled to Millicent night after night. "The boy doesn't think for himself at all any more."

"Well, I think she's a sweet girl, and very good for him," Millicent protested stoutly. "They are so happy together, Edwin. You can't deny it."

"Nor can you deny that she influenced our daughter. It was a bad day for us when the Pentecosts came on the scene."

"What nonsense!" Millicent said daringly, not quailing when her husband subjected her to a furious glare. He made no other response, however, and she felt pleased with herself for making the protest. Perhaps she, too, was becoming emancipated, like those brave suffragettes.

Matthew had full responsibility for sales and shipping now,

but the size of his salary depended on his father's somewhat capricious generosity rather than his worth to the company. "All this will be yours one day," Clay Tallon was wont to say with an expansive sweep of the hand encompassing the works and the office and the ships in Charlestown harbour. He seemed to think this an adequate reason for currently paying Matthew less than he was worth. Matthew found his father's attitude to money quite incomprehensible, while Loveday quoted Oscar Wilde, saying that Clay Tallon knew the price of everything and the value of nothing. His refusal to buy new equipment until the old literally fell to pieces was a case in point, and one that worried Matthew constantly.

He hated to part with a penny before he considered it strictly necessary; a state of affairs that was only partly ameliorated by occasional bursts of benevolence towards his family. There was a chance that he might pay for the new house; but equally, he might not, if its location or condition failed to please him.

Never mind, Matthew said to himself. If Loveday wanted Dr Geach's house, then she should have it. Somehow it would be managed. Surely no one could deny that it would suit them in every way?

In the event, no help was forthcoming from his father who had his eye on a house in the same road as Prospect Lodge and hoped to influence the issue by exerting financial pressure. It was one more mark against Loveday when Matthew raised a loan and the sale went through without the benefit of his blessing.

Sarah was thankful to see the light return to Loveday's eyes and the quickness to her step. The refurbishment of Dr Geach's house – more accurately known as Church Cross House – occupied the better part of 1908, proving to be of obsessional interest to its new mistress who, helped by the passage of time, seemed to have managed to push her secret back once more into the past where it belonged.

She would forget it, once and for all, she resolved. Sarah was right – she would ruin four lives if she continued to dwell on the matter. Nothing could be changed, and life was too full, too busy, to brood over it. The children were demanding in their different ways, but they were rewarding, too; and then, of course, there were all the other aspects of life in a small village.

Many still knew her as the daughter of the schoolmaster, and brought their troubles to her – their forms to fill, their official documents to explain. She was godmother to the baby born to Maisie Foster, who had married Joe Truscott, a St Ninn boy who nevertheless worked at Trelew. Their removal to one of the cottages in the main street close by the Methodist Chapel had been the cause of a great deal of discussion in St Ninn, the general consensus regarding it as only slightly less regrettable than banishment to Outer Mongolia.

"They'm a funny lot, over Trelew," Letty Foster said to all who would listen. "Still, work is work, when all's said and done."

Joe's mother was even less sanguine.

"Oh, 'tis terrible," she said to Loveday, meeting her one day in the village street. "Livin' with all they furriners."

Each season of the year, each month, each week seemed full of events; small in themselves, of no great moment in the great scheme of things, yet of infinite importance to Loveday and Matthew. They entertained their friends, and were entertained in their turn. They walked in the country and visited the beaches in due season, and from time to time Loveday took the children to Polruan, across the estuary of the River Fowey, where Dolly now lived with her coastguard husband, Percy Varcoe.

This was the most popular expedition of all where Sally and Oliver were concerned. It was necessary to take the ferry from Fowey, in itself an adventure, and to climb the long, twisting hill to the coastguard cottages, standing on the magnificent cliffs.

"Millionaires would pay a fortune to live on a site like this," Loveday said to Dolly as they looked out on a calm, blue sea and dreaming headlands.

"Oh, but the wind do blow come winter," Dolly said. "It do knock the breath from your body, and that's the truth. And the rain! Oh my dear life, Loveday, you'd never believe it."

"Days like this must make up for it. I feel as if I'm on the edge of the world – a beautiful blue and golden world. Smell the gorse!"

"Oh, you!" Dolly gave her a playful push. "You was always a dreamer. Come inside, do, and have your dinner, then we'll take the children along the cliff."

It was late autumn when Sybil paid a visit to Prospect Lodge at last, barely a month after Loveday and Matthew had moved into Church Cross House. Her decision to stay in London had grieved her mother and infuriated her father. Even when, not unreasonably, Sybil had pointed out to him that the resulting effect was precisely the same as if she had married – she was off his hands and out of his house – he was not mollified. It was the show of independence he resented; the thought that a daughter of his was managing to earn her own living.

"Among feckless, shiftless poets and scribblers," he grumbled. "What kind of life is that for a lady? And this Georgina she writes so much about – I don't like the sound of her at all. She's a bad influence. It wouldn't surprise me if she was mixed up in all this suffragette nonsense."

"Really?"

Matthew gave nothing away regarding Sybil's activities, but acted as if he had no knowledge of them. His father was repeating these oft-spoken observations over luncheon at the White Hart one day during the week before Sybil was due to arrive.

"You'll find her changed, Father," he said, thinking to prepare him. "And far, far happier. Surely that's of great importance?"

"The kind of life she leads is unnatural. She should have found a good husband who would make a settlement on her, but she made no effort. Easily influenced, was Sybil. I blame John Pentecost. She used to ride over to see him, you know, and he encouraged her in this writing nonsense, against my expressed wishes."

There was a time when Matthew would have argued against this opinion, a time when his voice might have been raised in irritation. Now the only thing he raised was a resigned eyebrow for he had long realised that nothing would change his father's views. They had been set in concrete years before.

At least Clay Tallon restrained himself from criticising Loveday for what he supposed was her part in Sybil's defection – in Matthew's hearing, at any rate. He had learned long ago that there was nothing to be gained in so doing, and was aware that over the years Matthew's attitude towards him had changed. The nervousness had gone. Half of him respected the change in his son, half was irritated by it.

There was one matter, however, which he had returned to over and over again of late, and this occasion was to be no exception.

"Have you thought any more about sending young Oliver away to school?" he asked now. "His mother is doing him no good at all."

"I wouldn't say that, Father. Loveday takes infinite pains with him and there is some improvement."

"She mollycoddles him. You must surely see that for yourself, Matthew. He needs to have all this nonsense knocked out of him. The rough and tumble of school life would do him the world of good."

"Loveday wouldn't agree."

"By God, he's your son as much as hers. You should make the decisions."

"We make them together. She knows more about children's needs than I do and I trust her judgement. He's only just eight, you know, and a sensitive little boy."

Clay Tallon thumped the table.

"That's precisely what he needs knocked out of him! Why, young Sally is twice the man that he is. Er –" He hesitated, looked up at a pretty young waitress who was hovering close by and smiled his charming smile. His voice, when he spoke, could have belonged to a different man. Gone was the note of impatient authority; all, now, was honeyed sweetness. "You're new, aren't you, my dear? And what do they call you? Betty, eh? Fetching little thing, our Betty – eh, Matthew? We'll take the bread-and-butter pudding, if you please, with plenty of clotted cream."

"Ess, sir, thank you, sir."

The waitress departed, and his expression reverted to its former aggressiveness.

"Think about it, Matthew. Oakby did you nothing but

good and it would do the same for Oliver, but first he must go to a good preparatory school. I'm perfectly prepared to pay the fees."

"That's generous of you, sir."

"And something must be done about Sally's education, too, eventually, though of course it's less important for a girl. Still, she will need a touch of polish in due time. She's the kind of daughter I would like to have had – pretty, and full of spirit. Strange that twins should be so different."

"Not really. They aren't identical twins, after all, and therefore have little more in common than normal brothers and sisters. In fact they are very close, very fond of each other."

"Think about it," Clay Tallon said again. "Exert your own authority, if necessary. Teaching in a one-horse school in a Cornish backwater hardly makes your wife an authority on education."

Matthew said nothing. He was, if the truth were to be told, more than a little uneasy about Oliver himself. He didn't doubt Loveday's dedication – but was her diagnosis right? And was it really the best thing to shield Oliver from what his father called the rough and tumble of school life? Perhaps Loveday was wrong to be so protective. After all, reading and writing weren't the only skills one learned in school. The art of getting on with other people played a major part – and heaven knew, it was an art for which Oliver had no natural talent.

"There's no hurry, surely," Loveday said fearfully when he told her that evening of his doubts and his father's offer. "Oliver couldn't bear going away from home. He's far too young and far too timid. I've never understood this upper-class wish to dispose of children as soon as possible."

"Maybe we should take advantage of his offer to pay the fees," Matthew suggested. "I suppose we should be thankful for small mercies."

"Hm." Loveday looked unconvinced. "If he paid you the rate for the job, it wouldn't be necessary."

"He wants to do something for Sally too, eventually. She'll need a little polish later on, he says –"

"Oh, does he, indeed?" Loveday looked cynically amused.

"Well, you may tell him that I have other plans for Sally. She is going to have a good education if I die in the attempt! A little polish, indeed – so she can make a good marriage, I suppose, like a lady should? Well, you may tell him that I should like her to go to university, if she is that way inclined. I think that she may be – who can tell?"

Matthew laughed ruefully.

"I imagine the offer of help would be swiftly withdrawn under those circumstances. Father is only generous if we live our lives according to his dictates. Like the house. Like Sybil. The moment she went off to do what *she* felt was best for her, he stopped her allowance!"

"Well, let's hope all is sweetness and light for her visit. Your mother has waited long enough for it, heaven knows, and I'd hate it to be spoiled for her."

Thankfully, there seemed no sign of that happening when Loveday saw the family together; indeed, for the first time in his entire life, Clay Tallon actually seemed to radiate a certain pride in his daughter. The wives of various friends had, it seemed, been expressing admiration for her work which was something which he found incomprehensible but intensely pleasing.

"I'm told they're excellent yarns," he said to her, and repeated to Loveday, who agreed wholeheartedly.

"I have always thought so," she said. "You should read them, Grandfather."

"Indeed, I shall make a point of it the moment I can find time," he said, his smile unusually benevolent.

"To be honest," Sybil said, a few days later when she was visiting Loveday at Church Cross House, "I should be most grateful if you would refrain from urging my books upon him."

"Oh?" They were descending the stairs at the time, for Loveday had been giving her sister-in-law a conducted tour of their new quarters. She paused with her hand on the banister and looked back at Sybil. "Why is that?"

Sybil shrugged her shoulders and looked confused.

"He wouldn't appreciate them," she said. "Particularly my latest, *Lorna Alone*."

"It sounds very sad."

"It's different from anything I have done before."

"You said something of the kind when we saw you in London last year."

"I'd only just begun it then."

"In what way is it different?"

"Oh, I don't know!" Sybil gave a light laugh. "It's more – emancipated, I suppose. More a picture of life as it really is, rather than life as we would like it to be – and much, much more ambitious. I can't tell you how I'd love to be able to talk it over with your father."

"No happy-ever-after and walking-off-into-the-sunset?"

"No." In the sitting room by this time, Sybil continued to appear ill-at-ease. "It certainly doesn't have a happy ending, but Georgina says –"

"What does Georgina say?" Loveday asked gently as Sybil paused, apparently engrossed in running her finger round and round a carved flower on the arm of her chair.

"She says it addresses important questions that women must ask," she replied at last.

Loveday considered this statement.

"I would say that on the whole you are right. It doesn't sound your father's kind of reading matter."

She caught Sybil's eye and they both laughed.

"He doesn't care for women asking any questions, important or otherwise," Sybil said. "Unless, of course, questions such as 'Here, darling?' or 'Now, darling?' "

She lifted her chin and narrowed her eyes as she spoke, and lowered her voice to a sultry, seductive murmur. Loveday looked at her in astonishment, half-shocked and half-amused. She had long recognised the fact that Clay Tallon had an eye for an attractive woman, but it seemed out of character for Sybil to comment on the fact. Except that she hardly knew, now, what Sybil's character was any more.

"Oh, don't look so amazed," Sybil said now. "We both know my father for what he is. He'll jump into bed with any woman who offers. What do you imagine he does when he comes to London on his so-called 'business' trips?"

"Sybil –" Loveday continued to look surprised. "I've never known you so outspoken."

"I've changed."

"You don't need to tell me."

"When I think what my poor mother has endured! I don't think he's ever been faithful to her, you know. He's incapable of it. Yet he sits in his pew at St John's, Sunday by Sunday, and insists on the maids coming to family prayers. Why, he's so righteous that when one of the maids became pregnant she was dismissed instantly without a character. Did you ever know such hypocrisy? And at the same time, he's so contemptuous of my mother – the way she looks, the way she dresses, the way she *is*! She's worth fifty of him."

"I know. I'm very fond of her."

"Loveday –" Sybil seemed to hesitate for a moment while Loveday looked at her questioningly. "Be careful of him," she went on after a moment.

Loveday frowned, bewildered.

"What on earth can you mean?"

Sybil laughed briefly and shrugged her shoulders.

"I hardly know," she said. "I only know that coming back like this, having been away so long, I seem to see everything more clearly. I can see how he strives to dominate everything, manipulate everyone, so that they do exactly as he wants. He'll use any means necessary, you know – bluster or charm or sarcasm. He never gives up, and he never forgets."

"He can't still resent the fact that Matthew married me instead of Gwendolyn Penberthy, surely?"

"He resents your closeness – the fact that Matthew does what you want rather than what he wants."

"Such as allowing me to teach Oliver myself?"

"Among other things. Mother points out what a happy family you are, but that hardly interests him. Oh, perhaps I'm being silly, Loveday. Truly, I can't imagine what he could do to spoil things; I merely feel you should be aware of what kind of man he is."

"I think I am, Sybil," Loveday said gently. "I once told him that I wasn't frightened of him –"

"He wouldn't have appreciated that. He likes to instil a little fear. You must be on your guard." Sybil spoke lightly. "Make sure that there aren't any skeletons in even the remotest cupboard."

She laughed, as if she had said something too outrageous for words, and Loveday, after a moment's hesitation, joined in. She wondered, even as she did so, if Sybil was convinced by it. To her it seemed to have a very hollow ring.

The pride which Clay Tallon had felt in his daughter proved short-lived. The review of *Lorna Alone* which appeared in the *Western Morning News* in the late spring of 1909 turned his face scarlet and led to an explosion of rage that made his wife look at him in alarm.

"What is it, Edwin?" she asked.

"Your daughter – your daughter –" So great was his anger that it was some moments before he could say more. "Read it," he said at last, thrusting the paper towards Millicent.

She fumbled for her spectacles and tremulously put them on her nose, scanning the column until she found the relevant review.

"Oh dear," she said faintly.

"Oh dear! Is that all you can say?" Clay Tallon leapt from his chair and paced up and down the sitting room. " 'The door of every decent home will be closed against her'," he quoted. "What can the girl have been thinking of? Well, she needn't think she can come running back here, because I won't have her. She's immoral, depraved – a disgrace to this family –"

"It's only one man's opinion, Edwin."

"You see the subject matter? A young woman leaving her home to live with a man and bear his child – a man she can never marry? 'An artist', it says in the paper, 'among whose questionable circle of friends is a prostitute and a pederast.' Is that a fit subject for Sybil Tallon to write about, eh? *My daughter?* Answer me that."

"We don't *know* –"

"It's that woman – that Georgina Thingummy! You can depend upon it, she's the one that's led Sybil astray. She's the one that's led to this disgrace. How am I to face society?"

"Perhaps people won't –"

"It'll be in the *Gazette* tomorrow, depend upon it. Those who don't see it here, will see it there. And I've told people. I've told them she has a book coming out – even told them the title! My God, I shall never hold up my head again." He stopped in his pacing and glared at himself in the mirror above the mantelpiece as if seeking for evidence of the mortal blow that Sybil had dealt him.

"Edwin, I do think we should read it before –"

"I forbid it." He swung round from the mirror to face his wife. "I forbid you to desecrate this house with such a filthy publication." He was breathing heavily and the finger he brandished at her was shaking. "And I forbid her, too. This is one house that is barred against her."

"Oh, Edwin –"

Millicent Tallon began to cry, softly and helplessly, but there was no compassion in the look her husband gave her.

"She is dead to me," he said; and strode from the room.

"It's not nearly so shocking as that wretched critic made it sound," Loveday assured her distraught mother-in-law. "Truly! I've read it, and so has Matthew. Believe me. You should read it for yourself."

"Edwin won't allow it in the house."

"I'll lend it to you and you can read it when he's not here."

"Loveday!" Millicent Tallon removed the handkerchief from her eyes and stared at her daughter-in-law as if the thought of such disobedience both disturbed and excited her.

"It's not fair to condemn it without a trial."

"But in the paper it said – it said –"

Mrs Tallon floundered, unable to speak the words.

"I know what it said. But honestly, the prostitute and the pederast –" Mrs Tallon gave a low moan. "They are the most minor of characters," Loveday went on. "She only brings them in to illustrate the almost divine character of the artist who can see beyond their outwardly depraved lives to the worth beneath."

"But the girl – the heroine, Lorna – she lives in *sin*! Oh, I shall never understand why Sybil did it. Who wants to read such things?" Pitifully Millicent dabbed at her eyes once more. "She might have known that she would shock everyone. Now her father says she may never come home. How can I bear it, Loveday? My only daughter!"

"Oh, please don't cry," Loveday begged her gently, putting her arms around her mother-in-law. "Surely all the fuss will die down soon."

"Will it?" Millicent looked despairingly at Loveday. "Edwin won't forget. He's not a very forgiving man, you know. I'm so worried that I'll never see her again," she said, beginning to cry once more.

"Oh, you will, you will." Earnestly Loveday did her best to reassure her mother-in-law. "If she can't come here, then you must go to visit her. We could go together."

"Could we?" Again Millicent's voice was full of a tremulous hope, but it was one that quickly died. She sighed heavily.

"Oh, Loveday," she said. "How little you know Edwin."

"I'm a match for him," Loveday said; but so softly that Millicent could not be sure that she heard.

❧§ 12 §❧

The firm of Tallon & Son, founded by Josiah Tallon, achieved its half-century in June of 1909.

First had come the Trelew works which had laid the foundation for all the family's subsequent prosperity. Now, with Josiah himself long gone, they owned no less than five workings: Wheal Charity, close to Trelew; Upalong, further towards Stenalees; Carbarrow in St Stephen's parish, and Wheal Florence on the Goonbarrow Downs.

From time to time, Clay Tallon would venture up to the clay country, just to smell the air and exult at the sight of the vast pits and all those white pyramids and the skips that ran up and down them depositing the waste that made them ever higher. Every inch they grew represented pounds in his pocket.

He felt, looking over the extraordinary, surrealistic landscape, like a lord of creation. All this belonged to him, and all this activity – the digging, the pumping, the loading of the skips – took place at his bidding. With a snap of his fingers he could put a stop to it if he so wished. The lives of hundreds were in his hands. It was a heady thought, and one that provided him with a great deal of pleasure.

He was determined to mark the fiftieth year of family ownership with a celebration of some kind; an outing to the sea, perhaps, for the workers and their families, with food provided. Races for the children, a band; that sort of thing. It needn't, he thought, cost a great deal, and the kudos would be great. It might quieten the malcontents who from time to time raised their voices against him, demanding membership of a trade union, compensation for their own careless accidents, and other such irrelevancies.

Planning the celebration had occupied his mind quite delightfully over the early months of the year. He would invite the other clay barons, of course – lay on a marquee and a special meal for them. Champagne. Little mementoes for the ladies. The prospect pleased him beyond words. The Penberthys would accept, he knew, for the unpleasantness caused by Matthew's stupidity in not marrying their daughter had been glossed over in the name of business long since, helped by the fact that Gwendolyn had made a good marriage to a minor landowner in Devon. Yes, they would accept and they would smile, but underneath there would be a touch of jealousy that he had thought of such a celebration whereas they had not.

Now this. Now Sybil.

He turned from contemplating the pit and the worker ants with their dubbers and shovels and their great heavy boots that trampled the ground into a thick white slime, and looked out towards the sea, grinding his teeth with fury and frustration. Instead of congratulations and compliments there would be scorn, amusement – even pity! Was it any wonder he had cut the girl off?

"You're making too much of it," Matthew had told him many times. "It's a nine days' wonder. It will all be forgotten by June."

Not by me, Clay thought, grimly determined, staring sightlessly at the glorious bay, bright silver in the morning sunshine. Not by me.

Sybil had always been a disappointment to him, there was no denying the fact; but even so the turn her life had taken was something he could never have foreseen. To call it astonishing was a mammoth understatement. She was so quiet, so timid, so self-effacing – who could have dreamed that she could ever have shamed him in this way?

That Georgina woman, he thought. All this liberal, New Woman nonsense! A bad influence. He'd said it before and he would say it again. But she wasn't the only one.

Sunk in bitter reflection, he stood on the very lip of the pit, his clothes incongruously elegant in that workaday setting, his shoulders sagging despondently, head thrust pugnaciously forward.

No – she wasn't the only one. His son's wife was equally guilty. She took a positive delight in thwarting him, and the way she led Matthew by the nose was little short of disgusting. She and her wretched father had played their part in encouraging Sybil, and no small part it had turned out to be. He was perfectly well aware of that.

It was all in the breeding, he thought bitterly. Once a Board School teacher, always a Board School teacher. Why couldn't Matthew have seen it? Set his sights a little higher? Oh, Loveday was pretty enough, of course; that had to be admitted. Good in bed, probably. She looked, to his experienced eye, as if she might be. Millicent, on the other hand –

He sighed and ran his hand over his face. No good dwelling on that. Millicent was inadequate in more ways than he could count, but at least she was a lady.

Swiftly he turned and slashed out savagely at a large, loose stone with his stick, sending it hurtling away from him. Cap'n Noah, approaching for a word about repairs to part of the pumping equipment, saw his expression and thought better of it. He hadn't reached his own particular pinnacle of power without learning how to manage Clay Tallon. This, he could tell with half an eye, was a day for keeping his distance.

There were mixed views concerning the celebratory picnic in the St Ninn household. Loveday was glad to think of the workers and their families having a day out by the sea. There was little enough to add variety to their lives, for they had no holidays apart from the statutory Bank Holidays; and even if free time were granted, only those who kept a shop or a smallholding as well as working on the clay would have had the money to enjoy it.

"They won't ask a lot," she said to Matthew. "Only that any speechifying will be kept to the minimum and that there'll be plenty of food and drink. I hope your father doesn't try to organise them too much."

"He said something about races for the children."

"Yes, well, that might be all right."

She was doubtful, though, that Clay Tallon would leave his work people alone to enjoy themselves, and even more doubtful about the possibility of enjoying the occasion herself. Making polite conversation with the Penberthys and the Trevoses, the Bethunes and all the other notables who would, without doubt, be invited, had very little appeal for her. She had long ago decided that they were a stuffy lot, suspicious of new ideas and critical of anyone even slightly unconventional.

She and Matthew found their friends more usually among the young professional people in the area: doctors, lawyers, architects. Even artists. The beauties of the county had drawn a number of these westward and she found them a delightful antidote to a surfeit of clay barons. Helen Farrar, the girl who had come to her rescue at the disastrous twenty-first birthday ball, had actually married one and now lived in cheerful penury in an old mill house just outside Mevagissey, full of children and assorted animals. Both she and her husband had become valued friends.

The tourist trade was developing, and more and more the local residents were finding strangers in their midst during the summer season. To Loveday it seemed as if a fresh breeze were blowing through the entire county; but it had done little to stir up those members of the old guard that were likely to be invited to this celebration.

Matthew regarded the occasion philosophically. It was, after all, something of a milestone, even if the less said about Grandfather Josiah Tallon's business methods the better. He just hoped that his father's inevitable speech wasn't *too* self-congratulatory, and that people were nice to his mother.

"If anyone says anything out of place about Sybil, I'll murder them," he said to Loveday.

"Oh surely, they wouldn't," she said. But there was a doubtful note in her voice.

Only the twins looked foward to the occasion with unalloyed bliss, and prayed earnestly for fine weather.

"We can paddle, can't we?" Sally begged. "We won't have to sit in the tent with you, will we? Please can we go in the races?"

Yes, yes, Loveday said. They could paddle and join in any games that were going, and no, they wouldn't have to sit in the tent, just so long as they minded what Susan said to them and behaved sensibly.

"Oh, we will, we will," they promised earnestly, and crossed off the days on the calendar as eagerly as the children of the clay country whose only excursion to the beach was the annual Sunday School treat.

The small railway which ran the three miles from St Austell to Pentewan had been built to take china clay to the harbour, but once a year its trucks were cleaned and swept and a small, wildly excited army of children was transported to the white beach of Pentewan.

It was this same destination and means of transport that Clay Tallon had chosen for his works' outing – only on this occasion the train would have to make two journeys, and there would be dozens of wagonettes besides.

"May we go on the train? Please, *please*, may we go on the train?" Sally was bouncing up and down in her eagerness.

"May they go on the train?" Loveday asked Matthew.

"I've agreed with Father that we shall arrive with him in the Rolls," Matthew said.

This was a new acquisition, barely used as yet. Clay Tallon had been determined to give his peers something to talk about besides his daughter's latest doings – a matter which doubts about the car's delivery date had almost nudged from his mind.

"Wouldn't you like to go in Grandfather's new motor car?" Loveday asked the twins.

"Oh, I'd much rather go on the train." Sally was in no doubt. Oliver had waited to see her reaction to the question, but now he nodded vigorously.

"Much rather," he agreed.

"They might as well," Matthew said. "Susan won't mind going to look after them, will she? We'll have our hands full, I expect, socialising with the bigwigs."

Susan pronounced herself delighted, and the matter was settled. She and the children would be dropped at the cattle market, railhead for the small train, while Matthew and Loveday drove on to Prospect Lodge, from where they would drive to Pentewan in the Rolls, arriving in state just before lunch-time.

"It won't be so bad," Matthew said comfortingly, hearing Loveday sigh.

Oliver, who had longed for the day to come; who had lain awake unable to sleep at the thought of it, could not understand why everything had gone so wrong.

It was all right for Sally. She had found a friend right from the first moment they had been dropped at the cattle market. Lucy, she was called, and she lived in Stenalees and had hair that was almost white, a turned-up nose and a wide, wide smile. Sally had grinned right back at her and in no time they were linking arms and were making plans; and once in the train, Sally seemed to be pretending she had nothing to do with either him or Susan.

"Don't worry, pet," Susan said. "There are lots of boys you can make friends with too."

The trouble was that he couldn't.

He didn't mind much on the train because there was so much to see. He had driven down the Pentewan road many times and knew it well, but the railway went through the wood which made the journey seem unfamiliar and exciting, as if it were foreign territory. The trees were thick on each side of the track, and the sun filtered down through glossy leaves. Anyone could be forgiven for expecting a lion or a tiger to leap out on the unsuspecting revellers.

Everyone was in high spirits. Even the grown-ups were shouting at each other and roaring with laughter, and although it was common knowledge that there was great rivalry, even enmity, between the pits, it all seemed forgotten on this day of days. All was accord and harmony – in more ways than one, because of course they sang. They always sang.

It didn't matter then that Oliver had no friend to push and shove and joke with. He was content to sit quietly in the corner, smiling at the sight of others enjoying themselves, listening to the songs.

"They'm singing a fair old mixture," Susan said; and they were. Hymns mingled with 'Shine on Harvest Moon' and 'Oh, oh Antonio', and it was this, in the end, that predominated. Even Susan, inclined to be shy in public, threw caution to the wind.

"*Left* me *on* my *own*io, *All* on my *own*io," she sang with gusto, swaying in time to the music.

Echoes of the song seemed to float over the beach long after they left the train – the long, white beach with the area of flat grass behind it where the marquee had been erected. The sea was blue, sparkling in the sunshine, with a big swirl of green heading out into the bay caused by the river that flowed white, like cream, all the way down from the clay country.

Family groups settled down together and the children dispersed all over the beach, like multicoloured beads spilled on a table. Girls played singing games; boys dug holes, made castles, skittered stones. They took off their boots and paddled in the sea, laughing and splashing and fighting.

Oliver stood alone and watched them, until suddenly he felt a violent shove in the back which made him buckle at the knees.

" 'Oo are ee starin' at?" a voice asked him aggressively.

He turned to see a boy of about his own age, but bigger, taller.

"I – I was just looking at the sea," Oliver faltered.

" 'Ai was just looking at the sea'!" Nose in air, the boy aped his accent. " 'Ow do ee get so la-di-da, boy?"

"I'm not la-di-da," Oliver protested. But the boy didn't wait to pursue the matter. Leaping like a springbok he was off towards the water, singing as he went.

"*Left* me *on* my *own*io –"

Oliver stood and watched him, regretting his disappearance even though he hadn't exactly been friendly. Maybe if he'd stayed and they'd talked for longer the boy would have found out that he was all right, not la-di-da at all.

He wandered back to where he had abandoned Susan, but she was talking to an old lady and her husband and gave him no more than a smile and an absent:

"All right, my 'andsome?"

She seemed to take his silence for assent, but he wasn't all right at all. He felt out of place and miserable.

He sidled over to where some smaller boys were making a castle and asked if he could help; but they only stared at him as if they couldn't understand him.

236

Sally didn't want him. She was playing Grandmother's Footsteps with a crowd of girls and had turned a closed, unfriendly face towards him when he tried to join in.

"Go away! They don't want boys," she hissed.

"But we always play together."

"Not *here*," she said. "Find some boys."

Unhappily he trailed back to Susan again, sitting with her to eat the pasties that were provided. The ox was already roasting, but wouldn't be ready until later.

"*Left* me *on* my *own*io."

The song came wafting across the beach, borne on the warm summer breeze.

"Can't ee find some friends?" Susan asked kindly. "See, they'm picking up sides for football over there."

They wouldn't want him, Oliver knew quite well. But clearly Susan didn't want him either. With a heavy sigh, he got up and wandered away from her.

Loveday came out of the marquee on to the beach where, just as she had dreaded, speeches had gone on interminably – and this was only the beginning! There would be more to the assembled workforce later, after they had partaken of the roast beef and baked potatoes.

She had smiled so much she felt that her face had been starched and ironed. Well, no one could accuse her of doing less than her duty as the wife of Clay Tallon's heir, though it had been no small feat to hold her tongue and retain a pleasant aspect when Sir Jeremy Bethune had given her his opinion of 'those appalling suffragettes' over luncheon, closely followed by an indictment of 'that mountebank, Lloyd George'.

"He'll not rest until we're taxed from cradle to grave and beyond," Sir Jeremy had said gloomily. "And why? To give old-age pensions to the poor. It'll discourage thrift, you mark my words. They'll not want to work now."

Loveday opened her mouth and closed it again, knowing that nothing she could say would alter his attitude.

It was a relief to be outside in the fresh air, and to hear the laughter of children – yes, and the quarrels too, for as was only to be expected with so many different factions, total

237

harmony had not lasted long. At a little distance, a group of boys seemed to be shaping up for a fight, while close at hand two small girls battled noisily for the ownership of a tin can, a necessary tool for the construction of sand pies.

She heard her name called, and turned her head to see Maisie coming towards her, holding the hand of a sturdy toddler.

"Maisie, how lovely to see you!" Loveday smiled at her delightedly. "You look so well. And little Edward –" She crouched down beside him. "How's my godson today? My, what a big boy! He's beautiful, Maisie. Such big brown eyes."

"He d'get they from his dad," Maisie said. "He'm growing away some fast, en em? But that idn't no surprise, the way he d'eat. He d'get that from Joe, too. He'm some fond of his grub."

"How is Joe?" Loveday straightened up, but continued to stroke the little boy's brown hair, relishing the soft, silky feel of it.

"Oh, Joe's 'andsome, Mrs Tallon."

"In more ways than one," Loveday said smilingly, seeing Joe coming towards them across the sand. He was indeed a handsome young man, tall and straight-limbed. It was clear from Maisie's expression as she greeted her husband that she adored him.

" 'Ow do, Mrs Tallon." Joe's smile was engaging, and his blue eyes crinkled attractively at the corners as he greeted her. He bent down to pick up his son who seemed intent on making a meal of sand and seaweed. "Maisie was saying she 'oped as 'ow she might see you."

"It does seem a long time since we've met," Loveday said. "You haven't been to St Ninn for weeks, though of course your mother gives me all the news."

Maisie bit her lip and giggled.

"Did she tell you I was expectin' again?" she asked. "I bin some sick – thass why I ent been down St Ninn. Still, don't last, do it? I'm better this week."

"That's wonderful news. Congratulations! Oh, it's good to see you so happy, Maisie."

Loveday's congratulations were warm and sincere. She was genuinely fond of the girl and delighted that she was so contented with her lot, but the pang of envy that she felt at her announcement almost took her breath away.

Impulsively, she kissed her, said goodbye, and walked away. It was then that she saw Oliver. He had been standing alone, looking at a group of boys who were kicking a ball about, the line of his thin shoulders, the way he held his arms, revealing his loneliness and vulnerability.

It revealed something else, too; and for a long moment Loveday stood, shocked into stillness, all other emotions forgotten, with her heart like a stone in her breast. It was as if the years had rolled back and she was once more in the playground at Fourlanesend, watching Henry – poor, misfit Henry, whom nobody wanted as a friend. The likeness was phenomenal. The truth seemed to scream aloud, and it seemed astonishing that no one else had perceived it. But why should they? Henry and his family had played their part in her life and moved on. Their presence, or absence, was of no significance to anyone but her.

She had, latterly, been aware that Oliver was growing more like Henry in appearance, though she had not allowed herself to dwell on it. Yes, she had said to Millicent Tallon, he did have something of the look of his great-grandmother, whose portrait hung on the upstairs landing; but if she had really been in any doubt about his parentage, if she could have closed her eyes to his small face with the pointed chin and over-large nose, she would have known by his skin with its slightly olive tint, the texture of the hair and the way it grew in a widow's peak. Oliver's might be clean and well-cut, unlike Henry's shaggy mop, but in essence it was the same.

But this – this *apartness*, for want of a better word, was something she had not allowed herself to acknowledge before. She had devoted all her energies to making Oliver feel confidence in himself and his abilities and had felt that she was making headway.

He tried so hard to please, and was desperately anxious for praise, particularly from Matthew. He no longer pretended to read things that were beyond him. Slowly and with difficulty, by dint of concentrating on one word at a time, he managed to get through readers that were not too far beneath a comparable standard for children of his age, though it took considerable patience to listen to him and encourage him. She couldn't blame Matthew for finding the task impossible. Almost anyone would.

Oliver had always been dependent on Sally, always looked to her for a lead in any joint venture, that was true, but Loveday had done her best to encourage self-reliance. She had given him love and attention; had protected him – over-protected him, some said – so that he need feel no sense of inferiority.

It wasn't enough. How easy it was to see that now, standing apart as she was, viewing him as a stranger. How clear it was now that Matthew had been right to query her judgement, how perfectly justified in urging her to consider carefully whether Oliver would not be better at school among other boys. Much as it grieved her, she would have to think again.

Matthew was both surprised and relieved when, the day after the trip to Pentewan, Loveday told him of the conclusions she had drawn.

"I've been wrong," she said miserably. "He must learn how to mix with others."

Matthew tried to reassure her.

"You've given him a good start," he said. "He would have sunk without trace in the average prep school without all your hard work – but now he'll be able to cope with it," he added hastily, seeing her look of uncertainty. "Honestly, I think this is the best thing for him."

"We shall have to choose the school carefully. Somewhere small and friendly, with an enlightened headmaster."

"Of course, of course. We'll make quite sure it's the right place."

He'd look at every school in England, Matthew thought, if it would please her and relieve his conscience. It seemed wrong that a father should be glad that his son was leaving home, yet he could not deny that this was indeed the case.

Why? he asked himself. What was it about Oliver that made him uncomfortable?

It was a question he found impossible to answer. He only knew that there was something that irritated him almost past bearing in Oliver's bony, closed little face, the secretiveness that was almost slyness, his ingratiating smile, his anxiety to please. He was ashamed of such feelings and would never have admitted them to Loveday. He could hardly bear to admit it to himself, it seemed so unnatural.

Poor little toad, he thought now, looking out of the window to where the twins played together in the small garden at the back of the house. Oliver tried so hard to keep up with Sally. His anxious, agonised little face was taut with worry as he tried to catch the ball she was throwing at him.

"There!" Matthew heard him say as he managed a catch. "That was better, wasn't it, Sal? Wasn't it, Sal? I did it right, didn't I?"

Don't be so *eager*, he wanted to warn him; but instead sighed and shook his head. Goodness knows what would become of him.

Poor little toad, he thought again.

It was early in 1910 that they found a school that satisfied all their requirements – a school that was small, well-run, staffed by an understanding schoolmaster and his kindly wife, with a few well-chosen assistants. It had the added advantage of being in the south-west, not far from Taunton, which made it easy to reach by train. Loveday, questioning the headmaster closely, discovered that his own brother had suffered from word-blindness. She had been favourably impressed from the beginning by the friendly, relaxed atmosphere, and this last discovery was the deciding factor. Oliver's fate was sealed.

"You'll have such fun," she told him. "The other boys seemed very nice. I talked to some of them and they told me they were very happy there."

Others were not so reassuring.

"You'll have to watch your p's and q's, my boy," Uncle Herbert Morcom said one Sunday luncheon at Prospect Lodge when the family had foregathered to celebrate Edwin and Millicent Tallon's fortieth wedding anniversary. "There'll be no hiding behind petticoats at Forbridge House. Any wrong-doing and you'll have to take your punishment like a man."

"Oh, there's a way to talk!" Aunt Clara looked reproachfully at her brother-in-law. "Have some mercy on the little lad, Herbert."

"It's right to warn him, Clara," Herbert insisted. "Any wrong-doing and there'll be six of the best. It's not what he's been used to."

"Ay, more's the pity," muttered Clay Tallon.

"I've never cared for the thought of boarding schools ever since reading *Tom Brown's Schooldays*," said Aunt Eveline. "All that dreadful bullying!"

"Forbridge House is not in the least like that," Matthew looked at his aunt with ill-concealed irritation. "We were most impressed with Mr Compton, the headmaster."

"It's not always easy to know." Aunt Eveline shook her head sadly. "One can be deceived."

"I feel sure Matthew and Loveday were not deceived," said Millicent Tallon, her voice so surprisingly incisive that everyone turned to look at her in astonishment. "Neither of them is anybody's fool, Eveline, and both care very much for Oliver's well-being. If you have finished, children, you may leave the table." Her colour heightened, she was dabbing at her mouth with her napkin. She said no more until the children had left, but once they had gone, she turned to Eveline again. "Oliver is quite nervous enough without such talk," she said, her voice trembling a little with the force of her feeling.

"Thank you, Grandma," Loveday said. She had never been able to bring herself to call the Tallons 'Mother' or 'Father' and had been vastly relieved when arrival of the children had suggested an alternative.

"I've no doubt he'll be beastly miserable at first." Brisk and forceful as ever, Aunt Jane seemed almost to relish the prospect. "But he'll get over it, mark my words. They always do. When Michael was at Charterhouse, he was physically ill on the eve of every term and looked as if we were sending him to his execution, yet a week later and his letters were bubbling over with all his doings. Of course, Charterhouse *was* something special."

Her two sisters exchanged covert smiles and raised eyebrows. Jane's Michael was the only member of the family to have gone to a major public school and she never neglected any opportunity to remind them of the fact.

"Well, Oakby was good enough for me," Clay Tallon said pugnaciously. "And Matthew, too. Whether young Oliver will be good enough for Oakby when the time comes remains to be seen. I can't imagine he'll ever make much of a scholar."

"Did I tell you what Michael's youngest said the other day?"

"No, Jane." Aunt Eveline and Aunt Clara exchanged glances again. "But it's quite certain that you will."

"It really was *so* amusing! He's such a bright little fellow. He takes after his father, of course, for although his mother is a nice enough little thing and quite sweetly pretty, no one could possibly call her intelligent. Well, he and I were walking up Lemon Street the other day –"

"Millicent!" Clay Tallon's voice cut through Jane's anecdote, reducing his sister to an aggrieved silence. "I rather think it's time you ladies retired to the drawing room."

"With pleasure, Edwin." Millicent smiled as she spoke, but beneath the amiable expression there was an undeniable touch of asperity. What on earth was the matter with her these days? Tallon pursed his lips thoughtfully, brows drawn together.

He wondered, sometimes, why he bothered with these family parties; they always resulted in boredom, argument, or both. Still, he was head of the family, after all, and it didn't hurt them to recognise the fact. The sisters seemed to enjoy coming. After all, Prospect Lodge was far superior to any of their residences. He could buy and sell any one of them, including the portly Herbert Morcom, the Truro lawyer, with his insufferably superior air and infuriating smirk and his politician son who went to Charterhouse. He turned to him now, expansively hospitable.

"A brandy for you, Herbert? Algernon? Joseph? Delightful as the ladies are, I feel sure you gentlemen won't disagree with me when I say that sometimes their chatter grows a little tedious."

"Quite," said Herbert, looking down his nose. He hesitated a moment, then coughed delicately. "Er – have you heard any news of Sybil lately?"

Clay Tallon struggled to keep the smile on his face, and afterwards congratulated himself on answering his brother-in-law politely. But was it any wonder, he thought furiously, that he inevitably suffered from indigestion after these occasions?

Loveday prayed that Aunt Jane would be proved right, and that Oliver would settle quickly at his new school. Clay Tallon, in one of his bursts of generosity, put the Rolls and its driver at their disposal for the day, and the novelty and excitement of this mode of transport were sufficient to distract the boy from the misery of the approaching parting until they were a few miles from Forbridge House; then, suddenly, the full impact seemed to strike him and he grew pale and silent.

"All right, old man?" Matthew asked, aching with sympathy for the boy but conscious at the same time of an impatience he was incapable of subduing.

"No," said Oliver briefly, unable to say more since he was, very tidily, being sick in his new cap.

Loveday knew she would never forget the sight of his small, distraught face as they said goodbye to him; however, in the weeks that followed, it seemed that Aunt Jane had been right in her assumption that he would settle down. It was not long before his ill-spelt letters assured them that he was 'wel and hapy with meny fredns' while Mr Compton, the headmaster, also wrote encouraging reports.

In spite of these, and of all he said in his letters, his first school vacation was a miserable, awkward affair. He was quiet and uncommunicative, giving nothing away either to Loveday or, more surprisingly, to Sally when asked about his life at school.

"It's all right," he said when pressed. "I don't mind it."

"What about your reading?" Loveday questioned anxiously. "Can you keep up with the work?"

He shrugged his shoulders in reply.

"Sometimes. Doesn't Mr Compton say in his reports?"

"I want to know what *you* say!"

"I manage somehow."

"Have you made a special friend?" Sally asked him. He thought about this, then shrugged his shoulders.

"Sort of," he said.

"I've got a best friend," Sally told him eagerly. "Her name's Caroline."

Caroline lived in St Austell and attended the small school where Sally now went daily. Caroline, it appeared, was tall and very pretty and had a lovely singing voice and was quite the best girl in the school at lacrosse.

"And she's got a pony of her very own," Sally said. "She lets me ride him. You'll like her. She's coming to tea on Friday."

But when Friday came, Oliver was nowhere to be found, and it was dusk by the time he came home. He had gone out exploring, he said, and hadn't noticed the time.

"Caroline was sorry you weren't here," Sally said.

"Was she?" Oliver was supremely indifferent. "Well, better luck next time."

But next time he was out, too; and the next.

"Where do you go? What do you do?" Loveday asked him, anxious about his welfare.

He shrugged again.

"Oh, I just explore," he said vaguely. "I walked all the way to Polkerris and over the cliffs to the Gribbin yesterday."

"I hope you're careful."

"Of course! I'm not a baby."

Even so, he looked close to tears when the time came to go back to school.

"It's not working," Loveday said worriedly to Matthew. "He doesn't mix with others any better than he did before. He didn't want any other boys here and he never talked about any friends at school. In fact, he never talked about anything. I felt as if I were having to make polite conversation with my own son!"

"You must give him time," Matthew urged her. "He doesn't seem actively unhappy."

The next holidays were a little better. He talked more openly and seemed more relaxed, even deigning to join in games of French cricket and croquet with Sally and Caroline. He still liked to go off on his own, however.

245

"That's just Oliver," Sally said to Loveday. "He's perfectly all right."

"If you say so," Loveday said doubtfully.

"He is, honestly. He likes to watch birds and things. He's dropped all sorts of hints about having binoculars for his birthday."

There was no doubt that the bond between the twins, stretched a little thinly during the previous holiday, had been restored to its old strength, though it had changed in character. Oliver was less dependent, less subservient. In the old days, he would have abandoned his rambles in the countryside if Sally had not cared for them. Now, perfectly pleasantly, he went his own way. She was welcome to go with him if she wanted to; otherwise he would go alone.

It was during the summer of 1911 that they rented a house on St Mary's in the Scilly Islands; two perfect weeks in which they swam and fished and lazed in the sun, Matthew sometimes joining Oliver on his bird-watching expeditions. It was the first time they had ever found a common interest, and Matthew was astounded at how far the boy's knowledge outstripped his own.

"What Oliver doesn't know about the life-cycle of the cormorant isn't worth knowing," he said to Loveday.

"And he's sensitive to beauty, have you noticed? Sally's first concern is people – will she meet a friend, will there be anyone for her to play with on the beach? – but Oliver's perfectly happy just looking. I found him staring into a pool the other day and asked him what strange creature he could see there. No creature, he said, just the light gleaming on the brown seaweed."

"Perhaps he'll be an artist –"

"Oh, no!" Hastily Loveday began gathering up the remains of their picnic to hide her agitation. "He has no talent in that direction at all."

Nevertheless, when Matthew bought him a simple camera, they were all astonished by the quality of his photographs even though Sally groaned at the time he took to pose a subject or decide on an angle.

"I've got a present for you, Dad," he said to Matthew at the end of the holiday.

It was a photograph of Loveday leaning against a rock with her face lifted to the sun, totally oblivious of the camera, and nothing could have pleased Matthew more.

"It's wonderful," he said enthusiastically. "I've never seen one I liked more. We must have it enlarged. Well done, Oliver."

"Did you see his face?" Loveday asked him afterwards. "You should praise him more. He looked as if he would burst with delight."

Matthew smiled at her.

"What a good holiday this has turned out to be. I feel we're all closer, don't you? St Mary's must have a beneficent atmosphere."

Loveday suspected that this had much to do with the fact that Clay Tallon was miles away in St Austell, but merely smiled and nodded and held his hand tightly.

"We must come again," she said.

Back in St Ninn, the summer almost over and school only just over the horizon once more, Loveday was thankful to see that Oliver appeared to view the prospect with equanimity, even pleasure. He would never be a great scholar, that much was clear from his end-of-term reports, but he seemed to have carved a place for himself.

"I just wish he would make more friends," Loveday remarked to Sarah. She and the twins had gone over to Carrivick for the afternoon and were walking in the grounds where some of the trees already were dusted with gold as if they dreamed of autumn.

"I suspect he will always be a solitary," Sarah said, watching his back-view disappearing into the woods. "But then, many people are. He's much, much more self-confident than he used to be. And better-looking, too. His features seem to fit his face now."

Loveday laughed at that.

"I do know exactly what you mean," she said. "Even his grandfather remarked on it."

"Do they get on any better?"

"Unfortunately not. Worse, if anything. Oliver used not to answer back, but now he tends to stick up for himself which can be disastrous. Clay Tallon doesn't take kindly to argument."

"Too bad! Does he still adore Sally?"

"Totally. It's become something of an embarrassment to her, though she's never less than kind."

"She wouldn't be." They were walking along a bridleway, trees and bushes on either side, and at this she stopped and looked back down the track to where Sally searched for hazelnuts. "She's a charmer; one of those children who one feels must have been here before, she seems so innately sure of herself, so – so intuitive about other people. You noticed, I am sure, how she seemed to know at once that Robert was feeling low today, though he said nothing."

"There's nothing seriously wrong, is there, Sarah?"

"Dr Hargreaves thinks not, but he's had this strange, nagging pain for some time now and we're both a little concerned about it. We thought we would go up to town for a bit and see a doctor there, just to set our minds at rest."

"I'm sure you're wise. I shall miss you, though. It seems you haven't been back five minutes since your last visit. You're not growing tired of Cornwall, are you?"

"Never, never. Unlike Sybil, I feel I belong here now, not in London. How is Sybil getting on, by the way? Have you heard lately?"

"Oh, yes. She writes quite frequently, and encloses a letter for her mother, just to save trouble. Her father still has a seizure at the sight of her handwriting on an envelope."

"So he's still adamant about forbidding her the house?"

"He won't have her name mentioned."

"Foolish man! I thought her book had much to recommend it. It was far better than all that romantic twaddle she wrote before. There was a painful honesty about it that made me think of her characters long after I finished reading about them. I hope she's busily engaged in something else."

"Probably." Loveday paused and looked back the way they had come to ensure that Sally was still with them. They were leaving the wood behind now and had reached the drive that approached the house. Reassured, she turned back and continued walking. "She's very much involved in politics, of course."

"Has she joined the Labour Party?"

"Yes – but the suffrage question transcends party politics. Keir Hardie supports the suffragists but there are plenty within the Party who don't. As for the Liberals – well, she can't abide Asquith, of course, since he's had the chance to act and has done nothing, and her opinion of Lloyd George is no better."

"There's not been so much militancy lately, has there?"

"They're giving the Liberals another chance, Sybil says. It seems that there's a rumour abroad that the Government might reconsider their position, so the suffragettes have called a truce until all's made clear."

"Oh, how I hope the rumour's right! I so admire the women's stand. One feels quite out of things here."

"I know. It's almost as if we lived in a foreign country."

"Have Sybil and her friend been involved in demonstrations?"

"I'm sure they have, though she gives few details. I imagine she's afraid of worrying her mother."

"I'll look her up when I'm in London. Maybe she'll come for dinner."

"Oh Sarah, pray do ask Georgina too! I simply long for a first-hand report. Matthew swears she must wear flowing, aesthetic sort of garments with no corsets, but I see her as being very masculine, with a shirt and tie, and an unadorned boater, worn very straight."

"And a ferocious expression. I know exactly!"

"Well, do find out. Make it your mission."

They were laughing together as they reached the paved forecourt and the terrace. How different it looked from that first time, Loveday thought, when everything was in such disrepair. Now the fountain was in full working order and the pillars were restored and every window gleamed in the spring sunshine. Her only mild regret was for the rhododendrons. They were as bright as ever but she rather preferred them as they had been before, untamed and magnificent.

"I hope Robert is having a good rest," Sarah said, as they walked round the side of the terrace to enter the house through the conservatory; but the words were barely out of her mouth when they saw him coming to meet them.

For a moment her step faltered as she saw his face, and instinctively she took Loveday's arm. When she spoke her voice was barely audible.

"Something's wrong," she said fearfully.

❦ 13 ❧

Matthew had telephoned, Robert told them. There had been an accident at Trelew – a cable fractured and one of the skips broke loose and hurtled down the tip. A young man had been killed.

Loveday caught her breath. She knew so many of those men. Some, of her own generation, were personal friends; others were boys she had known at school.

"Who?" she managed to ask.

"Joe Truscott. Matthew said you knew him – you might want to go to the widow."

"Maisie." Loveday's hand flew to her mouth and she turned her head away, unable to speak. Helplessly, she shook her head. "Could she bear to see me?" she asked. "I'm a Tallon, after all, and she has her mother."

She closed her eyes against the scene that was all too vivid in her imagination: the white tip with the sun on it, and the men – grumbling and chaffing and whistling and singing, and the heavy truck travelling up and up and up the pyramid. Then suddenly the screech of tearing cables and the sky full of blackness as death and destruction tore downwards.

"I rather think Matthew felt your sympathy and support would help her," Robert said.

She opened her eyes and stared at him wildly.

"But I'm a *Tallon!*" she said.

"How could it have happened?" Sarah's voice echoed her horror, and Loveday rounded on her.

"I'll tell you how it happened," she said, her face contorted with anger. "How do most of these accidents happen? They happen because Clay Tallon never buys a new piece of equipment if he can buy second hand, or patch or plate up an old one. Matthew has said as much a thousand times – has told him to his face that one day someone would pay for his meanness with their life, and now it's happened. And *I'm* supposed to comfort her! What must I say? 'Never mind about losing the husband you love, Maisie dear! Never mind about your two little children losing a father. It was all in a good cause. The Tallons are just that little bit richer because we made do with the old cables, so you see it was all for the best.' Am I to say that?"

"Hush, Loveday!" Sarah moved to comfort her. "It's a terrible accident, but accidents do happen, after all."

Loveday was close to tears by this time, but shrugged away from her, too angry to keep still.

"Last year a man at Upalong lost an eye because a lever flew off some ancient piece of equipment that Clay Tallon had refused to replace. There have been other needless accidents over the years – everyone knows about them. Cap'n Noah usually gets the blame, though we all know he's only carrying out Clay Tallon's orders. Together they scrimp and save and take short cuts. Ten to one that cable was old and rusted. Oh, it'll do a few more months, they'll have said to each other. They have hundreds of men's lives in their hands, and all they think of is the profit."

"Come inside and have some tea," Robert said, attempting to calm her. "This is pure speculation."

"Oh, no, it's not speculation." Loveday's face which had flamed with anger was now deathly pale. "Matthew knows – and I've heard what others have said over the years. For some reason Clay Tallon always manages to charm himself out of trouble. 'Good old Clay,' people say. 'Always a joke and a smile!' But profit comes first, and the men come nowhere. I know he's an old friend of yours, Robert, but it's time you recognised the truth. Clay Tallon's no better than a murderer."

"Loveday!" Sarah's voice carried a warning note, and she fell silent, turning to look behind her. In her distress and anger she had forgotten the twins. Now she saw that they had just turned the corner of the house and were standing within a few feet of her.

Oliver stood motionless, dark eyes huge and watchful in his pale face, but Sally ran to her, putting her arms around her waist.

"Mummy, what's wrong?" she asked.

"There's been an accident."

"Not Daddy?"

"No, no, not Daddy. Joe Truscott – Maisie's husband."

Oliver's face seemed to thin and his eyes blazed suddenly. "Did Grandfather kill him?"

Robert Morrow hastened to reassure him.

"No, of course not. Your mother is naturally upset. She didn't mean what she said."

Loveday looked at him stonily over the top of Sally's head. "Didn't I?"

"Of course not! Everyone exaggerates under stress, the children understand that. What happened to Joe Truscott was tragic, but an accident. Nothing but an accident. Now, pray let us all go inside –"

He cast a beseeching look at Sarah who immediately went to put an arm round Oliver, urging him towards the house.

"Come," she said. "There's some of Mrs Lane's very special cake waiting for your attention –"

Oliver resisted her for a few moments, looking up at her, his face pinched and old, not a boy's face at all.

"She's probably right about Grandfather," he said. "I wouldn't put anything past him."

Though Joe Truscott had lived and worked in Trelew, they brought his broken body to St Ninn for burial, where he had been born and where his forebears lay.

It was one of those damp days so common in the far south-west at any time of the year, summer as well as winter, a fine rain falling, steady and silent, shrouding everything in a grey and depressing mist. Loveday was glad that the children had gone back to school and were spared this dismal occasion.

Despite the weather a large crowd of Joe's workmates gathered to pay their last respects and Loveday, watching through the front window, marvelled at their number. She had not thought it possible that her desolation at the futile waste of life could grow any greater, but now, seeing these silent men – small of stature, for the most part, but powerful, with faces unused to showing emotion – she could sense their grief and outrage and knew an anger she had not experienced before.

"Are you ready?"

She turned as Matthew entered the room but made no move to join him, overwhelmed by the reluctance she felt to proclaim herself a Tallon. She had gone to see Maisie, as he had suggested, and had been touched by the fact that the girl seemed pathetically grateful and had uttered no word of blame, but this magnanimity had done nothing to lessen her own feeling of guilt by association.

She was being unfair to Matthew, and she knew it. He had argued against his father's penny-pinching methods time and time again without success, and was as saddened by the accident as she was herself – which did not alter the stark fact that, so far as the men outside were concerned, she stood with him and his father on the far side of a deep divide.

"Come on, Loveday," he said again, almost pleadingly. "The cortège will be here any moment."

Grim-faced, she joined him and together they walked the few yards from their front door to the churchyard, the crowd parting to let them through. No one spoke to them, though a few nodded briefly, unsmilingly, in acknowledgement of their presence. The atmosphere was heavy with a disapproval that sharpened to downright animosity when Clay Tallon, accompanied by Cap'n Noah, put in an appearance, the Rolls nosing up to the lychgate through the narrow lane that led to the square. Loveday had no need to turn her head to know that they had arrived, for a wordless mutter seemed to roll over the cemetery as once again the crowd parted to allow them through.

"Bastard," said a low, unattributable voice somewhere behind her.

She gave no sign of having heard, but was conscious that Matthew stiffened slightly. Don't worry, she thought bitterly. It's Cap'n Noah they hate. Clay Tallon will soon have them eating out of his hand once more.

Poor Matthew! Could anything be worse than to feel so responsible, yet be so helpless? She felt sorry for him – but oh, he should have fought harder! Even if she was being unfair, she couldn't avoid the thought.

Another shifting of the crowd heralded the arrival of the coffin followed by members of Joe's immediate family: the young widow, heavily veiled, supported by her mother and sister. Joe's mother, bowed and weeping, leaning on the arm of her husband. Joe's brothers, faces white and grim. And all the while the rain seeped down relentlessly, grey as their misery, and the trees dripped silent tears.

"Man that is born of woman hath but a short time –"

The hateful, familiar words droned on, no more than a background to her anger. The waste, she thought repeatedly. The tragic, criminal waste. She stared at the back of her father-in-law's head and wondered what, if anything, he was thinking. Was there, inside that expensively barbered head, any vestige of guilt? Somehow she doubted it.

At last it was over, the clods thrown, the principal characters departed.

"You'll come in for something to warm you, won't you?" she heard Matthew asking Clay Tallon and Cap'n Noah.

She turned, and without waiting for anyone, walked swiftly back to the house. Matthew was free to ask whomsoever he wanted, and she would be polite; nothing, however, would make her accompany Clay Tallon through the small crowd that still lingered in and around the churchyard.

"Is something amiss with your wife?" Clay Tallon asked, standing before the fire in the drawing room of Church Cross House, whisky glass in his hand. Only he had accepted the invitation, Cap'n Noah muttering that he was expected back at the Truscotts' cottage in Trelew. "By Jove, it was cold in that churchyard. She may have caught a chill."

"She was upset," Matthew said.

"It was an upsetting occasion." Tallon put his glass down on the mantelpiece and patted his pockets, seeking his cigar case. He drew it out, offered it to Matthew who shook his head, taking a seat by the window.

"They're already making a noise about compensation," Tallon said, bending down to the fire to light a spill, frowning as he held it to his cigar. "Those brothers," he went on, between puffs. "They're a vocal lot."

"Hardly surprising," Matthew commented dryly. "I hope you're prepared to be generous."

"Of course. I thought, perhaps, fifty pounds? That should tide the widow over the first year. After that she should be able to work."

"No," Matthew said.

"What?" His father exhaled in surprise and stared at him through the smoke.

"It's not nearly enough. That poor woman has two small children. Fifty pounds comes nowhere near what we owe her for the loss of the breadwinner."

"What we owe her? What *we* owe her? My dear Matthew, what can you mean? The young man was careless and inattentive –"

"And the cables were old and needed repair, if not replacing. You know it, I know it, the men know it. They're sullen and discontented – even Cap'n Noah told me he could get little work out of them this week. Is that the way to run a profitable business?"

"Now, listen!" Clay Tallon pointed his cigar at Matthew. "I was running this company before you were born –"

"With the intention, I imagine, that I should continue to run it after you are dead. Well, I'd say that was questionable unless we alter our ways. Times are changing, Father. Men demand more, and rightly. You read the papers, you know what's going on all over the country."

Tallon gave a short, scornful laugh.

"You mean all this union activity? I'll have none of it here. Nor will you when your time comes, if you've a brain in your head."

Wonderingly, Matthew shook his head.

"You're like Canute, trying to hold back the waves, Father. Ask Cap'n Noah. He knows what the men are saying."

"His views are the same as mine. The men will knuckle under if they have to."

With an impatient movement Matthew rose to his feet, and stood looking out of the window, hands thrust into his pockets.

"Maybe they will," he said at last, his voice tight with anger. "Maybe they will because they have no alternative. There's little work in the tin mines, and fishing's not what it was. Many have emigrated, of course –" He swung round and faced his father, his face set. "Which is what I shall do if you don't agree to make some changes. I'm not joking, Father. I'm perfectly prepared to go abroad, and go I will if you don't bring the machinery up-to-date. I'm in touch with several firms in several different countries who would be only too pleased to employ me. I will not stand by and see all this patching and plating and making-do –"

"*Go abroad?*" Tallon roared. "You're mad! Business is business no matter where it operates. You'll find nothing different in America or Australia or South Africa. You can't uproot your wife and your family over a matter like this, take them to some far-flung outpost –"

"As a matter of fact, Loveday is right behind me. She's always wanted to travel and has relatives in America."

His father stared at him.

"I might have known," he said, his voice no more than a hoarse whisper. "This sounds like one of her tomfool ideas. She's never been anything but trouble."

"That's not true! I'll not have you talking of her like that."

"What other way is there to talk of her? She's one of them, Matthew, not one of us. There's been nothing but discord since she joined this family. Sybil would never have left home without her encouragement. She and her pernicious father, anarchists both –"

Matthew couldn't avoid smiling at this absurdity, which seemed to enrage his father more. His face became suffused with colour, his handsome mouth distorted.

"You'll laugh the other side of your face when the men are striking and the pits are idle," he snarled. "Anarchy I said, and anarchy I meant."

"Is it anarchy to insist on safety?" Matthew asked. "Is it anarchy to hate and detest the patching and plating of worn-out equipment, the making-do with old, rusted cables? It was making-do that killed Joe Truscott. For God's sake, Father, profits may be important, but they're not everything."

"You've been glad enough of them. They've given you a comfortable home, paid your children's school fees –"

"Well," Matthew said tightly, "you'll be relieved of that, won't you?"

Angrily Tallon ground out his cigar and threw it into the fire with an abrupt, dismissive gesture.

"Go, then," he said. "Emigrate. Take your chit of a wife and leave everything I've given my life for. Break your mother's heart."

He waited for no reply, but stamped from the room, roared for his coat and hat and slammed out of the house.

Seconds later Loveday appeared in the doorway, a startled look on her face.

"What happened?" she asked. "No – don't tell me, I can guess. You gave him an ultimatum."

Matthew looked at her for a moment without speaking. He saw her eagerness, the dawning hope in her lovely eyes replacing the sadness that had been there ever since the news had come about Joe. He saw the questioning tilt of her chin that never failed to fill him with delight. What did anything matter so long as he had Loveday? Even the remotest corner of the world would be home to him, if they were together.

"Do you really fancy living in America?" he asked.

For a moment she did not move, but her eyes blazed.

"You did it," she said softly. Then louder: "You did it!"

She ran to him across the room and twined her arms around his neck and for a long moment, as he held her close, they kissed more and more hungrily.

"I propose," Matthew said a little shakily, drawing away from her at last, "to go upstairs and change out of this funereal black. May I suggest –?"

"That I do the same?" Smiling tremulously she kissed him briefly. "The thought had occurred to me. It just seemed a bit –"

"Disrespectful?"

"I suppose so. I feel ashamed of being happy – but oh, Matthew!" Her arms tightened again and she pressed her face against his. "Are we really going?" A new life, the lifting of the shadow, the past well and truly put behind her. The thought filled her with excitement.

"Unless Father meets my demands," Matthew said.

The light in her eyes died a little and her lips twisted wryly.

"I expect he will," she said. "When he has time to think about it."

Much as flight appealed to her, it was, she thought as they went upstairs together, too neat and easy a solution. She would be surprised if she could escape her memories and fears as easily as all that.

They cast a long, long shadow, she thought bitterly. They were like an albatross about her neck, a burden she could never shed. Not even in Matthew's arms did she feel herself free of them.

"First Sybil," Clay Tallon said through gritted teeth, storming up and down the drawing room of Prospect Lodge. "Now Matthew. Were there ever such thankless children? They've had the best of everything, never wanted for any luxury, and do I get any thanks? No! There's no gratitude, no thought of filial duty –"

"Edwin, do sit down." Millicent's voice was mildly exasperated. "It's time you took Matthew's views seriously. After all, he's over thirty and should surely be taking more and more responsibility. It's not as if you're getting any younger."

"Oh, no doubt he'd be glad to see me dead and buried so that he could have everything his own way! Certainly that wife of his would. She's at the root of everything. Well, let him go, I say."

"You don't mean that, Edwin." Millicent spoke calmly, but with a quiet certainty that made him look at her with new eyes. Why wasn't she crying? Normally by this time she would have turned on the waterworks – a habit that irritated him yet, at the same time, made him feel superior. Now she continued with her embroidery, the needle going in and out in an unbroken rhythm, and it threw him off balance.

"Oh, don't I?" He glared at her belligerently.

"Of course not. You don't want him to emigrate any more than I do. What have you been building the business up for all these years, if not to leave it to your only son?"

"I didn't know my only son would marry a wife like that, did I?"

"Don't forget that she's Sally's mother, as well as every-thing else," Millicent persisted. "Where she goes, Sally goes. What do they say about cutting off your nose to spite your face?"

Sally! Shocked into silence Tallon rose from his chair and moved to the window, staring out at the slanting rain and the grey sea. In furious thought he chewed his lip. He had not, for some obscure reason, given Sally more than passing consideration, so angry had Matthew made him. But now he thought of her and his heart sank.

She was his darling, his Achilles' heel, the only living soul he truly cared for. If only he could have had a daughter who looked like that – bright-faced, full of charm and intelligence with a smile that would undoubtedly bring strong men to their knees all too soon. She was growing up so fast, fulfilling all the promise of her childhood. Her beauty delighted him. Giving her presents was one of the keenest pleasures he had ever known. Loveday objected to that, of course – said it wasn't fair either to Sally or the boy, and even Sally reproved him.

"What one has, the other must have, Grandfather," she said from time to time, adorably solemn. Well, now the boy was out of the way and he could give her what he liked. His thoughts went off at a tangent. She would like a pony, he knew that. He'd look around, make a few enquiries. Perhaps he could ride with her himself, though it was many a long year . . .

He forced his thoughts back to the present, to the possibility of losing her.

He was at his best with her. There were times – infre-quent, it was true – when he thought about his ultimate end and wondered if he would be called to account for his life. The recording angel could set that down, he thought defiantly. No matter what his sins of omission and com-mission had been, he would go through fire and water for his granddaughter. Surely he would receive a little credit for that?

He let out his breath in a sigh and his shoulders sagged.

"America!" He spoke the word in a voice heavy with disgust.

"I believe there is much to recommend it," Millicent said. "Wide open spaces, and a less class-ridden society."

"I fail to see why either should be regarded as an advantage."

"There are more opportunities, they say. Mrs Trevose's nephew has done most awfully well there. She says he's already a dollar millionaire."

He snorted, disbelievingly.

"Poppycock! That woman wouldn't know the truth if it jumped up and bit her." He passed his hand over his face, turned from the window and wandered aimlessly for a few moments, up and down the room, pausing at last as he came face to face with the window again. There was the round table with the inevitable jigsaw puzzle on it. He had spent the entire evening of the previous day working on this one; now, however, he merely stared at it as if it were totally beyond him.

Millicent's needle went in and out as she glanced at him once or twice. He looks old, she thought; old and beaten and sad. And though his arrogance had often infuriated her, she could not avoid feeling a pang of pity.

For a while he stood in silence, his shoulders bowed.

"There must be no breach," he said at last, barely audible. "I can't let them go."

Millicent's sigh of relief was inaudible.

"Of course not," she said, and smiled as she sewed.

Oliver came home at Christmas. He seemed to have shot up in the short time he had been away. Bony wrists stuck out of his jacket sleeves, and trousers hung at half-mast.

Just before Christmas Loveday took the twins to Truro to order new clothes and complete their Christmas shopping. It turned into a riotous day, full of enjoyment for all of them, even though they had their usual difficulty in deciding on the joint presents they always gave and Oliver grew restive at having to stand still to be measured.

The shops were full of gifts and the lighted windows shone out brightly in the early dark. Plump turkeys hung from hooks in butchers' windows and carol singers rattled collecting boxes under their noses.

"Oh, why doesn't it ever snow in Cornwall?" Sally asked. "Still, even so, it really feels like Christmas, doesn't it?"

Loveday had to agree with her. She had half thought that she would take this opportunity to refer to her outburst in the garden of Carrivick on hearing of Joe Truscott's death, but now she thought better of it. It was best forgotten, she decided, especially at this season of the year when all the family was bound to be thrown together in close proximity.

Soon after the event she had spoken of it to Sally who had appeared to understand that her words had been uttered in the heat of the moment. Without doubt, Oliver would think the same, if he thought anything at all. He might even have forgotten it completely, in which case it would be a mistake to revive the matter.

It was not in Clay Tallon's nature to admit mistakes, but in this case he had backed down. Matthew must stay, he said, and would be given a partnership. He had more authority now and an enhanced salary, and he made sure that though there was no extravagance, economies such as those that had killed Joe Truscott and threatened other men's lives were a thing of the past.

Working practices had undoubtedly improved. Maisie Truscott had been awarded compensation of £150 – still not enough, Matthew had thought, but it had been sufficient to buy her a small shop with a house attached at Carclaze and she seemed contented enough. Clay Tallon had been badly rattled and for the last few months had been treating Matthew with kid gloves. He had even, Loveday thought with grim amusement, forced himself to be almost pleasant to his daughter-in-law.

No; best to pretend that those unguarded words had never been uttered. Best to regard this season of goodwill as the beginning of better times, better relationships.

Among the Christmas cards was a tastefully expensive snow scene from Sarah and Robert, still in London, enclosed in a long letter.

"You were absolutely right and Matthew was wrong," she wrote. "Miss Georgina Burrell-Hobbs wears mannish shirts and extremely serious hats – at least, the one she sported when she came here was definitely not a hat to be trifled with. Nor, I may say, is Miss B-H herself, being a lady of definite views which she has no hesitation in stating forcibly, brooking no argument. Within the first half-hour she had informed us that (a) moving pictures are an artistic aberration and will be dismissed as an irrelevance within five years; (b) Kaiser Wilhelm is the best friend that Britain ever had, though the German people generally are no better than barbarians, and (c) the emancipation of women will undoubtedly see the demise of the fashion industry as women free themselves from the need to please their menfolk.

"Though I found myself disagreeing root and branch with every statement, I regret that I said nothing, apart from a weak 'what about Beethoven?' in answer to (b), such is the force of Miss B-H's personality. Sybil appears well, if entirely in thrall. Robert and I have been arguing ever since their visit about the nature of their relationship which he feels certain is *unnatural* – need I say more??? Personally I am not so sure, simply because of the way that Sybil fluttered her eyelashes at him under the influence of a glass of his best Château Lafite. I am of the opinion that if a suitable man should demonstrate an interest, she would probably show Miss B-H a clean pair of heels.

"What cannot be denied is Sybil's health and happiness. She seems, as they say, to have Found Herself, both in her writing and in her political life, though I am a little perturbed about the latter. As you know, the Conciliation Bill from which the suffragists expected so much was little more than a damp squib, and the truce which held good all last year has been swept away. No doubt you have seen in the papers that a new era of militancy seems to have dawned. Shop windows are broken almost daily and pillar-boxes set alight. Can such actions be right, no matter what the cause? When all the suffragists did was heckle and fly-post and chalk pavements they had all my support. Now I am not so sure they are going about it in the right way.

"Sybil entertains no such doubts and told me openly that she is ready and willing to do whatever is required by those that run the WSPU (i.e. Christabel Pankhurst, who is nothing but a despot). I gather she has not yet been arrested on any of her sorties, though she sounded to me as if she positively relished the prospect. Miss B-H certainly bears a great deal of responsibility for this attitude. She herself suffers from a bad back sustained as a child in a riding accident, and this, it seems, precludes her from taking part in demonstrations, etc., much to her grief, she would have us believe. 'Sybil is my surrogate', she proclaims enthusiastically, and Sybil beams with pleasure at the honour thus bestowed.

"I only hope that Sybil's surrogacy does not lead her into trouble: This having been said, I can only report favourably. I wish Millicent would come and stay with me and see for herself. I am by this same post writing to her to suggest that she makes the trip after Christmas, and rely upon you to persuade her to be bloody, bold and resolute. Dear Edwin can hardly clap her in irons, can he? On second thoughts . . . ! !

"We are having a gay time here, with a great deal of entertaining and theatre-going. Robert's health is much improved, but we have decided to stay on for a little longer and will perhaps go to Baden-Baden to take the waters before coming home in March. No, I have *not* deserted Cornwall, nor shall I ever wish to, but I'm enjoying the flesh-pots, just for a change."

Loveday, coming to the end of the letter, folded it thoughtfully. Could she possibly persuade her mother-in-law to go to London? It was not, after all, such an outrageous thing to do. Other women did it all the time, but apart from an annual visit to her sister in Devon, Millicent Tallon never seemed to want to leave her own home and garden.

She longed to see Sybil, though, Loveday knew that. Was it enough to persuade her to defy her husband? Only a short time ago, such a thing would have seemed out of the question, but there was a new self-confidence about her now that made Loveday wonder. She would mention the matter to Matthew, she decided, and would make an opportunity to speak to her when they went to Prospect Lodge on Christmas Day.

It was to be a quieter Christmas than usual this year, with no aunts or other relations in attendance. Edwin, who complained bitterly of being taken for granted by his sisters, was put out that they had all arranged to visit offspring in other parts of the country.

"They were always unpredictable," he grumbled.

"It's hardly unpredictable to want to be with your children at Christmas," Millicent said. She was looking down at her plate as she spoke, but Loveday knew that she was thinking of Sybil.

For herself, she was glad that the aunts and their attendant husbands were not to be present. Singly she could cope with them; en masse, they were overpowering. It was better like this, she thought, even if unexciting. Clay Tallon, apart from the odd, acid comment concerning his sisters, was in mellow mood, at his most charming. Not that a great deal of charm was directed towards her, Loveday noted with wry amusement, or towards Oliver. Beyond a tug at the boy's ear – a greeting which Oliver had always detested – he was largely ignored, though Sally was subjected to a display of attention that was almost embarrassing. After luncheon, sitting beside the fire, he drew his granddaughter on to his knee, and her discomfort was obvious. She held herself stiffly away from him.

"I think I'm a bit old for this, Grandfather," she said awkwardly after a few moments.

"Nonsense!" Winningly he smiled at her and dropped a kiss on the top of her shining head; but she did not smile back, and without a word slid off his lap at the earliest opportunity and went to join Oliver.

It was then that Millicent Tallon invited Loveday to go and inspect a new and exotic plant that her husband had given her for the conservatory, and seeing this as the perfect opportunity to broach the subject of the visit to London, she rose from her chair with alacrity.

"Do come too, Matthew," she said, fixing him with a meaningful stare, happy that matters had organised themselves so neatly. "It might be exactly the plant I'm looking for to put in the window."

"Matthew doesn't care for such things," his father said.

"Oh, indeed I do," Matthew insisted. "You'll excuse me, Father?"

Meanwhile, in benevolent mood, no doubt engendered by

the Christmas fare, Clay Tallon had invited the children to assist with a new jigsaw puzzle, and seeing Sally's dark head bent over the task, he smiled with pleasure. She might feel herself too old for his caresses, but here, at least, was a chance to engage in a joint venture, even impress her with his expertise.

"It's a lovely picture," she said, as he leaned over the table beside her. She smiled up at him a little tentatively, knowing that she had hurt him. "And you've managed to do an awful lot of it."

"We'll finish it together. There, that's right, well done, darling. That's a piece of the carriage wheel. No, no, boy – what can you be thinking of? Use your head, for the love of heaven! Here we are, Sally. Here's a piece of the green dress."

He had seldom felt happier, or more at peace.

"Edwin wouldn't like it," Millicent said.

"Mother, for heaven's sake –" Matthew's voice was exasperated. "He'd get over it. Why shouldn't you have a short holiday with Sarah?"

"I've never done much travelling. It's years since I was in London."

"All the more reason to go! You'll enjoy yourself."

"Your father would be dreadfully put out."

"Isn't it worth a little put-outness to see Sybil?" Matthew asked.

"Oh, you know how much I would love to, but he's still dreadfully angry. I can't believe he would agree to it."

"It seems such a good opportunity," Loveday said. "Sarah would love you to stay with her. She begged me to try to persuade you."

"I don't know," Millicent's voice was tremulous with doubt. "It's a long way to travel on one's own – but oh, I do long to see Sybil! Perhaps I might do it, if only . . ." Her voice trailed away, then strengthened again as an idea struck her. "Why don't you come with me, Loveday? I should feel quite differently about it if you would. It's silly to be so nervous, I know, but I am no traveller and never have been."

Loveday exchanged a questioning glance with Matthew.

"Why not?" he asked. "I'd come too, if I could, but there's

a lot on hand at the moment. You wouldn't be away for too long, would you? Two weeks, perhaps? Listen – I have an inspiration! I could suggest that Sally and I come and live here while you were away. Father would love that."

They huddled together like conspirators, laughing with delight at their plans. Millicent clasped her hands together.

"Oh, what fun!" she said, then sobered and shook her head. "But I still can't imagine what Edwin will say."

"Leave everything to me." Matthew hugged her reassuringly. "He's being rather docile of late."

It was then that they heard the raised voices, the infuriated roar like the bellow of a bull.

"Who said such a thing? I'll have an answer."

There was the sound of a slap and a yelp of pain, and without waiting for more Matthew sprinted down the passage towards the drawing room.

Both children were screaming as he flung the door open, but it was Oliver who was clearly at the receiving end of Clay Tallon's wrath. Scarlet in the face with rage, Tallon was shaking him with one hand and boxing his ears with the other.

"Father, have you gone mad?" Matthew shouted, seizing him from behind. "Leave the boy alone, for the love of heaven."

Sally ran to Loveday who was only a second behind Matthew, and flung her arms around her, her face contorted with sobs.

Matthew forcibly wrested Oliver away from his grandfather, who, fury unabated, now turned and swept every piece of the jigsaw to the ground.

"Never let that boy within my sight," he roared.

"Take the children away," Matthew said quietly to Loveday. "He's gone mad."

"If I have, he's to blame," Tallon shouted, pointing a shaking finger at Oliver. "He called me a murderer – me, his grandfather –"

"Sit down, Edwin." Millicent Tallon, who had been standing by helpless and appalled, now took charge. "Sit down and calm yourself. You'll have a seizure. Go, all of you. Take the children home, Matthew. I can manage your father."

"I don't like to leave you –" Matthew began, but imperiously she gestured him away.

"Go," she said again. "The children need you more than I do. I haven't been married to him for forty years without learning how to manage his rages."

They had almost reached the door when Clay Tallon spoke again. He had ignored Millicent's instruction to sit down and was still standing, one hand on the table for support, his head thrust forward. The breath still rasped in his throat and his eyes glittered, his gaze fixed on Loveday.

"It's you I blame," he whispered. "You. The boy told me what you said. You called me a murderer in front of my grandchildren – poisoned their minds against me. Poisoned Sally's mind against me. I'll never forgive you for this – never, never."

Transfixed, Loveday stared at him. She opened her mouth, then closed it again. What on earth had possessed Oliver to repeat her unguarded words? Yet how could she deny that she had ever uttered them?

"What on earth was all that about?" Matthew asked when at last they were at home.

Sally had continued to sob intermittently and Loveday had concentrated on comforting her on the journey, asking no questions. Oliver had sat hunched into a corner, silent and withdrawn. It was not until they were indoors in their own sitting room that Matthew attempted to question them.

"I can tell you," Loveday said. "We were at Carrivick on the day I first heard about Joe Truscott. I was angry and upset, certain that your father was to blame, and I said to Sarah that he was no better than a murderer. I spoke in the heat of the moment. I thought the twins were miles away. They weren't meant to overhear."

"Honestly, Oliver –" Matthew looked at the boy with the exasperation clear on his face. "Have you no sense at all? What on earth made you repeat such a thing to your grandfather?"

Sally rushed to her brother's defence.

"Grandfather was being beastly," she said. "He's always beastly to Oliver. He finds fault all the time and makes him go in a dither and then finds fault all the more. It's not fair,

Daddy. He keeps asking Oliver why he can't be more like me, and I hate it. He's always done it, and Oliver used to be too frightened to speak up for himself –"

"But now I'm not," said Oliver defiantly. "And I don't care that he doesn't want to see me again, because I don't want to see him either."

"That's the least of it." Matthew was coldly, bleakly angry. "You realise you have virtually betrayed your mother? Isn't there a code against telling tales at this school you go to? Go to your room, Oliver. I don't doubt you had provocation for what you said, but I expected a little more discretion. You must have known how hurt and angry your grandfather would be."

"I'm going too," Sally said. "It wasn't Oliver's fault."

"Go, then." Matthew sounded too dispirited to argue. "Just when I thought," he said bitterly when the children had left the room, "that he was becoming a little more mature. Is the boy a complete idiot?"

"You're not being fair to him." A small core of anger burned through Loveday's shame and regret. "Your father must take some of the blame. He's never done anything but disparage Oliver. It's too much for any child. Anyway –" the anger burned out and she slumped dispiritedly " – the blame should be mine. I spoke hastily, and I couldn't regret the consequences more."

Hands clasped between his knees, head bowed, Matthew was silent for a few moments. Then he looked up at Loveday and gave a bitter laugh.

"I'm as much at fault as anyone," he said. "If I'd given Father an ultimatum earlier, Joe Truscott might be alive today instead of leaving a grieving widow and two fatherless children to face their first Christmas alone. I must say," he went on after a moment, "I have had more festive Yuletides!"

Loveday reached out and took his hand.

"Next year can only be better," she said.

❦§ 14 §❦

It took Loveday an entire morning to compose a letter of apology to her father-in-law which expressed her heartfelt regret at the souring of relations without compromising her sincerely-held beliefs that he had indeed been negligent in the Joe Truscott affair. The last thing she wished to do, she told him, was to spoil in any way the relationship between him and his granddaughter:

"For I know how deeply you feel for her," she wrote, "and give you my assurance that I would never seek to do any such thing. I have always regarded your love for her as one of the blessings of her childhood and know that she will think of you with affection all the days of her life.

"The words I spoke, I spoke out of shock and outrage, and Sally understood this. I cannot conceal from you, nor should I want to, that I am at one with Matthew in feeling that safeguards were not always considered adequately, but all this has now changed and I beg you not to allow my foolish outburst nor the unthinking words of a boy to cause any rift in the relationship between us which I have felt was improving of recent months.

"I would not, at this time, willingly cause you any hurt and I apologise most sincerely if I have done so."

This elicited no reply from Prospect Lodge, until one day in the middle of January the Rolls drew up in front of Church Cross House, heralding an unexpected visit from Millicent Tallon. She had never been a frequent caller. Though always on good terms with Loveday, she had never lost a certain diffidence, not allowing her too near, never permitting confidences.

To see her now was something of a surprise, but Loveday welcomed her warmly.

"Can I dare hope that this is to say I'm forgiven?" she asked, when her mother-in-law was seated in the drawing room. "My apology was sincere, I assure you. I can't tell you how bitterly I regret my ill-considered words."

"I know, dear." There was sympathy, Loveday felt, in her mother-in-law's helpless gesture. "As for ill-considered words," she went on, "Edwin should be the expert on them! I wish I had a five-pound note for all the times he's been guilty of speaking hastily. Not that he means to wound, of course –" Her voice trailed away as if she was remembering many occasions which made her less convinced of the truth of that statement. Hastily she dismissed the past and returned to the present. "The whole episode was most unfortunate, and certainly reflected little credit on him. To attack Oliver with such violence was unforgivable."

"Tempers were high on both sides. Oliver wasn't badly hurt. I was so sorry for my part in it – and at Christmas, too!"

"I – I understand that, my dear." Millicent looked acutely uncomfortable and seemed to hesitate before she continued. "I know you are sorry, but – oh dear, I'm afraid it will be some time before Edwin forgives and forgets."

Loveday sighed unhappily.

"I know. Oh, what a mess it is! Matthew tells me that whenever they meet to discuss business, the atmosphere is like ice. Is there anything I can do to mend matters?"

"Well –" Millicent began, and sighed. "I came to see you about the trip to London we spoke about. Sadly, it's out of the question for me now –"

"Oh, I'm so sorry."

"Edwin wouldn't consider it for a moment and I don't want to upset him by suggesting it." She hesitated again. "Loveday – please, I beg you –" She paused, biting her lip, clearly embarrassed. "Don't take this amiss, will you? What I came to say is this." She drew a deep breath, seeming to rally her forces of persuasion. "I think *you* should go. Remove yourself from the scene for a few weeks, if Matthew agrees. Edwin is still very upset, but time will help all round, and if

Matthew and Sally come to live at Prospect Lodge while you are away, they may well be able to heal the breach between them."

Astonished, Loveday stared at her, fighting down a certain amount of indignation. Matthew's on *my* side, she wanted to say; I've done nothing to warrant being banished. Yet, on the other hand, he had to work with his father. Anything that might make his life easier was worth considering.

"We'll talk it over," she promised at last. "I wouldn't want to go for too long – nor would Matthew want me to."

"You're not offended that I should suggest such a thing?" Millicent's neck had flushed scarlet, a sure sign that she was agitated and embarrassed. Loveday's indignation left her. It must be a hard life, attempting to smooth the path of such a one as Clay Tallon, she thought.

"I'm sure you have the good of everyone at heart."

"You could bring me first-hand news of Sybil. That would be almost as good as seeing her for myself."

"Not for her, it wouldn't. Truly, you must try to go up at some time."

"I will. Tell Sybil that's a promise. Tell her –" She hesitated and Loveday looked at her enquiringly. "Tell her, I'm so *proud*," she said at last. "I tell her in letters, of course, but I want you to emphasise the fact. I know what she's doing, you see. Assure her that she has my support – she and all those other brave, brave women. They make me feel so – so unworthy! Tell her I do try, in my own little way, not to be too subservient. It's not always been so. It is not truly in my nature, and Edwin is a very forceful man, as you know. In the past I have – but that's of no consequence now. These days I try to stand up for what I believe in. Tell Sybil I know that in the end she and those like her will win through and the vote will be ours. It seems so long since I've seen her, but my thoughts and prayers are with her constantly."

"I'll tell her," Loveday said, unexpectedly moved. "If I go, that is."

Reluctantly, Matthew agreed with his mother that the idea had some merit though he begged Loveday not to stay away for too long.

"How long is too long?" she asked. "How long is long enough? Two weeks? Three weeks? A month?"

"No more than three weeks, if you love me," Matthew said.

The length of her stay was still an open question when Loveday boarded the train that took her to London. She was conscious of a touch of resentment as she kissed Matthew goodbye; had she really acted so heinously that she had to be sent away from home like this? But as the train steamed over the Tamar Bridge any such feeling melted away, its place taken by a pleasurable anticipation. If only Matthew could have been with her, everything would have been perfect.

He had made her promise to telephone him the instant she arrived at Sarah's house. The telephone was a new toy – it, together with a Ford motor car, had been bestowed on them as part of the new deal which marked Matthew's decision to stay in England after all. With neither did she yet feel particularly at ease; however, it was a comforting thought, that she could actually hear Matthew speaking over the miles even if his voice proved to be distorted by the strange noises and atmospherics that manifested themselves over even short distances.

Both Sarah and Robert met her at Paddington – Robert, she thought, looking thinner and older than he had done before, as if his illness had taken a toll of him. Sarah, on the other hand, never seemed to age at all. She was wearing one of the latest hobble skirts and a hat with the crown made entirely of violets, and still turned as many heads as she had ever done, her vitality undiminished by the years.

"You must tell me precisely what has been going on," she ordered when they were in the taxi. "I simply don't understand a word of it! Whatever it is, it's had a frightful effect on you, my dear. You look as if there's been a death in the house. Robert, it's our solemn duty to cheer this young woman up."

"Oh, I'm cheered already, just being here." Loveday sat on the edge of the seat, delightedly looking from one side to the other, enjoying the novelty of all the bustle and the traffic and the people. "I needed to get away."

"Why isn't Millicent with you?"

"Edwin was upset. I told you."

"I could make no sense of it. Edwin flew off the handle, you say, because Oliver repeated what you said –?"

"About being no better than a murderer. You remember – you were there at the time. He assumed I'd been going about slandering him, poisoning Sally's mind against him. That was the worst aspect as far as he was concerned. So my name is mud, and here I am!"

"For us to rehabilitate you! Well, so we shall. Tonight we are going to a delightful French farce – *almost* naughty, but not quite – and afterwards to supper at Maxim's; and for tomorrow we have tickets for the Queen's Hall to hear the London Symphony Orchestra."

"I must buy some clothes. Matthew said I might."

"My dear, of course! Oh, what fun we shall have."

Loveday lay back in her seat with a sigh of contentment.

"I feel as if I have shed ten years already," she said. "You simply can't imagine what the atmosphere has been like."

"Forget it. Erase it from your mind," Sarah ordered. " 'Here shall ye see no enemy, but winter and rough weather' – and I dare swear we'll have plenty of that."

"Are you feeling quite better, Robert?" Loveday asked, thinking him very quiet.

"Much better, thank you." When he smiled, he looked much as he had always done. "And all the better for seeing you. You must give us all the St Ninn news."

The recital of it lasted them all the way down Park Lane and round Hyde Park Corner. They were coming up towards Harrods when the taxi slowed to a halt, held up by a small, milling crowd that blocked both the pavement and the road in front of them.

Sarah's smile died as she peered out of the window.

"Suffragettes," she said tersely.

"They're fighting – look, they've broken the shop windows! Oh Sarah, see how the police are dragging that tiny woman along as if she were a criminal!"

Sarah, much distressed, was shaking her head.

"They *want* to be arrested," she said. "They feel it's their only weapon now, to keep the Cause before the public and the Government. But I don't know, I don't know. I hate the destruction. They slash pictures in galleries, burn historic buildings. I can't believe it to be right, no matter what the cause."

A handful of women, no more than four, were slammed into a police van and driven away. The crowd dispersed and the taxi drove on, its occupants silent, preoccupied.

"How brave they are," Loveday said.

"Brave – misguided, I don't know."

"Not misguided to demand the vote –"

"No, no, of course not. It's quite monstrous that it should be denied to us, but I don't think this will help. Rather the reverse."

"And this is the sort of thing that Sybil does?"

"I don't know what she does exactly. You must ask her yourself."

Inevitably their mood had changed, become sombre. In imagination Loveday followed the police van. How did they feel, those women inside? Triumphant? Fearful? Defiant? She admired them even if what Sarah said was right, and they were misguided in the tactics they used. At least they had the courage of their convictions, even unto prison and the dreaded forcible feeding that she had read about. Even thinking of it made her feel sick.

Her thoughts were distracted by their arrival. Sarah and Robert lived in a typical town house, three steps with a brass rail leading to a wide door with a graceful fanlight and a gleaming brass handle. Inside was a large square entrance hall with black-and-white chequered tiles, and the invaluable Marnie to welcome them.

"You see, you're among friends," Sarah said. "Marnie will take you to your room so that you can freshen up before tea, but pray don't bother to change."

Her portmanteau was unpacked and a fire was flickering in the grate, Loveday found, when she went up again after tea. Poor things, she thought, looking at her dresses hanging in the wardrobe. Really, coming to London was the most chastening experience! Even the shop girls and office workers she had seen in the street seemed to be wearing clothes that were of a different and presumably more fashionable cut. She had not realised she was quite so out-of-date. Never mind. She would soon change all that. Matthew was always generous and had insisted that she provided herself with everything that she wanted.

"Within reason," he had added. "Keep the mink coats to the minimum and the diamonds within bounds."

"I shall be my usual frugal self," Loveday assured him.

Sarah had other ideas, sweeping with her around all the big stores where they sat on little gilt chairs while assistants modelled the gowns for them.

"You realise," Loveday whispered to Sarah, "I shall have to remove every bit of lace from all my dresses? No one wears it any more."

"Absolutely not," Sarah agreed. "Buttons are the thing when it comes to trimming, with bright colours for evening, no wishy-washy pinks and mauves. And the oriental look is in. I think it would suit you."

"All these salesladies are smarter than I am. I can positively feel them despising me! The first thing I must buy is a really elegant costume to go shopping in –"

"French navy," advised Sarah authoritatively. "There – *that* colour, but in a slightly heavier material. A two-piece, with the jacket cut fairly long, rather like a man's tail coat. They're all the thing. Perhaps they can show us something more suitable now we know exactly what we want."

"Do we?" Loveday asked, bemused by the choice that was paraded before her, but delighted and entertained by it at the same time.

Together they bought clothes, visited exhibitions, strolled in the park, met friends. Loveday was included in invitations to dine and to dance, and thoroughly enjoyed the opportunities provided to flaunt her fine new feathers. Sarah took her to a coiffeur in Grafton Street, and she felt an entirely different person after submitting to his ministrations, as if at last she had the right to mix with all Sarah's glittering friends on equal terms.

It was all in great contrast to the meetings she had with her sister-in-law.

She had telephoned her soon after arriving in London, and Sybil had come to dinner in Cadogan Square. She was dressed in a dark gown, unfashionably high-necked and badly creased as if she had hastily delved into a crowded wardrobe to find the garment most conveniently to hand, but had clearly made an effort not to appear under-dressed by hanging a selection of necklaces, vaguely Aztec in design, about her neck.

Her hair was drawn into a low knot at the back of her head. ("Scraped," Sarah said afterwards. "But at least the wisps were under control. She looked rather like a Russian ballerina with a Peruvian father – rather distinguished, I thought.")

"Are you busy on a new book?" Loveday asked her after she had delivered all her mother's messages.

"I've just finished one – perfectly respectable, you may tell Father, with not a prostitute to be found in its pages. I'm so thankful it's done. I can concentrate on my other work now."

Beyond saying that it was work for the WSPU she refused to be drawn on the nature of it, preferring to talk of the family and of news of home. Interested as she was, Loveday didn't press her. She was to go to the flat Sybil shared with Georgina within a few days and was quite sure that she would hear all about it then.

Nor was she disappointed. The flat, situated in a narrow Bloomsbury street, was reasonably spacious, but was made to look small by the clutter of books and suffragist pamphlets and literature that were piled everywhere, as well as bolts of coarse cloth which, Georgina confided, it was her task to distribute so that it could be turned into banners.

She was a tall, rangy woman with a hearty handshake and an incongruously sprightly manner.

"My job's at HQ," she told Loveday breezily when sufficient assorted goods had been moved from the chairs to the floor to enable them all to sit down. "I'm one of the worker bees who get no glory. Have you put the kettle on, Sybil? Good, good." She rubbed her hands together briskly and smiled at Loveday.

She was, Loveday thought, a handsome woman, despite an over-large, thin-lipped mouth and a high-bridged nose. Her eyes were a light, bright blue, her complexion clear and highly coloured, and her hair a brassy gold. She was a little older than Loveday had, for some reason, expected; well over forty, she judged, and totally self-assured, confident of the worth of her lightest utterance. Even so, Loveday thought she could see why Sybil had been so enraptured with her, and seemingly continued to be so. Such assurance had its own attraction, even if the converse was also true. It was almost impossible, she imagined, to feel neutral about Miss Burrell-Hobbs.

"We had a girl until a short time ago," she told Loveday, "but really, it's a waste of money. Two able-bodied females in a small flat should be able to take care of themselves without exploiting the under-class –"

"Doris was really sorry to leave," Sybil said. "I don't think she felt exploited. She hasn't found another job yet, Georgina. She came to the centre the other day."

"She'll find something, depend on it."

Georgina's smile, Loveday thought, reminded her of the shark that someone had caught at Mevagissey last summer. Her teeth were small, even and pointed – and surely more numerous than normal?

"Sybil is nothing more nor less than a *brick*," she said in a low, throbbing voice when they were alone together, Sybil having gone to make the tea. "She has such energy! She'd never allow me to lift a finger if I didn't insist upon it."

"Really?"

"And *tireless*, of course, in her work for the Cause. I gather that you are in sympathy?"

"Oh yes, naturally. Of course women must have the vote – but we seem to hear so little about it all in Cornwall. There have been demonstrations in Truro and Plymouth, but it's not at all the same as here. I saw several women being arrested on my way from the station soon after my arrival."

"No doubt, no doubt. Ah, here comes tea. Well done, Sybil – place it here, beside me, if you please, and I shall pour. Oh!" Her smile died and she stared down at the plate of biscuits on the tray. "Shop-bought, I see." Head on one side, she looked from the plate back to Sybil and asked, with a touch of reproachful coyness: "Couldn't we have done better than that for our guest, dear?"

"I had no time. I'm so frightfully sorry –"

"Honestly, I don't mind. I like shop-bought biscuits,"

Loveday assured her; but Sybil, mortified by the rebuke, hastened to explain.

"You see, I was in the office at Clement's Inn almost the whole of yesterday and only had time to rush home and get changed and rush out again to a meeting at the Holborn Hall –"

"Please don't apologise, Sybil. I think they look awfully nice. I'm so looking forward to hearing all about your WSPU work," Loveday went on. "What do you do, exactly?"

"Sybil is a *brick*," Georgina said again with a forgiving smile, leaning over to pat her friend's knee. "You must know how shy she was when we first became friends, but now you would never believe how confident she is when it comes to speaking in public. Can you imagine it, Mrs Tallon?"

Loveday smiled at Sybil.

"It is something of a new departure, I must say. Congratulations, Sybil."

"Georgina has encouraged me," Sybil told her. The words were accompanied by a brief, grateful smile at her friend, who reached out to clasp her arm in response.

"Sybil speaks where I cannot," Georgina said, in a voice that once more throbbed with emotion. "Once, not so many years ago, I could speak tirelessly, Mrs Tallon, but owing to a defect in my larynx, inherited from my dear father who was afflicted in exactly the same way, these days I cannot project my voice without suffering frightful pain. Such a sadness! Can you imagine my frustration, when all I want to do is to proclaim our Cause from every street corner?"

"I," said Sybil proudly, "am Georgina's surrogate."

"I see. However," Loveday went on deviously, smiling over her teacup, "no doubt you make up for it by attending all the demonstrations, Miss Burrell-Hobbs?"

In response Georgina's large mouth drooped at the corners and she lowered her eyes.

"Alas," she said. "My back – a riding accident – impossible to stand for any length of time. The pain I suffer cannot be described. No, no, I have to confine my support to paperwork, of which there is plenty."

"Oh, plenty," confirmed Sybil. "And really it's the most important part of all –"

"No, no, my dear." Georgina laughed gently. "You do yourself an injustice. Marching and fly-posting and chalking pavements and speaking are vital, absolutely vital." She paused for a moment, contemplating one of the despised biscuits which she held delicately between thumb and forefinger. "Fun, of course," she said, a little regretfully. She wore a brave smile. "I can't tell you how I yearn to be part of all that corporate activity! But still – someone has to do the dull, boring things."

"And there are few who could do them as efficiently as you, Georgina dear," Sybil said staunchly.

"What about breaking windows?" Loveday asked. "That's what the women were doing in Knightsbridge."

"My dear." Georgina's voice was solemn. "Such activity is necessary. Unfortunate, but necessary. Nothing else has had any effect –"

"But do you honestly believe this will make the Government think that women are ready for the vote?"

"I confess I'm not comfortable about it," Sybil said. "Nor about the giving of false fire alarms. That's a widespread practice and seems to me to be dangerous in the extreme. As for the destruction of old buildings and works of art –"

"You cannot make an omelette without breaking eggs," said Georgina, with more sententiousness that originality. "I totally agree with Mrs Pankhurst on the matter."

Sybil continued to look worried but said nothing and Loveday did not pursue the subject. The talk turned to more general matters during which Georgina Burrell-Hobbs positively assured Loveday that the previous month's National Insurance Act marked the end of world bourgeois parliamentarianism; that Shakespeare's crown had been taken by Shaw and he no longer commanded respect as a playwright ("Poet, *yes*," she allowed. "Playwright, *no*."); and that it was a well-known fact that a class of six-year-olds had been encouraged to paint at random with their fingers, the results being exhibited as the work of an avant-garde Impressionist painter and sold for vast sums to art critics who should have known better.

After an hour in her company, Loveday felt battered and

exhausted. How could Sybil bear it? Back in Cadogan Square she attempted to analyse the situation with Sarah.

"I think she must like being a victim," she said. "She was her father's for long enough. I swear she would put her head in the gas oven if Georgina told her to – first having cooked a tasty dinner, of course. As for Georgina's ailments that keep her cosily inside while everyone else does the dangerous part, I don't believe in them at all."

"But you'll agree that Sybil is happy?" Sarah asked.

"Yes, I suppose so." Loveday admitted it with some reluctance. To say she had not taken to Miss Georgina Burrell-Hobbs was the understatement of a lifetime.

"And she looks well."

"Yes." There was a silence as she considered the question further. "She's not entirely convinced of the need for all this increased militancy, though. She's being egged on by dear Georgina. I do hope she doesn't get into trouble."

"Ah, the little surrogate!" Sarah sighed and shook her head. "Well, no one can say that Sybil doesn't know the dangers."

"She was arrested once, she told me, but Georgina paid the fine for her."

"I expect she's like all the others, and won't be happy until she's arrested again. Oh, those men in parliament!" Sarah went on angrily. "Why can't they see sense and give us the vote *now*! In the end it's bound to come, but until that day there'll be untold suffering and misery. Can't they see that? Are they blind?"

"Thank heaven all men aren't the same," said Loveday, thinking how much she was missing Matthew and how she longed already to see him again.

It was two days later that she received a letter from Sybil asking whether she would care to accompany her to a meeting in Notting Hill.

"We don't expect any trouble," she wrote. "It's nothing more than a routine speaking engagement, and on the whole we find plenty of support among men and women alike on these occasions. A group of four or five of us are going to drive from Clement's Inn in an open carriage, suitably decorated. I thought you might like to see how we operate."

"I would advise against it," Sarah said cautiously when

Loveday told her of the invitation. "It's all very well for Sybil to say she doesn't expect trouble, but one never knows."

"It seems rather lily-livered to refuse." Loveday was rereading the letter, chewing her lip. "Shouldn't I go for Millicent's sake, so that I can give her a first-hand account? And after all, I do support the Cause."

"That's as may be." Sarah was unconvinced. "I do, too – but I also feel slightly responsible for you and your welfare. I don't want you getting into serious trouble up here."

Loveday laughed at that.

"Oh, Sarah – how could I? I don't propose to do anything but listen."

"You'll be riding in their carriage," Sarah pointed out. "Why not say you'll see Sybil at the hall in Notting Hill? It'll be miserably cold, driving in an open carriage, apart from anything else. We could both go – take a taxi. I'd rather like to hear her speaking myself."

"Very well," Loveday agreed, relieved, if the truth were known, to be presented with a valid reason for refusing.

She wrote to Sybil saying that as both of them would be attending the meeting, they would see her at the hall; and in reply, on the morning of the meeting, there was a telephone call for Loveday in the unmistakable tones of Georgina Burrell-Hobbs, saying that two seats would be reserved for them in the front row.

"So no chance of sliding in at the back," Sarah said when this was conveyed to her. "Oh well, never mind. Put it all down to experience."

It was an afternoon meeting, beginning at half past three, and promptly at three o'clock the taxi drew up to take them westwards to Notting Hill. It was shortly before three-fifteen when they arrived, but already the hall was over half-full with more and more women arriving all the time. Among them was a scattering of brave, masculine souls, but for the most part the audience seemed fairly evenly divided between working-class women, some with children, and ladies of the more leisured class. Sarah even saw an elderly actress she recognised as she and Loveday made their way to the front row of the dingy hall, ushered there by a young woman sporting a WSPU sash in green and purple and white across one shoulder.

"Good Lord!" she whispered to Loveday as they took their seats. "There's Dimpled Daisy du Marr! Whoever would have thought it? Where have all the dimples gone? She looks like a plucked chicken!"

"Do you want her to sit with us?"

"Heaven forbid," Sarah said piously.

"You know," Loveday said after a moment, "I feel rather bad sitting here. I think I should have waited to see the arrival of the carriage. Sybil would have expected it."

Sarah pursed her lips and shook her head.

"It hardly matters now, surely?"

"Perhaps not."

Loveday was, however, not comfortable about it. Sybil was about to arrive with a certain amount of fuss and fanfare. There were others in the carriage with her, of course, but undoubtedly it was her sister-in-law to whom Sybil had wanted to display this moment of importance – of triumph, even, for it was a triumph that she who had been so timid and unsure could now stand up and speak in front of a sometimes hostile audience. Not that this one appeared hostile. Loveday, looking over her shoulder to see how the hall was filling up, judged that there would be few voices raised in dispute on this occasion. She also saw that the hands of the large clock on the wall at the far end of the hall had still not reached the half-hour.

"I think I'll go outside and wait for her after all," she said to Sarah, suddenly making up her mind. "There's no need for you to disturb yourself."

"You're not leaving, surely?" the girl with the sash said as she made her way to the door.

"No, no. I'll be back in a moment," Loveday assured her.

She found she was only just in time to see Sybil's arrival. The hall was in a side-street just off the main thoroughfare, and just as she emerged from its double doors she saw the WSPU carriage, lavishly decorated with swags of purple, green and white material and emblazoned with a 'Votes for Women' banner, turn the corner and approach her. She could hear the arrival as well as see it, for Sybil was standing up with a megaphone to her lips and a bell in one hand and her message reverberated round the narrow street.

"Votes for Women," she shouted, clanging the bell. "Votes for Women."

A horde of small boys ran behind, catcalling and shouting and laughing, but the knot of women who stood at the entrance of the hall applauded. Loveday applauded too, cheering and clapping with her hands held high.

Everything seemed good-humoured, even high-spirited; a little like St Ninn feast, she thought, when people decorated farm carts and rode in procession and afterwards danced the Flora.

There was even music to add to the similarity. Someone in the carriage had a gramophone and had been winding it furiously while Sybil was declaiming; now the music blared out, and it was to a tinny, distorted version of the *Marseillaise* that the carriage drew up to the kerb, the song which, with revised words, had become the suffragettes' battle hymn.

Two policemen were watching closely from the opposite corner of the road, but their interest seemed benevolent. They were smiling, relaxed. Loveday had given them a brief, concerned glance, but quickly dismissed them as a threat, as all the other women gathered there had apparently done.

Suddenly, in the twinkling of an eye it seemed, the atmosphere changed. Four more policemen appeared from the other end of the street and came ominously close, their truncheons held loosely in their hands as if ready for trouble. The two original policemen came across, not smiling now, but shouting at the women in the carriage to remove the obstruction.

"Can't hear!" the woman with the gramophone shouted smilingly, miming deafness. The smile died when one of the men attempted to seize the horses' heads and lead the carriage away. "Don't!" she cried, turning off the music. "Let us get down and we'll take the horses round the back."

A small, dark figure was on the box, muffled against the cold wind in a purple cloak on which the legend 'Votes for Women' was sewn in white and green letters. As the policeman continued to drag one of the horses, she stood, flourishing her whip, screaming abuse.

The women on the pavement took up her cause, one of

284

them darting out and pulling at the man's arm. Thoroughly frightened, the nearer horse reared and whinnied, and Sybil, half in and half out of the carriage, was thrown backwards.

Loveday was only one among several women who ran to her, barely noticing that the police reinforcements had moved closer. Afterwards she found it impossible to recount the sequence of events. She only knew that from somewhere – perhaps from the small boys who had been running along with the carriage – a stone was thrown. Destined for the women? Who could tell? The target it found was the policeman at the horse's head who was hit on the side of his face, and with a roar he abandoned the horse and came round to the side of the carriage to pull from it the woman who had been playing the gramophone.

The four reinforcements closed in, swinging their truncheons. Confused by the startling change in the atmosphere, Loveday ignored the blows even though her heart was pounding with fear. She bent down to help Sybil regain her feet; then, suddenly, she felt herself seized from behind, strong arms pinioning her, holding her helpless.

Instantly her fear was swamped by a feeling of passionate outrage. A tide of fury and disgust, blood-red, seemed to flow over her, obscuring her vision and her thoughts. She was no longer Mrs Matthew Tallon, aged thirty, come to the rescue of her sister-in-law in a London street, but eighteen-year-old Loveday Pentecost, attacked and abused and degraded in a Cornish wood.

Ferociously she kicked backwards at the man who held her, flinging herself sideways, fighting loose from him, seeing through the mist of red that somehow his face was now towards her, pitted and scarred, with a ragged moustache and a mouth full of bad teeth that roared obscenities at her.

She reached up and raked it with her nails, panting with horror, wanting only to smash and destroy him. She saw the blood burst out in beads, and clawed again, howling like a banshee. It took two of them, holding her with all their strength, to get her into the police van that had appeared in the street as if from nowhere. Others joined her: Sybil, the woman with the gramophone, and the small, dark, furious girl who had been holding the reins.

Afterwards Loveday could remember that day only hazily. The passion left her. There was only endless waiting, and a fearful, numbing misery. And there was the cold – the bitter, bitter cold, so that no matter how tightly she wrapped her arms about herself as she waited on the hard, narrow bench at the police station where they were taken, she couldn't stop shivering.

The past seemed very near, very threatening. A vision of Joely Tregilgas, hugely distorted, seemed to loom towards her out of the ether, causing her to cower and hide her face. How could she have deluded herself that it could be buried and forgotten? There were two pits awaiting her, she saw with a sudden, intense clarity: discovery or madness, and in both there were heartbreak and the disintegration of her world.

She could hear laughter echoing around – scornful, triumphant laughter – and she knew it belonged to Clay Tallon, vindicated at last for his dislike of her.

"See?" he seemed to be saying. "I was right all along. The girl is worthless."

Ultimately there would be no escape. One or the other of the pits would claim her. Or perhaps both. Somehow she felt quite certain of it.

She had, the prosecution maintained, attacked a policeman to the extent that he might well be scarred for life.

As I am, she thought, standing in the dock at Bow Street on the following day. As I am. Wildly she looked around the crowded court; at the reporters scribbling and whispering and sniggering, and the faces, faces, faces. She recognised nobody. She felt alone in the world.

"Have you anything to say in your own defence?" the judge asked her.

"Votes for Women," someone called from the back of the court, and the judge banged his gavel in an irritated manner.

"Silence in court. Usher, remove that woman. Well?" he said, turning once more to Loveday.

She shook her head, unable to frame any words – unable, even, to make sense of the judge's summing-up. Vitriolic hysteria, pernicious disregard for authority, mindless violence that must be stamped out wherever it is found – he had a dry, precise little voice that rambled on without pause, but though she heard the words they meant nothing to her.

"Not one word of regret for the constable she disfigured," he went on.

Disfigured? With her bare hands?

Shakingly she lifted them in front of her, curving them a little as they must have been when she made the attack, staring at them as if she had never seen them before.

He raped me, she wanted to say. I was helpless and he threw me down and he raped me.

"And even now you seem to be glorying in your monstrous violence," the judge said with disgust. "I sentence you to twenty-eight days' imprisonment, and in view of your total lack of remorse, I order that these should be served in the Third Division. Take her down."

Briefly, before she was taken to Holloway Prison, she saw Sybil again and they were able to embrace and clasp hands.

"My dear, I'm so sorry," Sybil said. "They tell me you are in the Third Division. It's so unfair."

The words meant nothing to Loveday. She did not know that prisoners in the Third Division wore prison uniform, coarse and ill-fitting, and were allowed no personal possessions. She could not have envisaged the brutal, dehumanising procedure that had them marching barefoot from one place to another, dressed only in a short cotton garment, to give up their money, to be searched, to take a bath in filthy, scummy water already used by heaven alone knew how many prisoners.

Even those who had been bold and defiant were by this time cowed. The wardresses yelled at them to hurry, hurry, as at random they were given stockings of harsh wool, coarse cotton underwear, dresses of dark, chocolate-coloured serge daubed with white broad arrows and a white cotton bonnet that tied under the chin.

Loveday moved like one in an horrific dream, pushed and pulled and shouted at by the wardresses, the last one to finish dressing, the last one to tie her stiff, heavy shoes, several sizes too big. She welcomed the solitude of the cell, even though it was cold and dimly lit and utterly bare of comfort. A wardress instructed her, not unkindly, how to make her plank bed and showed her the tin plate, the wooden spoon, the tin pint measure from which she would drink her 'skilly', the hard yellow soap, the basin and the slop-pail.

The mattress provided was hard and comfortless, the round, bolster-like pillow apparently stuffed with some scratchy shrub, totally unusable. The cold was intense. All night Loveday lay sleepless, shivering, dazed with misery and disbelief, listening to the disembodied footsteps that passed and repassed in the passage outside, starting at the occasional cry, hardly believing, even yet, that she was in prison – she, Loveday, wife of Matthew Tallon, mistress of Church Cross House, St Ninn, in the County of Cornwall.

Yet why should she be surprised? she asked herself hopelessly, trying once again to cover herself with the narrow, inadequate blanket provided. She was guilty, guilty, and if anyone deserved punishment, then surely it was she. Her sins were as scarlet and this prison cell the destination that had long awaited her.

Matthew, called to London by Sarah, was steaming into Paddington less than twenty-four hours later. He looked pale and shocked as he stepped down from the train, but was calm in comparison with Sarah who hurried down the platform to meet him.

"Thank God you're here," she said, clasping his arms. "Oh Matthew, I can't tell you how sorry I am –"

"What's the position?" Matthew asked tersely.

"Robert is seeing someone at the Home Office at this moment – someone he's known for years. He feels sure he'll be able to pull some strings."

"Can I see her?"

"No. I've been pestering the authorities all day, but it's quite hopeless. Robert says I am to take you home, and he'll either come there or telephone as soon as he has any news."

"How *could* she?" Matthew burst out. "What possessed her to get mixed up in something like this?"

"She wanted to support Sybil –"

"*Damn* Sybil!"

"It wasn't her fault."

"Of course it was. Loveday wouldn't have gone to this wretched hall –"

"You're being unfair, Matthew. No one expected trouble, least of all Sybil. She speaks at meetings like this several times a week, but for some reason the police were out to get them this time and the whole thing just erupted from nothing. It's just –" She broke off, shaking her head helplessly. "I was going to say 'unfortunate', but if ever there was an understatement, that must be it. Heaven knows what poor Loveday is going through. I can't bear to think of it. But we'll get her out, Matthew, or at least get her moved to the First or Second Division. I gather that's bearable."

Tensely Matthew sat in the taxi, seeing nothing of the passing scene.

"What I can't understand," he said after a moment, "is why Loveday should be given harsher treatment than Sybil. After all, she was no more than an onlooker."

"She did defend herself rather ferociously."

"Sarah –" he paused, hardly able to frame the question he wanted to ask. "Sarah, she won't go on hunger strike, will she? So many do, don't they? I'm afraid she might. She's such a determined character when she thinks she's in the right."

"I don't know." Her face drawn with worry, Sarah tucked her hand through his arm. "We can only hope and pray, Matthew. I'm more anxious –" She broke off, biting her lip.

"Well?" Matthew turned and looked into her face.

"I'm anxious about her state of mind," she said. "I saw her in court. She seemed – oh, disorientated. Dazed, as if she had no idea how she got there or what was going on. I don't think she saw me. Certainly she gave no sign of recognition."

Matthew stared at her.

"Could shock do that?" he asked after a moment.

"Probably. But we must help her. I wonder if Robert is back yet?"

He was not, but it was not long before he joined them.

"It's hopeful," he said. "I've been to Clement's Inn and have a signed statement here that Loveday is not, and never has been, a member of the WSPU, and that she had gone to the meeting merely out of curiosity. Philip Thomas, my friend at the Home Office, helped me to word a petition saying that she had been attempting to help her injured sister-in-law when she was seized from behind with unnecessary force, and the so-called 'attack' on the policeman was no more than a startled woman's defence against unwarranted violence. In any case, the damage she inflicted was wholly exaggerated and we have statements to that effect. He has promised to present this for me in the right quarter –"

"*When?*" asked Matthew desperately.

"Tomorrow, first thing."

"I shall go to Holloway immediately. Perhaps I can see her."

"There's little point –" began Robert, but Sarah shook her head at him.

"Let him go," she said. "He feels he must."

It was late when he returned and he looked exhausted.

"You were right," he said as he lay back in an armchair, his eyes closed. "I got nowhere. But at least I was *there*! Perhaps she was aware of it, in some remote part of that terrible building."

"Tomorrow will see some action, I'm sure," Robert said, handing him a glass of brandy. "Get that down you, then try to sleep."

"Sleep!" Matthew laughed mirthlessly. "There's not much hope of that."

"You'll need all your strength for tomorrow," Sarah said.

Loveday dreamed. She was a girl again, walking up the lane towards the schoolhouse under a blue sky, with primroses in the hedgerows and birds singing. Someone was waiting for her just beyond the turn of the road and with a sudden surge of joy, she knew quite certainly that it was her father who waited and that he was not dead at all – had never been dead.

And all the sadness, all the fear – that had never happened either. She was free; free of prison, free of guilt. Joely Tregilgas hadn't attacked her, the children were Matthew's after all, she was not in prison –

A voice, shouting in protest, echoed hollowly through her dream and she was awake on the instant. For a moment the dream held her captive. It was still dark. Then, suddenly, there was a great clamour – a ringing of bells, heavy footsteps, shouts. The light was turned on and she saw the reality; the dingy cell, the small barred window, and hanging on a nail, the disc of yellow cotton bearing the number twenty-one.

That's what she was now; not Loveday Tallon, but No. 21, and as such she was required to wash in the little basin, dress in the hateful garments, emerge from the cell to empty the slops at the shout of command, roll up her bedding, clean and polish the tins with the scrap of torn rag provided and brick dust scraped from the floor.

Breakfast was thin gruel, poured into the tin measure, and a hunk of bread. She couldn't eat it.

"One of those, eh?" said the wardress, coming into her cell a little later, bringing a sheet for her to hem.

Loveday looked at her dumbly. She had not eaten because to do so would have made her sick, not for any other reason. The woman's words made no sense to her. She had forgotten that there were such things as hunger strikers. Nothing seemed real. Her life seemed to have narrowed down to nothing more than the need to take one breath after another.

Chapel came later, and numerous inspections: a doctor; the governor and matron; a visiting magistrate. They were announced by the wardress, but none gave her more than a cursory glance, passing by along the passage in silence. Perhaps they were phantoms, she thought. Perhaps she was a phantom.

It was afternoon, the light fading, before a wardress came and with no word of explanation ordered her out of her cell, along the corridor and down some steps.

"In there," she said, with a jerk of her head. "You're one of the lucky ones."

"What?" Uncomprehending, Loveday stared at her.

"Go on in. A friend's waiting for you."

Uncertainly Loveday turned the knob and opened the door. She found herself in a bare room with dark, discoloured walls furnished only with a wooden table and two straight chairs. Rising from one of them, to her astonishment, was Sarah, her arms held wide, her expression reflecting the shock she had received at the sight of Loveday in her prison clothes.

I am dreaming again, Loveday thought, not moving from

the threshold. I shall wake at any moment to find myself back in the cell.

"Oh Loveday, my dear –" Sarah stepped towards her and took her in her arms. "My poor darling, what have they done to you?"

"Sarah, is it really you?"

"I've come to take you home."

"I don't believe it!"

"It's true. The sentence has been set aside. Look, I have your clothes here –"

Loveday buried her face in her hands. She was trembling, Sarah saw, and crying weakly.

"Come, let me help you," Sarah urged her. "Let's take these horrid things off. Matthew's waiting for you below. I was the only one they would allow upstairs. Come," she went on, growing even more concerned, certain now that Loveday was suffering from some mental shock or breakdown. "You're coming home, and we're going to look after you and pamper you and make you well again. It's all over, Loveday."

Loveday lowered her hands. There was something strange about her eyes, Sarah thought. They looked unfocused, as if the spirit had gone from them. She shook her head.

"No," she whispered. "I can't ever escape. They're waiting for me, just round the bend of the road. I thought it was Papa, but it wasn't."

"Come," Sarah said again, more gently than ever. And with infinite compassion reached to untie the cap.

15

Soft pillows, the scent of hot-house flowers, whispering voices, the pattering of rain against the window-pane. Loveday was aware of them, but in the grip of a lassitude such as she had never known before, she did not move – could not move. Her eyelids were too heavy to lift, words too cumbersome to be spoken. She was wrapped in cotton wool, insulated against anything that was happening in the room beyond the bed.

"I don't know what to do."

Matthew's voice – muted, desperate.

You must leave me, she wanted to say. I am not fit. But she was too tired to speak, too tired to listen for Sarah's whispered reply.

She was floating; floating on air, floating on cotton wool, layers and layers of it like fleecy clouds. Not happy, not unhappy.

"She hasn't stirred," she heard Matthew say, his voice a little closer now.

"She's sleeping away the shock."

"I can't understand –" Matthew went on; but she heard no more, did not even wonder what he couldn't understand, just drifted away away away, sinking deeper and deeper into sleep.

"All over the papers," Clay Tallon said tightly. "The *Western Morning News, The West Briton*. Look at it – 'Clay Owner's Wife Arrested – Mrs Matthew Tallon in Holloway'! I thought I'd plumbed the depths with all that book scandal, but there seems to be no end to the disgrace, no end to what my family inflicts on me. How the devil did they get hold of it?"

"I suppose it's their job to get hold of such things," Millicent said. "It's not such a disgrace, Edwin – in fact some would say quite the reverse. I can't see why you're in such a state. After all, poor Loveday isn't there because she's a common criminal. You'd be better off worrying about how she's getting on instead of what people will think. It must have been simply frightful for the poor girl."

"She's got enough people worrying about her. Five days, Matthew's been up there –"

"You know what he told us on the telephone. She's ill. He has to stay."

"She's got Sarah Morrow and all her flunkeys dancing attendance. Matthew's needed down here. All hell is about to break loose."

Millicent opened her mouth and closed it again, but she gave him an exasperated look before bending once more to her sewing. She was mending one of Sally's pinafores, torn in an encounter with one of the bushes in the garden, taking pride in her small, neat stitches. She felt delightfully purposeful, having a child about the house again, with proper, useful sewing to be done instead of the everlasting embroidery.

"One meeting in the Public Rooms hardly constitutes hell in my opinion," she said.

Edwin rattled the paper in annoyance.

"Straws in the wind, my dear Millicent. Straws in the wind," he said. "A year or so ago the clayworkers would have had more fear for their jobs than to attend a union meeting. I'll not have it, and it's no use their thinking I will. I propose to visit the pits and tell them so."

Millicent's hand froze in mid-air for a second before she continued with her work.

"It might," she said almost casually, "be politic to wait for Matthew's return. It's possible that he might have a more diplomatic approach."

Her husband lowered the paper and glared at her over the top of it.

"You're saying I'm not capable of handling this?"

"I'm saying he's closer to the men."

"Nonsense, Millicent! They like me. I've always got on well with them."

"Things are different now. Matthew understands their way of thinking."

"Ha!" Clay Tallon went back to his reading. "Instructed by his jailbird of a wife, I suppose."

Millicent shook her head at him disapprovingly.

"Oh, really, Edwin!"

"Well, it's true, isn't it? Why he couldn't have married someone more – well, someone more like you, I will never know. You would never have got yourself in prison, would you?"

"I might have done. Under the same circumstances."

"Nonsense, Millicent. You were always much too –" He hesitated.

"Ineffective?" Millicent said.

"No no, of course not. Too much of a lady."

Millicent gave a small, acid smile, knowing that her own suggestion was nearer the mark.

"Sybil was arrested too, you know, even if her treatment wasn't so harsh."

"I will not have that girl's name mentioned in this house."

"She is still our daughter, and I admire her for the stand she's taking."

"Well, at least the papers have ignored her on this occasion, I'm glad to say. Not that it's a great deal of comfort, with these photographs spread all over the place."

"They're the fiftieth-anniversary photographs, aren't they? The papers must have had them in the archives. You were glad enough to see them then."

Angrily Tallon threw the paper aside.

"Well, I'm *not* glad to see them now. I'm totally appalled by the whole incident. And equally appalled that Matthew seems to find it necessary to hover by his wife's bedside when there's work to be done here." Restlessly he rose from his chair and stood for a moment rocking from heel to toe, apparently undecided what to do next.

"Where's Sally?" he asked abruptly.

"Up in her room, I think. She said she was going to write to her mother."

Tallon pursed his lips and nodded, appearing to hover on the brink of a decision. Then he smiled.

"I'll go and find her," he said. "She can help me with the jigsaw. One more effort and we shall have finished it."

"But Edwin —" began Millicent, then fell silent, shaking her head. He had gone, and no words of hers could stop him.

"She's going to be all right," Sarah assured him. "She's awake now, and fully conscious."

"But so strange." Matthew looked distraught.

"It's shock. The doctor is convinced that with love and care she will be back to normal quite soon. You must give her time."

"She kept talking of a road and a pit. A claypit, do you think? And what road? I don't know what she meant. Something — or maybe someone — was waiting for her just around a bend, she said, and she couldn't avoid it. The thought seemed to upset her. Sarah, are you sure that doctor knows what he's talking about?"

"Dr Aynsworth is the chief authority on such things, I promise you. We could get no one better."

"I want to take her home."

"Not yet, Matthew. Please, not yet. There may be no one better than Dr Hargreaves for measles and whooping cough and broken legs, but this is something different."

"You said all she needed was love and care."

"Not all. She needs expert attention, too."

"But surely, in her own home, with her own family and her possessions around her —"

"She's not fit to travel yet, and may not be for some time."

"But I can't stay here for much longer."

"There's no point in your doing so. Though it seems like it sometimes, Cornwall isn't the other end of the earth. You can come up from time to time —"

"From time to time! My God!" Matthew looked at her wildly. "How long will it be before she's well?"

"You heard what Dr Aynsworth said." Sarah spoke patiently and with infinite compassion. "Such things are impossible to forecast, but with love and care she *will* get better. Hold on to that, Matthew. Meantime she is as well

296

off here as anywhere – better, for Dr Aynsworth is within call and I am here to nurse her myself."

"And I am to leave her?"

"I think it makes sense. You can do very little here –"

"I can support her. Let her know I love her."

"You can telephone –"

"I hate the damned thing! Half the time it's impossible to hear properly, or one's cut off in mid-sentence. And *all* the time one's conscious of the wretched woman at the exchange in St Austell noting every word. It wouldn't surprise me at all if the local papers got wind of it from her. Father's furious."

"No doubt," Sarah agreed, adding as if the mention of Clay Tallon had reminded her: "Matthew, whatever you do, you should see Sybil before you leave London. She's out of prison now."

"I don't know that I can bring myself to. It's she that brought all this on us."

"That's grossly unfair. Loveday went of her own free will as much to satisfy your mother's curiosity as her own, and no one could have foreseen the outcome."

Distractedly Matthew sighed and ran his fingers through his hair.

"Oh, very well," he said. "You're right, of course."

He went to see his sister the next day and reported her none the worse for her prison sentence and more than ever determined to continue with her campaigning.

"She agrees with you that I should go home," he said. "She had a letter from Mother only yesterday, worried to death about the situation. It seems that Father is taking this union business very seriously and proposes to use strong-arm tactics to force the men to drop the idea. He's panicking, she says." He shook his head hopelessly. "It won't do, Sarah. They're in a mood to stand their ground and he'll precipitate a strike as sure as eggs. I can't understand why he can't see it. The whole country is going through an unprecedented time of upheaval. We've had miners' strikes, dock strikes, every sort of strike. Why should he think the clay industry will escape?"

"Go," Sarah said urgently. "You're needed there far more than here at the moment. All Loveday needs is rest – the doctor has said so, and it's true. You can come as often as you please and can write every day, and I feel certain she will understand."

"Well –" Still Matthew hesitated. He sighed deeply. "I can't tell you how I hate the thought of leaving her, but perhaps you're right. I feel so useless here, so completely surplus to requirements. I'll go tomorrow and come back –" He thought for a moment. "Not this weekend but the one after. Now I'll go and try to explain it all to her."

Loveday listened to him, passive as ever.

"Darling, you do understand?" he asked urgently. "I'm needed urgently at home, and there's nothing much I can do for you here. Promise me you understand."

"Of course. You must go. The road –"

"What about the road?" Matthew asked as she seemed to hesitate. But she shook her head, frowning, and did not answer.

Sarah was brushing her hair the following day, soon after Matthew's departure, when she noticed, to her great distress, that tears were slipping silently down Loveday's cheeks.

"Oh darling, what is it?" she asked, putting the brush down and bending to clasp Loveday in her arms.

"He hates me," Loveday whispered, so quietly that Sarah could barely hear her.

"Hates you? Who?"

"Matthew – who else?"

"What? Matthew? Don't be silly, darling. He adores you. He always has and always will."

"He's gone –"

"Only because he had to get back to his work. You understand that, surely? He explained everything to you." Tenderly Sarah wiped her tears away. "There, there, my love, you mustn't upset yourself over such a foolish idea."

"He's disappeared round the bend of the road where I can't see him."

"He's gone to St Austell and he'll be back in ten days. He loves you."

"He loves me?" There was a dawning, disbelieving hope in her eyes. "In spite of everything?"

"Of course."

There was silence for a moment, a silence in which Sarah continued to hold her, and when Loveday spoke again she sounded normal, even carefree.

"What a relief!" she said. "Such a relief, after all these years. I thought he would hate me –"

"Loveday?" Sarah drew away from her a little and looked anxiously into her face. With a sinking of her heart she realised that she had been mistaken. The voice might sound normal but it was only a delusion. "Loveday?" she said again.

Loveday gave a breathless little laugh.

"Around the bend of the road he can see everything," she said. "He knows it all now."

"I don't understand, darling."

Uncertainty clouded her expression again.

"He knows," she said, almost fretfully. "All about –" she paused before adding on a dying note: "everything."

Sarah was silent, but in her silence Loveday read the truth.

"Doesn't he?" she asked. "Doesn't he know? Didn't I tell him? I thought I did – oh God!" She buried her face in her hands and began to cry again. "I thought he knew. I thought he knew and still loved me and that I was on the other side of it."

For a moment Sarah watched her, stroking her hair, her face bleak with pity and regret.

"And I thought the past was dead and gone," she said. "You have seemed happy for so long."

Loveday stared up at her, then shook her head – slowly at first then faster and faster as if she would shake herself free of the guilt that had plagued her.

"Oh, what am I to do?" she cried piteously, tears spilling uncontrollably from her lovely eyes. "Help me, help me, help me!"

But Sarah, her heart wrenched with pity, could say nothing. For the first time she wondered if, perhaps, she had not already helped too much.

The farmhouse was in a lonely place, down a long rutted lane with nothing but an empty expanse of moorland to be seen between the high hedges to right and to left.

" 'Tis the last place God made," Ellen Kelynack grumbled

to her mother whenever she went back home to Bodmin. "I might as well be dead and buried, never seeing no one but that long streak o' misery, with 'is face like a poor lemon. He'm sour as sap, I'm telling ee, and taisy as a snake."

"Well, you stick to it, girl," her mother said. "Work don't grow on trees."

" 'Tis driving me some daft, Ma! Measures out the lamp oil, 'e does, and counts out the slices on a side of bacon, and never a smile or a kind word –"

"Poor soul, too. Didn't un lose 'is wife no more than three months back? 'E's grievin', thass the truth of it. Where's your Christian charity?"

"Charity? Huh!" Ellen turned her eyes to heaven. "That un dun't know the meaning of the word. 'E'd not give a cup o' water to a dying beggar. Mean as dirt, 'e is."

"Careful, maybe," her mother suggested; but Ellen would have none of it.

"Mean," she said. "Mean, mean, mean. I'll see this month out but not one minute more. A girl could die there and no one would know. I'm young, Ma! Sixteen! I want a bit o' life, a bit o' fun, not to be buried alive in the middle o' Bodmin Moor."

She wouldn't tell the old buzzard though, she thought, as she walked the five miles down the lane to the farm, having been set down on the main road by an obliging neighbour. Not till after he'd paid her at the end of the month. Only ten more days to go; well, she'd put up with three months. She could manage ten more days.

It wasn't the work she minded. Only the loneliness; the lack of any kind of companionship apart from the old buzzard – and what sort of companionship was that, with him out in the fields all day and never so much as a kind word when he was at home? She'd look for something in town, she resolved; or anyway, close to a village. Anywhere so long as there was another human with a smiling face with whom she could pass the time of day.

"You'm cheerful," said the old buzzard when she got home, making it sound like an accusation. She didn't tell him why. Ten more days, she thought.

It was on the seventh that the stranger came to the door

She had heard the old collie bitch barking, but had taken no notice for she'd been restless lately. She'd got puppies in the barn and seemed as worried by them as any human with too many fractious children.

She had just taken a tray of pasties from the oven and had put them on the table when she looked up and there he was, looking over the top half of the stable-type door that led into the back yard.

"Where did ee spring from?" she asked, startled but not unduly worried. The man didn't answer, but stood there, grinning at her. She didn't much like the look of him, on second thoughts. He was unkempt and dirty; but at least he was alive. At least he was human. "Master's out," she said. "Gone to market."

"They pasties smell a treat."

"Well, you can't 'ave un, not without the master says so. 'E d'count every morsel goes in and goes out this kitchen."

"You'm a tasty morsel yourself, my bird. I d'dearly like maids with yellow 'air and a bit o' shape to un."

Ellen tossed her head, not displeased.

"Give over! What do ee want, anyway? 'Ave ee come for one o' they pups?"

"Naw." The stranger reached over and unlatched the door, still with the grin on his face. "Give I a cup o' tea, my bird. I'm some parched."

Human or not, she didn't like him, Ellen decided. There was a nasty, sly look about him, and she'd swear he hadn't seen soap and water for a month of Sundays. Still, he was parched, he said. *She* wouldn't be like the old buzzard, not willing to give so much as the time of day.

"You can 'ave some tea, but keep out o' my kitchen," she said. "The master wouldn't like it."

"But the master ent 'ere, is un?" Laughing softly, the man came inside.

"Keep out! You'm trackin' mud."

"Bugger the mud." Well inside now, he reached out with one hand and pulled her towards him. "You'm a lovely liddle maid, right enough. 'Tis a long time since I had my hands on a maid."

Ellen struggled and managed to pull away from him; but

her efforts were as useless as Loveday's had been so many years before. The laughter died and all thoughts of tea seemed forgotten as the man's eyes grew hard and bright, his jaw rigid with purpose.

Her struggles only seemed to inflame him. Inevitably he caught her and gripped her and struck her, and reaching for a sharp kitchen knife, he held it to her throat while he tore off her garments, baring her full white breasts, her curving belly and flanks.

His own excitement was growing. His breath was ragged, the noise of it mingling with the sound of Ellen's terrified whimpers. He pushed her to the ground and crouched over her, fumbling with his own clothing, carelessly allowing the knife to droop harmlessly for a second.

She saw her chance and did her best to take advantage of it, pushing at him with all her strength and rolling away from him. Frantically he grabbed her and in his excitement he fell on her, feeling her body go limp, aware of his dominance and glorying in it, for that was how it should always be: Joely Tregilgas, all-powerful, all-conquering. For too long he had been imprisoned, despised, sworn at, degraded. Shudderingly he reached the pinnacle and knew that he was now the master.

Spent, he rolled off the girl.

"There, my 'andsome, 'twadn't bad, was it? Now give I the tea." She didn't move, and he laughed. "Shall us do it again?" he asked, and lifted his head to look at her.

In his excitement he had forgotten the knife. It had a black handle, the kind of knife that women used for preparing vegetables. Not a long knife, but long enough.

It had entered her throat right at the centre, and above it her eyes, bulging and terrified, stared at him blankly from a mottled face.

Ellen Kelynack, the girl who had longed desperately to have fun, would never see any sort of life again.

Joely stood up, staring at her, wiping his hand across his mouth. He fastened his trousers, buckled his belt, breathing almost as heavily as before but with a different emotion.

He was frightened. He knew he had to get well away, put as many miles between him and the girl as possible, lie low. But where was he? He didn't know, exactly. He only knew he had come out of prison in Bodmin two days before and had struck east towards Launceston before turning off the road somewhere before Blisland. He'd wanted time to think about his next move and intended to hole up somewhere while he made his plans. This latest turn of events altered matters.

His eyes darted round the kitchen. He would take the pasties and whatever else he could find: the remains of a loaf, a couple of apples. A pile of newspapers was stacked in a corner, no doubt waiting for the girl to tear them into squares for the privy. He snatched one, wrapped up the food and stowed it in the small bundle of belongings he had left outside.

At the door he paused and looked back at the girl on the floor. His mouth moved in an uncontrollable grimace and he shook his head impatiently. He didn't believe in regrets.

"Silly bitch," he muttered, shouldering his way through the door. He heard the dog barking, barking, as he ignored the lane and took a narrow path that led over a field towards heaven alone knew where.

"I must tell him," Loveday said.

Sunshine was pouring through the wide windows. Just like spring, Sarah had said, setting down a bowl of early daffodils, and Loveday had agreed. Hearing her words, Sarah sat down opposite her, and for a moment said nothing.

"I shall have no peace until I do," Loveday went on.

Sarah looked at her. She had improved a great deal. She read books and wrote to the children and had even embarked on knitting some golf stockings for Matthew. He had taken to golf recently.

Sarah knew, however, that the shadow had not lifted. Though for a great part of the time nobody would have guessed that she had suffered a breakdown, normality was nothing more than a thin veneer that could crumble at any time. Often the knitting needles were still or the book abandoned. Then Loveday's eyes would be blank again and her lips would droop. Frequently she wept. Not yet had the ghost been exorcised.

Sarah sighed.

"Perhaps you're right," she said. "Dr Aynsworth said much the same to me only yesterday. Loveday –" She paused and Loveday looked at her enquiringly. "Loveday, if I was wrong all those years ago, then I'm so sorry. I meant it for the best. I couldn't bear your life to be ruined. For some reason, the thought that there might be a child – children – never entered my head."

"Nor mine. But there they are. Matthew must be told. Until he knows, I am living a lie and it's breaking me."

It seemed simple and straightforward when she said it, a matter that brooked no argument, but the following weekend when Matthew came to see her, it was all very different. For one thing, he had spent Friday in Taunton and had seen Oliver.

"And he sent you this," he said, producing an eight-by-ten photograph. "He must have taken it in the holidays. He entered it for a competition at school, and would you believe it? He actually won! He was delighted with himself."

"Well!" Diverted in spite of herself, Loveday took the photograph and looked at it with interest. It was a study of two clayworkers taking a break from the loading of sand, leaning on their shovels and enjoying a joke together. They looked completely natural, totally unaware of the camera, in harmony with themselves and each other and the giant pyramid that formed the backdrop.

"It's a picture," she said at last. "Not just a photograph."

"He's making quite a name for himself, it seems." There was an unmistakable note of pride in Matthew's voice. "Other boys ask his advice and there's such an air of authority in the way he answers them. It's wonderful to see it, when you think of how he used to be. Do you know, Loveday –?" Matthew moved in his seat and leaned towards her, hands clasped loosely between his knees and a look of pleasurable remembrance on his face. "We talked, Oliver and I. Man to man. I think it was the first time we've ever done such a thing – the first time I've ever really felt close to him. I suppose the process began last summer in the Scillies, but even then I felt –" He hesitated and gave her a somewhat shamefaced smile. "Well, he's always seemed such a pathetic little creature to me. That's a terrible thing to say about your own son, isn't it? It's true, though. He's always been in Sally's shadow – always difficult to know."

"But not this time?"

"No. He seemed different."

"And photography has done this?"

"Perhaps not entirely, but it's played a part. He's known for something – valued for something. It doesn't matter that he's slow at reading and can't spell. Suddenly he's being praised for something that he *can* do, and clearly it's done him the world of good. I tell you, Loveday, it was the best day's work we ever did, sending him to Forbridge. I have the utmost respect for Mr Compton."

"Did you speak to Oliver about Christmas – about your father?"

"I did." Matthew's smile died and he sighed. "I don't think I've ever realised quite how Oliver's suffered over the years, or how like my father I am. I've treated the boy nearly as hamfistedly as he has. I'm not proud of it. Sally's always been the one for both of us, hasn't she?"

"Yes." Loveday touched his hand, robbing the terse word of any harshness.

"It's amazing that Oliver's still so fond of her."

"She's a lovable girl and she's always stood up for him. Besides, I've always said that he has a sweet nature."

"We talked about the upset at Christmas. He's sorry about it and ashamed of the way he landed you in such trouble – but you know, I can understand now how it happened. Well, that's all over and in the past." He dismissed it with a gesture. "We went to an hotel for tea yesterday." He was smiling again, thinking of the occasion with remembered pleasure. "There was some rare bird on the lawn; a brown lesser-spotted crested thingummy-jig – God knows what it was, I certainly didn't. But Oliver did. There was a woman there, quite elderly, another enthusiastic bird-spotter, and she was intrigued by him and talked to him for minutes on end. You would have been proud of him, Loveday. He was so polite, so quietly confident. She congratulated me afterwards on having such a delightful son."

"I'm pleased." Loveday smiled, her hand on his arm. This was when I was going to tell him, she thought, that I have lived a lie and the children are not his. But I can't do it; I can't. Not just yet.

"You look so much better," he said. "Everyone sends lots of messages, Sally especially. She misses you desperately."

"Oh, I miss her, too. She writes such sweet letters."

They talked of her and of home, and of Oliver again. *Now*, Loveday thought; but she couldn't find the words.

"Sarah had an idea," she said instead. "Next month she and Robert plan to go to the South of France. They're taking a villa just outside Nice. Robert is like me, a lot better but he gets tired very quickly, so they're spending a couple of months in the sun, just to complete the cure. Sarah suggested that I should go too, and that you and the children should come for a couple of weeks over the Easter holiday. Then the four of us could all come back together."

"You want to go?" Matthew smiled at the eagerness in her eyes. He could hardly believe that this was the same person as the weeping, pathetic creature he had seen on his last visit, even though Sarah had told him that Loveday was still prone to bouts of depression.

"Oh, yes! I've always longed to go to the South of France. I've never seen the Mediterranean."

"Poor darling. We haven't been away much over the years, have we?"

"I haven't minded. The Scillies were lovely."

"We'll do it," he said, making up his mind on the instant. "The children will love it, and so will I."

"How's the union situation?"

"Trouble averted for the moment, but there are rumblings beneath the surface. It's as well I went back."

"Can you be spared for the last week in March and the first in April?"

"They'll have to chain me down to keep me away." Bending towards her, he kissed her lips. "I'm already counting the days," he said.

Joely Tregilgas walked all day and saw no one, except a man rounding up some sheep and a halfwit boy with a round, red, vacant face swinging on a farm gate. He needed to find shelter before nightfall – and warmth, too, for although the weather was bright, it was cold, and there would undoubtedly be frost before morning.

He thought he would head for Plymouth where surely it should be possible to find a ship heading for some foreign port whose Master needed an extra hand.

They'd be after him by now; or would they? His initial fright had subsided for, to the best of his knowledge, no one knew he'd been in the district. The man with the sheep had been too far away to have gained any idea of what he looked like and the idiot boy wouldn't remember. It was three days now since he had been out of jail. For all the authorities knew, he might have gone miles away. Maybe he'd go to London instead of Plymouth and drop out of sight there.

He'd had plenty of time to think as he walked – to weigh up the alternatives and make plans. One thing was clear above all others. He needed money. He couldn't do anything without that, not eat or travel or anything.

He'd have to steal it, which meant that he'd have to go where there were people and houses. Plymouth again? He wished he knew exactly where he was. This was a part he didn't know at all. Camborne or Redruth now, that was different. Or Trelew, of course. He knew every nook and cranny of Trelew and Carrivick Woods and St Ninn.

But Bodmin Moor! A man would need to be mazed to want to live here, it was so cold and bare, with bogs and rocky outcrops and nothing but sheep, one part of it looking so like another.

He came across a small hamlet at nightfall, with a farm and barns and outbuildings. He waited in a ditch until the farmer had plodded back to the house and the men had gone, then climbed out and found a barn with a pile of straw where he could burrow for warmth, and where not even the rats disturbed him all night. Say what you will, he thought as he drifted off to sleep, on the run or no, it's better than Bodmin Jail.

It was light when he woke, and though early he could hear the tread of boots in the yard, and cows mooing, and someone shouting to them. The noise receded a little, and he crept out, straw clinging to his clothes and in his hair.

At midday he stopped to eat one of the pasties, and it was

during the eating of it that his eye fell on the newspaper he had snatched up from the floor of the kitchen. For the first time he looked closely at the picture on the inside page and he swore in disbelief. His jaw dropped open. There was no mistaking it. It was Loveday Pentecost. Master's girl.

Reading didn't come easily. His attendance at school had been too spasmodic for that, but slowly he managed to get the gist of the story; and when he did, it was the best antidote to fear and panic that he could have imagined. He laughed until he thought he would die. She was in prison – or had been when the story was written! Just like him! Who'd 'a thought it? Two old lags together, he thought, and laughed again.

She was as pretty as ever. Pretty and neat and toffee-nosed, with a big hat on with feathers and netting and whatnot, smiling towards the camera as if she hadn't lain under him on the floor of the hut with her legs all abroad and her skirt around her neck. How long ago was that? It was hard to remember. He'd been sentenced twice since then, and had that time in Camborne, and lived with the whore in Redruth.

It had been spring 1899, he decided at last. And now it was February, 1912. Thirteen years.

He studied the picture again, munching on a pasty as he did so. There was her husband and the kids. Girl and boy. *Boy!* His jaw stilled and with his latest mouthful of pasty half in and half out of his mouth, he brought the paper closer to his eyes. He hadn't taken particular notice of the children before, but now the boy who stood by his mother's side commanded all his attention.

It was the living spit of Henry – Henry who had died of the consumption ten years back, but who had looked like that, with that face and that funny way of standing, as if he hated everyone and wanted to run away.

Laboriously he spelled out the caption.

"'Mr and Mrs Matthew Tallon with their twin children, Sarah and Oliver, aged thirteen.'"

He began laughing again, quietly this time. Thirteen, he thought. Thirteen, and the living spit of Henry. How had she managed it? Did the toff know – him with his claypits and his moneybags? Or had she kept it dark? Either way, they wouldn't want it known. There had to be something in it for him. Thirteen! Oh, it was a good joke, the best he'd heard.

Thirteen, he thought, and chuckled as he went on his way. Well – lucky for some. That's what they said, didn't they?

He felt that luck was on his side right away, for very soon he came to the main Bodmin to Launceston road and a spot that he recognised. Easy now to find the lane to Lostwithiel and cut across to St Ninn that way. That's where they lived, so it said in the paper. Lucky it was such a small place. Anyone would be able to tell him where to find them, anyone at all.

A long walk was ahead of him, but he'd be in St Ninn well before evening. He thought about his plan of campaign. Would it be better to approach her or him? How much should he ask for? Whatever it was, they could afford it. A hundred pounds wouldn't be too much and would see him right. He could go to Australia on that, and still have cash left when he got there to get settled. Two hundred would be better, though. He could buy land then. He began to laugh again. Joel Tregilgas, landowner. It had a good ring to it.

Though he and Sally continued to live at Prospect Lodge in Loveday's absence, Matthew went back frequently to Church Cross House. The old man who worked as a gardener and handyman was living there with his wife, who worked in the kitchen. They kept the place aired and in good order, but they never intruded into the drawing room or the dining room or the family bedrooms, unless it was to clean them, choosing to sit by the kitchen range in the evenings and sleep in the attic bedroom which had been theirs for some years now. Mrs Grigg never failed to ask him when the family was coming back home, and Matthew never failed to give the same answer.

"Just as soon as we possibly can, Mrs Grigg."

"The 'ouse do seem very big without ee," she said. "It don't seem right."

"Everything will be back to normal soon."

He never stayed very long, but would sort through papers in his study or sit for a while in the drawing room, taking strength from the fact that this was his place – his and

Loveday's – and that it was waiting for them to take up the threads of their lives again. He liked the peace of it; the harmony of the furnishings and pictures, the lightness and the sheen of the pieces of furniture they had chosen together.

Prospect Lodge was all heavy, solid prosperity; richness-made-manifest, Loveday said. Church Cross House was altogether more homelike and comfortable. And best of all, it was theirs.

On this evening in March he had come to the house just in time to meet Mr and Mrs Grigg on their way out. There was a concert in the church hall, they said. Mr Tallon ought to drop in. It would cheer him up.

Do I really look that miserable? Matthew wondered. It was perfectly possible. Loneliness for Loveday was like a physical ache, but it was not the sort of ache that could be assuaged by a church concert – nor, in all honesty, was it in any way relieved by these visits home. Quite the reverse. He was merely indulging himself, luxuriating in his loneliness. Sometimes he would close his eyes and think he could hear her footsteps coming lightly down the passage; or would catch a faint breath of her perfume, or hear her laugh. If anything ever happened to her –

His thoughts swerved away. He was growing morbid. Nothing was going to happen to Loveday. She was getting better. There had been a letter from her only that day sounding bright and carefree, as if the Mediterranean was just as wonderful as she had always imagined. Soon they would be together there, and everything would be just as it had been before.

Was it normal, to feel like this about one's wife of thirteen years? Was it weakness?

Loveday led him by the nose, his father would say. It was a charge that he met by laughter or exasperation in turns, but now that she was not here he could see that there was a grain of truth in the charge. Loveday was his strength. Without her he felt lost and rudderless, at the mercy of conflicting currents.

I am two men, he thought, sunk dispiritedly into his chair. For Loveday I strive to be – I *am* – slow to anger, altruistic, amiable, considerate.

Without her, he was conscious of the man he might have

been – a mirror image, a man who bore a disquieting resemblance to his father. She was his anchor, his lodestar. If that was weakness, he thought, then so be it. As to whether it was normal, he couldn't tell. Other men seemed so matter-of-fact about their marriages, their feet so firmly on the ground that one couldn't imagine that they had ever experienced the flights of ecstasy that were part of youth and love and passion. What was Loveday's secret, that she should keep him so enthralled even after so long?

He picked up the photograph that stood on the mantelpiece in a silver frame, and looked at it, long and carefully. He smiled and shook his head.

"Witch!" he said softly, setting the photograph back on the mantelpiece.

It was then that the doorbell rang, clanging throughout the house, over-loud in the stillness.

Someone from the village had seen the light, Matthew thought, and had come to invite him yet again to the church concert. He and Loveday had been keen supporters over the years. He had even sung a solo once. But he had no enthusiasm for going without her and it was with a polite refusal ready upon his lips that he opened the front door.

It was no one from the village who stood there, but a stranger – a tramp, by the look of him, come to beg a shilling or a crust, or perhaps both.

"Yes?" Matthew was not encouraging. The man looked particularly filthy and repellent.

"You'm Mr Tallon, en ee?"

"Yes." Matthew's assent was cautious.

"I got somethin' to tell ee. Somethin' ee'll want to knaw."

"Something about the clayworks?"

"Maybe yes and maybe no. 'Tidn't right to talk of un out 'ere. 'Tis important, see."

For a moment Matthew hesitated. He disliked the man on sight, both his appearance and his attitude. There was a jaunty arrogance about him, a kind of sly contempt. His instinct was to slam the door in his face, but one never knew – these were strange times in the clayworks. Talk of strike action rumbled on. Whatever this chap had to say, it might have a bearing.

"You'd better come in." Matthew opened the door wide again and nodded towards his study. "Take a seat, won't you?"

The man ignored him and remained standing. As Matthew followed him inside the room he was looking around him with interest.

"Where's your missus to?" he asked.

"What's it to you? She's away, as it happens."

"Thass a proper shame, that is." The man was smiling, showing his rotted, discoloured teeth.

"Well?" Matthew was not disposed to prolong the interview. "What's this important information you have?"

"Loveday," the man said simply.

It took a second for Matthew to react. His face flushed scarlet and he stepped towards the stranger, his hands clenched.

"How dare you," he said, his voice trembling with outrage. "Don't speak of my wife in that familiar way."

The man laughed softly.

"Oh, I'm familiar," he said. "I'm some familiar with 'er, I am."

"Get out! I thought this was business."

" 'Tis business, sure enough. Just shut your face and listen." He tapped his own chest. "I'm the father of Loveday's children. You must o' wondered."

"You're mad." Matthew's anger died, its place taken first by bewilderment and then by pity. The poor fellow, he thought – must have escaped from Bodmin Asylum – what shall I do? "Come along now," he said heartily, putting out his hand to coax him towards the door. "Perhaps a little fresh air –"

"I ent mad, Mr Tallon. 'Tis true as I'm 'ere. I 'ad 'er in the woods afore she was wed. I fucked 'er, Mr Tallon, good and proper, and 'tis my belief she never bloody told you, not if your face is anything to go by. Thass a proper joke, that is – she never told you she was up the spout. Those are my kids you got, my tackers. Thirteen, they are. Thirteen. That boy's living spit of our Henry, I'd know un anywhere."

Matthew's rage was a thick, drumming, all-consuming tide that made his head spin. It wasn't true, of course it wasn't true, but to have such a man as this speak so of Loveday –

"Get out," he whispered hoarsely, his voice trembling with anger. "Get out before I kill you."

" 'Ow much is it wuth? I'd say one hundred pound, Mr Tallon. I'll keep my mouth shut then, not say a word, not to no one. You don't want your high and mighty friends to laugh at ee —"

Matthew took a step towards him, breathing heavily. He brandished his fist in the man's face.

"You're a filthy liar and I'll give you nothing. Now get out of here, and if I ever hear that you've —"

Joely Tregilgas caught hold of his upraised arm.

"I need the cash, Mr Tallon."

"Take your hands off me."

" 'Tis God's truth, I 'ad 'er up there in the woods —"

Matthew's fist smashed into the grinning, lying mouth with a satisfactory crunch. He had never known such rage, such a desire to smash and kill and pound into a pulp.

Tregilgas recovered and came towards him, his lips drawn back in a snarl.

"If thass what ee wants —"

The one thing he could do was fight. He had done it all his life, in prison and out, and now the odds were high. He could take what he wanted and run, once Tallon was floored.

It was a rough and bloody fight; a matter not of fists and Queensberry rules but of clutching and smashing and butting with heads and knees, of ramming against the walls and the wide desk, and gouging of eyes.

Matthew knew it was a fight he could not win. The man was tough and ruthless, with vast experiences of encounters such as this. With blood pouring down one cheek, an eye that was closing rapidly, one arm wrenched to the point where it was all but useless, it seemed only a matter of time before he was knocked senseless.

He backed away and held up his good hand.

"All right," he said, bowed and panting. "I hope you rot in hell but you can have the money. A hundred, you say?"

Tregilgas licked his lips and his eyes flickered.

"Two," he said.

"Very well."

313

Matthew went behind the desk, opened a drawer and felt inside it. He withdrew his hand, and in it was a pistol.

"Now get out," he said. "And if I ever see or hear from you again, or hear that you have been bothering my wife or any of my family, or spreading your filthy lies, I give you my solemn word I shall seek you out and I'll kill you." He motioned with the pistol. "Go on, move. Get your evil carcase out of here."

The black eyes flickered in Joely's face. He looked uncertain, fearful. For a moment he hesitated, staring at the gun. Then he shrugged his shoulders.

"Money or no, I told ee the truth," he said.

"Get out. Now."

He went, and Matthew slammed the front door behind him, leaning against it for a moment, sick and trembling.

He went back to his study and withdrew the velvet case from the desk drawer. Inside was an exact twin of the pistol he held in his hand. They were ancient, decorative, quite useless – the only articles he had been tempted to buy at the Carrivick sale all those years ago. He had been thinking of having them restored ever since, but had never done so.

He replaced the pistol and slammed the drawer shut. He felt tainted by the sheer depravity of the man. To think he could speak of Loveday –!

Oh, it was horrible, horrible. He should have killed him, *would* have killed him if he could, should surely have silenced that hateful, lying mouth for ever. He would never have believed that such a pacific man as himself could have experienced such a powerful urge to destroy. The mirror image, he thought, returning to his earlier thoughts. The man within.

But what other reaction was he supposed to have? It was Loveday – *Loveday* – whose name had been dishonoured.

Sick and aching, he went into the dining room and helped himself to a drink from the decanter which stood on the sideboard, noting that his hand still trembled.

I should have killed him, he thought.

❦ 16 ❧

In the vain hope of protecting Sally's innocence, Millicent Tallon forbade her to read the papers which reported the Murder on the Moor, as the case came to be called. She reckoned without the burning interest of the girls of Trenerry School, who were familiar with every last detail of the case – even its sexual connotations, which Millicent barely understood herself.

"That poor girl," they said to each other, pleasurably aghast. "All alone on the moor. What could she have *felt*?"

"She should never have let him in."

"But she was at his *mercy*! Just imagine!"

"Perhaps she invited him."

"There was evidence of a struggle, the papers said. Oh, it doesn't bear thinking of!"

But they thought of it just the same and discussed it endlessly. Could the word of that mentally defective boy who said he had seen a stranger be trusted? Could the farmer really be sure that someone had slept in his barn *that* night and no other? Was an apple core and a cigarette-end conclusive evidence?

"If you ask me," said Pauline Jago, "he'll be clean away by now. My father says he'll have hopped a ship –"

"The police are swarming all over the Plymouth docks," Vera Penrose informed them importantly. "My father was there and he saw them."

They swarmed to good effect. On a Saturday morning towards the end of March the papers reported that one Joel

Tregilgas of no fixed abode had been apprehended for the murder of Ellen Kelynack at Moorland Farmhouse.

"He looks perfectly beastly," Sally said to her father, shuddering theatrically.

"I don't think Grandma would want you to read that," he replied absently, himself engrossed in *The Times* and the Irish Question which continued to plague Mr Asquith almost to the exclusion of everything else.

They were alone at the table, for Millicent Tallon had slept poorly and was taking her breakfast in bed, while her husband had gone to Bristol, making business his excuse. The matter was nothing which could not have been resolved by post. Matthew was well aware of that, but pretended not to be. Such sorties had been part of his father's way of life for too long to be in any way remarkable.

"Oh, Grandma's behind the times," Sally said airily. "All the girls at school know about it. It's horribly gruesome. Ugh!" Extracting the last ounce of enjoyment out of the horror, she shuddered once more. "Look at him, Daddy. You can tell he's a murderer, can't you?"

"He's innocent until proven guilty," Matthew said tolerantly, humouring her by glancing towards the paper she held towards him. "Wait a minute," he added in a different voice, paying closer attention. "Let me see that, Sally."

He took the paper from her. The picture was no more than an inch square and was far from clear; even so there was no doubt in his mind that the man arrested in Plymouth was the same man who had come to him making his preposterous allegations and demands. He himself still suffered from the consequences, and had been forced to explain his cuts and contusions by saying he had tripped and fallen down the front steps of Church Cross House in the dark – an explanation that his mother, he was well aware, regarded with deep suspicion. Her private theory was that he had been assuaging his loneliness in the bar of the Trengrose Arms and had become involved in some stupid brawl, about which the less said the better.

He became aware of Sally's voice, full of eagerness.

"What is it, Daddy? Do you know him?"

"Grandma's right," he said. "This is not the sort of thing

you should be reading." He stuffed the paper into his jacket pocket and stood up. "The man was clearly perverted, a danger to himself and everyone who came into contact with him."

"What about being innocent until proved guilty?" Sally asked cheekily.

"I think I agree with you. He looks quite capable of anything. Now come along – if I'm to drop you at Caroline's house on my way to golf, it's time we were off."

He left his daughter at her friend's house on the Truro road and proceeded to the golf course where he played a reasonable round, talked clay prices and labour problems with others equally involved, and drank a pint of ale. Deliberately, he closed his mind to the shock and revulsion the newspaper report had roused in him. There was no one here he wished to share it with.

On his way home, some way before he reached Prospect Lodge, he brought the car to a standstill at a wide part of the road, and pulling out the paper which he had thrust so unceremoniously into his pocket, he read again the account of the arrest and the murder which, largely ignored by him, had been the talk of the rest of the district for weeks.

The full horror of it made his gorge rise, and the hands that grasped the paper grew clammy. When he reached the end, he grasped it still, but stared fixedly through the windscreen, seeing not the lane and the hedgerow, but the leering face of the man called Tregilgas – the man now branded as a rapist and a murderer, the evil creature who had uttered foul things about Loveday and had done far worse to the poor girl on the moor.

This was the man he had grappled with – a man who would certainly not have hesitated to kill him, for what had he got to lose? – had it not been for the ornamental, useless pistol he had remembered so providentially.

He chewed at his lip, racked with indecision. His evidence would be further proof of the man's criminal violence and he should undoubtedly go to the police with his story. And yet – and yet . . . Suppose they asked *why* Tregilgas had demanded money from him? Suppose later, on oath, he was required to repeat the man's foul allegations – drag Loveday through the mud?

No – he couldn't risk it. He would keep quiet, say nothing. After all, there was surely more than enough evidence to convict Tregilgas without any word from him. Loveday was too precious to him to allow the merest breath of scandal to touch her, however false – and God alone knew, she had suffered enough just recently. There were the children to consider, too. No, no. It would be folly to mention the matter to anyone.

Resolutely he did his best to put it behind him, for there were pressing problems at work – an American contract Tallons were in imminent danger of losing unless new terms could be agreed, the sudden illness of the captain at Upalong. Quite enough to worry him without continuing to think of Tregilgas.

Tregilgas. A good Cornish name. Why did it nag at him so? Where had he heard it before? Was there someone on the workforce of that name? He didn't think so. He felt certain, somewhere in the back of his mind, that it was in some quite different connection that it had been brought to his attention.

Forget it, he told himself impatiently; yet each night, in his lonely bed, he found himself going over and over the evening that Tregilgas had come to him.

The man was mad, that was the only conclusion. He had to be mad, to do what he had done to that poor girl. Suppose it had been Loveday –

He found himself staring wide-eyed into the darkness.

Suppose it *had* been Loveday! Suppose Tregilgas had raped her too?

Nonsense, he told himself. Impossible nonsense. The man was a liar, a criminal, and Loveday was honest as the day. And John Pentecost had been honest, too. Neither could have kept such a frightful happening to themselves. As for what he had said about the children – well, it was almost laughable, the stuff of a penny dreadful.

But how would he have reacted, just supposing the unthinkable had happened to Loveday?

He would have been compassionate, he told himself

318

stoutly. Nothing could have come between them – not then, not ever.

But it didn't happen. So everything was all right.

"All that wisteria!" Sarah said, lying in a wicker chaise longue on the terrace and looking up at the blue sky through the clustering leaves. "This place must be so beautiful in summer."

"It's beautiful now."

Loveday spoke without moving, luxuriating in the sun. Like a cat, Sarah said; and warned her constantly against allowing it to ruin her complexion. But it seemed so long since she had experienced its beneficent touch and she loved the feel of it. It seemed to soothe and straighten all the tangles that had knotted her nerves for so long.

It was unseasonably warm, old Lady Wilding said. She was their neighbour who had taken up permanent residence on the Riviera; a small, wizened, highly sociable woman whose wrinkles were pasted over with make-up inches thick and whose hair was an improbable, unflattering jet black. Her husband had been quite disgustingly rich, she told Sarah, but had been considerate enough to die just after buying the Villa Rossignol and leaving his fortune to his widow.

She remembered Sarah from her heyday in the theatre, and had invited the Morrow household to all manner of entertainments, most of which they had politely declined.

"My husband and my friend are convalescing," Sarah told her, making the most of it. She had nothing against Lady Wilding; indeed, she was rather attracted to the colourful and eccentric widow, but the last thing any of them wanted was to be forced to scream inanities at a collection of people they had never met and were never likely to meet again; nor did gambling, which seemed to be Lady Wilding's major preoccupation, very much appeal to them.

"Though we ought to have a little flutter before we leave," Sarah said, and the others agreed that indeed they ought. One day. Perhaps when Matthew came.

Meantime they moved through the days rather like sleep-walkers, taking the beauty in through their pores as well as their eyes, growing calmer and stronger day by day. Even Sarah's vitality had failed her recently and she was uncharacteristically content to read and look at the view and walk into the nearby village of St Just to sit in the *place*, a glass of local wine on the round metal table in front of her, doing nothing but watching the passing scene.

The Villa Mignonette was not large, as villas went, and as a piece of architecture it undoubtedly left something to be desired. It had irrelevant little turrets here and a castellated tower there, as if it couldn't make up its mind whether it was going to be Versailles or Windsor Castle when it grew up. It didn't matter. The garden, cut from a pinewood and planted with all manner of exotic shrubs unknown to Loveday, had forgiven all and enfolded all.

There were still pines at the end of the lawn and between them the sea glimpses dazzled and glinted. Much too cold to swim, Sarah said; but Loveday had done so and had enjoyed it, plunging in off the rocks at the edge of the bay just below the house.

She felt renewed and invigorated; in balance once more.

"I was wrong," she said to Sarah one day when they had climbed down to the rocks and were sitting watching the waves curdle round them. "I know now that the guilt is something I have to bear. It is the price I have to pay for deceiving Matthew in the first place. What good can it do now to tell him about the children? It can only do harm, to him and to them. I must protect all of them."

"I've always believed that," Sarah agreed. "So long as *you* believe it –"

"I do. Holloway and all that experience unhinged me a little."

"Hardly surprising!"

"Oh Sarah, I'm so weak. When one thinks of all that other women have endured, and continue to endure, I'm ashamed of myself."

"They go into it knowingly – they even welcome it. Your case was different."

"My namesake, Loveday Hambly, went to prison, you know. She was in Launceston Jail for – oh, I don't know how long. A long time. But she never ceased to praise God and preach her beliefs. My father admired her so. I wonder what he would think of me?"

"Do you need to ask? He loved you."

"You don't think he would be disappointed in me? I'm not particularly proud of my life."

"Your story isn't told yet."

"I hope there's not too much drama in the rest of it and that it has a happy ending."

"Well, this week has a happy ending, anyway, with Matthew and the children arriving."

Smiling, Loveday lifted her face to the sun.

"They're going to love it," she said. "I just can't wait."

The reunion was as rapturous as anything she could have imagined, and even after a week she found herself watching her family and smiling foolishly with the sheer joy of being with them again.

"You've grown," she said to Sally, walking with her to the village to buy a pair of espadrilles.

"Not grown," Sally objected. "Grown up."

"Well, perhaps."

"It's Oliver who's grown."

"He certainly has. He's taller than I am now."

"He's such a pest with that camera of his. Do you know, he made me sit on the grass for ages and ages yesterday with those daisy things in my hair and one in my teeth. He kept yelling at me to look soulful when all I wanted to do was giggle. I nearly swallowed the daisy."

"So long as you shook the ants off first."

"Oh Mummy, how beastly! That was bad enough, but you know that Grecian urn on the terrace? Well, he wants me to drape myself in a sheet and lean against it gracefully, holding up a bunch of grapes."

Loveday laughed at her.

"You enjoy dressing up."

"But I don't enjoy keeping still."

Oliver explained his obsession with his camera by saying he couldn't resist the light.

"It makes everything look different," he said. "You can understand why so many painters come from France."

"You've not been tempted to paint instead of photograph?" Matthew asked him. Loveday found herself waiting for his reply, expelling her breath with relief when he denied it. She wanted to see no likeness between Oliver and the boy who liked to draw 'birds and cats and rabbuts and all that trade'.

Indeed, the physical likeness was much less than it had been a few years before. Oliver's face had somehow lengthened, nose and chin becoming more in proportion.

"He has the sort of looks that improve with age," Sarah said. "It wouldn't surprise me if he became quite good-looking in a beaky kind of way."

"Just as long as he's happy," Loveday said, in the way of mothers.

He certainly seemed happy and relaxed. He no longer agonised about trying to please, or strained every nerve to keep up with Sally. He liked his own company and quite often went off for a walk by himself in the hills above the village, but equally was at ease with the family.

In particular he was at ease with Matthew. Sometimes they walked together. Towards the end of the holiday they hired bicycles and went off for an entire day.

"You don't mind, do you?" Matthew asked Loveday anxiously when the idea was mooted.

"Of course not. I'm delighted," she said.

Hand in hand, they were strolling along the lane which led away from the villa, the light fading a little, every leaf and blade of grass clear and intense. The scent of fruit blossom drifted towards them and from somewhere far away in the hills, a bell tolled.

"How magical this is," Matthew said after a moment. "Why haven't we come before?"

"I don't know. Why haven't we?"

"I feel –" He looked at her, shaking his head, unable to put his feelings into words. "It's what I imagined," he said at last. "Better than I imagined, when we were apart and you were so ill."

"I'm sorry to have caused so much worry and fuss. And as for Oliver – you must know how delighted I am that you and he are getting on so well. It makes everything perfect."

"Being all together again makes everything perfect."

"Where do you think of going tomorrow?"

Matthew groaned.

"Up to the hills, can you imagine it? Oliver wants to go to one of those *villes perchées* we can see. I feel certain it will kill me."

"Think of free-wheeling down!"

"With that wonderful view in front of us. I suppose it will be worth it – if I survive."

"I hope you do. Did Sarah tell you we are invited to Lady Wilding's tomorrow night for dinner? She's asked all of us, children as well, for an informal meal – just us, nobody else, and Sarah couldn't think of any reason why we shouldn't go. We've made polite excuses for so long that we've really run out of them."

"Damn! I like our evenings."

"Don't we all?"

"And there are so few left!"

"I know. But remember, Sarah and Robert are staying on another month and they don't want to offend her. It's very kind of her to want us. Just so long as she hasn't invited a horde of her socialite friends –"

"I know. I'm sorry. I'll be good." He grinned at her, and they paused and kissed; happy and serene, no shadows between them. "I love you so much," he said softly. "I can't tell you how I hated it when you were away."

"But you have told me," she said smiling. "Often and often. Heaven send it doesn't happen again."

While Matthew and Oliver were away on their bicycles, the others went to Nice. Robert went to change some money and Sarah had her hair washed, but Loveday and Sally – not for the first time – wandered around the flower market and the surrounding streets, looking for presents to take back to the grandparents and various friends, feeling faintly sad because this indicated that the days were running out and this magical holiday would soon be over.

"Mark my words," Lady Wilding said, much later when the cyclists had returned and had bathed and changed. "Cornwall will never seem the same again."

They had dined off *bouillabaisse* and *salade Niçoise* and *pollo pepitoria*, washed down with a fresh and fragrant wine of

323

which even the children were allowed half a glass. It was all so different, Sally thought delightedly. Imagine being allowed wine at Prospect Lodge! And people were different – more relaxed, happier, easier in their manner. They were all grouped around the large table in the dining room of the Villa Rossignol which had one wall almost entirely made of windows, so that although it was too cold at this time of the year to dine on the terrace still it seemed as if they were dining al fresco. The curtains remained undrawn, the garden appearing part of the room.

The other walls were covered with Impressionist paintings in pale, shimmering colours. Loveday, not at all knowledge-able about art, had no way of knowing if these paintings were good of their kind; she only knew that she found them harmonious and restful, in tune with the mood of the evening. No doubt, she thought, Georgina would have a little more to say about them, were she present. And thank God that she wasn't!

Lady Wilding ('Call me Davina,' she said, but nobody did) was dressed in a flowing gown with enormous rings on her claw-like hands, and earrings like gold chandeliers; but she was vivacious and welcoming, equally so to the children as to the adults, which warmed Loveday's heart. She encouraged them to join in the conversation, sought their opinions on such matters as education for women and social reform, was charmed by Oliver's interest in her pictures. It was he who ventured a mild protest at her remark about Cornwall.

"It's very beautiful, you know," he said.

"But cold!" She shuddered, illustrating the point. "And less colourful."

"Cornwall is milder than anywhere else in the British Isles," Matthew said defensively, and Loveday smiled. One word of criticism, she thought, and we all close ranks. It's where we belong, after all.

"You'll admit it's less dramatic. No, that's not the word. Land's End and the Lizard are as dramatic as can be. Less *melo*dramatic, is perhaps what I mean. Everyone's affected here by the sun, you know, and the colours. They go to our heads and we behave in an exaggerated way. It makes for an exciting life. People take lovers and shoot their husbands and pursue vendettas – in short, we who live here are all, quite delightfully, off our rockers."

"What happens to your British phlegm?" Robert was laughing at her extravagance, as she had intended.

"Gone, gone!" Her voice had a hollow ring.

"Along with the pen of your aunt?"

"We have murders in Cornwall," Sally said. Marie, Lady Wilding's, maid had half-filled her glass with wine when no one was looking, with the result that she felt elated, sophisticated, mistress of the situation. It was hugely enjoyable. "An awful thing happened to a girl on Bodmin Moor."

"That will do, Sally," Matthew said repressively, but Lady Wilding beat her little claw on the table and glared at him with mock ferociousness.

"No, it won't do at all," she said. "Let Sally tell me! There's something particularly appealing about murder on a Cornish moor. Brontë-esque, one might say. Was it a jealous lover?"

"It was an extremely sordid case," Matthew said. "Not suitable for discussion in polite society."

Lady Wilding raised her eyebrows.

"My, how stuffy you sound! This is France, you know, not Little Grovelling in the Marsh. We call a *bêche* a *bêche* here. I'll wager fifty francs your daughter has all the facts at her fingertips. Did the village bobbies manage to make an arrest?"

"They were jolly clever," Sally assured her earnestly. "They found him at Plymouth. Tregilgas, his name was. Joel Tregilgas. It sounds like a murderer's name, don't you think? He'd only been out of Bodmin Jail a few days."

"That's enough, Sally."

Matthew had seldom sounded more stern and Sally, wounded, stared at him in astonished embarrassment. She bit her lip and looked down at her plate. Everything seemed a little out of focus, her elation gone. Why did Daddy have to be so sharp with her? It wasn't fair. She was only trying to be bright and social, like Lady Wilding. That was the trouble with grown-ups – you never really knew what they wanted of you.

Robert leapt in to cover an awkward pause.

"Do you come to England at all, Lady Wilding? You must visit us at Carrivick. We could, perhaps, demonstrate that the country has much to recommend it, particularly our corner of it – isn't that so, Sarah?"

"Oh – oh, yes." Sarah sounded as if her mind had been elsewhere. She smiled brightly at Lady Wilding. "Yes, of course you must come."

"How kind! But I doubt that I will. One travels very little these days.– too comfortable by half, you see. And of course one has one's chums –" She paused and looked searchingly down the table towards Loveday. "Are you feeling unwell, Mrs Tallon?"

Loveday's smile was the merest twitch of her lips.

"No, no – I'm perfectly well." She raised her glass and took a sip of wine, setting the glass down with unusual clumsiness, spilling a little on the table.

Matthew had felt it a point of honour not to look at her when Sally had mentioned the murderer's name. It seemed like an insult, even to think for one moment that she would recognise it. But now, slowly, he lifted his head as if he had no control over it.

She was deathly pale, her white face and pearly dress shimmering in the light of the candles. She was so still and expressionless that one might have thought she had suspended breathing, suspended thinking. She does know it, he thought. The realisation was a sudden, physical pain.

And all at once, as if a shutter had opened in his mind, he knew where he had heard the name before. Henry Tregilgas, he thought. Henry Tregilgas, the boy Loveday had taught before they were married; the boy who was backward in his reading, the boy who lived in the wood with his peculiar mother and jailbird brother. Dammit, the murderer had mentioned Henry! How could he not have remembered?

She lifted her head and looked, not towards him, but straight ahead at Sarah who was sitting opposite; and Matthew, glancing sideways, saw that Sarah returned the look for a long moment before turning towards their hostess.

"Such a delightful evening, Lady Wilding –"

"My dear, *Davina*, please! We're to be neighbours for another month."

"Davina, then. Thank you so much – it's been wonderful, but I really think –"

"You're not going? It's not late."

"The children –" began Matthew, but Lady Wilding brushed him aside.

"No one bothers about children in France!"

"Even so –" Matthew, glancing at a strangely mute and passive Loveday, stood up decisively. "I think we should go. Thank you very much indeed, Lady Wilding. You've been most kind."

Somehow they managed to take their leave, with their hostess protesting to the end that they were being just too, too, utterly English, and back at the Villa Mignonette, Sally and Oliver were dispatched to bed.

At last Matthew and Loveday were alone in their room. There was silence between them; not an easy silence, born of familiarity and companionship, but a silence that loomed and chilled and threatened.

Like one in a trance she undressed and sat in her pale-green wrap brushing her hair in front of the dressing-table mirror until, oppressed by the quality of Matthew's silence, she put the brush down and bowed her head.

Matthew, sitting on the edge of the bed, watched her.

"The man Tregilgas," he said at last, the words wrenched out of him. "You recognised the name."

Loveday lifted her head slowly and looked at him in the mirror. He saw the muscle in her throat move as she swallowed.

"Of course," she said, her face expressionless. "I taught his brother."

"And that's all?"

Let her say 'yes', he prayed. I'll believe her; I won't question it. Just let her say 'yes'.

Slowly she turned round to face him. She parted her lips as if she was about to speak, then closed them again. Once more she bowed her head.

"Loveday?"

She gave a deep sigh and looked at him. How sad she is, he thought. It filled him with apprehension.

"Matthew," she said, so softly that he had to strain to hear her. "Matthew, you know that I love you?"

"Well?" He could feel his heart racing and it was difficult

327

to breathe. She came and sat beside him, taking one of his hands and holding it between both of her own. "Well?" he said again.

Her eyes were fixed on their joined hands as if she found it impossible to look at him. Her grip tightened.

"I don't want to hurt you," she whispered. "I've never wanted to hurt you. That's been the trouble."

"Dammit, Loveday!" Matthew stood up abruptly, snatching his hand away. His voice was harsh. "Before Tregilgas murdered that girl, he raped her. He told me that he'd – he'd had you, too."

Loveday stared at him.

"He *told* you?"

"He came to see me, demanding money. I didn't believe him. Not then. Now –" He broke off and moved away, twitching the curtain aside to stare out into the darkened garden. A lighted ship was passing a long way out in the bay. "Now I don't know what to think," he added huskily at last.

After a while, when he did not move, Loveday went to join him. She put her arms around his waist and rested her head on his shoulder. It felt hard and resistant. For a moment neither of them spoke.

"You should have told me," he said at last, and Loveday sighed.

"I wanted to," she said. "I've always wanted to. I'll tell you now."

The night was bright with stars and somewhere in the hills behind the house a nightingale was singing. Matthew, having rushed from the bedroom, stood irresolute at the side of the lawn. Where could he go? What could he do? There was no refuge anywhere.

Flight seemed pointlessly melodramatic – bleakly he remembered Lady Wilding's use of the word – yet he could not have stayed in that room one moment more, now that his world had apparently crashed around his ears.

He looked back at the house. The terrace was in shadow, the room above it where Robert and Sarah slept in darkness. To the right, beneath the tower in the room he shared with Loveday, there was a light. He knew that she was weeping there, and it tore at his heart; but he was weeping too and could be of no comfort to her. He turned from the house and walked down to the edge of the lawn where the pines began; to the steps and the rocks and the sea.

It was the deceit, he told himself – the thought that his wife, the girl he loved, the woman he had placed on a pedestal, had thought of as the guiding light of his life, had all along deceived him. He thought he had known her as well as any living person could know another. But he hadn't known her at all. It had all been an illusion.

He didn't blame her for the rape. He pitied her. How could he do anything else? She had been so young and innocent. Fourteen years on, he felt certain that it would have made no difference to him. But the children! That was a different matter. For over thirteen years she had knowingly hidden the truth from him. All those years when he had struggled to treat Oliver with the same patience and affection as he had effortlessly shown towards Sally, she had deceived him. It might not have mattered so much then. Sometimes, he had to admit, it would have seemed a positive relief to know that the boy was not flesh of his flesh.

But now, *now*, when he and Oliver had discovered each other, it hurt to think what blood ran in his veins. And in Sally's veins. Oh, Sally! He sat on the rocks and buried his head in his hands. How could he bear it now, watching them, fearing for them? And how could he ever trust Loveday again? What on earth was he to do?

He lowered his hands and stared blindly at the sea. It was calm tonight, barely moving. He felt a loose stone on the rock beside him and hurled it into the water, seeing the starlight catch the circle of droplets that shot upwards.

I could do that, he thought. I could shatter our circle, our family circle – destroy the security the children have always known, send Loveday away. But to what purpose? To live in isolation in Church Cross House?

Perhaps it had all been too perfect. He had doted too much, idolised too much. Other people seemed to manage happily with lower expectations; other marriages survived long after illusions were shattered. After all, nothing really had changed.

She loved him, she said; and perhaps, when the shock had worn off, he would find that he, too, felt the same – that this sense of betrayal had dissolved like mist in the sun.

He was cold, he realised, and bone tired. Half of him wanted to make a dramatic gesture; to walk away from the villa, disappear in the wild hills to the north, or the streets of Nice. The other half insisted that this would be childish and would solve nothing. Wearily he got up from the rock on which he was sitting and went back to the house.

Loveday was not asleep, though she had gone to bed. She sat up immediately she heard him come into the room and held out her arms to him.

"Thank God," she said. "Thank God! Oh darling, please come to me."

The sight of her tear-stained face tore at his heart and swiftly he went and held her. She wrapped her arms around his neck and strained towards him, and sobbing again, ran her fingers over his face as if tears had blinded her and she was reminding herself of the shape of his brows, his nose, his lips.

Their mutual fervour increased, familiar yet more intense than it had ever been. He kissed her lips, her neck, her breast, wanting her now so much that tenderness was forgotten; there was only hunger and passion and an insane desire to hurt and subdue.

And then, suddenly, the desire left him, taking him by surprise. He moved away from her, one arm across his eyes.

"I'm sorry," he said after a few moments.

She lay beside him. He felt her lips on his shoulder.

"It doesn't matter. So long as you're back. So long as you stay."

"I'll stay," he promised dully.

Long after she fell asleep, he lay staring into the darkness, seeing it thin and lighten as dawn approached. Yes, he would stay. He would swear her to secrecy for the sake of the children. They must never know from what frightful stock they came. No one must know.

And eventually everything would be as it had been before, the past forgotten. The feeling between them was not such that it could be wiped out so easily. Hadn't she proved her love for him that night, turning to him with unprecedented passion?

Or had that been a ploy? Had she thought the matter most easily settled in bed? Was that nagging doubt the reason he had failed her at the last moment?

Wearily he closed his burning eyes. Somehow he would have to learn to trust again. Life would be unendurable if he did not.

"They Tregilgases was never no good," Mrs Beswarick said. "Never nothing but trouble, all the days of their lives."

For once Mrs Penhaligon could only agree with her, and even Letty Foster, always ready to take a more lenient view of humanity, could find nothing to say in Joely's defence.

"They say as 'ow 'e was 'ere, in St Ninn," she said. "I don't know if 'tis true or no."

Loveday, who had come into the post office to buy stamps, left suddenly without them. It was the same everywhere she went. The whole village was a-buzz with this latest sensation – that Joely Tregilgas, who had lived among them, was on trial at the County Assizes for the murder of Ellen Kelynack.

She walked swiftly away hardly noticing where her steps were taking her, aware suddenly that she was on the way to Fourlanesend, to the schoolhouse and the moor. To her youth, she supposed. If only it were possible to go back in time as well as in space!

It was winter now – not the weather for walking on the moor, yet somehow its bleakness was in tune with her mood.

Nothing had been right since they returned from France. Matthew was kind, but there was a strange deadness between them.

"Why, why?" she asked Sarah desperately, for at last she had sought refuge from the chill at Carrivick. "He says he has forgiven me for deceiving him, yet I can't get close to him. Sometimes I think he hates me and hates the children. Yes, even Sally, if you can believe it."

For a moment Sarah did not reply, but busied herself with pouring tea. Then she set the teapot down with a sigh.

"It's the evil," she said. "The darkness that was in Tregilgas."

Loveday frowned, not understanding her.

"What on earth can you mean?"

"Evil reaches out and touches others, just as goodness can. I believe that strongly. We're such complicated beings, Loveday. I don't doubt you're aware of guilt, even if it's misplaced – and with that comes remorse, and maybe a longing for revenge. Dark things, all of them. Evil things. I expect it's the same for Matthew."

"Why should he feel guilty? He's done nothing." Sarah looked at her with compassion. She did not speak, but Loveday seemed to divine her thoughts. "You think him unable to cope with the fact that his woman was violated, is that it?"

"It's possible. Instinctively he hates the thought; intellectually he feels guilty at having that reaction when so clearly you were blameless."

"I don't feel blameless about Ellen Kelynack. Perhaps if I'd brought charges against him, she'd be alive today."

"Nonsense! In the unlikely event that he'd been found guilty and imprisoned, he would have been free long ago. Be thankful that *you're* alive!"

"I am, I am," Loveday said, and shuddering, buried her face in her hands. "Oh, when will it be over, Sarah? The trial seems to be going on interminably."

"The paper says the summing-up is tomorrow. It won't be long. Then that monster will hang from the neck until he is dead, and I for one can't find it in my heart to pity him."

Loveday's eyes had darkened with a desolation she could neither understand nor contend with.

"May God have mercy on his soul," she whispered.

Book Three

§ Book Three ❧

❧ 17 ❧

Over by Christmas, everyone said; but then had come Mons and the Marne and Ypres, and casualty lists read out in church on Sundays, and Kitchener's finger pointing from hoardings, and young men disappearing only to reappear again, briefly and proudly, in khaki or navy blue. Carrivick was turned into a hospital for naval personnel and Loveday went there several days a week to do what jobs she could, from cleaning and dusting to writing letters for the men unable to do so because of their wounds.

The china-clay industry was suffering, now that only the old men were left and export to Europe virtually at a standstill. Cap'n Noah still bullied his workforce at Trelew, but even he found it hard to get a good day's work out of men long past their prime. Other pits closed altogether.

"They don't need me," Matthew said, and Loveday looked at him hopelessly.

"You're not thinking of enlisting?"

He was, she knew. For a long time now he had been restless and unsettled, looking for an excuse to leave. Or was that her imagination?

They had cobbled up a reconciliation, papered over the cracks. Helen Farrar, now Folgate, who lived a tempestuous life with her artist husband, informed Loveday that she and Matthew were quite the happiest couple she knew.

"My dear, when I think how many pots I've broken on Gerald's head, and the number of times he's stayed out all night, your marriage seems positively idyllic."

"Ah, but think of the fun you have making up!" Loveday said.

In total contrast to Helen and Gerald's marriage, there was a dearth of fun and laughter in theirs. They were kind to each other; polite, considerate, a little distant. Joely Tregilgas was never mentioned, but sometimes Loveday felt that his evil presence was with them always, poisoning the very air they breathed. There were no recriminations, but little love-making, either. Work took up more and more of Matthew's time – which was hardly surprising in view of the fact that the year following their visit to France there was a protracted and damaging strike in the clay industry, with police drafted in from Glamorgan to deal with the ensuing violence. That had been a bad time, not least because Matthew seemed torn in two by it.

His sympathies had been with the men to a great extent. They were, after all, asking for very little – only five shillings more a week, an hour off for lunch, an eight-hour day. He would have given in without a struggle had the matter been left to him, but there were the other owners, not least his father, to contend with.

It had all fizzled out in the end. The workers, shocked by the violence, knew that they had lost and drifted back to work – and then, of course, had come the war and the departure of many of them into the Army and Navy. It was history now, but had been a trying time without doubt, one that seemed to leave Matthew more restless than ever – angry at compromising his principles by giving in to the other owners, angry at feeling the need to defend himself to Love-day. Yes, a bad time all round. The only positive result, Matthew said afterwards with grim humour, was that Clay Tallon and Granville Penberthy were on speaking terms again, united in their condemnation of his more liberal atti-tude. If the strike had accomplished nothing else, it had accomplished that.

It had all been the perfect excuse for a withdrawal from home and family. Or was she being unfair? Loveday won-dered. It was hard to tell. They never seemed to talk much any more, not about things that were really important. And when they did, they often disagreed – as they seemed to do almost constantly whenever Oliver's name came into the conversation. He was at Oakby now, and was finding it very different from Forbridge House where he had been so happy. Loveday had seen him change from the brighter, more confident fourteen-year-old that he had been in France to a withdrawn youth with eyes that were dull with misery.

Matthew, however, couldn't seem to see it, or if he did, he refused to believe that the school was at fault. Oakby was a grand place, he said heartily, and Oliver would soon shake down. It would be quite wrong to allow him to leave. He would have to learn that giving in and giving up was not the answer.

Though there were times when Matthew made her angry, Loveday still couldn't bear to think of him going away. Somehow, somewhere in some golden future, she cherished the hope that everything would be as it had been before. The thought of losing him with this echoing void between them filled her with panic.

Millicent Tallon died in November 1915, just a few days after the twins' sixteenth birthday. She had gone into hospital for what had seemed no more than a routine operation – an appendix that had bothered her on and off for years – but afterwards had succumbed to septicaemia.

It was wet on the day she was buried. Did it always rain at funerals, Loveday wondered, remembering Joe Truscott? Somehow it seemed appropriate. But then she thought about the day they buried her father, which had been bright and sunny with a skittish wind and cotton-wool clouds, and remembered that that had seemed appropriate too.

After the funeral, family and friends gathered at Prospect Lodge. Oliver had come home for the night from Oakby. She looked around the room for him and saw him standing with Sally talking to Sarah and Robert. At least, Sally was talking. Oliver was drooping beside them looking pale and withdrawn, the new suit bought only last term already short in the arms, a sprinkling of spots on his chin. He looked utterly dispirited. *Damn* Oakby! Both Matthew and his father seemed to revere the place, but she couldn't see that it had done anything for Oliver, other than make him miserable. Why couldn't Matthew see it?

She would miss Millicent. A good deal more than the aunts would, she thought with a touch of cynicism, looking at them in their funereal black. They were putting up a very good show of restrained grief, not arguing at all but talking in low voices of Millicent and her kindness and the huge number of flowers that had been sent and the beautiful way the minister had spoken of her. They were taking small, joyless sips of sherry as if to do otherwise would have shown a lack of respect. Impossible, somehow, not to remember the times when they had quelled their sister-in-law with a cutting word, reduced her to a quivering mass of nerves, treated her as a nonentity in her own home.

"I imagine the change is purely temporary," said a voice in her ear.

Sybil – at last allowed back home, now that her mother was gone and could extract no pleasure from it.

"I'm taking bets on how long this respectful accord will last," Loveday said. "My guess is another five minutes."

"Something of an over-estimate. I think they've started already." Sybil looked around her. "How Mother would hate this," she went on. "People standing about, making small-talk. It was quite her least favourite form of entertainment. I hope they don't stay very long. Most of them hardly bothered to give her the time of day when she was alive. As for Father –"

She broke off, a small, sour smile crooking the corner of her mouth.

"I think it's really hit him hard," Loveday said.

"Do you?"

"He can barely speak of her without emotion."

"My dear Loveday, how long have you known him? He is playing the part of the Broken-hearted Widower! Oh, I'm not saying that when the dust settles he won't miss her quite dreadfully, much more than he imagines, but right now the brave little smile and dewy eye is for the benefit of his public."

"How bitter you are," Loveday said.

"Do you wonder at it?"

"No, perhaps not." After all, she knew more than most all that Sybil had suffered at her father's hands – even so, she thought, such bitterness was doing her sister-in-law no good at all. There was a sharpness in the way she spoke now, a sourness in her expression. The schoolgirl gawkiness, the anxiety to please, seemed to have gone, its place taken by a spinsterish acerbity. "But perhaps he is remembering, and feeling remorse. Who knows? This may be his only way of coping with it."

"Hm. You're more charitable than I."

"How long are you staying, Sybil? I hope we have time for a really long talk."

Sybil shrugged.

"There's not a lot to tell you. No more action on the WSPU front, of course, because of the truce. My guess is that this war will help our cause. How can they refuse us the vote when women are doing men's jobs right and left?"

"How's Georgina?"

Sybil helped herself to another glass of sherry proffered by a passing maid, and said nothing for a moment. Her face seemed to grow harder, the little smile more fixed.

"She's gone," she said. "There was a man – a frightfully weak sort of fellow who was sympathetic to the Cause and who used to help out with the accounts at HQ. I never liked him. He moved up to Liverpool at the beginning of the war. Something to do with the docks, I understand. Georgina decided to go with him. I say –" she looked around the room once more. "Do you think anyone will be frightfully offended if I have a cigarette?"

She did not wait for a reply from Loveday, but extracted a cigarette from her bag, dealing with holder and matches with practised efficiency.

"I'm – I'm sorry about Georgina," Loveday managed to say after a moment. "That must have been a blow."

Sybil blew out a puff of smoke.

"Not really," she said. "A surprise, yes. But now that I'm on my own I have come to realise that it's better this way. I'm writing full-time again, and it's a great deal easier with only myself to think about."

"I can see that it would be."

Sybil looked at her, the crooked smile twisting her mouth again.

"Shall I tell you something frightfully amusing?" she said.

"Having denied me the right to come home when Mother was alive, last night Father suggested I should actually come back here to live. Can you imagine?"

"You see? He's more affected by your mother's death than you give him credit for."

"Nonsense! He wants a housekeeper, that's all. 'All forgiven and forgotten', he says, but mark my words, the moment I unpacked my case, he would be trying to run my life for me, trying to turn me into the person he wants me to be. What's the matter with Matthew?"

"Matthew?" The sudden change of subject took Loveday by surprise. She frowned at her sister-in-law. "Nothing, as far as I know, except that he's grieving for his mother, of course. They were always very close."

"Yes." Sybil's face seemed to soften. "Yes, they were. But it's not that. He's aged since we last met. For the first time I can see how like Father he is. In appearance only," she added hastily.

"The strike was a great strain on him."

"That was two years ago!"

"Things are difficult now, with men leaving all the time and markets lost. He's having to scrape around to find new ones. And of course –" Loveday paused, then continued in answer to Sybil's enquiring look. "He feels he ought to go," she said. "He wants to join the Army."

"I can understand that. One feels a compulsion to join something." Sybil drew on her cigarette and looked thoughtfully across the room to where her brother was talking earnestly to Michael Morcom, now a Liberal Member of Parliament for a constituency in the far west. "I suppose that could account for it."

She said no more for Clay Tallon was approaching them. He was as immaculately clad as ever, the gold of his watch-chain and tie-pin glowing richly against the black of his waistcoat, the silver hair and moustache well brushed.

"My dear." He touched Sybil's shoulder. The expression on his face was one of sadness, tinged with reproach. She looked at him impassively, blowing out a wreath of smoke. "I must say I'm a little disappointed," he said. "Aren't you showing a lack of respect? We both know how your mother would have hated it."

"To see me smoking? I don't think I agree, Father. Mother would have been delighted to see me smoking during the years you kept me from my home. She would have been delighted to see me doing almost anything."

His eyes widened and hardened with anger at her response, but before he could reply Hugh Trevose had joined them, proffering his hand and his renewed condolences, saying that he had a pressing appointment and would have to leave.

"Of course, of course." Clay Tallon was gravely kind once more. "And tell your dear wife that I appreciated her letter of sympathy."

Mr Trevose left, and Tallon's smile died as he turned towards Sybil.

"You've wounded me, Sybil." His lips trembled a little and there was a moist brightness in his eyes. "I had hoped we could forget the past."

"Really?" Sybil smiled at him brightly and unforgivingly. She surveyed the room again. "How long is all this going to last, do you think? Isn't it time everyone went home?"

Her father drew a breath, collected himself.

"Mr Sinclair wants to read the will while all the family is together," he said. "It will save him another trip from Truro."

"Are the aunts required? The Penwith lot look as if they're about to leave, thank God."

"No, no – only the immediate family. You, Sybil, and Matthew and Loveday and a few of the servants. Millicent, bless her, didn't have a lot to leave."

He left to say goodbye to the departing guests, leaving Sybil and Loveday exchanging amused glances.

"Millicent, bless her," said Sybil, "had been persuaded to part with practically everything she owned many a long year ago."

"You're forgetting Piper's Piece."

"I'm willing to bet that Father isn't. Underneath all that bravely-borne grief, he's rubbing his hands in glee that soon it will be his."

"Mummy, are we going home soon?" Sally asked sotto voce, appearing at Loveday's elbow. "I don't want to be

341

rude, but Oliver and I have got oceans to talk about, and if he's going back to school tomorrow –"

"Your father and I have to stay to hear Grandma's will read."

"Then couldn't we beg a lift with Aunt Sarah and Uncle Robert? We could walk from Carrivick."

"That sounds a good idea, if the Morrows don't mind."

"They won't," Sally said, with certainty. She darted away to arrange matters.

"How delightful to be Sally," Sybil said dryly. "How very enviable to be sixteen and to look like that. Oliver's growing up very nicely, too, though I must say adolescence isn't the most attractive stage for a young man, is it? He looks rather doleful. Is he happy at Oakby?"

Loveday hesitated.

"Well – it's not Forbridge," she said at last. "I suppose the answer to you is no, he's not. Matthew says he must stick it out. It's good for his character, he says."

Sybil raised an eyebrow at the touch of bitterness she detected in Loveday's words.

"I've heard it said that public school is the best preparation for the trenches it's possible to get," she said.

"Please don't!" Suddenly Loveday's voice was harsh.

The thought that Matthew might choose to enlist was bad enough. The knowledge that Oliver might have no choice in the matter was something she couldn't bear to contemplate.

"It just didn't seem to have anything to do with Grandma," Oliver said.

"I know. I kept expecting her to come in –"

"With that sort of hunted look she used to get when there were too many people about the place. The aunts do go *on*, don't they? They get so passionate about who said what to whom in eighteen-o-whatsit. As if anyone cared."

They were in what was known as the muddle room at Church Cross House; a small room upstairs furnished with a square table covered with a chenille cloth, two sagging armchairs, a nursery screen embellished with cut-out pictures that they had known as long as they could remember, and numerous bookshelves. Evidence of their interests was all around them. Oliver's photographs were on the wall. Sally's piano occupied a space between the two windows. Tennis racquets leaned in a corner.

They had drawn the curtains against the dark, and Sally, cheeks glowing, was bending close to the fire with a slice of bread speared on a toasting fork. Oliver, watching her, feeling the comforting ambience of the long-loved room all about him, was dangerously close to weeping.

"Didn't your heart bleed for the Grand Old Man?" he said, wanting to distract his thoughts.

"Don't be mean, Oliver."

"Well, honestly." He tipped his chair back and managed to reach one of the tennis racquets which he subjected to a minute inspection, straightening each string. "I thought it a pretty sickening display."

"You can't really know what he thinks, can you? I mean, how do you know what anybody thinks? There was Mummy, f'rinstance, being terribly nice to the aunts and saying how she hoped she'd see them again soon and all of that."

"She likes Aunt Clara, all right. Anyway, that's politeness. The GOM was just playing for sympathy, blinking back his non-existent tears, making brave little jokes."

"Here, this one's done," Sally said, unspiking the toast. "Put that racquet down and butter it while I do another. You really are mean about Grandfather, you know. Oh, I know he can be difficult, but he was pleased as punch when you got into Oakby." When Oliver didn't answer, she took it as disbelief and looked over her shoulder towards him. "He was, you know," she said. "And do butter that toast while it's hot."

"To hell with the toast." Oliver threw it down on a plate. He put his elbows on the table and held his head between his clenched fists. "And to hell with Grandfather and Oakby and everything," he said. His voice sounded strange, thick with unshed tears.

"Oliver, what is it?" Sally laid the toasting fork down in the hearth and looked at him with concern. He shook his head, not able to speak, and she went to him, drawing a chair up close and taking hold of his shoulders. "Oliver, tell me. It's not just Grandma, is it?"

He shook his head, but said nothing.

"What, then?" she persisted.

He sniffed and wiped his eyes with the heel of his hands.

"Do you swear not to tell?"

"Don't be daft! We never tell."

"Swear!"

"Of course I swear." She lifted a hand shoulder high. "By the blood and the bones of St. Ninn. Will that do?"

"Sal, I'm not going back," he said.

"What?" She stared at him. "What do you mean? They'll make you."

"They can't. I'm going to get off the train in Plymouth and join the Navy. Sixteen's old enough."

She grasped the arm that lay on the table and held it tightly with both hands.

"Oh, Oliver! Are you sure?"

"Absolutely. I can't stand another day."

"But if you talked to Mummy and Daddy –"

"I've talked to them! Dad won't listen. I don't know what's the matter with him. He used to be all right. We used to be able to talk, but not any more. He says it's good for me, all this misery. He thought Oakby was marvellous, and maybe it was for him. They didn't call him 'Loonie' and gang up against him and rag him and get him into trouble all the time. Oh, I know it sounds wet –" He had his head in his hands again. "Maybe it is. Maybe I *am* wet! I only know that I can't stand one more beating, one more day of being made to feel stupid."

"You're not stupid!"

"I know. But I'm slow at reading, Sal, you've got to admit that, and my spelling's awful. It was all right at Forbridge. Old Compton understood and nobody hurried me, but Oakby's different. I don't know why they ever let me in, and nor does anyone else. It was only because of Dad and Grandfather being Old Boys, with their names all over the Rolls of Honour and sports trophies. I hate the place, and everyone in it. I'd rather join the Navy. I'd rather be dead."

"Oh Oliver, don't talk like that. I can't bear it." She tightened her grip on his arm.

"Don't be silly. Nothing will happen to me. I just meant

that I'd rather take any risk than stay at Oakby. Anyway, I want to go. I'm old enough to do my bit."

Sally looked at him in silence for a moment, biting her lip, her eyes shining with emotion.

"I suppose it is rather splendid," she said. "Your King and Country Need You."

"Well, Oakby doesn't, that's certain."

"I wish I could come too, like Sweet Polly Oliver."

"I don't know her."

"Silly! She's a song. She 'dressed as a soldier and followed her love'."

"Well, you couldn't. You've got bosoms, for one thing."

Sally squinted downwards.

"Yes, I have rather, haven't I? Oh Oliver, I do envy you, though. It's really rather romantic, when you think about it – running away to sea. You will let the parents know what's happened quickly, won't you? They'll be worried."

Oliver grunted disbelievingly.

"Mum might."

"Daddy would too."

"Would he?" Clearly he was unconvinced. He sighed. "I wish things could have stayed the same," he said. "Like when we went to France. Remember when Dad and I had a day up in the hills on bicycles? I've never forgotten it. It was really great." He sighed again. "I don't know what went wrong. Oakby, I suppose. I just turned out a great disappointment."

Sally said nothing and when he glanced at her he saw that she was not even listening but appeared to be lost in some reverie of her own. By the look on her face it was not a happy one.

"What's up?" Oliver asked. Not looking at him, she bit her lip and shook her head. "Go on," he urged. "It's your turn, after all."

"I wasn't going to tell you. It's sort of sneaking."

"Oh, honestly!"

"Swear to keep it a secret?"

Oliver groaned theatrically and collapsed on the table in front of him. He seemed almost cheerful now that he had delivered his bombshell.

"Get on with it," he said.

Sally rubbed at a stain on the cloth that had been there for as long as she could remember. It looked like a map of Italy and had always fascinated her.

"It's Daddy," she said.

"Well?"

"You know Caroline?"

Oliver sighed.

"She's only been your best friend for the last five years!"

"She's got an older step-sister called Verity – *much* older, about twenty-eight – who's married to a naval officer. Well, he's away somewhere and she's come back home to live. She's awfully pretty and stylish, and sort of larky." She turned tragic eyes on her brother. "And oh, Oliver – Caroline says that she really likes Daddy and that they flirt together like anything. And it's true! It doesn't matter how busy he is, he'll always take me over to their house and he sparks up like billyo when Verity is there. And she nearly always is."

Oliver considered the matter.

"I don't suppose there's anything in it," he said.

"I can't bear to think he could have fallen in love with someone else."

"You're talking rubbish!" Oliver sounded scornful. "Dad and Mum have always been potty about each other."

Sally looked unconvinced.

"Well, I hope you're right. I couldn't bear to think he was getting like Grandfather, always flirting and twinkling and being generally blush-making. It's the thing I've never been able to stand about him."

"No," Oliver said again. "He wouldn't do that. I'm sure of it." He thought about it a little longer. Dad was different these days, there was no denying it. "Almost sure, anyway," he added uneasily.

Mr Sinclair, the Truro solicitor, had a monotonous voice and was clearly enjoying his role, omitting none of the 'heretofores' and 'whereases' and 'hereinafters' contained in Millicent's will.

As Clay Tallon had said to his daughter, there was not a great deal to leave. He sat with his head slightly bent and a small, sad smile on his lips, listening to the interminable voice as it droned on, dealing with the shipping shares that were to go to Matthew; the South African mining shares for Sybil. Small stuff, unimportant stuff. He required none of it and had expected none, for Millicent had, as Sybil mentioned to Loveday, long ago made over to him all the land around Trelew and Carrivick that had been her inheritance. All except Piper's Piece, and soon that, too, would fall into his lap. And about time. It was quite extraordinary the way that Millicent, so compliant in most respects, should have held so tenaciously to this small parcel of land.

He missed the part about her jewellery, but it didn't matter for she had discussed with him the disposal of it. Her pearls, the ruby necklace and her solitaire ring to Sybil; the gold chain, the diamond bracelet and earrings to Loveday; the rest, less valuable, to be amicably divided between them; her dear granddaughter, Sally, to be allowed to choose between the cameo and the gold chain bracelet.

Get on, get on, Clay Tallon thought.

There were bequests for a few of the long-serving maids, and for the butler. *Now*, surely.

"And finally," Mr Sinclair continued. " 'Unto my said daughter-in-law, Loveday Ruth Tallon, for her absolute use and benefit, I bequeath that land known as Piper's Piece, extending to about two roods and four perches and bounded to the north by Piper's Brook and to the south by the Trelew clayworks –' "

Loveday!

Tallon's head came up, astonishment wiping from his face all vestige of grief. He could feel the anger swelling, had to grip the arms of his chair to prevent himself leaping to his feet and shouting a protest. What, by all that was holy, could Millicent have been thinking of? The land was his! It had to be his. Common sense dictated it. She knew its importance to him – knew that he needed the stream for both Trelew and Wheal Charity. What on earth was the point of this capricious bequest?

His eyes met hers, the woman he had always regarded as an adversary; the woman who had taken his son and imprinted her own standards upon him so that he barely recognised him. She looked, he had to admit, as startled as he was.

Then he saw her eyes blaze with triumph – triumph tinged with amusement, and it was as if a knife twisted in his gut. There was nothing he could do now to rid himself of her. He was just as much tied to her now as he had been to Millicent, and she knew it. Oh, what could Millicent have been thinking of?

It was over now, the great farce. He forced a look of pleasantness on his face, shook Sinclair by the hand, offered him a whisky that was mercifully refused. He returned from seeing the solicitor off the premises to find the servants gone and Matthew, Loveday and Sybil sitting in silence.

He had had time to compose himself – had stopped by the huge gilt mirror in the hall and smoothed his hair and squared his shoulders.

"Well, well," he said, and smiled at Loveday. "So you are a landowner now! I don't mind telling you it came as something of a surprise."

She had the decency to hide her triumph and in fact now looked more embarrassed than pleased.

"I'm sure it did," she said. "I'm absolutely astonished. I had no idea this was in her mind."

Sybil laughed, her new, hard, cynical laugh.

"Mother's little bit of insurance we called it," she said. "Perhaps she thought you needed some insurance too, Loveday."

Loveday looked at Matthew and smiled.

"Well, I'm grateful, of course," she said. "But I can't imagine why. It naturally won't make any difference to anything."

"I should hope not," Matthew said, and smiled at her in return.

She could not help noticing that it didn't reach his eyes.

They put Oliver on the train on Wednesday morning. He seemed, Loveday thought, more cheerful than was usual on such occasions. She had come to dread saying goodbye to him, seeing the helpless misery in his eyes and feeling herself powerless to help him; but on that day, though he seemed keyed up, she could swear that there was an air of suppressed excitement about him as if he were positively looking forward to going back to school.

"You see," Matthew said, driving away from the station. "I said he'd settle down."

"I hope you're right. I can't help thinking Oakby is quite wrong for him, though." Matthew said nothing, but Loveday sensed that he had stiffened with impatience. "I've nothing against the school itself," she went on. "It's just that they don't know how to cope with Oliver's difficulties. It seems to me that he's slipped back since leaving Forbridge."

"Do we have to go over this again?" Matthew sounded weary. "Oakby is a damned good school and he's lucky to be there. The discipline is tough, I know that, but he *needs* discipline –"

"With his background, you mean?" Loveday's voice was bitter. "Oliver is gentle and sensitive and something of a solitary. Public school is probably the last thing he needs."

"Discipline never hurt anyone."

"Especially the son of a rapist and murderer?"

"Shut up!" Matthew's voice rose with anger. "When have I ever brought that up? I never think of it." He knew as he said it that it was only partly true.

"I'm sorry." Loveday stared out of the window, seeing nothing. "I shouldn't have said that."

"No, you shouldn't."

There was silence between them as they drove through Carclaze, up to the clay country with the blue sea sparkling on their right, bright as on any summer day, the rain of the previous day quite gone. Loveday laid a hand on Matthew's knee.

"I really am sorry," she said. "You're a good father, the best of fathers. I worry about Oliver, though, and sometimes it seems that you don't care. You seem – detached from us."

"I suppose I am preoccupied, I have to admit it, but I'm busy, that's all. I care – of course I care. But there's a lot to think about. It hasn't been the easiest of times."

"I know." He had made no acknowledgement of her apologetic touch and she removed her hand. She gave a brief laugh.

"I still can't get over your mother leaving me Piper's Piece.

349

Your father must be furious. Was it some sort of joke, do you think?"

"Rather some form of feminist solidarity, I imagine. It's been the ace up her sleeve for years. No matter what Father has got up to, he's been prevented from going too far because he's known damned well that without Piper's Piece life would be very, very difficult."

"Hm." Loveday cocked her head. "I suppose it could be useful." She smiled at him. "You'd better behave yourself, then."

"I always do," he said.

He took Loveday home, then drove to the office. The telephone seemed to beckon and entice, but he succeeded in ignoring it while he dictated letters to the worthy Miss Pike who had been his secretary for the past year. Only when she had gone to lunch did he succumb.

Verity answered immediately.

"You blighter! You said you'd ring this morning," she said.

"It is this morning. Well, very nearly." The church clock was striking half past twelve as he was speaking. "I'm sorry, Verity, but I had to take my son to the train, and work had piled up at the office –"

"My dear, you don't have to explain." Her voice was warm and sympathetic. "You've had enough on your mind recently without my adding to it – besides, I know how busy you are. I'm just so thrilled you thought of phoning me at all. Isn't it a grand day after all that rain?"

"Wonderful. Shall I see you up at the Golf Club this afternoon? I could pick you up."

"Why not? My dear step-mama is out at some sewing-bee luncheon and I am under a cloud of disapproval for being a lily of the field, neither toiling nor spinning."

"Is two o'clock too early?"

"Not a bit. I'll see you then."

He replaced the handpiece and stood for a moment, rubbing the side of his face. He felt guilty. Why, in heaven's name? What could be more innocent than a game of golf? Verity was damned good, for a woman, and a breath of air at

Tregongeeves was just what he needed to blow away the miseries of yesterday. He'd never known a more depressing day. Seeing his mother's coffin lowered into the ground –

He shuddered and turned away from the phone. Time for lunch at the White Hart. Just as well Father wasn't in today. Not that he'd be censorious about stealing away for the afternoon; far from it. He'd done it often enough himself.

And that, of course, was the trouble. He couldn't bear the thought of Father's man-to-man twinkle, the sceptically raised eyebrow at the mention of golf, the understanding pat on the shoulder. He couldn't bear to think that he was stooping to the same level – that somehow he and his father were in league against Loveday.

He was doing nothing wrong. It wasn't as if he were being unfaithful. What, after all, was a game of golf? He had played truant before, many times. He kept a change of clothes at the club for just such a purpose as this. What was the use of being the boss if he couldn't take advantage of the odd fine afternoon? The fact that he was playing with a woman was quite immaterial.

The inner argument wouldn't go away, however, and continued to plague him all through lunch, teasing at his conscience. It was infuriating and quite unnecessary. Verity Spalding amused and attracted him. That was all there was to it. He relished the illicit thrill of the chase and it was an undoubted boost to his ego to realise that she clearly found him attractive too, but he had no intention of taking the matter further.

So any feelings of guilt were misplaced, he told himself firmly. He would waste no further time on them.

The telegram from the school arrived the following morning, not long before lunch-time. It read: Please wire revised time Tallons arrival.

Loveday stared at it, at a total loss. It had been sent, she saw, at ten o'clock that morning. What on earth did it mean? Oliver had set off at nine the previous day and should have been at Oakby by two-thirty at the very latest.

She put a call through to the school and waited for an hour

before Letty Foster rang back to say that she didn't seem to be getting an answer.

"Could be they wires are down," she said apologetically. " 'Tis nothing but an old buzz, no matter what I do."

Loveday sent a telegram.

"Oliver left 9 a.m. train yesterday kindly inform if arrived stop am worried."

Matthew, generous in almost every other matter but this, would have cavilled at the last two words, but she didn't care. She *was* worried, and so ought the school to be.

They were, it seemed. They managed to telephone late in the afternoon to say that there was no sign of him; that they had met yesterday's train, as arranged, but that he had not arrived on it.

"What can have happened to him?" Loveday asked frantically. "Should I contact the police?"

"No, no." Over the miles the housemaster's voice was soothing, even with its accompaniment of crackles. "He'll be in contact, I feel sure. Boys do take it into their heads to run away sometimes, you know."

"Not if they're perfectly happy," snapped Loveday. "I hold Oakby responsible for this."

"Come, come – my dear Mrs Tallon!" There was a touch of steel in the voice now. "You're understandably upset. Perhaps I could speak to your husband."

"My husband is not here," Loveday said. "But I have no doubt he'll be in touch with you as soon as he arrives home from the office."

"Why isn't he here?" she demanded of Sally, turning from the telephone, wringing her hands. "Oh, what can have happened to Oliver? Did he say anything to you, Sally?"

"He said he wasn't happy at Oakby," she said carefully.

"Well, I knew that, of course. But where on earth would he have gone? And where on earth is your father?"

She telephoned the office, to be told that he had not been in all afternoon. She telephoned Prospect Lodge, but he was not there either.

"I must find him," she said desperately to her father-in-law. "Oliver has disappeared. He never arrived back at school, and

I'm desperately anxious. Have you any idea where Matthew might have gone?"

"None whatsoever. Hold on, hold on. Sybil is trying to say something. She's been in Truro all day – only just got back."

"Hallo, Loveday?" Sybil had taken possession of the telephone. "I gather there's an emergency."

"Yes, I must find Matthew."

"But my dear, he's in Truro – at least, his car was. I didn't actually see him, but he was parked outside that little hotel at the top of Lemon Street, or rather just round the side of it. You know, right up the hill. I'd never have gone up there in the normal way, but I went to see Sophie Angrave – you remember, Sophie Nugent as was? I couldn't imagine what it was doing there, but there was no mistaking it –"

"I see. He must have been meeting someone – business, you know. Shipping." There was a strange, fluttering feeling of panic in Loveday's stomach. "He'll be back soon, I'm sure."

"Don't worry about Oliver," Sybil went on. "He's not a babe, after all. He's probably joined up."

"Joined –? Oh no, Sybil! He's not old enough for that. He's only sixteen, after all."

"Sixteen is old enough for the Navy, isn't it?"

"Yes, but – oh Sybil, he wouldn't have gone without telling us, surely? Not without saying goodbye?"

"I don't know, my dear. But I'm sure you needn't worry."

"Are you?" Loveday said tonelessly. What would Sybil know about it? She felt angry, suddenly, at her sunny complacency and replaced the receiver. "Sybil thinks he's joined the Navy," she said. She looked at Sally for a long moment. "And so do you, by the look of you," she added.

Worry and indecision and unhappiness seemed to chase themselves across Sally's face. She couldn't say anything, she couldn't! She'd sworn!

"He did say something, didn't he?" Loveday asked.

"Oh, Mummy!" Sally cried miserably, and ran into her arms.

She had almost decided to begin dinner without Matthew when at last she heard him come in. She could hear Sally in the hall, telling him about the telegram and the telephone call.

"What's all this?" he asked, coming into the room where she was sitting. He looked impatient and angry rather than concerned.

She explained the situation.

"The general consensus seems to be that he's joined the Navy," she said.

"The silly young fool!"

"I told you he was desperately miserable. You took no notice. We must get him back, Matthew."

"Where from? There's no conclusive proof that he's joined the Navy, is there?"

"Sally seems to think that was his intention. We can't just let him go."

"Why not? If he thinks the Navy is a soft option, then let him try it."

"Matthew!" Loveday's voice was no more than a shocked whisper. "He's only just sixteen, and there's a war on, in case you've forgotten. We must do something."

Matthew lifted his arms out to the side and let them fall again.

"I'm going to change, and I'm going to have a drink, and I'm going to have dinner, in that order," he said. "Then I'll be more capable of coming to a sensible decision."

Helplessly Loveday watched him go towards the door.

"Matthew!" she said, just as he reached it.

He halted, turning back towards her.

"Yes?" He looked so cold, she thought. So distant. Almost a stranger.

"Where were you?" she asked. "I tried to get hold of you when the school rang."

"Oh." There was a moment's hesitation. "Sorry about that. I was – I was chasing up the prospect of a contract. In Bodmin."

She looked at him without expression

"Satisfactorily, I hope?"

"Oh yes, yes indeed. I went and had a drink on it, as a matter of fact, with the chaps involved."

"In Bodmin," Loveday said.

"That's right."

He smiled at her briefly and went on his way.

❦ 18 ❦

"Now that," said Clay Tallon with an upward brush of his moustache, "is what I call a damned fine filly."

Matthew, lunching with his father at the White Hart, had his back to the door and was prevented by good manners from looking round to corroborate this opinion.

"A damned fine filly!" Clay drew the words out, smiling appreciatively. "And coming this way, what's more. She's with young Caroline's mother –"

Matthew turned his head seeing, with a feeling of inevitability, that Verity was approaching with a somewhat reluctant-looking Mrs Trevail in tow. Both men rose as they drew level.

"Mrs Trevail – Mrs Spalding –" Matthew, dabbing at his mouth with his table napkin, gave an awkward little bob of his head towards each. He felt at a disadvantage, conscious of his mouth half-full of baked salmon and of Verity's amusement at his predicament. Utterly self-possessed, she had not waited for a formal introduction but had dimpled prettily at Clay Tallon and offered him her palely-gloved hand.

"I can't tell you how I've longed to meet you, Mr Tallon. I've heard so much about you."

"Nothing but good, I trust." Another brush of the moustache. "Are you ladies lunching alone? Can you be persuaded to join us?"

"How kind of you!" Mrs Trevail smiled uncertainly. "However, I don't think –"

"Oh Mama, why not?" Verity pouted coquettishly at her

step-mother. "I can't tell you how I long to talk to Mr Tallon."

"We should be an unwelcome disruption, I'm sure."

"Not unwelcome!" Clay Tallon protested. "Never unwelcome. Sit down, sit down, I beg you –"

"We have a table reserved, Mr Tallon, and my husband may be joining us later. Come along, Verity! You're condemning these poor gentlemen to a cold meal."

Rather to Matthew's relief they at last moved on, Verity with a provocative smile over one shoulder.

"A *damned* attractive little filly," Clay said once more. Matthew grunted noncommittally and continued with his rapidly cooling salmon. "Such a figure!" his father went on enthusiastically between mouthfuls of lamb cutlet. "Did you notice her waist? My God, if I were twenty years younger –"

"Aren't you forgetting you're still in mourning?" Matthew said coldly.

"No – no, of course not." Clay Tallon's smile died and for a while he ate in silence. "Your mother understood me," he said at last. "I miss her, I assure you."

Matthew's conscience struck him.

"I shouldn't have spoken like that, Father," he said in a gentler voice. "I know you miss her."

"Can't help appreciating a pretty woman, though," his father said defensively. "*She* knew and never complained. You'd never get away with it, I appreciate that. Loveday's more demanding."

"I think most wives would be."

"Perhaps." The mischievous twinkle reappeared, unsubdued. "Even so, if I were you I'd try my luck with the luscious Mrs Spalding. You have to admit she's an enchanting creature – with an eye for you, unless I'm much mistaken. And I seldom am on such matters."

"She is married, Father."

"My dear boy, married ones are the best! Who misses a slice from a cut loaf?"

Their heads were bent close together, their voices low, like two conspirators. Two of a kind, Matthew thought, and for once did not reject the notion, conscious of a feeling of amused resignation as if he had at last been persuaded to join a club that he had long rejected. The urge to confide was almost irresistible, for he knew it would bring him nothing but approbation if his father were to know that he and Verity were already lovers. There would be a touch of envy, perhaps, but vicarious enjoyment too, laced with admiration that his son had attracted so worthy a prize.

He said nothing, however. To tell his father would be a double betrayal of Loveday – and heaven knew, one was bad enough. His conscience troubled him quite sufficiently as it was.

He had decided several times not to see Verity again but had found it impossible to stick to his decision. She answered an overwhelming need for – what? Revenge? Was that what this was all about?

No, it was more than that. He had been unsure of himself ever since Loveday's revelation, their love-making perfunctory at best and at worst, a total failure. It didn't matter, Loveday said. Everything would return to normal soon. But she was wrong. It mattered terribly, to him if not to her, and far from returning to normal things only grew worse. Their closeness was a thing of the past, and he felt he no longer knew what she was thinking, or if she meant what she said. Since France, he knew that she had never been the open book he had imagined.

There were no uncharted depths in Verity – or at least, none that affected him. She was frivolous and fun-loving, with a quick wit and a ready laugh, and though she was not conventionally pretty, she had a piquant, intelligent face and, as his father had noted, the figure of an angel. She wanted nothing from him that he was not prepared to give, demanded no promises, no protestations of undying love.

Soon, when her husband found a flat in Portsmouth, she would go away, and that would be the end of it. Meantime she provided the cheerful and uncritical company he needed. In her arms, he felt himself to be an adequate lover once again – more than adequate, if Verity was to be believed – and no matter that his conscience plagued him, he knew he would continue to see her just so long as she lived in the town. It was fun, that was the top and the bottom of it – fun to plot and scheme to have afternoons together, fun to pretend they barely knew each other whenever they met in the company of others, and oh, such fun to fall into bed together!

Just so long as Loveday never found out. But she never would. How could she? He and Verity were discretion itself.

On the day when Sally announced at dinner that Verity's husband had found somewhere for her to live in Portsmouth, Loveday went on helping herself to vegetables, giving no sign of the surge of thankfulness that flooded through her.

"Verity will no doubt be pleased about that," she said calmly.

"You'd think so, wouldn't you? But Caroline says she's been in a foul mood ever since she heard."

"Really?"

Loveday's voice expressed only a mild interest. She avoided looking towards Matthew, for she wanted to see no reflection of that foul mood in his face; but when, after a few moments, he spoke about some minor incident at the office, his voice gave nothing away.

Perhaps, Loveday thought, she had been wrong about Verity Spalding after all. Perhaps Mrs Trevail had been wrong to come all the way to St Ninn for the purpose of warning her against her step-daughter. Clearly there was no love lost between the two women – one had only to see the look in Verity's eyes and the twist to her lips when she addressed Mrs Trevail, older by no more than twelve years at the most, as 'Mama, dear'. Spite could have been the motivation.

In her heart, however, she knew that the warning was justified, even though she made light of it to Mrs Trevail. To Matthew she said nothing at all, hoping against hope that the pretty grass-widow was a transitory aberration. It was far from easy to stand by, noting his elation, knowing he was making occasions to see her, wondering if the journeys he began to make to Bristol and Swansea and other centres were necessary or simply the kind of so-called business trip that Clay Tallon had indulged in so frequently, yet she could never bring herself to question him.

There was no alternative but to ride it out. Sooner or later Verity would go and it would all blow over, she told herself miserably – but she only half-believed it. In her heart of hearts she was convinced that she deserved no better treatment.

Now that the time of Verity's departure was so near, Loveday found she had no idea how Matthew would react. She tried not to watch him too obviously, carefully avoiding any evidence of possessiveness. He must, she thought, have room to breathe – and was unaware that she gave every appearance of being remote and uncaring. Even after Verity had gone, the distance between them seemed to remain as unbridgeable as ever. There were small, foolish misunderstandings, hurt feelings and hasty words, and when Matthew at last enlisted in the Duke of Cornwall's Light Infantry at the end of 1916, it almost came as a relief.

At the age of thirty-eight, he need not have gone, though with nothing but bad news pouring across the Channel and an increased recruitment drive, pressure to do so was great and his desire to be involved even greater. Or was it, Loveday wondered, his desire to be away from home that was greatest of all?

It was not as if he had anything much to keep him in Cornwall. His father was still quite capable of running the much reduced business in his absence, and indeed appeared to be doing so with a great deal of enjoyment and energy. Good old boy, dear of un, the workers said. Ent no one like old Clay Tallon. Never passes without a word and a laugh.

Matthew joined the Pioneer Battalion, which seemed appropriate since he had practical knowledge of burrowing and blasting. Loveday had been cheered by the thought that he would not, after all, be in the thick of the fighting. It had not occurred to her that the Pioneers were often in front of the front line and that always, when needed, they were detailed to defend the line as well as construct it.

He was sent to Salisbury Plain for his basic officer training, then to the Isle of Wight for further instruction. Relations between them, on his infrequent leaves, were repaired to a certain extent. They were kind to each other, and very polite, but always when he had gone, Loveday was conscious of a deep sadness. Nothing was the same, and now she was truly fearful that it never would be.

*　　*　　*

All but one of the gardeners had left and the rhododendrons had almost taken over again at Carrivick. Loveday looked at them with appreciation, happy to see them as she bicycled down the drive, rutted by the passage of ambulances, their colours shouting aloud that no matter how black the wickedness of man, nature would in the end have the last word.

The panniers on her bicycle were filled with soap and toothpaste and cigarettes; blue wool for Chief Petty Officer Marley's petit point, a yachting magazine for Lieutenant Gray, a fine-nibbed mapping pen for Leading Seaman Woolley, and a motley selection of books brought to the church hall in St Ninn for distribution.

There were two ambulances parked in the forecourt, newly arrived from Falmouth. She knew they were from Falmouth because the drivers were old friends, frequent visitors. The orderlies from one of the ambulances were manoeuvring a wheelchair in through the wide front door, but the others were preparing to leave.

"Lovely day," one called out. Loveday smiled and nodded, leaning her bicycle against a wall. "Never think there's a war on," he pursued. She nodded again.

What could one say? It was the peace, when it came, that would seem unbelievable. The war seemed to have been going on for ever, the stream of wounded never-ending. Terrible things were going on in Flanders, though she had a shrewd idea that those at home didn't know the half of it. Still, one had only to hear the lists of those killed to know it was hell out there. Ned Crowle had been lost only a couple of weeks ago; Missing, believed Killed, the telegram had said. She had been to Roskelly Farm to see his parents.

" 'Tis God's will," old Walter had said, wiping away his silent tears.

"But there's hope," she pointed out.

"There's always hope, my 'andsome. Underneath are th'Everlasting Arms, that's what the Good Book d'say, and that's where our hope d'rest."

Hope rested in the Americans, too, who had newly joined the fray. Over a snatched cup of coffee in the housekeeper's room, Sarah and Loveday agreed that their arrival in Europe would make all the difference.

"We're all so worn, so tired," Sarah said. "I have come to the conclusion that there is nothing more exhausting than the imminent expectation of dread news. Whereas they are fresh and strong, and as a race so energetic. Have you –?" She broke off, looking shamefaced.

"Have I what?" Loveday prompted.

"Nothing. I shouldn't have asked."

"You mean, have I heard from Matthew? Not since the last time I mentioned it." And a thin, unsatisfactory letter it had been, full of meaningless phrases. She smiled brightly, hoping to hide from Sarah the disappointment she had felt in its emptiness. "And if you dare to say to me that no news is good news," she went on, "I swear I shall crown you with one of those strategically placed bedpans."

"I wouldn't." Sarah held up her hands in an attitude of denial. "Though it probably is, you know. Well –" She stood up and smoothed the pale-blue checked overall that covered her skirt and blouse. "Lights, music, beginners, please. We must get this show on the road. We're short-staffed in the kitchen. Mrs Beswarick has Come Over Peculiar and little Kathleen Blamey hasn't come at all. Her fellow's home from France, so I gave her a few days off."

"I'll look in to see if I can help when I've finished my rounds."

"Oh, bless you! If you could –"

She was gone. Sarah was quite stout these days and her hair was grey, pulled back in a knot. Her erstwhile public would probably not have recognised her, but her energy was still prodigious, her personality such as would lift the spirits of the most devitalised sailor. At the beginning of the war she had merely allowed Carrivick to be used by others and had herself taken little part in its running; however, the difficulty in obtaining domestic staff and her own forcefulness soon changed all that. She had taken on the catering 'for a few weeks' when almost everyone else in the entire establishment had been laid low with influenza. Somehow, weeks had stretched to months, and then to years. Those in authority discovered a truth which she and Robert had always known:

she was an excellent housekeeper. The fine table she had kept before the war had been no accident. With Robert away in London at the Board of Trade, she had made the choice to stay on in Cornwall – to keep an eye on Carrivick, and to work her passage at the same time.

Largely her work was administrative; on this day, with difficulties in the kitchen, it was she herself who, with one of the VADs, brought the trays into the ward where Loveday was manning her trolley.

"This will bring the roses back into your cheeks," she said to one young lieutenant, smiling at him in such a way that she hoped would disguise the tears that she shed in her heart. He had been blown up in Scapa Flow. Twenty-two years old, with the shoulders of a rugger player, but he'd never walk again.

But no time for that; on to the next bed where a tray almost slipped out of her hand and she had to perform a quick juggling act to save it.

"*And* for my next trick –" she said. The men roared with laughter.

"Would you believe," Loveday asked the young lieutenant when she had gone, "that you have just had your lunch served by Sarah Sangster?"

"Who?" he asked, and Loveday laughed, shaking her head.

"Tell your parents," she said. "They'll be impressed even if you're not."

There was a good atmosphere at Carrivick. For the most part, the nurses were young, and although much in awe of the Matron, a deceptively sweet-faced woman in her fifties whose sharp tongue could almost reduce battle-hardened sailors to tears, there was a great deal of laughter.

Loveday knew, without question, that she couldn't have endured without it. Anyone could have carried out the menial work that she did, but for her it was a lifeline, filling the hours which might otherwise have been spent worrying about her menfolk. As it was, their safety, their comfort, dominated her thoughts whenever she had an idle moment. Well, she wasn't alone in that, she reminded herself constantly. Every woman with a husband or son in the forces felt the same. She hardly dared to admit to the thing she feared most: that

Matthew would be taken from her before matters were happily resolved between them.

Surely, surely, they had loved too much, been through too much, for it all to count as nothing? There were days when she felt happily confident that this must be true – but equally, there were long and sleepless nights when doubts flooded in and she felt certain that he had gone from her for ever.

Letters, both from Matthew and Oliver, were infrequent and uninformative, and of the two Loveday sometimes thought that Oliver wrote with more warmth. Even from him there had been nothing since a letter a month ago posted in Rosyth – a communication which told her little except that he was still alive. Cold waters, Loveday thought wretchedly, and was unwise enough to ask one of the men at Carrivick what it was like in the North Sea in the kind of gales the country was at that time enduring.

"Hell," he had replied simply. "A man would be cold and wet and frightened. Maybe hungry as well."

"My son's out there."

"Then I'm sorry for him," he said.

"I'm sure he's all right, Mummy," Sally said on one of her visits home. "I'd know if he wasn't."

She and Caroline were living with one of Caroline's aunts in Plymouth, working in the office of a naval shore establishment. Loveday hadn't been in favour of the enterprise at first, but had been won over by Sally's earnestness and determination. She couldn't help wishing she was with someone other than Caroline however, unfair to the girl though that might be. It was too great a reminder of the bewitching Mrs Spalding, no doubt currently causing as much havoc in Portsmouth as she had done in St Austell.

Of course Caroline was not to blame for anything, Loveday was fully aware of that. Neither was her mother, and most definitely not her aunt, who was the most respectable lady it was possible to meet. Still she would have preferred Sally to be living almost anywhere else, illogical though that might be. And so, very emphatically, did Matthew. His last leave before going to France had been marred by constant arguments on just that subject.

He was against the Plymouth project altogether, no matter

with whom Sally was living – was determined, indeed, to go roaring up there and bring her back to St Ninn. What on earth could Loveday be thinking of? he demanded. Didn't she have any idea what Plymouth was like?

"I know what Sally's like," Loveday had retorted. "She's a sensible girl, Matthew, with both feet on the ground. She's enjoying the work and feels needed and useful. I beg you not to make her give it up. She'll not easily forgive you."

"But all those sailors, Loveday, and two impressionable girls! What's this aunt like? Will she look after them properly? See they're in at a reasonable time? There are some terrible people about –"

"I know," Loveday said quietly. And they had looked at each other for a moment, until Matthew turned away with a sigh. Always the shadow, Loveday thought. He'll never forget. It reaches out, just when I least expect it.

"Well, I would have thought you, of all people –" he began, and sighed again. "I don't like it, and I think you're wrong. The whole world seems to have gone crazy. I shall tell her this weekend when she comes home that she's to give notice and pack her bags."

"Don't!" Loveday had begged unavailingly.

His orders to Sally had been equally unavailing. She had stared at him, open-mouthed.

"But Daddy, I can't possibly leave now," she said. "I'm needed. They're depending on me."

"Rubbish! There are plenty of girls."

"There aren't. Not like me. I understand all the rosters and the schedules. It's taken me weeks to learn the job and I'm very efficient at it."

They had battled and Sally had won; but it spoiled the weekend and the precious five-day embarkation leave.

Not that Sally's affairs were totally to blame for the uncomfortable atmosphere which characterised his short stay. Matthew himself seemed to have retreated from the partial warmth of recent months, almost as if he wished he hadn't come after all, Loveday felt. Almost as if he regretted the time spent away from his unit. He seemed irritable, with her and with everyone else. His father, cursing the Germans, had been treated to a burst of impatience that had, perhaps for the first time in their acquaintance, made Loveday feel quite sorry for him.

"Well," she said dryly to Matthew as they drove away. "At least you're not frightened of him any more."

He had not smiled.

"That sort of attitude makes me sick," he said. "The Bosch have a job to do, poor bastards, the same as we do."

"You were a bit hard on him, though. He is on your side, you know."

He had grunted at that and said nothing, until later when, staring out at the square and the church and the chestnut tree by the lychgate he had muttered a few words which might, perhaps, be taken as an apology.

"Nothing seems real," he said drearily. "I'm behaving rather badly, I'm afraid."

If only she could have reached him across the arid wasteland that seemed to divide them! Even in his arms, she knew it still existed. Now he was gone and there were only those stilted letters – letters full of clichés and banalities, saying nothing of any importance.

Oh, when would it all be over? Soon, soon, please God, so that they could all pick up the pieces and get on with their lives. She paused for a moment with her trolley at the doors of the conservatory to take a deep breath and will herself into a more cheerful frame of mind.

"Rag and bone," she called gaily, flinging open the door, greeted by a chorus of welcoming voices.

No one, she thought, conscious of a nagging pain behind her eyes, would ever know quite how tired she was of being so damned bright.

Matthew writhed and struggled, fighting the barbed wire. He was held in the entanglement – could not move, up or down or left or right, was being strangled, throttled –

He woke, panting. He was not caught in a barbed-wire entanglement. He was lying in his flea-bag on the floor of a dugout, somewhere close to the shattered village of Herleville.

The barbed wire belonged to tomorrow, when his small team was to move up to the Front. Wide awake now, he lay and thought about it, tried to prepare himself, knowing it was pointless. It was impossible to know exactly what to expect. Some said the Germans were preparing to pull out of the Somme area, but it didn't sound like it. He could hear the shellfire from here.

Tomorrow. The thought of it was like a cold, depressing weight on his stomach. It wasn't the right sort of mood in which to embark on such a project, he knew quite well; but what, in God's name, could one do about it? Only Generals and Field Marshals in Whitehall thought that war was glorious. For those on the ground – the muddy, rain-soaked ground – it was utterly depressing, more and more pointless, so many lives lost over so few yards of ground.

Not just names, either. Faces. People. Young Parker, for instance; no older than Oliver, with bright blue eyes and carroty hair and a mouth that was always ready to break into a grin, or a song or a cheerful obscenity. He'd gone last week, in the middle of uttering some of the choicest swearwords that Matthew had ever heard. Did that mean he'd go straight to hell, his mate Edyvean wanted to know? He was as young as Parker, a St Ninn boy, equally cheerful.

"I think this is our hell," Matthew had replied. "The devil himself couldn't dream up anything worse."

The sector of the line where they were going tomorrow had been held by the French who had now been relieved. He'd come across French trenches before. On the whole they were poor things – too shallow, without enough traverses. Their job was to move in and improve matters, both by increasing the number of traverses to limit the damage of the trench-mortar shells and by raising the parapet. It sounded simple enough; the trouble was that the French all too often left relics behind. Corpses were buried too near the surface. There was often the odd hand-grenade. One of his most reliable men had lost a hand just recently, picking up a smoking grenade discovered just below the surface of the earth and attempting, too late, to throw it into a shell-hole outside the trench.

It had been quiet that day, too, and they'd been off their guard. No, one didn't know what to expect. He ought to sleep. Morning would come soon enough.

The others seemed to be able to sleep anywhere – sitting down, standing up, even on the march. They slept with Woodbines drooping between their lips, a forkful of food halfway to their mouths, a word half-spoken. He wished that he could. Too old, maybe? Dad, they called him. Like Oliver.

He didn't want to think of Oliver. It was too painful – almost as painful to remember the sudden brief friendship that had flared between them before the war as to remember their last meeting when they had been so at odds, snarling at each other about the merits and demerits of Oakby. Oakby! Good God, could anything be more irrelevant?

Where and on what ocean was Oliver now? He hoped he was safe. Even his own comfortless situation seemed preferable to the icy sea, especially now that the submarine war was hotting up. George Spalding was gone, drowned in the North Sea, so Verity had written. Poor bastard. He hadn't replied to her letter yet – didn't know what to say or what he was supposed to feel. The truth was that he felt nothing very much. George Spalding had never been a three-dimensional figure to him and it seemed a little late to start feeling sorry for him now.

He had not meant to see Verity again, once she left Cornwall. He had tried to mend his marriage – he was sure he had tried, but Loveday had seemed unapproachable. Hurt, perhaps? No, why should she be? She couldn't have known anything about Verity, he felt quite sure of that.

The Isle of Wight's proximity to Portsmouth had not escaped him, but he had done nothing to seek her out. Meeting her had been pure chance, and had come at a time when he had been in a curious mood – bored with drilling and training, exasperated by the Army's petty rules and restrictions, apprehensive about what lay in store, guilty because somehow the odd weekends he was able to spend with Loveday always seemed to turn out so unsatisfactory. He knew he was drinking more than was good for him and that he was uncharacteristically moody and ill-humoured. When David Thorpe, a brother officer, invited him to go along to a party, held at the home of old friends in Portsmouth, he had refused at first.

"I'm not in the mood for parties," he said. "I'd put a blight on the proceedings."

"Rubbish! It'll do you good. You've got a face like a wet week, and speaking for myself, Tallon, I'm fed up with seeing it around. Come on, spruce yourself up, man, and come with me. You haven't been off the island for weeks."

He had done so at last – unenthusiastic, but too lethargic to hold out against Thorpe's persuasion. The unknown friends, a Mr and Mrs Colville, were effusively welcoming, and a glass of over-sweet punch was pressed upon him. Introductions were made to a dozen strangers, to whom he could think of little to say. Desperately he smiled and smiled and wished he had stayed behind at camp, until suddenly he had looked across the room where, to his total astonishment, he saw Verity framed in the doorway. It had not, in all honesty, occurred to him that she might be a fellow guest. Portsmouth was a big place, crammed with naval personnel and their wives. How could he have known that the Spaldings had become tenants of property owned by the Colvilles and were now close neighbours?

"Oh, here's dear little Mrs Spalding at last," his hostess had said. "You must come and meet her. She's being just too terribly brave all on her own, with her husband at sea in the most frightful danger."

"I simply couldn't believe it," Verity said afterwards. "My heart turned at least three somersaults when I saw you coming towards me. Oh, say you were pleased, too, Matthew. You know you were!"

"Of course I was," Matthew agreed. How could he not have been pleased? It seemed the most cheering thing that had happened to him in ages. Even now, ten months later, he could smile at the thought of it.

He must have dozed at last, for suddenly it was light and time to move. A sleety rain was falling, cold and penetrating, as they marched along narrow lanes, through a grim, deserted landscape. Could this be springtime? There was nothing but devastation on either side; ruined villages, trees no more than jagged stumps, no leaves or blossom or colour to be seen.

There would be primroses along the Cornish hedgerows now, amid the ferns and aconites and ivies. Primroses, too, in Hampshire no doubt, though it had been bluebell-time when last he saw it. Trudging dispiritedly through the French lanes, he thought of that last weekend with Verity, seeing again the carpet of flowers beneath the new, young beech leaves, and Verity Spalding's piquant face cupped in his hands.

"After the war –" she had said, reaching up to kiss him.

"We said we wouldn't talk of after the war."

"But I can't help thinking of it. You'll come back to me. To *me*! You *must*! It's fate, Matthew, meeting again like this, after we'd said goodbye."

"It's not what we agreed, Verity."

"To hell with what we agreed! That was then. This is now, and everything's different."

"We're both married. We can't ignore that."

She had pulled away from him at that, snatching angrily at a leaf and twirling it between her fingers. She pouted, like a hurt small girl.

"You know how little my marriage means to me. I married far too young, and I hardly knew George at all. I only agreed to it to please my father. I've never loved anyone like this – as for *your* marriage, it's my guess that it's no better than mine."

"I've never said that."

"You said things had gone sour."

"I said –" Matthew had fallen silent, bitten his lip and shaken his head hopelessly. He was no longer sure of what he had said or what he thought. He only knew that though the world in which he had strayed with Verity had a brittle kind of gaiety, it lacked something indefinable. Reality, perhaps?

It was the following weekend that he had gone home for his embarkation leave and Loveday and he had fallen out over Sally's job in Plymouth. That she was living with Verity's aunt gave the whole thing an ironic twist. Every instinct he possessed screamed aloud that it was dangerous for her to be there, in that household – or was it he who was in danger? What was wrong with him? Everything he said or did seemed to upset someone. He was at odds with Loveday, at odds with Sally, at odds with his father, and most of all at odds with himself.

If that's reality, he thought, there's precious little to be said for it – and found it a relief to get back to the uncritical, undemanding company of Verity. Was it Verity he loved after all? Had Loveday, guarding their love by hiding the truth, finally managed to kill it off altogether?

And did it really matter, all this heart-searching? Only this was real – the rain and the mud and the weight of the pack he was carrying, and the longing for a hot drink and the fear of what they would find, what would happen to them tomorrow. And the men. They were real.

The trenches were proving hard to find and an early dusk was falling as they approached their general area through rain that had thinned to a drizzle. They came at last to a small Command Post, and as they trudged towards it they were met by a captain in the Welsh Regiment. The orders had been changed, he said. The Pioneers were to proceed to a trench abandoned by the Germans about five kilometres further on.

"Are you sure?" Matthew asked wearily.

"Positive, old boy. It came over on the field telephone less than an hour ago. I've been waiting for you to get here. You look as if you could do with a drink."

"We all could. I think we'll stop and brew up. A hot drink and a smoke will cheer everyone up a bit."

It wasn't much, but it helped. The irrepressible Edvyean produced his mouth-organ and played a few tunes of the moment – "Everybody's *doing* it, *doing* it, *doing* it," sang the men, without a great deal of fervour.

Willis, the subaltern, had disappeared towards the Welsh captain's dugout. He was a willowy young man, barely out of the sixth form of his public school, who had only just recently joined the unit. Matthew had not warmed to him. He seemed arrogant and aloof – had hardly said a word the entire day. But fear often took strange forms. Perhaps silence was to be preferred to the excessive garrulity which seemed to strike many men in a similar situation. Maybe a tot or two of the Welsh captain's whisky would do him good.

They were supplied with guides to take them to the abandoned trenches, but somehow even they managed to lose the way and it was pitch dark by the time they arrived at their destination. They were to begin work early next morning, extending the trenches and setting up field telephones back to the Command Post, and a hot drink followed by sleep seemed to be the priority for the exhausted men; however, they had barely fallen out before a runner arrived with a verbal order. The area was to be patrolled at once.

Matthew swore, comprehensively. Many of the men were already asleep where they sat. Willis, it now appeared, was suffering from some sort of gastric complaint; had been suffering all day, but had been prevented by his stiff upper lip from mentioning the matter, even back at Command HQ where something might have been done about it.

No-man's-land stretched before them, dark and impenetrable. Everything was quiet. How near or far were the new German positions was unknown. Matthew felt very vulnerable with his small band of Pioneers, as if he had brought them to the edge of the known world. Neither Loveday nor Verity had any place here, and he had long since put them from his mind. Only these men, these boys, this patch of earth, had any significance.

"Sir?" Edvyean was calling to him, holding up a mug of tea. Matthew came down into the trench and sipped it gratefully.

"I'm going on patrol," he said. "Pass the word along. I don't want to get shot by some gun-happy insomniac."

"Who else is on duty, sir?"

"I don't know." Hopelessly, Matthew looked down the trench at the huddled figures. He wasn't officer material, he decided, giving a small and mirthless inward laugh at this somewhat belated conclusion. He didn't want to wake any of them.

"I'll see how it goes. You youngsters need your sleep. Lieutenant Willis isn't well."

They were a small unit – a team that had worked together for some time, apart from the lieutenant – and there was little formality observed. Edvyean, in particular, felt himself in a privileged position. In his previous incarnation as a delivery boy working for Snell's Butchery in St Ninn he had delivered pork chops and the weekend joint and strings of sausages to Church Cross House.

"You got to 'ave someone to relieve ee, sir. You cain't

walk around all night, stands to reason. Thass a mug's game, that is."

"Strictly between us, Charlie, I don't want to walk around anywhere, but everyone's dead on their feet."

"You get some sleep, sir. I'm all right for a bit – no, true as I'm 'ere," he went on. " 'Tis all quiet. I'll take first watch."

"Well, if you're sure." The offer was more than tempting.

"Dead sure, sir."

"Thanks, Edyvean. I appreciate it." He was suddenly so tired that he hardly knew how to hold his head up. "Mind how you go. The ground is sure to be peppered with shell-holes and I don't want you breaking an ankle."

Dead sure, he'd said. Afterwards Matthew couldn't get the words from his mind, couldn't rid himself of the guilt, couldn't rid himself of the hideous, shameful relief. What sort of a man was he, that he could feel thankful that it was young Edyvean who had stopped the sniper's bullet? He was hardly more than a boy, his whole life before him. He could see him now, with his cap on the back of his head, whistling as he rode up to the door of Church Cross House on his delivery bike, not a care in the world.

Somehow, against the odds, he had always believed in his own invincibility. Not any more.

Edyvean's death and his own instinctive reaction to it had jolted and humbled him. Who was he to think that some special providence would ensure a safe home-coming for him?

I am nobody, he thought; and from that night on, he knew he did not deserve to survive, felt quite sure he would not survive. A pity, he thought with dreary resignation, just when he seemed to be recognising essential truths more clearly than he had done for a long time. It was as if by dying in his place, Charlie Edyvean had shaken the kaleidoscope that was his life so that all the pieces fell into place. There were things to do, he realised with sudden urgency, before he could go in peace.

He grew even quieter and more thoughtful. The men regarded him warily, aware of the doom-laden aura that emanated from him, knowing instinctively that there were demons that haunted him.

*　　*　　*

373

Loveday, pushing her bicycle up the steep hill which led to Church Cross, was not looking where she was going. There was a stiff breeze blowing and her head was down, all her energies engaged in making her way homeward, her main concern being whether she would reach Church Cross House before her hat blew off and was never seen again.

It had been a hard day at Carrivick. One of her favourite Ordinary Seamen had been told that there was no hope, after all, of saving his leg, while another older man, a Chief Petty Officer, had been taken to Truro for an emergency operation just when he seemed to be so much better. On a less dramatic note, Petty Officer Hoskin couldn't seem to settle to anything because his wife was imminently expecting a baby, and Ordinary Seaman Rosewall had been annoyed about the green wool she had brought him because it didn't quite match the original colour. It had been fruitless to explain that St Austell was not exactly the hub of commerce – that tapestry wool was as scarce as hen's teeth, and he had only been moderately appeased by her promise to look for the right colour in Truro on her next visit.

Thank heaven matters on the domestic front seemed less fraught with problems. Kathleen Blamey was back at work sporting a brand-new diamond-chip engagement ring, and Mrs Beswarick was restored to health, making Sarah's life a great deal easier.

"Excuse me," a voice said, interrupting her thoughts.

She became aware of legs encased in a pair of sailor's trousers standing in her way and came to an abrupt halt. Her eyes seemed to travel up endlessly, past the jersey and the square collar to the face above it; a beaky face, burned brown by the wind and fuller now than when she last saw it. Brown eyes, merry eyes –

"Oliver!" she cried, letting the bicycle fall to the ground and throwing herself upon him. "When did you get home?"

"Less than an hour ago. I was going to come and meet you, but Susan plied me with tea and yeast cake."

"How long –?"

"Forty-eight hours."

"Oh darling, such a short time!"

"But totally unexpected, so let's be thankful for small

mercies. We had to come into Plymouth for repairs and I wangled leave, being so near home. I saw Sally last night. She looks marvellous."

"So do you. You're so big!"

"Amazing, isn't it? I'll be able to look down on Dad now. And Grandfather."

He picked up the bicycle and together they walked towards home.

"Give me all the news," he said. "How are you getting on, all on your own? And how's Dad? Have you heard from him lately?"

She told him all she could, stealing glances at him as if she could hardly believe that this tall stranger was her son.

"I shall take tomorrow off," she told him when they were at home. "Sarah let Kathleen Blamey take time off when her soldier came home. She'll be equally kind to me now that my sailor is home from the sea. Oh darling, tell me everything! I imagine such terrible things."

"You mustn't," he said. "Honestly, it's not bad – it's better than Oakby, anyway, and a damned sight better than the trenches." He looked at her and bit his lip. "Sorry," he said. "That was tactless. Dad's there, I know. He'd probably say it's a lot better on dry land, but personally I'm glad I chose the sea."

It was still blustery the following day, but bright – just the day, he said, for going up to Trelew.

"I think about it when I'm out there," he said. "I can't wait to get back."

"To Trelew?"

"I love it up there. It's so clean and high and windy. I used to go there all the time."

"I didn't know."

"I took that picture –"

"The one that won the competition. I still have it. I thought it was just a chance thing."

"Not on your life. I used to go up there and hang around until Cap'n Noah gave me a job to do."

"You never said!"

"Well –" He shrugged and grinned at her. "I suppose I liked to think I had a secret life."

('Twasn't nobody's business but mine,' Henry had said.)

"Do you want to go up there on your own now?"

"No." He put an arm around her shoulders and hugged her. "Let's walk up together. We can take a pasty and eat it on the moor – if you'd like to, that is."

"I'd love to," she said.

She could not believe that this was Oliver – this calm and confident young man who chatted to her of his hopes and fears and who, in turn, listened to her problems and gave her the benefit of his advice. He'd noticed, he said, that there was a tree fouling the guttering. He would fix it before he went back. And it seemed to him that the brakes on the bicycle weren't very good. He'd look at them as soon as they got back from the moor.

"I'm good at fixing things," he said as they sat and ate their pasty in the shelter of a Cornish stone hedge. "It'll come in useful after the war when I'm in the business. Do you think Dad will want me?"

"Want you? Of course he'll want you!"

She was not as confident as she sounded. Would he want her? Would he want any of them? It was these sort of questions that kept her awake at nights.

"Hope you're right," Oliver said.

"Of course I'm right. I'm just a bit surprised you want to do it."

"What else would I do? Pure clay runs in my veins, you know, not blood."

"I always thought you'd want to go in for photography. You're so good at it."

He pulled a face.

"No! Oh, it's a great hobby and I enjoy it. I'll always enjoy it, but I never thought of making a living at it." He rested his head against the grey stones behind him and for a moment said nothing, his eyes following the path of a bird in flight. "Yellowhammer," he commented idly. He came back to the subject of the future. "It's all going to be different, you know, after the war. I mean, everything's going to be mechanised. I was thinking, we ought to get hold of army surplus lorries and get rid of those great carts. Come on –"

He stood up and reached out to help her up. "Time to be on our way."

Loveday felt she hated time; hated to think of the hours rushing past. She took her watch off so that she could pretend to herself that it was standing still.

But at least Oliver was giving her much to think about after he had gone – and much to write to Matthew about, which was something to be thankful for. Sometimes she felt her letters must seem no more than a boring recital of the same events, repeated over and over.

Now she could tell him of Oliver's enthusiasm; of the way Cap'n Noah had greeted him as if he were an old and trusted friend. How Oliver had greeted Cap'n Noah, man to man, not in the least frightened of him, and of the men at the clayworks who had come up to him and shaken him by the hand – had joked and laughed with him.

"We didn't know him at all," she wrote to Matthew when Oliver's forty-eight-hour pass was no more than a memory. "All those times when he went off on his own – many of them, anyway – he was up at Trelew, pottering about, doing odd jobs, helping Cap'n Noah. And the men like him so!

"We walked all day, and we talked and talked and talked. He reminded me so much of – you'll never guess! None other than my father. His features are different, but he is equally tall and thin and there is a likeness of expression and something about his eyes. His care for me was rather touching. He has changed so much. He says the Navy has done that, and that the Army will have changed you, too. I wonder if it has? I hope not too much – but be assured that I shall still love you, my darling – now and for ever."

Had she said that often enough? Vehemently enough? Did her letters convey her feelings adequately? It was so hard to know. It was an article of faith with her to write as if nothing was wrong between them, but it was impossible not to be affected by his restraint. He was always conscious of the censor, he said – of some third party reading what he wrote to her. It made, she sometimes thought, a most convenient excuse.

She sat for a long time after she had finished her own letter, thinking about him. Would a stranger come back to her?

Sometimes she felt it was a stranger who had gone away. Sometimes it was hard to picture him as he had been before her revelation.

One step, she thought sadly. One chance step had led to this and had brought the shining edifice of her marriage crashing down. God alone knew if it could ever be rebuilt.

❧ 19 ❧

Clay Tallon suffered a stroke while visiting Trelew early in 1918. Accustomed to robust health, the fact that he felt distinctly unwell that morning had been the cause of annoyance rather than concern.

"Why don't you stay at home?" Mrs Wilkinson, his housekeeper, asked him, in the cosy, nannyish voice she kept for him. "Have a day in bed, all tucked up nice and warm with your new jigsaw."

He glared at her in reply to this entirely well-meant suggestion. She would have to go, he thought. She was just precisely the sort of fussy, busybodying sort of woman he had never been able to stand, with a moustache on her that any man might envy. How Loveday had thought her any improvement on her predecessor – or, come to think of it, the housekeeper before that one – he would never know.

"I shall be perfectly all right as the day wears on," he said, with icy dignity. She wasn't a woman he felt merited any exercise of charm.

But he had not been all right. The day wore on, but it brought chaos and panic and an ambulance, and a terrifying paralysis down his left side.

He was confined to a hospital bed for two weeks, but afterwards came home to Prospect Lodge, his handsome face pulled sideways a little, his left leg dragging slightly. He had to use a walking stick now, but otherwise his vigour seemed unimpaired.

Sarah sought Loveday out one day at Carrivick to tell her that he had come looking for her, that he wanted to talk to her urgently and that she had shown him to her own sitting room where he was even now waiting for an audience with his daughter-in-law.

Loveday, engaged in teaching a young seaman to knit socks, looked at her in bewilderment.

"What on earth can he want?" she asked, conscious of the shiver of apprehension that visited her so often these days. She asked the seaman to excuse her and together she and Sarah walked up the corridor. "It's not Matthew, is it?"

"Of course it's not," Sarah reassured her. "How could he know anything that you don't?"

"I don't know." Still she felt uneasy. He couldn't surely have found out – no, of course he hadn't! Joely Tregilgas had lain in his unhallowed, murderer's grave for years and there was no one else who would tell her secret. But still, it was a strange and uncharacteristic thing for Clay Tallon to do, to come looking for her. Whenever he had wanted her to sort out his domestic arrangements, he had never done other than to send for her.

"Ah, Loveday, my dear –" He rose as she came into the room where he was waiting for her, and favoured her with his most charming smile.

My dear? Alarm bells rang in Loveday's head. She trusted that smile no more than she had ever done, but still she smiled back and greeted him politely. Since Millicent's death an armed truce seemed to have existed between them. Wariness still undoubtedly existed, but now that Matthew was at the Front there was an acceptance of the fact that they needed each other.

"You're looking much better," she said.

"And you're looking as lovely as ever."

"Thank you. Did you have some special reason for coming to see me today?"

"Reason? Do I need a reason?" He cocked his eyebrows at her, the impish smile not quite what it was now that his face was slightly distorted. "I was in the area inspecting some of my properties and thought I would call to see how you were getting on – and incidentally, to ask if you had any news. It seems some time since I heard anything."

The pang of pity took her by surprise. He was lonely, she

realised. He missed Millicent and Matthew and Sally and in his loneliness he turned to her.

"Sit down," she said. "I'll go and get some coffee and be back in two shakes."

"Thank you, my dear. You're a good girl."

Good girl, indeed! He must surely be very lonely, Loveday thought amusedly as she hurried away. It was a great pity that there wasn't a way of transmitting by some miraculous means the image of this new, chastened Clay Tallon, so that Matthew could see him at first hand. He would certainly find it difficult to believe his eyes.

Once back in Sarah's sitting room with the coffee, Loveday told him all her latest news, such as it was. Sally, she informed him, was planning to come home for Easter, and to bring a young man with her.

"A naval lieutenant," she told her father-in-law. "A most charming young man. I was introduced to him the last time I was in Plymouth. Now pray, don't look like that even before you've met him! I feel sure you'll approve of him."

"Is she serious about him?"

"I think so."

"She's much too young."

"No younger than I was. Please, don't spoil things for them by being unpleasant. You'll be the loser, you know."

"You mean I'll lose her the way I've lost Sybil? She didn't come near me in hospital, you know. She's a hard woman. An unforgiving woman."

"She's also a very busy woman."

"Well, perhaps." He sighed gustily. "Still, you would have thought – her old father, seriously ill . . ." His voice trailed away, then picked up again. "I suppose I must bite on the bullet where Sally is concerned."

"I think so." Loveday looked at him with compassion. "It doesn't mean a lessening of her love for the rest of us, you know. Love isn't rationed, like sugar. There's always more of it where the last lot came from."

"What?" He beetled his brows at her as if she were speaking in an unknown language. Then slowly he nodded and sighed. "Perhaps you're right," he said. "I hope you're right."

From Matthew, she had had no letter for the past two weeks.

"I suppose," Clay Tallon said, "that no news is good news."

"I try to believe so," Loveday agreed, with no sign of the fury with which she would have greeted this statement had it been made by Sarah.

There was a pause in their conversation, but looking at him across the hearthrug that separated them, Loveday felt certain that there was some further reason for this visit – something quite apart from his quest for news.

"It must be a worrying time for you," he said at last. He put his cup and saucer down on a table beside him and surveyed his nails, pursing his lips and frowning as if something about them displeased him. "Impossible for you not to think what might happen."

"If you are asking if I ever think about the possibility of Matthew not returning," Loveday said, "I suppose the answer is 'Yes' – but only in very low moments. I try to keep hopeful, to think positively. There is no point in doing otherwise."

"Very sensible." He smiled at her. There was, she thought, something much more appealing about this new, slightly lopsided smile than the old one. It gave him an appearance of vulnerability. "I merely wanted to say –" He hesitated a moment before continuing. "It's just that – I want you to know that whatever happens, you are a most valued member of my family. It – it hasn't always been so," he said, hurrying on. "We've had our differences, I'm well aware, but life goes on and things change. I wanted you to know that you will always have a home with me, should you need it."

Loveday stared at him in total astonishment.

"That – that's kind of you," she said. "May I ask what has brought about this change of heart?"

He hesitated again.

"This dreadful war, for one thing," he said. "And also the fact that in the past few weeks I've been aware of growing old and of the need to face my own mortality." He cocked his eyebrows at her. "We all make mistakes, you know. I was wrong about you, Loveday. You've been a good wife to

Matthew, a good mother to your children. I suppose, in a way, I was jealous . . ."

"Jealous?" She stared at him in astonishment.

"Of what Matthew had. You and Matthew. The closeness."

Little did he know, she thought dryly.

"You could have had the same."

"Never! It was different. Millicent –" He broke off and stared down at the carpet. "It wasn't the same," he said after a moment.

"No." She could only agree with him. "You dominated her, or tried to."

"Didn't always succeed, though. She went her own way, if she felt strongly enough." He stood up. "Well, mustn't keep you, my dear. I know you have valuable work to do, and I admire you for it. Matthew will come home safely, I'm sure of it, but I wanted you to know that I'll be here, to look after you."

Being faced with his own mortality, Loveday thought as she put the cups on the tray after he had gone, seemed to have done him the world of good.

It was not until she was home again that she had leisure to think over Clay Tallon's extraordinary visit. More than extraordinary, she thought. Was it truly family feeling that had prompted it – a sudden upsurge of love and concern for his son, and with it, concern for his son's wife? Were they friends, she and her father-in-law? Did this signal the end of all enmity? Such a change of heart seemed almost too good to be true.

Almost certainly, loneliness accounted for it. He was lost without Millicent, even though he had done his best to keep her under his thumb.

Not that he had always succeeded, as he was the first to admit. There was, after all, Piper's Piece –

Piper's Piece! She sat bolt upright in her chair. She had forgotten Piper's Piece – Millicent's insurance policy. Was that the answer? Oh, the wily old fox!

That was it, of course. He had suddenly thought to himself: what if Matthew doesn't come back? What will she do then? And having thought, he had gone into action – played the part of the loving father-in-law, neutralised any bad blood between them. The wily old fox, she thought again, and laughed to herself.

Later still, she wondered if she had been too harsh in her judgement. After all, he had had a shock – had woken up to find himself in hospital. Perhaps it had affected him. He had never been ill before, not in all the time she had known him.

She laughed again. It didn't really matter anyway. Whatever happened, she would never be disloyal enough to sell Piper's Piece to a competitor – but it wouldn't do Clay Tallon any harm to wonder a little, she decided. To find him wooing her with his charm as she had seen him woo so many others was a pleasant novelty.

Anyway, it was all academic. Nothing would happen to Matthew. He would come home and all misunderstandings would be swept away. This, for some reason, was a day when she felt quite certain of it.

The rumours were that there would be a spring offensive. The Germans were planning a big push, so the word went, and no one was inclined to disbelieve it.

Matthew, for the moment enjoying a quiet period in a billet behind the lines, refused the prospect of company other than a bottle of whisky, and began a letter to Loveday.

"My dearest," he wrote. "If you should receive this, you will know that I'm not coming home."

He paused and chewed the end of his pen. He had written such a letter before, but always, on reading it afterwards, it had seemed stilted and unsatisfactory, expressing little of what he truly wanted to say. How to start? He had never been particularly fluent when it came to letter-writing and this, surely, must be one of the most difficult tasks known to man. The only thing was to put down the words just as they came to him, hoping that she would know they came from the heart.

"As I write," he continued, "I am full of sadness and contrition. I love you with all my heart. I have always loved you, and should it not be given to me to come home and assure you of this in person, 'I shall but love thee better

384

after death' as some poet-Johnny said. Shakespeare? Anyway, you'll know.

"I am such a fool, Loveday. I can't think why you love me, though I know that you do. We had such a bright, shining thing between us and somehow I managed to ruin it – because of what? Pride, I suppose. Stupidity, certainly. Somehow I created a no-man's-land between us where communication on any loving level was impossible, and now we may never have the chance to recapture the happiness we had before.

"I have men under me who seem like children. I agonise for them, make allowances for them, try to make their lot as easy as possible, even though I can do very little. Loveday, those children are older than you were when you were faced with the decisions that shaped your life. How can I have shown so little understanding?

"The decisions you made were made because of love – love for your stupid, obtuse husband. I know that now, and I know that nothing else is of any importance in this crazy, hateful, ugly world. Only love matters. Love between you and me, love between us and our children. That only will endure long after we are dust.

"You were the best part of me and this part, like the fool I am, I did my best to destroy. I can't begin to explain or excuse it. Here, in a world gone mad, I stand in total amazement at my own attempts at self-destruction. Regret is a sour taste in my mouth.

"So forgive me, my darling, I implore you. Forgive me for my lack of understanding about Oliver. I read your letter about his leave with such happiness. Of course he must go into the business. We want the name of Tallon to live on, don't we?

"And such news, too, of Sally! Is the young man good enough for her? You say so, and therefore I must believe it. At any rate, I will not emulate my father who, I dare swear, will huff and puff and want to blow the young man's house down, but will only say that with my dying breath I shall pray for her happiness.

"Remember me with love, my darling, however little I deserve it, and thank you for the wonderful years we had."

He read through what he had written. It was still inadequate, he thought, but it was an improvement on his last attempt.

Should he have said more about the children? He picked up the photograph of Loveday that he carried in his wallet – had always carried in his wallet, now that he thought about it, even during the Verity days. Shouldn't that have told him something? He looked at it for a long time. She was smiling a little and looked as if she was about to speak. It was impossible, somehow, to look at it and not to smile back, in spite of the weight of unshed tears that constricted his throat.

On reflection, he thought he had said enough. Who knew what eyes might see it? He wanted her secret to be kept. She would break the code – would see that everything he had written shouted aloud his acceptance and his love. Once again he read it through, signed it and folded it – then paused for a moment and picked up his pen once more.

"P.S." he wrote. "I think it was Elizabeth Barrett Browning."

He smiled, folded the letter again and sealed it in an envelope. He'd give it to Colonel Shaw, he thought. He'd make certain it was sent, when and if necessary.

He was pouring himself a tot of whisky when the bombardment started. A fragile peace had suddenly given way to war at its noisiest and most shattering and for a moment he stood, incapable of movement, while the earth shook under him.

Good old Fritz, he thought dryly. Damned if he wasn't right on cue.

Loveday and Sàrah were snatching a few moments to drink their coffee in the sunshine at Carrivick, sitting on a bench that was sheltered by a wall where roses rioted in untended abandon. The air was full of their scent and of the sound of birdsong. Any moment now, Loveday thought, closing her eyes and lifting her face to the sun, I shall undoubtedly find myself remarking that nobody would know there was a war on.

"How is your sainted father-in-law getting on with his new housekeeper?" Sarah asked. Loveday sighed and opened her eyes.

"Quite well," she said. "But she insists she's only temporary. I'm beginning to think I have no alternative but to go and look after him myself. That's what he wants, believe it or not."

"My dear Loveday! That would be a fate worse than death."

"Maybe. Or maybe not. We don't get on too badly these days."

"You say Edwin likes this new woman?"

"He seems to. She's rather pretty, in a buxom sort of way, and gives him a bit of backchat, which he enjoys."

"Can't you persuade her to stay on?"

"Not a hope. She never stays anywhere, she tells me."

"I wouldn't like that," Sarah said after a moment, looking out at the unchanging view, the folded hills, the blue and sparkling sea. "Funny how a place can get you, isn't it? I loved it here from the moment I came, and now I feel part of it. These past four years have only rooted me deeper."

"Mm. I know what you mean." Loveday was silent for a moment. "Someone said to me once," she went on, her voice tripping a little as she remembered who had said it, and where, "that I would travel far but never leave the clay. It didn't seem to make sense at the time, but I suppose you could say that for a little girl from Fourlanesend I've travelled a fair way – especially if I go and live with Clay Tallon in Prospect Lodge! Could I stand it, do you think?"

Sarah smiled and shook her head, unwilling to commit herself.

"He's changed, you say."

"Oh Sarah, I don't know! I don't trust the old rogue – never have, never will. One moment I feel sorry for him, the next I feel quite sure he's playing me like a fish on a line."

"But you're getting along better than you used to do."

Loveday laughed.

"Yes, I admit it. I accused him the other day of only being nice to me because of Piper's Piece and in turn he accused me of being a cynic – but I swear it's that little bit of land that's effected the change. It's as if he started to force himself to be friendly towards me, and now can't get out of the habit."

"Perhaps Millicent was wiser than we all guessed. Is he

managing to cope with the business, now that he's only working half-time? Who's running things?"

"There are a few clerks, and Miss Pike, of course. She's been a tower of strength."

"There'll be an enormous job for Matthew to do after the war, to get the business back on its feet."

"He'll have Oliver to help him, if he chooses to allow it. Isn't that a strange thought? I never imagined it, somehow. He and Matthew didn't always see eye to eye in the old life, but things will surely be different after the war. Oliver has changed so much. I wrote and told his father all about it, but I haven't had a reply. After the war!" she repeated, savouring the words. "It's like talking about a far country, isn't it? Some place that's quite alien to us all. I suppose we'll reach it one day." She sighed heavily. "But how long, oh Lord, how long?"

"Not long," Sarah said. "Somehow it feels to me as if we're getting towards the end of Act III. Soon the curtain will be rung down –"

"Let us hope," Loveday said wearily, "that it is to the sound of tumultuous applause."

Somehow, in spite of the sunshine, she could not feel hopeful. It was one of *those* sort of days.

The sound of the railway porters' voices at Newton Abbot made Matthew realise that, against all expectations, he was back on West Country soil at last. The knowledge filled him with a feeling of unutterable bliss. Not until he crossed the Tamar Bridge would he feel that he was truly home, though, he told himself severely. This, after all, was still foreign territory to the true Cornishman.

"Seems to be going on for ever, doesn't it?" said the woman in the corner of the first-class carriage brightly, snapping round and eager eyes. She had thin, high-coloured cheeks and a twitching mouth, and ever since joining the train at Reading she had done her best to draw the rather interesting army officer in the opposite corner into conversation. Now that the aged couple who had occupied the other two corners had left the train at Exeter, she felt less inhibited. Now, perhaps, he would respond.

"I beg your pardon?" Matthew leaned forward a little.

"The journey. Such a long way."

"But worth every mile, and every hour." He smiled at her, but said no more, awkwardly picking up his book and immersing himself in it once more, putting it down on his knee every now and again to turn the page. Poor man, she thought. Perhaps he was in pain. His left arm was heavily strapped and supported by a sling, so he must have been wounded. Perhaps that accounted for the fact that he seemed to want to keep himself to himself – or was he merely shy? It was all rather a pity. She would have enjoyed a little chat to pass the time.

She was on her way to Penzance to stay with her old schoolfriend, Hetty Wells, and as the miles passed she made up a little story with which to enliven her arrival.

"My dear, *such* a delightful man," she would say. "And so frightfully brave. We chatted all the way down. Direct from France, he told me. From the Front. Wounded. I could see such suffering in his face, such gratitude for a woman's company and a little amusing conversation, after what he must have gone through. He wanted to see me again, of course, but it wasn't possible. He had other commitments."

Or had he? She really had to find out.

"I expect your wife will be feeling so excited at this moment," she said roguishly as he put his book down once more to turn the page. He smiled back politely.

"She doesn't expect me. I tried to phone last night from London, but couldn't get through. Nothing much seems to have changed since I've been away. I thought of sending a telegram, but decided I'd simply catch the early train."

"Oh, but what a *surprise* for her!" She caught her lip between her teeth and hesitated for a moment. "Is that really wise, I wonder? I mean – supposing she's – " She came to a full stop.

"Entertaining her lover?" His mouth twitched with amusement.

The woman was covered with confusion.

"No, no, of course not. Out, I was going to say. Shopping, or something."

The officer smiled again.

"I know where she'll be."

Carrivick. Where it all began.

He could see her now, standing on the stairs looking down to where he stood at the foot, dark hair showing beneath her tam-o'-shanter, the delicate oval of her face tinted like a wild rose, and eyes that could bewitch at one glance.

"I had a friend," said the woman, "who was in the same sort of position. I mean, her husband came home when she didn't expect it and it so happened that she had gone to stay with her mother who had been ill –" She chattered on, and Matthew dreamed.

How could he be sure that she would welcome his return? God knew he hadn't been particularly pleasant the last time he was home. She might have met someone – some wounded naval officer to whom she had ministered at Carrivick. Someone who had taken one look at her and had been enslaved, just as he had been before he had somehow lost his way.

"And then, of course, this friend – this *other* friend, the one my friend had lent her flat to, she heard this banging in the night and she thought she was being burgled –"

She wouldn't have changed. Steadfast was the word for Loveday.

"The policeman insisted on taking him – oh!"

Thank heaven for small mercies, Matthew thought. At least the arrival of the ticket collector had managed to shut her up, though he had something of a problem retrieving his ticket from the pocket of the holdall where he had been unwise enough to put it. Sticking it in had been easy enough. Taking it out with his shoulder strapped and his arm in a sling was proving all but impossible.

"Oh, do allow me," the woman said, seeing his difficulty. She plunged her hand into the pocket. "Here we are – oh, no! Silly me!" She giggled, showing little rabbit teeth. "It's a letter. I'll try again."

"I'll take it, thank you," Matthew said.

He kept hold of the letter while the ticket was found and taken away, and for a while he sat and held it, merely staring at the sealed envelope. Colonel Shaw had come to see him in the Casualty Clearing Station just before they'd moved him back to the hospital in St Omer, and it was he who had stuffed it into the pocket where it had lain forgotten until this moment. With difficulty, he at last began breaking the seal. The woman half rose from her seat.

"Oh, do let me –"

"No, really, I'm quite competent. You'd be surprised."

He was uncomfortably conscious of her watching him with ill-concealed interest, her avid eyes making him feel as if he were undressing in public. Wretched woman! Why couldn't she read her library book and leave him alone?

He got up and lurched into the corridor, wincing a little as the movement of the train brought his shoulder into contact with the door. But once outside he was able to wedge himself more or less comfortably in a stationary position that allowed his one good hand to remain free.

It was eerie, reading the letter again after such a long period – just as if it had been written by a stranger. Not that it was such a long time ago, really. Only three months. It was the unremitting, heart-stopping, belly-churning horror of it that had made it seem so endless.

He had been so certain he would never return; and now here he was, not dead at all, but on his way back to Loveday, and the war, if not over, was undoubtedly in its last stages. It was unlikely that he would see action again – and how thankful he was for that! No, he thought now, grinning ruefully, he wasn't true officer material. Still, he wasn't sorry for the experience. It had shown him what was important and what was not.

They were rattling alongside the sea at Dawlish now. There were children playing on the beach – a little girl there who looked like Sally from the distance. Not that there was anyone quite like Sally! It seemed no time at all since she'd made sandcastles, and now she was a woman grown, engaged to be married. He couldn't wait to see her. Nor Oliver, the son he had found and lost again, and now hoped to find once more. He would stay in the corridor, he decided. Anything was better than having his thoughts and dreams interrupted by his fellow passenger's banalities. He didn't want to miss a moment of all this normality through which they were passing.

When the train came to a halt at Plymouth he let down the window and leaned out, grinning to himself. Still not quite Cornwall, he thought, but getting on. Soon they would be crossing the Tamar – now *that* was a moment he wouldn't miss for anything – and then he would know that he was home. But for the moment, Plymouth was better than nothing. He had been here so many times – to the panto-mime at Christmas, and on shopping sprees – buying school uniform with his mother, choosing furniture with Loveday. He had brought the children to Navy Days and had walked with them on the Hoe, taking them to the Barbican to see where the Pilgrim Fathers had embarked for the New World. They had gone for a cream tea, he remembered, and Oliver had distinguished himself by dropping his scone, jam-side down. How many years ago? Ten? Twelve? It seemed like yesterday.

North Road Station was busy, the platform thronged with sailors carrying kitbags, stirred into action now that the train had arrived. Presumably they were on their way to Falmouth. Why didn't they go by sea? The thought amused him. It didn't, somehow, seem much of an advertisement for the Senior Service to have so many of its personnel travelling overland.

A group close by his carriage had been squatting on the platform playing pontoon. Others were by the chocolate machines. One, a little apart, sat on a luggage trolley and read a letter. He had a doleful expression which was somehow at odds with the round hat that clung by some miraculous means to the very back of his head. Now cards and letters were stowed away, kitbags shouldered. The men called to each other, rallying their special mates.

"They look rather *rough*, don't they?" said a breathless voice at his elbow. He turned to see that he had been joined by the woman from his carriage.

"They've probably had quite a rough time," he replied mildly.

"Oh, I wasn't criticising, believe me!" She had gone quite pink with agitation. "I've nothing but admiration for them – for all you men who've sacrificed so much for all of us at home. I have a very dear friend in the Navy –"

The vicar, actually, but it wasn't a lie, not really. He was a sort of friend.

"Are you travelling far into Cornwall?" Matthew asked, taking pity on her. She smiled at him. Oh, this was better! This was what she had wanted all along – just a nice, pleasant little chat. She began to tell him all about Hetty and how they had been friends since the Fourth Form and how they both went into the Civil Service together – *both*, if you please, being sent to the Admiralty, such a coincidence!

She was just embarking on an account of Hetty's Aunt Fanny who had left her a tidy little sum, just enough to allow her to retire from the Civil Service and buy a cottage near Penzance, when she became aware that she was talking to herself. The officer's attention had gone back to the window and the platform and the look on his face seemed to suggest that he had seen a ghost. She paused in her narrative and asked him if anything was wrong, raising her voice as the guard was now blowing his whistle and the train was moving off.

"What? No – nothing's wrong. Excuse me, please."

He squeezed past her, almost forcing her back into the carriage. Really, she thought, perhaps he wasn't quite the gentleman he appeared! Undoubtedly he seemed to be in the grip of some strange emotion. Curious, a little outraged at his abrupt departure, she watched him lurch along the corridor. Perhaps he was ill, she thought. Perhaps she should summon a guard – pull the communication cord. After a moment's thought, she did neither but instead sat down in her seat and folded her hands in her lap, gazing out at the expanse of water they were about to cross.

There was this pathetic, shell-shocked army officer in my carriage, she would tell Hetty. Really, it was impossible to carry on a conversation with him, he was quite incoherent. When one *thinks* what he must have gone through . . .

Surely it had been Oliver, Matthew thought, as he stumbled down the corridor. He had only caught sight of him at the very last moment. He had been largely shielded by others until the general move towards the train, and even then his face had been half-turned towards his companion.

Loveday had mentioned his height. This man was tall. He

was dark, too, with the same aquiline features – just like Oliver, yet not like, for he had last seen Oliver as a boy, and even a partial view of the sailor on the platform had shown that this was a man, with the shoulders of a man and the stance of a man.

He was in the uniform of a Petty Officer. Was Oliver a Petty Officer? Loveday hadn't said. Perhaps it was a recent thing – assuming this *was* Oliver! It was hard to be sure, the train had swallowed him so fast.

The engine roared and thundered over the Tamar Bridge, but though the river, the county boundary, had been the one sight he longed to see, he barely noticed it. He felt like a bird with a broken wing, unable to balance, thrown this way and that with the movement of the train, but still he staggered on. He had left First Class behind him, with its half-empty carriages and little lace antimacassars. Now he was in another, crowded world where the air was thick with Woodbine smoke and sailors crouched in the corridor playing cards, and kitbags blocked his way.

Inside the carriages, those lucky enough to find seats were settling down to sleep, or were passing bottles between them, or reading newspapers. Curious faces turned to look at him as he opened each door, scanning the occupants. On the whole they were hostile, suspecting unwarranted interference – and who could blame them? He was invading their territory – but it was a dumb hostility that expressed itself in ribald jokes and suggestions only after he had closed the door again. He could hear the laughter and had a shrewd idea of its cause. Sailors, he imagined, were not so very different from soldiers in this regard.

"Excuse me – sorry!" Clumsily he lurched on, trying to shield his shoulder, wincing when he failed.

Over the couplings and into the next carriage, the noise from the track as loud as a banshee's scream – but still no sign of Oliver, or anyone like him.

There were civilians, of course, as well as sailors. A fat lady in purple glared at him when he fell against her as if she suspected him of making improper advances, while a small boy with a penetrating voice asked his mother what that funny man wanted.

His heart leapt with hope as he peered into the next carriage. There was a dark-haired Petty Officer sitting by the window, looking away from the door, but before Matthew could make his presence known the man turned round as if sensing his scrutiny, revealing the face of a stranger.

Disappointed, Matthew sagged against the door wearily. Pain had flared in his shoulder, more piercing than for days past. Clearly he had been wrong, he thought – hallucinating, seeing what he wanted to see. Oliver wasn't on the train. He was probably miles away, out in the Atlantic or up in the North Sea. Still, he was almost at the end of his search now. It would be pointless to give up at this stage.

Less urgently and with little hope, he edged his way along the corridor, and it was there, in the next carriage, that he found him. The train was stopping at St Germans, and an elderly man and his wife were on their feet, taking luggage down from the rack, preparing to leave. The tall Petty Officer had been sitting beside them, but he, too, was standing now, helping them, smiling at them, and for a moment Matthew stayed at the door of the carriage, looking at him, his heart pounding both with his physical exertion and with emotion.

He had no doubt now that this was Oliver. Loveday had said he reminded her of her father, but he had been inclined to dismiss this as wishful thinking. Now he saw that she hadn't been mistaken. The station platform was on the far side of the carriages and Oliver had his back half-turned towards Matthew as he handed out the luggage. It could, Matthew thought, have been John Pentecost himself. Yet when he turned to sit down and looked towards him, the fleeting resemblance had vanished and now he could see the boy he had known, but with none of the pathetic uncertainty. He had grown up, filled out, become an authoritative figure.

The unguarded delight, the look of pure pleasure on Oliver's face as he caught sight of him was something that was to stay with Matthew for a great many years.

"Dad!" his voice was breathless with astonishment. "My God – *Dad!*"

Suddenly unable to speak, Matthew held out his one good arm, and Oliver stumbled towards him, knocking into knees, treading on feet, apologising right and left.

"Dad," he said again as they clasped hands, rocking as the train gathered speed. "You're home! What have they done to you?"

Matthew gripped his shoulder, grinning widely with the pleasure of seeing him, mindless now of the pain in his shoulder.

"It's nothing – honestly, nothing of any importance. I'll be right as rain in no time. And you – look at the size of you! Are you on your way home, too?"

"Not immediately. Soon. Oh Dad, it's good to see you."

"It's good to see you, too. Better than good. The best surprise I could have had."

"I had a letter from Mother only yesterday. She didn't say you were on your way home."

"She doesn't know. I couldn't get through on the telephone."

Oliver threw back his head and laughed delightedly.

"Oh, I wish I could be there to see it! She'll be in her seventh heaven."

"Will she?" Matthew spoke lightly. "Will she really?"

"Oh, come off it, Dad! It's the moment she's lived for all this time."

"Me, too," Matthew said. He cleared his throat, finding himself a little husky for no good reason. He turned to the window. "Look out there," he said, tipping his chin towards the Cornish countryside, keeping his balance with his one good hand. "Home! I can't tell you what it means to me to see it again."

"I know what it means. Believe me."

"Yes." Matthew looked at him. "You and me – we know."

He turned again and saw the dreaming countryside, lying as peaceful and unchanged as it had throughout the centuries; a countryside drenched not in blood but in sunshine. He felt weak with gratitude that he had been spared to see it again.

He had been so sure that he would never come home. It seemed melodramatic now – the feeling of doom, the letter he had written. He was conscious of it still folded in his pocket. What should he do with it? Tear it to shreds, scatter

396

it from the window, create a minor snow-storm to disrupt this perfect June day?

Or should he keep it to remind himself how much he had nearly lost?

"You and me," he said again, with a sideways grin towards Oliver. "We're going to work together one day, aren't we?"

"I'd like it, if you would."

"Can't think of anything I'd like more. My God, there's so much to talk about –"

"It'll keep," Oliver said. Calm. Authoritative. The word occurred inevitably to Matthew again, and he saw with certainty that the old Oliver had gone for ever, his place taken by this confident young man – a young man that any father would be proud to own as his son.

Even after they parted – Oliver to continue his journey, Matthew to proceed to the cab rank outside the station – the thought of him was more of a delight than he could have dreamed possible. But there were other, more pressing things to occupy him now. Soon he would be with Loveday. She'd be in her seventh heaven, Oliver had said. Dare he really hope for that after all that had happened? Could he honestly expect her to forgive him? Yes, yes, and yes again! She was Loveday, wasn't she?

Maybe, he thought as the old station fly bore him towards her, maybe he should show her the letter after all. It was as true now as the day he had written it.

Or maybe he wouldn't. It was of no consequence, either way. This was a new beginning. He was home and they loved each other. Nothing else mattered.

ᎀᏹ Epilogue ᏹᎀ

The sun shone so brightly that the clay was dazzling in its whiteness, and beyond it stretched the moor and the sea and the arms of the Gribbin and Black Head.

"Home," Matthew said softly, Loveday's hand in his. They turned to smile at each other, their eyes full of love. "I'd kiss you," he went on, "if it weren't for the curious gaze of half a dozen workmen – not to mention Cap'n Noah!"

"There'll be time for kissing later. All the time in the world. Come, my darling. You mustn't tire yourself."

He yielded to her gentle pressure and walked with her away from the pit and the men who dug at its surface, and the pyramid with its small railway and the skip that travelled up and down.

Men smiled and touched their caps as they passed.

"Couldn't ee keep away, sir?" they said; and "Good to 'ave ee back, Mr Tallon."

"Oh, Matthew – it *is* good," Loveday said softly.

"Oliver was right in what he said to you, you know," Matthew said. "After the war, we must mechanise."

"There'll be army lorries going begging, he said –"

"He's got his head screwed on the right way, that boy." Matthew paused as he made his way to the car which waited for them. "You go on, darling. I must have a last word with Cap'n Noah."

"Don't be too long, then. Sally will be arriving soon."

She watched him go, then turned and slowly walked on.

Changes will come, she thought, and we shall grow old.

But they would grow old together, and the thought failed to dismay her.

Sally would marry her naval officer and give them grandchildren to love, and even if they didn't live on the doorstep, they would come to see them frequently. And Oliver was bound to marry before too long – a Cornish girl, she felt sure, for he would never stray far from home.

And Matthew?

Well, perhaps one day she would take for granted this intoxicating freedom from worry. Perhaps one day she would look at him without feeling the surge of gratitude that now swept over her, every time she thought of how easily she could have lost him.

Perhaps, too, she would take for granted the harmony that existed between them – the breaking down of all the barriers that had divided them for so long; the feeling that this was a new beginning, with the way before them full of love and hope.

She leaned against the car with her face turned towards the sea, aware that she was smiling. He wouldn't stay long with Cap'n Noah. The waiting was almost over.